Robert Greenfield is a former international fashion designer, once dubbed 'Britain's answer to the Italian Look', and a well-respected interior designer, whose work is often featured in the press.

In 2011 Robert's autobiography *Samphire Coast* – driven by his experiences of owning a quirky award-winning boutique B&B in North Norfolk – was published by Vanguard Press (Pegasus): it continues to be one of their best sellers.

Robert is currently working on a crime thriller, from his new woodland home on the North Norfolk coast: it's based on his dreams for a Worldwide Dog Protection Law.

If you enjoyed this book, a review would be really appreciated by the author, even if it's just a couple of words on Amazon or any online retailers of *The Cedar Cage*. Reviews help expand the author's audience.

Twitter: robscape
Facebook: Robert Greenfield
www.robertgreenfield.co.uk

By the same author

Samphire Coast

The Cedar Cage

Robert Greenfield

The Cedar Cage

Pegasus

ISBN 978 1 910903 05 6

*Pegasus is an imprint of
Pegasus Elliot MacKenzie Publishers Ltd.*
www.pegasuspublishers.com

First Published in 2017

**Pegasus
Sheraton House Castle Park
Cambridge CB3 0AX England**

Printed & Bound in Great Britain

Dedication

For Barnaby – somewhere over the rainbow – and Toby, my rescue.

Acknowledgements

Thank you… thank you… thank you

To my life partner, Michael, for three long-suffering years of patience – here's to the next three as my third book comes down the pipeline.

To my brother Tony for being the perfect sounding board.

To my father and mother: I wish you were here to read *The Cedar Cage.*

A special dedication to my grandfather – Private Michael Jacob Jackson (Royal Army Medical Corps/82nd Field Ambulance B Section) ID-tag no. 2622 – awarded the Military Medal for outstanding bravery at the second battle of Ypres in 1915.

A salutation to the gallantry of the 8th Norfolks.

To my brilliant editor, Roland Clare, at www.wordfix.org for being an unwavering guide in bringing out the best in me as an author.

To Spiffing Covers at www.spiffingcovers.com for their stunning book jacket design.

And by no means least: Pegasus Elliot Mackenzie for believing in *The Cedar Cage.*

CONTENTS

CHAPTER ONE
TILLY

'Wood Feels' – odd name for a dwelling, but here I was pacing the deck of my cedar boathouse, built just before the Great War. The dusky marshlands, their snakelike creeks flushed by a Nordic sea, struck me as a sort of no-man's-land. There was even a dilapidated lookout bunker a half-mile or so down the coastal path.

I was checking my mobile phone for a text alert: the only network hotspot was right at the end of the jetty, which stood reassuringly proud of the recent high tide. But it was not good news: 'Poor Mother – whole ground floor flooded – could be away for weeks. Sorry, Bertie. Call me. Luke x.'

Ironic, amid all the talk of climate change: we go and buy a boathouse, on Norfolk's north coastal frontline, where the sea defences are eroding. Yet it's Luke's mum, way up in Geordie country, who gets flooded out.

Back in June, the moment I had stepped over the threshold of Wood Feels (not 'Woodfields', as I'd heard it over the phone with the estate agent), I had fallen for its timber-framed integrity, its sequestered location, perched on a dense bank of pinewoods like some exotic aviary.

But I hadn't bargained for Luke disappearing up North for weeks on end. Naturally, he was doing the right thing to support his mum in a crisis, and he was lucky to have the chance. My own, bohemian mother had resisted any such help, and spent her life running away from a stream of upheavals of her own making. But our boathouse was going to feel awfully lonely without him, and I did worry this might reignite the OCD – the checking and rechecking that nobody had slipped into my home – that had plagued me off and on since a violent episode in childhood. Surely, with my forty-third birthday fast approaching, I was old enough to ignore such wretched thoughts. At least I still had my chilled-out whippet, Boo, for company. He was hardly a guard dog, though: had he been human, he would have been a cross between David Niven and the Dalai Lama.

This unexpected separation from Luke gave me a chance to get the place together for his return, personalise it with some trademark twists from my former career. For six years we'd run a flourishing interior design consultancy from our base in bohemian Muswell Hill (mother would have loved it, had she lived), catering to clients with money to spare.

Now where had Luke left the spare set of boathouse keys? I had to locate them, before I could sit down to dinner. What if he had dropped them outside somewhere? I could be murdered in my sleep...

'*Calma*, Roberto.' An inner voice – what some people might call a guardian angel – was back in my head. I hadn't heard it in years, though I'd never forgotten its first manifestation: after a visit to the National Gallery – my hippie mother getting her homesick fix of the Italian Renaissance – I'd been allowed, with characteristic *laissez faire*, to climb the banisters on my way to bed. As my child self plummeted headlong down the staircase, this dulcet voice had spoken – '*Calma*, Roberto' – and I'd found myself brought in to land gently on the floor below.

And later, on holiday, ten-year-old klutzy me had tumbled off a diving board and cracked my head in the deep end, unobserved by mother or her new partner, my self-styled 'Uncle' Roy. It was the little voice – I imagined it emanating from a *putto*, a plump angel from the da Vinci exhibition – that saved me from panic, and certain drowning.

'*Calma*, Roberto,' in my head again. So many years since this reassurance had offered itself... so why now?

The understairs coat cupboard was a logical place to look for a door key. But could mulling over the cherub's re-emergence, in a space without electric light, revive memories of the childhood trauma that had triggered my OCD affliction? No – years of therapy had surely put paid to such nonsense in my adult self.

I started to rummage through Luke's pockets – a quilted puffer jacket, a reefer coat, a tweed blazer with gun patches – but without success until, as panic loomed, my foot scuffed something across the floor and I heard the jangle of keys.

Aha, so they'd dropped out. I scrambled around on the floorboards, reaching into the recess under the bottom step of the staircase. And as I dragged the knobbly keys towards me, I felt a wad of newspaper, wrapped around something solid.

Back in the light I discovered the papers had been protecting – or concealing – a finely carved oval frame, decorated with Art Nouveau branches, all made from a single piece of reddish-brown wood. Sadly there was no photograph or other clue about its one-time owner. I sniffed it, and it had the same piquancy as the whole understair; in fact the entire boathouse retained a cedary aroma.

Judging by the dates on the yellowing newspapers, the frame had been hidden around the time the boathouse was constructed. But fish soup was simmering, so I shoved papers and frame back in the cupboard and hurried to the stove. My samphire chowder was bubbling over. Luke would have smarted at my carelessness: he can't bear mess.

I put the soup on our kitchen tabletop, an upcycled monastery door once earmarked for a client's chapel conversion. I fancied myself as a bit of a chef – or a *souscharlatan*, as Luke would waspishly remind me. Just as I was about to tuck in, I thought I heard a voice call me by my nickname. But where? Sounds can travel deceptive distances over the marshlands.

"Bertie? Bertie, sweetheart, where are you?" Nobody called me 'Bertie' except my beloved Luke: it was his pet version of Robert.

An athletic figure bounded lightly down the jetty and up the steps to the veranda decking. Low tide made this intrusion possible; otherwise access to the boathouse was only by boat, or down through the woods on the secluded track from the coastal road to the south. As I opened the French doors on to the deck, Boo slipped out.

"So, so sorry to bother you..." The visitor looked fraught. "I've lost my wire fox terrier. I don't suppose..."

Up came Boo, coursing the little mite up the ramp from our small front garden, which cross-linked under the jetty, and merged imperceptibly with the marshes. The stranger swept this Bertie, my canine namesake, into her arms like a lovesick mother.

"Well, I guess you've found each other now." I smiled.

"Oh, thanks to your handsome blond... what's his name?"

"Say hello, Boo," I told him. "Silly, aren't we?"

I could have been forgiven for thinking this vision was the prettiest of posh boys, but obviously now she was the handsomest of women. A close shock of side-parted raven hair, with a tomboyish cut, framed Hepburnesque brows, set over deep incandescent eyes with a violet tinge. A rare beauty...

"Well, hello: Tilly Offord." Her handshake was firm.

"You might as well call me Bertie." I felt my mouth widen.

"How funny..." she laughed. She set wire-haired Bertie down on the ground, where he, or she, promptly had a puppy accident.

"Oh my God, I am so sorry!" Tilly said, while the terrier looked up sheepishly.

"No probs, I have a pooper-scooper." Boo cantered over for a sniff of his guest's calling card.

"Don't worry, just a little doggy *faux paw*."

Tilly grinned at my attempt to lighten the moment. I felt comfortable in her company, and invited her to join me for some chowder. She eyed me over curiously, then accepted. She threw her parka on to the veranda balustrade with a swagger. In a gingham shirt with narrow braces, her skinny jeans cuffed over Oxford boots, she looked a 'tough mudder' today; but I could imagine her, at a moment's notice, morphing into a slinky *femme fatale*, dressed to thrill both sexes.

The sun skimmed the horizon, a bronze discus thrown by the gods. For a beatific moment the cedar shingles of the boathouse threw back a Titian glow, and fine strands warmed Tilly's gamine features.

I darted through the French doors into the kitchen, rummaging for a bowl in a half-unpacked box of kitchenware. I also grabbed a jug of elderflower homebrew from the fridge on the way out: powerful stuff.

"Do sit," I said.

Tilly pulled a rattan chair to the table, while I laid her place. She rolled up her shirtsleeves, as if she wanted an arm-wrestle, and I glimpsed her vintage gent's Rolex: six o'clock. With a napkin over my right arm, I served her like a *maître d'*. Luke would have frowned, as the starched cloth dangled in her soup; Tilly made no mention of it.

"Mmm, thank you. You live here alone?"

"No, with my partner Luke, but he's had to rush up North, to bail out his mum. Near Whitley Bay, she lives: storm water, the works."

"How terrible. The floods, I mean, not that you have a partner." She coyly blew on the soup, and took a sip.

"We've only just moved in. We were looking for a hideaway no one can find, not Google Earth, not SatNav. Only you, Tilly." I smiled. "We've got no network coverage for mobiles, and no landline, and it suits me fine. Even our mailbox is right up by the main road."

"What fun!" There was a Famous Five thrill in her voice. "But you and Luke: are you retired, or what?"

"Christ no, just some time out, after selling up in London, a whisker before the credit crunch and the next Great Depression."

"Oh, what was your... thing?"

"Stuff like this," I said, tapping the glass tabletop with my spoon.

"You recycled oil-drums?"

"The fifty-gallon ones are brilliant for outdoor furniture. Get them from a boatyard, just add glass."

"Cool. So you're some kind of designer?"

"Yeah. Interiors and exteriors: houses of course."

"Ah, that explains... your taste." It was flirty, but she was also sending me up. I reached for my sweatshirt, which hung over a deckchair, and pulled it on over my grubby vest.

"So, you sold up and moved out here." She hiccupped, and giggled: my potent cordial was going down like Evian.

"We did. How about you? You don't sound like a native."

"Well, I did my MA in Fine & Decorative Art at Sotheby's Institute. I would have stayed in London, but I landed a pretty interesting job, just near here, with the Norfolk Heritage Society. Restoring a historic hall."

"Congratulations," I said, trying at the same time to guess her age. The coltish charm made a puzzling contrast with her worldly sophistication: approaching thirty was my best guess.

"Really it was a good excuse to flee the city, and my woeful love life," she added. "By the way, your soup is wicked. Chin-chin." She helped herself to more elderflower wine.

"There's plenty on the stove."

"I couldn't. But thanks. I see BFT loved it too." Boo and the fox terrier had collapsed on the deck in an *après-dinner* heap.

"BFT?"

"Yah, we use an acronym: Bertie fox terrier."

"Makes sense," I said, puzzled.

"So tell me about this wondrous place." I let the subject change, though I was more than curious to hear all about my guest.

"Okay. But let me warn you, I'm a hopeless data-geek."

"Bertie, feel free. I love a house with history."

"This place is called 'Wood Feels' – crazy name huh? 'Sleef Doow' spelt backwards if you like." I thought it might as well be spelt backwards: it was an idiosyncrasy by which I always hoped to make sense of strange names. It'll pay off one day. She looked at me oddly.

"It was originally a wedding gift, from a local aristocrat to his American bride. All built from a single ancient Cedar of Lebanon on his sprawling estate," I explained.

"How marvellous."

Just as I was about to name the estate, a breeze whipped up and carried Tilly's jacket off the balustrade on to the jetty below.

"I'll get it."

"Bertie, you're such a gent."

Back on the veranda, I hung her parka over the deckchair, then excused myself to go and light the woodburner in the lounge.

"You were saying?" she said, when I returned.

"Ah yeah, my boathouse was a wedding gift for a titled lady. Some present, eh?"

"She must have been a knockout, to deserve a love nest like this." Tilly sounded wistful.

"Somewhere in this tonnage of wood, we've been told, there's a Tudor inscription saying 'Anne Boleyn', inscribed on the tree by the doomed Queen herself."

"Nooo?" She looked enthralled. "Any idea where it is?"

"Christ knows," I replied, "But it could easily be true. Apparently Anne did spend time at Blickling Hall, not that far from here. So I like to believe it."

"Blickling is fab – all topiary and Dutch gables," she said. "Mind you, where I'm working seriously gives it a run..." A flock of pink-footed geese suddenly honked overhead.

"What did you say?"

"I said... oh never mind." And she shook her head.

"Ah. Well, as I was saying, my aristo was darkly eccentric and, according to the locals, he blew his brains out on this very veranda in 1929, time of the Stock Market crash. The body was never found."

"So he fell in the sea, right?"

"Perhaps."

"Her ladyship must have been trouble," Tilly said, with a bewitching glint. She offered me a cigarette from a silver Deco case, but I'd given up years ago. Luke and I were health freaks now.

"Do you mind?"

"Please go ahead." I held up the storm lamp, so she could light it from the flickering candle. Hell, her eyes were so arrestingly violet in the evening light: she could turn a gay man straight.

"I'm been trying to quit. It's either the booze or the ciggies. One has to go. So what happened next?"

"Well, I asked around: the place was empty a long while, then some local boatbuilder rented it for a couple of years, patched it up – on a shoestring, by the look of things – but leaving the period features intact. Then it came on the market. Sadly, by the time I wanted to get in touch with him, he'd drowned. Off Blakeney Point, where the seals hang out."

"Bertie, not to worry, most old homes have tragic pasts."

"Oh, I'm not worrying," I told her. "Really."

"And then?"

"I saw this ad in *The London Evening Standard*: 'Quirky Boathouse – Stunning Sea Views'. Luke and I, we fell head over heels in an instant. Not literally *heels*, as we weren't exactly wearing slingbacks." Tilly grinned, but took a long hard drag, right down to the stub of her Marlboro, and blew a plume of smoke seaward.

"Are you okay?" I asked. She looked pensive, poured more wine and seemed to loosen up, like someone in need of a friend.

"Oh, it just feels so peaceful here, far from the madding crowd."

She didn't strike me as a Hardy fan, and I said so.

"It's a question of happy endings," she said. "You can trust Hardy, because he knows better. Where's Mr Sex-Bomb Right in real life?"

"So you're a fatalist?" I said. "It was definitely fate that I met Luke. A blind date some mutual friends arranged: and... *voilà*."

"Well, I guess I am paying for the sins of my parents."

"Oh?"

"Daddy was a workaholic: he'd have preferred a son for his only child, so I turned out a tomboy. It really didn't work, but the image stuck."

"And your mother?"

"Mummy?" Tilly rolled her eyes. "She was a top model in the seventies, jet-setting around the world, a hopeless alcoholic with more issues than *Vogue*." She passed me her smartphone. "That's Mummy. Oh, and Daddy too. Stockbroker. The marriage was a sham. She committed suicide in the end. I was twelve." We two have a lot of background in common, I thought.

"Your mother was beautiful," I told her. I could see where Tilly had inherited her looks.

"Yah, but totally, totally, insecure."

The temperature dropped, and she wrapped the parka round her shoulders. Her vulnerability needed caressing, but I didn't dare.

"Coffee?" I asked, moving the wine jug casually out of her reach.

"No thanks, and sorry to bore you with the semantics of my woeful love life. Far too depressing for such a gorgeous evening."

"No probs." She didn't know me at all, yet she spoke as you might to a therapist. We could be great mates, I thought, if I ever saw her again.

"So when's the next bus back to Brancaster Staithe?"

"Long gone, I'm afraid. Don't worry, I can drop you home later, if you like?"

"I've encroached on your time already."

"It's no trouble. Really..."

Conversation continued to flow as the light rapidly faded. A well-lit ship slipped by in the distance like an ocean liner, though in reality it was just transporting maintenance workers to the offshore wind farm; time was finally catching up here too. We wandered into the main lobby of the boathouse, between the kitchen – open-plan, if we pulled back its heavy louvered doors – and the living room. The dramatic ceiling trusses looked like an upturned hull.

"Wow," said Tilly, slowly.

"Oh, excuse the packing boxes." Five tall cardboard crates, like vertical eco-coffins, encircled her. I'd only opened one since we moved in.

"Do you really play baseball?"

I laughed; but I saw what had caught her eye, and pulled it out.

"It's not a baseball bat, this. I ought to keep it hidden. Luke doesn't like people to see it."

"What, a huge pencil?"

"We won a big Designer award in 2005, and this was their hip trophy." I hefted it. "Some exotic hardwood, I suppose."

"Fab. What's the writing?"

"That's gold leaf."

"I mean, what does it say?"

"It's nothing really, but if you must, that's the name of our consultancy."

"Really? You know your acronym spells 'DILDO'?" She hiccupped loudly.

"No, '*Designed in London*' was us and 'Designaward.org'. We were their inaugural winners in the 'Eco-Interior' category. You're right, though: Luke calls it the Dildo too."

"Chunky!" Tilly took it from me.

She shouldered it like a rifle and saluted, then started to march towards me: I gently disarmed her. I'd obviously been a bit slow removing that jug of wine. Tilly steadied herself on one of the freestanding crates. It rocked as well.

"And this is a cobbly... cobbled-flint wall?

"Yeah, right up the west gable end, through the bedroom upstairs. It houses the chimney: hence the Swedish woodburner."

"Bertie, it's heavenly, the whole boathouse."

"Cheers."

"Ced... cedar, you said?"

"Yes. Potent, eh?"

"Save you a fort... a fortune on burning oils," she said; yet another stammer.

The dogs had crashed out by the woodburner, which blazed seductively. I thought of inviting Tilly to sit there, for a nightcap; but I backed off, thinking things might get awkward.

"Come on, boy." I made for the kitchen door, which opened straight on to the wooded track, where my VW campervan was parked. I flicked on the wall lantern, and the dogs followed us out.

"Ooh, classic pale blue," she said, climbing in with boyish swagger.

"Westfalia 72, and it's never let me down. Well, Luke's the mechanic." I rapped the dashboard and started up, praying it wouldn't make me look like a dork.

There was no need to turn on the radio; the journey brought up plenty of topics, and Tilly and I were definitely in tune. We both remarked on Boo's chivalrous attitude to BFT, whom he had not tried to mount.

"I hadn't realised your 'Bertie' was a girl," I said. "Perhaps Boo hasn't either?"

"She's really Victoria Albertina," Tilly explained. "Named after my favourite museum on earth."

"On that basis, I'd have called Boo 'Smithsonian'," I said, and Tilly laughed.

I unloaded my new friend, and Victoria Albertina, near the harbour front, outside a nicely-lit cottage, all blue-painted clapboard, where she had a six-month let. Driving back slowly, I tried to push adulterous fantasies out of my dirty, inquisitive mind.

At home the smell of cedar was intoxicating. While Boo wandered through, I opened up the French doors and ambled down the steps, to the end of the jetty, to pick up a phone signal. It was 10.30: the boathouse stood solitary, dwarfed on the edge of its sylvan ridge under a vast, shimmering starlit dome of jet-black night. It put childhood memories of the London Planetarium to shame.

"Hi, Luke. Sorry I didn't call you earlier." He sounded groggy, as if I had wakened him. I clung to the end post, and gazed skyward.

"Aye. Bertie. You okay?"

"Fine. How's Mum?"

"Suffering badly, what with her condition. The salvaging is an ordeal – the floodwater stinks – but Uncle Vin has been great."

"Do you need me to come up?"

"No, you just get the boathouse sorted, I can take care of Mother. We're sleeping at Vin's bungalow, which is sound: it didn't flood."

"I miss you," I said, swallowing.

"And I you. The walls are paper-thin so I can't speak up. Let's talk tomorrow."

"Oh okay. G'night."

"Aye. Love ya..."

And we signed off. I hadn't had a chance to mention Tilly. She'd be all alone at home right now, though at least Victoria Albertina was company. As I turned the key in the mortise lock of the French doors, I felt myself rocked by a wave of emptiness, a sickening flashback to my own loneliness, my terror of an empty house, which had started so soon after Mother died.

My secret dread: it all came down to keys, and not even Luke knew the exact details. I hadn't told him about the stalker who'd hung around one of my many childhood homes. I'd believed – as far as children ever understand these things – that he was after my mother. The joke was that he was one of her many suitors, and my Uncle Roy referred to him as 'the Secret Admirer'.

When Mother died I suppose Roy and I had both thought the Admirer would vanish off the scene. But events had quickly revealed the sickening truth: it was not the crazed Italian hippie he'd been secretly admiring, but her pretty little son.

I was eleven again. My bereaved stepfather and I were being consoled at a neighbour's place and, as it grew late, Roy gave me our house key to let myself back in, promising to be home in ten minutes himself. The responsibility had made me feel all grown-up.

What was this compulsion, to go over the vile events, again and again? There I was, turning on the breakfast room light to pet Oscar, my shaggy black poodle, when the Secret Admirer's horrible face appeared at the window, leering in at me. It was ajar, but at least it was latched securely, on the first hole of the stay. He loomed scarily, grasping the frame with one hand, and warned me in a growl that, if I ever told of this visit, he would break my spine.

I gathered Oscar up and ran to hide in the understairs cupboard, my Panic Room. My heart was thumping so loud I thought it would give me away. Such a huge relief when I heard the click of the front-door lock: it seemed Roy was home sooner than expected, and I was on the verge of calling out to him when I heard crashing noises, as if the place was being ransacked. Only then did I realise I had made the most appalling mistake of my young life: by leaving Roy's key in the front door, I had inadvertently left an open invitation to the Secret Admirer.

God, I hated these endless memories, how I hugged my dog close, how the understairs door had been wrenched open, how the warty hands had grappled Oscar from my arms. My dog snarling as the Secret Admirer made to strangle him. Me begging him not to, crying hysterically. Oscar squealing.

I can't forget the cigar breath, and his psychotic "You're next!" Somehow I'd scrambled past him, up the stairs, desperate to evade this nightmare by hiding in Mother's room, under her cold bed. My first time in there since she'd died; I find I've wet myself.

An uneasy hiatus. He's standing in my mother's doorway. My eyes track his oxblood Doc Martens as he prowls round the bed. He crouches down.

"You ain't invisible... yet," he sniggers. Still chilling, the thought of that bulbous face, the yellow teeth in Lilliputian close-up.

'*Calma, piccolo. Calma*, Roberto.' That had been the last time I'd heard the *putto*'s comforting voice. Then, in the brush of a tear, my drunken stepfather Roy was ringing the doorbell. The Secret Admirer fled through the balcony doors into the back garden below. I ran down the stairs, pulling up on the second-last step where my poor dog Oscar lay, his back broken, kicking and writhing in his own blood and faeces. How had I coped, at that age?

Boo pattered over and rested his muzzle on my knee. Never again, I thought, with a flare of anger. Losing the comfort of my first, sweet companion – on top of Mother's recent passing – I'd withdrawn into a blur for a long, sad time. Coming into the house – any empty house – was a wellspring of renewed terror, fear that someone else had a key, that the Secret Admirer would somehow have got into the bedroom cupboard or be lurking in the loft, ready to come sidling out and take me in my sleep.

Years later, of course, his infamous face was splashed across the newspapers, the mess of fiery red hair, the glazed feral eyes: a notorious child-molester, he'd been sent down for many years. The idea that he was behind bars was a continuing comfort to me. But when would I get over the trauma of a violated home, or this guilt over my carelessness with a vital key?

Back in the now, the embers in the woodburner fizzled out a squall of shadows, hip-hopping over the cobbled flints of the boathouse. Boo growled, as if the Admirer had escaped from my imagination. I hastened around to close all the shutters, checking their latches were secure. I revisited all entry points, from the kitchen to the French doors, to be sure the deadlocks had clicked firmly into place. I double-checked, I treble-checked: there could be no margin for error. Like an addict in denial – swept up in this flurry of paranoia – I felt myself relapsing into a *very* bad habit.

"Boo? Come boy, bedtime."

I switched out the lights. Precious Boo followed me faithfully upstairs to the galleried landing; the second-last step always creaked like mad, a haunting echo of the madman. I must try to feel safe, in my cedar cage, fortified for the night. Boo climbed into his basket, nestled in an alcove under the porthole window, dark now, but by day offering far-reaching views over the coast.

I hung my clothes over the banisters and wandered through the bedroom: it stretched across the entire first floor, under myriad ragged rafters exposed to the roof ridge. In the old bathroom, which overlooked the dark woods, original sanitary ware, still in good order, stood testimony to its Edwardian creator. The latest conveniences of the day must have impressed the American bride, not least a copper slipper-bath on a Moroccan-tiled platform, an erotic stage where her new husband could view her half-submerged beauty.

Yawning my way back to the bedroom, I climbed into the baroque monster of a bed, carved with swags of curlicues, intertwined with *putti*, bleeding red paint from the patina of their antiquated gilt. We had inherited this incongruous piece with the boathouse: it felt as though it had been teleported from some louche château.

There was no denying, 'Wood Feels' exuded charm, but – my mind darting about as I lay staring up into the cupola – I worried that Luke and I were still strangers here. In fact it somehow felt that I was intruding into somebody else's fantasy.

Boo shuffled around to find his comfy spot, then slipped, with a twitch and a yelp, into a dream. The stars petered out, and the place was shrouded in the moonless cloak of a Norfolk night. Soothing silence, but for surging waves: capricious Nature at its deadliest. The mass of muscular timber began to creak and groan, as if I were encased in a great galleon. Disquiet engulfed me with a shivery chill, akin to motion sickness, and begged one niggling, recurrent question: why call a boathouse 'Wood Feels'?

Not your average house name like Woodfields, as Luke and I had first thought. 'Feels' somehow implied it was a living entity, with an animate force still running through its woody veins. The night grew long as I tossed and turned, prey to unsettling thoughts. Eventually, I began to slip into a dream-ridden sleep – haunting echoes, from dark corridors, beckoning me into labyrinths of anxiety

CHAPTER TWO
BODY ART

All night in a carpenter's workshop, the scent of the wood, the sound of sawing. A dream perhaps: but it ended with a thud that startled me awake. Boo's ears pricked up.

The outsize trophy-pencil lay on the bed, *en route* for some wall-space far from visitors' eyes. Grabbing it for self-defence, I made my stealthy way to the staircase. The blasted second step off the landing creaked loudly, and my heart raced. Damn: whoever had broken in would know I was about. I crept into the lounge, trophy poised like a club.

But there was no sign of a forced entry, no whiff of a Secret Admirer. It must have been one of my 3D-HD dreams: Luke was forever bemused by my vivid early morning accounts.

After breakfast I took Boo for a constitutional: a clement morning for October, just the notion of a chill on the marshes. A light plane, low overhead, broke the silence. The polar-white wind turbines, motionless on the horizon, were not earning their keep today. The tide was freshly out.

As we headed toward Blakeney Point I found myself singing an old ragtime tune, probably dating back to World War I:

'Oh! You beautiful doll, you great big beautiful doll! Let me put my arms about you: I could never live without you...'

I stopped for a second: what had revived this earworm? Some old film I'd seen? Boo had also frozen, on the muddy brink of a creek, cocking an ear as if he too heard the sentimental lyric, faintly rising from unseen dugouts on the Western Front. It was his rapt gaze, into this empty trench, that reawakened last night's dream in full: horrific images welled afresh in my mind – mortar fire, shattered forests through which soldiers limped like marionettes, barely coping on their prosthetic limbs...

This gruesome recollection left me in no mood to enjoy the landmarks that punctuated the coastline beyond. The blue Lifeboat House looked like a beached whale, and the old redbrick Watch House radiated desolation. Originally a smugglers' den, it had declined into a Spartan holiday let, and even that was now shut up, awaiting repair. I turned for home.

On approaching Wood Feels I spotted a figure, moving aimlessly, with the bedraggled air of a drifter. Luke and I had noticed this man when we'd moved in – he often came trudging along our shore at low tide, presumably imagining his stare to be unobtrusive. Maybe it was his unwanted presence that had reignited my anxiety about strangers getting into my house? I looked away, but he had turned and was already approaching me. Soon we were just yards apart: an encounter was unavoidable.

"Hey, dude, nice mornin'." Broad Norfolk with a dose of *California Dreaming*, I thought.

"Er... certainly is," I replied.

"Aren't you one of the dudes from the boathouse?"

The question was disingenuous: he had watched us settling in for weeks.

"Yeah."

"Thought so. I am Jud. One 'd'." He shook his unkempt strawberry-blond hair, stroked a beard in urgent need of clipping, and unexpectedly lurched towards me to high-five. I gingerly reciprocated, so as not to offend.

He crouched down and petted Boo's head with one of his heavily tattooed arms: at least he was dog-friendly. Boo gave him a good, exploratory sniff. But as the sun came out, Jud got up and pointed at Wood Feels.

"Hey man, guess who built your boathouse?"

"I don't have to guess," I said evenly. "His name was Lord James Newton-Grey."

"No, that was just the squire, up at ol' Samphire Hall. He had his master carpenter build your boathouse, years ago: and that was my great grandpappy. He died in there an' all."

A 'master carpenter' dies in my house, and I dream all night about frigging woodwork?

"Wood was his name, same as mine. Not long married and a couple of kiddies an' all." Jud yanked up his fluorescent T-shirt sleeve, and there on his shoulder, below a flaming aircraft nose-diving, was a further tattoo. "That's him: Skipper Wood." He pointed out a fair-haired strongman, depicted with a megawatt smile. A caption, 'London 1908', was framed with five interlocking circles.

"Remarkable," I began.

"I know, you're gonna tell me them 'lympic rings weren't invented in 1908."

I was glad he couldn't read my actual thoughts. He couldn't be more than thirty, but I guessed he'd had no parents to warn him that the whole gallery – his grinning ancestor was brandishing a crosscut saw, I now noticed – looked downright unsettling.

"Is that supposed to be a medal?"

"Gold," said Jud proudly. "Skipper were Cap'n of the team what won the tug-o'-war."

"So what happened at the boathouse?"

"Oh man, you don't wanna know..."

"Well I do, now you've mentioned it."

"Accident that were, so they said: he fell on his saw – slashed his throat – almost lost his fuckin' head."

I didn't know what to say. '*Calma*, Roberto,' came the angel's voice in my mind.

"Look, gotta get back to my Winnebago. See ya." With a shrug of his shoulders, Jud turned to slope off in the direction of Wells.

"Hey, I need to know more about Skipper Wood!" I called. "Jud?"

He didn't look round.

Damn, I mustn't panic, but this living canvas of a man had really got to me. I started running home, and Boo easily overtook me. He likes a chase. Uneasy thoughts were coalescing in my head as I clambered up the ladder steps from saltmarsh to jetty. Boo took the ramp, speeding to his water-bowl, while I hurried on upstairs to the veranda, cursing as I grappled the locks on the French doors, and headed for the kitchen. I needed a drink too.

I thrust my head under the tap on the wall. This poor carpenter, Skipper Wood, might have done the same thing on the same spot, before he lost his. Wasn't Anne Boleyn beheaded too? The tap heaved up a few short, bile-like spurts. Ideas joined up in my mind, deaths linked with the boathouse. Previous owner, drowned; Lord James Newton-Grey, suicide on my balcony. I fiddled blindly with the copper lever, and suddenly clean, icy water gushed over me. In a moment, the pattern was washed away. Strange coincidences do happen, I promised myself: they don't have to mean anything.

It was easy to get paranoid – Luke would dismiss this as 'overthinking'. I needed to give him a call, just casually, and did my best to saunter back down the jetty, and find the network hotspot. Gulls screamed as the call connected; I counted to ten.

"Had to rush Mam to A&E this morning," he said, without preliminaries. "5 a.m., heart attack."

"Oh no, is she...?"

"No, she's okay. But she broke her hip in the fall. Titanium replacement, they've offered. Can't believe the waiting list." His voice quivered.

"Oh God. Luke, this is dreadful."

"Aye, one thing after another and at her age as well."

"I'll drive up this afternoon."

"There's nothing you can do, Bertie: get on with things at home. Just realise, I'm likely to be up here longer than we agreed."

"Sure, totally understand."

"Uncle Vin is helping on the house front. He was a builder, you know."

"You've got a load to deal with. Sure you don't need me?" The gulls screamed again.

"I'll give you a shout if I need to. Missing you madly, and Boo."

"Me too you."

"Aye. Sounds like a scene from *The Birds* down there."

"It's Hitchcock central at the moment." Luke didn't know the half of it, I thought.

"What did you say?

"Nothing."

"Look, I got to go, doctor wants a word. Speak soon."

"Love to Mum – bye for now." I shut off my phone, almost wishing I hadn't called and heard this distressing news.

Squadrons of Brent geese flickered across the sky, on their autumn migration from Iceland. I had the campervan: I could wing it up to Tyneside by late evening. But it would only add to his problems if I arrived unexpectedly. Instead I had a tidy-up, pondering his predicament; but as I ate lunch, I couldn't stop my thoughts slipping back to the era of Skipper Wood.

"Hey Boo, fancy a ride?"

We headed the camper for the car park at the Blakeney Hotel, my other signal hot spot. Cheeky, perhaps, but I needed a Wi-Fi connection for my laptop, and we'd learnt the security password – 'twitcher', lower-case – from a veteran birdwatcher in the public bar. I was online in moments, typing 'Skipper Wood obituary' into the search bar.

We regret to announce the accidental death, which occurred on Thursday 10th April 1913, of Mr Skipper Wood of Stiffkey, master carpenter and Olympic athlete.

His widow, Mrs Beulah Wood, reports that the craftsman had been attending to adjustments at the cedarwood boathouse he has lately constructed, for Lord James Newton-Grey, on the Samphire Hall estate. Falling, in the course of repairs adjoining the first-floor landing, Mr Wood regrettably severed his carotid artery with his own saw, and expired at the foot of his own stairway through catastrophic loss of blood. He was just 28 years old.

Coroner Mr George Bishop recorded a verdict of 'Death by Misadventure' on the deceased, whose Olympic gold medal at Shepherd's Bush in 1908 brought him fame far beyond his native Norfolk.

His children Archibald, three years old, and little Pearl, one year old, were permitted among the funerary celebrants at the church of St John & St Mary in the Parish of Stiffkey.

It was hard to imagine how an athlete, a dextrous craftsman to boot, could have suffered such a clumsy accident. Falling downstairs on to a saw seemed intrinsically unbelievable, until I made a chilling connection: Luke on his hands and knees, a few days into our tenure at the boathouse, vainly scrubbing at a cloud-like mark ingrained on the cedar planks at the very foot of the stairs. So Jud had been telling the truth.

A cacophony of birdwatchers, returning from their safari to the headland, gathered annoyingly close to my van, banging on about sighting some rare pipit. I climbed over into the kitchenette, pulling down the blinds, to concentrate on my furtive research. Skipper Wood's story, I found, had been printed and reprinted, over several weeks, before his star faded into obscurity, eclipsed by the coming Great War.

On returning to the boathouse I made for the foot of the stairs, where the supposed accident had happened nigh on a century ago, hoping the spot would have more to reveal. But something about it made me shudder. '*Calma*, Roberto,' pleaded the little voice, back on duty with a vengeance, it seemed. I tried to pull myself together, put the past behind me, where it belonged. "Sod it," I sighed, "I'll be dead myself if I don't get this place together for Luke's return."

For the first time since our arrival at the boathouse, I sat down to work, at the post-war steel desk Luke had bought for my fortieth birthday. Under the marvellous sea-view window, it fitted our front bay as if one had been made for the other. I flipped open my laptop and loaded *Vectorworks*, the nifty software package I'd always relied on to show clients my vision for their buildings and living spaces, rendered in whatever finish they desired. Now I was both designer and customer, I fancied a room-by-room tour through the skeletal structure of Wood Feels. I'd fed in the dimensional data months ago: line-by-line the X-ray of the building came back to life on the screen.

Luke and I both wanted to preserve the authenticity of the boathouse. I tinkered with a few cosmetic changes only, and was plotting a rewire of the archaic electrical system, when a chill came down. Freezing the screen on 'save' a moment, I went to get fuel from the log-pile outside the kitchen door.

"Jud," I gasped, "What are you doing here?"

"Dude, sorry to startle you at this hour..." he replied unconvincingly. He appeared somewhat agitated, and evidently saw the same emotion in my own face. "Didn't mean to shock you about Skipper Wood earlier."

"Well, I survived," I retorted, trying to appear nonchalant at the prospect of a stranger lurking outside my door in the twilight.

"Cool, no harm done then?"

"No, Jud, no harm done." As we eyeballed each other I found myself wondering if he was planning to show me more tattoos, further inky clues about Skipper's story, perhaps. "Anything else I should know?"

"Ah, man." He stroked his beard nervously.

"Would you like to come in for a drink? There's a bit more to tell, eh?"

"No, it's gettin' dark, I've got to get back to Wells. See you out on the marshes some other time."

Again he turned on his heel, this time heading up the wooded track towards the main road. Blimey, I hope he didn't think I was chatting him up? And suddenly I felt stupid and reckless, inviting in a complete stranger who might, after all, have acquired his strange idioms and intricate body art in some stateside penitentiary. Once again I took my keys and cruised round the boathouse, checking all entry points like a prison janitor.

"So where were you, my big butch guard dog?" Boo shrugged his shoulders and trotted, like a show pony, in the direction of his bowl. Dinnertime. I lit the woodburner and slumped into my favourite club chair –

distressed tan leather, shabby chic, squashy – and it was not long before I drifted off. I found myself back at school, in the carpentry shop: clamped in a vice was a tiny leg made of cedarwood, and shavings twisted round me in long curlicues, tentacles ready to strangle me. The workroom was stifling: sawdust clogged my windpipe and I felt myself spluttering for air.

And then... vigorous sawing so audible, the smell of cedar so palpable: it was as though Skipper Wood was still at work on the boathouse, and whistling a grating tune that seemed all too familiar. Boo darted about. At the foot of the stairs he froze in a trance, gazing skyward into ether. Kangaroo-like, on his hind legs, he jumped up to acknowledge some other presence. The room went Baltic cold. The fire in the woodburner died in an instant. Boo yelped, ran to his basket cowering. I leapt over the side of the armchair, to comfort him and myself at the same time. Terror had me in its grip.

Then the fire was raging afresh, as if a switch had been flicked. The room was light again, and warm. I jolted from sleep, disorientated, unable to tell how much of this had been nightmare. I was on the floor, moist with sweat, alongside Boo's basket. He was quivering as whippets do when stressed, leaving me even more bewildered.

'*Calma,* Roberto. *Ci sei solo tu.'*

I'd forgotten that tag line of the *putto*'s, 'There's nobody here but you'. Yes, his advice had reassured me in the weeks and months following the violation of my childhood safe place. But this time it was misplaced: the enemy was within.

Determined to concentrate on something normal, I made a cup of tea. The kettle, whistling like an ocean liner leaving the quayside, should have served as a wake-up call to my intuition. Why couldn't I suss that 'Wood Feels' name? It was tempting to see 'Wood' as a reference to the Olympic carpenter, but surely Lord James could not have intended the building to stand as a kind of mausoleum, following Skipper's death here? That idea came with a very unpleasant frisson; I really needed to focus on something more agreeable.

Tilly! She'd mentioned working on 'a large estate' nearby: surely it must be Samphire Hall? I hadn't mentioned James Newton-Grey by name, or she'd surely have picked it up at once. This was the excuse I needed to drop her a line, once it was light. I wished I'd asked for her mobile number.

I was never going to sleep now, so I took a sandwich and more tea over to my desk. The computer lit up, out of standby, and the timber bones of my boathouse hung centre-screen, hovering 360° on a north-south axis.

I scanned down to the corner where I'd listed the construction materials: cedarwood, cobble and flint. "*Cedrus Libani*, the Cedar of Lebanon," I whispered. Boo glanced up. An ancient tree, revered in the Bible! Damn, I wished I had access to the Web.

But somewhere I had just the right reference book. Mother had gone through another of her phases, trawling antiquarian markets to impress her latest lover, before he was inevitably shown the door: my inherited *Natural History of the Bible* was a first edition. I'd never opened it until the day our estate agent told us that a single, eight-hundred-year-old cedar had been felled at Samphire Hall, to build the boathouse. By his account, some forbear of the Newton-Grey dynasty, supposedly a Crusader, had brought the sapling home from the sacred slopes of Mount Lebanon, now a World Heritage site. This was way before Capability Brown, the garden designer, had planted magnificent cedars on just about every fashionable estate in the country.

I rummaged in one of the large crates in the hall, where our books were waiting while I thought about building some shelves. The one I needed was easy to spot: I slipped it out of its bubble wrap and went to a section I'd bookmarked. The writer spoke of his rapture at encountering 'the Monarchs of the Forest' at the turn of a pass atop Mount Lebanon. What if I was living inside the very first cedar of Lebanon to grace this country, grown from a sapling off that hallowed mountain grove? Its ravishment, by an infidel foe, would have seemed sacrilegious in the Arab world, might have resulted in some kind of curse descending on the boathouse, on Samphire Hall, and even on the ill-fated Anne Boleyn. She had supposedly even *signed* the damned tree! Not that I could ever prove that, without taking the boathouse to pieces, plank by plank.

Then I remembered another resource too, my data-geek's stash of postcards, in the vintage steamer trunk we'd reinvented as a coffee table. Here it was: the tatty Adidas shoebox, and my fingers trembled as I riffled through the contents. Several dozen cards were filed as 'Middle East', and many had useful blurb on the back. I took them to my desk and turned the anglepoise on.

Discarding a few humdrum duds, I soon came across a striking card showing the green cedar on the Lebanese flag, and another referencing cedar oil's importance in the ritual mummification of the pharaohs. The postcards tumbled about the desk, as I scrabbled for one showing Old Jerusalem, where the Great Temple had been constructed partly from cedar.

"Oh Boo, you're standing on it..." His doe-like eyes looked up at me, while I carefully slid the fallen card from under his paw. '*Shalom* from Jerusalem', read the caption, but the info on the back was what I wanted. Yes! 'A mythical House of Cedar, built by King Solomon for his favourite wife, the Pharaoh's daughter'. Bingo! The romantic notion that had surely inspired Lord James

Newton-Grey with the idea of a cedar dwelling for his American bride.

And now, I wondered, had we done the right thing by buying the boathouse? People in the pub had said we'd got it at a steal, when prices in the area were supposed to be recession-proof. Why hadn't the place been snapped up sooner? Had nobody wanted to live in a jinxed property with a chequered past, whatever its unique setting, its rustic charm?

Not for the first time I felt myself overpowered by the tomblike aroma of the place, just as I'd been so long ago, tending to my bedridden mother in rooms reeking of incense. A parallel memory started to trouble me now: poor Luke's mum, laid up in hospital after her fall. True, she was hundreds of miles away, yet I found myself wondering if her misfortunes were another manifestation of the curse.

Too anxious now to stomach my sandwich, I flopped into my club chair, staring restlessly at the postcard from Israel. A Biblical story, a sacred tree: my far-from-ordinary house, which should have been a little piece of paradise, had begun to feel more like a hot slice of hell.

I pictured the cedar frame I'd found – doubtless an offcut from the original tree – so conspicuously lacking any picture, any understandable clue. I fetched it out of the understair cupboard, and as I unwrapped it for a second time the old newspaper headlines grabbed my attention: doom-laden stories, from the sinking of the *Titanic* in 1912 to the outbreak of the Great War in 1914. Was all this part of the pattern?

The oval frame, the size of a human face, slid into my hands. I placed it on my desk, running my fingers over the finely-carved decoration, stems and branches surely paying homage to the parent tree. I was convinced Skipper Wood himself had made it. Conceivably, it had been left as some kind of memento. It had waited all these years for a photograph: but by whom, and showing what?

CHAPTER THREE
THE AUDIT HOUSE

First thing next morning I drove up to Tilly's cottage, in the surfer-realm of Brancaster, hoping for a chance to exchange mobile numbers. Disappointingly she had left for work, so while Boo and Bertie fox terrier exchanged yelps and snuffles through the front door I scribbled a note and slid it through the letterbox. Tilly wouldn't mind the intrusion: we were both aware of our special rapport.

The next hour or so I spent strolling along the white sands of Brancaster beach, mulling over Skipper Wood's death at the foot of my stairs. The kite-surfers were out in force, making the best of the brisk autumn breezes. Boo scampered in and out of the froth under a host of colourful kites, criss-crossing a big sky in the style of a Miró.

My mobile sang. The signal was surprisingly good, and the sound of her voice only enhanced the scene.

"It's me, Tilly, just popped home and happened to find your note."

"Well hi... thanks for getting in touch so soon."

"There's something you need discuss, urgently?"

"Yeah, where you're working, is it by chance...?"

"Samphire Hall," she cut in. "Why, Bertie?"

"I'll explain – can we meet up later?"

"Love to."

I had to be careful she didn't get the wrong impression, though the thought of seeing her did leave me mildly aroused. But I had the legitimate excuse of telling her the boathouse's connection with her workplace, which she might find useful.

"How about four o'clock on the estate mews, the Audit House?" she was saying. "It's the only right turn off the north drive, about a hundred yards inside the entrance: you can't miss it."

"Perfect." It sounded like a date, albeit a platonic one.

Later that day I drove over to Samphire Hall, stopping at the entrance before some imposing iron gates topped with sharp arabesque finials, their foreboding implication: 'Keep Out'. I sensed a world that maybe I should not dare to enter. Yet Tilly had given her instructions, and off the north drive I found the cobbled mews, which still contained functional stables, apparently used by a local riding school.

Tilly was there to meet us, dapper in a Harris Tweed suit; her short hair, styled with a Marcel wave, evoked a twenties' fashion plate from *Country Life*. We greeted each other by a half-open stable door.

"So, Bertie," she began, stroking the head of a dappled grey, "What's *so* important?"

"Well – apart from seeing you again of course – I'm pretty certain the cedar tree, the one my boathouse was built from, grew on this very estate."

"Really? It's Blickling Hall that has the well-known Boleyn connection."

"No, no: definitely Samphire Hall. Anne Boleyn must have come visiting here, as a child, before she went off to France."

"Bertie, I'd like to tell this to the NHS." My confusion must have looked quite comical. Tilly snorted with laughter as she explained her acronym which, as far as the rest of the UK was concerned, stood for National Health Service.

"The Norfolk Heritage Society, silly. They'll be really keen on news like this, especially as we've got a Tudor escritoire as the star exhibit for our Gala Opening in November. A writing desk, the earliest one in the country. And also..." But then she lapsed into thought, twisting a heavy key on its chain, as if she were Samphire Hall's caretaker, not its young archivist. "Shush, I have an idea. Follow me."

She led Boo and me down the mews. I stopped to read a plaque over one stable door: *Pocahontas, beloved bay mare – killed in action on the Somme (date unknown) – owner: Lord James Newton-Grey.* One of a million hapless horses sent to the Front in the Great War, never to return.

"Come along, Bertie," Tilly called, like a hockey captain. We approached a hexagonal brick and flint building where the heavily panelled door bore a brass sign: Estate Office.

"The Audit House," she exclaimed. "Come in, before anyone spots us." She led me up worn stone steps into an intriguing room, again hexagonal, on the top floor.

"I might get shot for this, but some diaries were discovered at the Hall the other day, written by the last-ever Lord Newton-Grey. I had them brought over here for cataloguing: bet you'd like to have a read?"

"Tilly! You're sure this is okay?"

"Look, they brought me in to do archival stuff, at the eleventh hour really. The opening's only on Bonfire Night and there's a lot of family treasures to curate before that: so this will help me as well as you."

"Last-minute dotcom, eh?"

"Yah, their curator – ex-V&A as well – got really sick. So that's how I landed the job. I'm a kind of understudy around here, unless I really prove myself with the NHS."

"Okay, great. If I unearth anything of interest, I'll let you know, promise."

"Bertie, I've got to get back to the Hall, it's manic over there. Can I leave you to browse for a few hours and pick you up later?

She strode over to a wall of shelves, floor to ceiling filled with identical ledgers. The well-fitted suit accentuated her figure as she stretched up for a stack of small books: the Newton-Grey diaries.

"Enjoy."

"Thanks, Tilly; I was!"

"I'm glad I found you," she smiled, flicking dust off her jacket shoulder, as if making ready for a parade.

"Likewise."

"*Ciao*," she said. Her lips parted, emphasising her dimples.

"*Ciao, bella: ci vediamo*," was the shameful best I could manage in what was, in principle at any rate, my mother tongue.

Tilly blew me a kiss before pulling the heavy door to: my attempt at sexy lingo had struck a chord. The sound of her brogues echoed down the steps, the outer door shut and I was alone in the Audit House.

I put the bundled diaries down on a draughtsman's table, marked with indentations, scratches and circular vestiges of ink. Maybe Lord James Newton-Grey had actually sat here, poring over his designs for the boathouse, in collaboration with the luckless Skipper Wood. The room was stuffy. As I hung my jacket on a chair I spotted a plum leather-bound tome on a shelf nearby: its spine, embossed in gold, read *Maps & Plans / Samphire Hall*.

The diaries could wait: here was a plethora of charts and diagrams, mostly of the estate, some of the county, food for my fascination with old cartography. One particular lithograph outlined the curtilage of the Samphire Hall estate – some twenty thousand acres, according to a handwritten annotation. With my forefinger I followed the boundary to the north of the coastal road, and felt myself drawn across contours – characteristic of North Norfolk's rolling terrain – to a bank of trees. In an elevated clearing beyond, overlooking the saltmarshes, the plan view of a simple structure grabbed my attention. Putting on my glasses, I read the tiny print: *Boat Store 1726*.

So Wood Feels occupied the site of a much earlier, *bona fide* boathouse; but it had become a somewhat larger dwelling, more like an Art Nouveau cottage, cannily built on higher ground to avoid flooding. Flicking through the book I came across plans folded inside a card sleeve, and laid them out: Boo sniffed at the edges, which overhung the draughtsman's table like a printed tablecloth.

Here it was, my boathouse in all its glory: Edwardian architectural blueprints. Excitingly, moreover, most were signed by Skipper Wood, with what looked like a flat carpenter's pencil, the sort I'd seen – sharpened by a good old penknife – used for scrawling plans on plaster walls at many a commissioned restoration of my own. No less a person than Lord James Newton-Grey, using a black-ink fountain pen, had elegantly signed off each detailed elevation. They were dated 1911.

But then my eye was caught by a surprising detail, a note in the same black hand: 'To be known by the old name, Woodfields'. This made sense, since the site was a field among woods. But it deepened the already-perplexing question about 'Wood Feels': when, and by whose decision, had the name been changed to this unnatural, self-conscious expression? It seemed to be trying to convey a message in some kind of clumsy code. I felt like a spy in need of an Enigma machine.

I started snapping the plans on my old camera phone. It occurred to me that I could print up one of the diagrams and put it in that oval frame from under the stairs. Luke, with his love of period detail, would adore both the frame and a blueprint of the boathouse, preferably showing Skipper's signature. It would make an unforgettable Christmas present.

Soon I found myself scouring the shelves of estate ledgers. I pulled one out and blew years of dust from the tops of the pages. A sharp sneeze came from under the table.

"Sorry, Boo."

Routine entries dating back to the mid-eighteenth century were uninspiring for my particular research, but they made me realise this was a series. Knowing when Skipper Wood had worked on the boathouse, I sought out *Estate Accounts – 1911*, with its pay-log for estate workers, house staff, agricultural labourers, physicians, veterinary surgeons, gamekeepers and so on. Leafing through the statements, I took special note of payments to Skipper, which rose steeply towards the end of 1911. So... he had died in April 1913. Sliding back my chair, I sought out the accounts ledger for that year as well. Among numerous entries of no great consequence one odd line stood out: '£600 paid to Mrs Beulah Wood, May 1913'. Rather a sizeable fortune back in the day: according to the calculator on my mobile, something like £56,000 in today's money. I guessed this was some kind of reparation made by Lord James to Skipper's grieving widow, a month after his fatal accident.

But my time with this hoard of diaries was running out. There were eight in all, bundled together with shaggy garden twine. A5-ish in size, and green Morocco-bound, they were dated 1910 to 1918. Some were knotted shut with silk tapes. Adrenaline surged like a tide as I opened the earliest one: the black handwriting on the first page was indeed that of Lord James Newton-Grey, last incumbent of Samphire Hall.

How could I have known – as I randomly chose an entry and started delving into Lord James's deepest, most private thoughts – what an impact this would have on my life henceforward?

4th March 1910 – p.m.
I cannot get Alice out of my mind this evening, a delicious vision as she stepped from a landau provided by dear Countess Daisy. A most memorable day – clement weather – Alice and I strolled arm-in-arm through Hyde Park to our rendezvous at the Ritz, with the Countess and His Majesty the King.

Despite the estimable company it was Alice, with her Titian hair, her emerald eyes, and her beauteous poise, who transfixed me – a man can most certainly lose his wits in the presence of so exquisite a creature. It has to be said that the King, with his roving eye, was clearly also taken with the West Virginian.

But my eye soon settled on a much less sophisticated entry.

5th April 1910
Pater's gout has returned, making him more lugubrious than ever. He blasts directives at the servants like a round of heavy artillery. We rowed at breakfast most fiercely. Why does he think he possesses me, as if I were an obsequious stable boy?

Conflicts with Papa... I felt sorry for the man, but at least James had known who his father was. Most of my mother's partners had been presented to me as 'uncles'. Drunken Roy, the last of these father-incarnations, had got saddled with me after Mother died, her system full of uppers, downers and heroin as I later found out. To his credit Roy did stick around to see me through my Eleven

Plus, which secured me a place at grammar school. Then he pissed off. I was curious to see how James's troubles resolved.

10th April 1910

Lest I forget the harsh treatment I endured as a child, let me record Pater's punitive measures: the beatings with a riding crop, the welts across my naked flesh, the ice-cold baths, the solitary confinement – in order to make me ready for another war, so he said! Mater and Nurse Henderson's pleas, on my behalf, were invariably fruitless. But now I am a gentleman of twenty-one years, I stand six-foot two *sans* riding boots, taller than my great mare, Pocahontas. Pater has grown feeble with age, and I am his only heir – so my time is coming, and Lord Randolph's is expiring…

Father or not, my Uncle Roy had been a pussycat in comparison to Randolph Newton-Grey.

1st June 1910 – p.m.

A telegram this morning from poor Daisy, deep in mourning from the passing of our King on the sixth day of May, despite their entanglement being long past. She has troubled herself to confirm arrangements for Alice Fitzgerald's imminent arrival for a country weekend at Samphire Hall, to be chaperoned by her Mama, Constance.

Mater's rose garden, with its fragrant arbour, will be the perfect rendezvous in which to venture my proposal. Or, perhaps better, the romantic shade of The Boleyn Cedar?

This was something indeed for Tilly: Lord James mentions a cedar on his estate, the 'Boleyn' reference surely clinching the legend that Henry VIII's future queen had carved her name there.

3rd June 1910 – a.m.

Dawn beckoned through the damask, a Friday full of promise. The Hall stirred with a clamour of activity. I passed Ida along the passage. Dependable Henderson: my governess, my nurse and, it has to be said, my surrogate mother, since mater's untimely passing, when I was a mere stripling. Indeed, Ida knew what my heart felt this morning.

After breakfast, I took Pocahontas down Peddars Way into Holkham, making good time back to Samphire Hall to dress for lunch.

Lord James at full gallop along the Roman coastal path, which runs past my boathouse: an arresting sight, no doubt. Already identifying with his miserable childhood, I now pondered how traumas past would have affected his adult self, without the benefits of counselling as we know it today.

3rd June 1910 – p.m.

Bailey sounded the motor-horn to announce their arrival on the forecourt. Pater, had he not been bedridden, would have insisted the servants stand to attention, all starched, to greet visitors, but I dismissed them as an act of defiance.

Alice mesmerised me as she stepped out of the Rolls: her emerald eyes evoked the deepest pools of Shenandoah and her gaze, under the brim of her picture hat, would have inspired Gauguin.

3rd June 1910 late

Pater was wheeled down to dinner this evening. Mama Constance was charm personified! But why would she not be, when the wealthiest man in the county was vetting her beautiful daughter? She fussed excessively over Pater's sickly countenance. The bastard is nearing his maker – begone, old man – my time draws closer!

I got up to stretch my legs. I was only starting, gleaning first insights into the curious thinking of James Newton-Grey. How could I possibly trawl through eight years of diaries before Tilly returned? She'd been so considerate, letting me see them: would it be so impertinent to ask for their loan? The research and information I could provide, while she was under pressure in the couple of weeks before the Hall opened, could only be to her advantage.

"What d'you reckon, Boo?" But he was fast asleep at my feet.

4th June 1910 – a.m.
Yesterday my love, having secured her Mama's approval, accepted my proposal! The old house danced with a gaiety and song I have never known before.

Pater retired earlier; he deteriorates with each passing day, and I rejoice. I may sound ignoble, but to you, my diary, trusted *confidant*, I confess all my innermost truths. It is little wonder that despairing mater chose to go to an early grave.

So it was suicide? This parallel between Lord James's life and my own spooked me even more than Tilly's similar story, the other evening, had done. Considering how grievously I'd suffered after my mother's desertion, I felt alarm for James's mental state.

Luke might enjoy moaning about his old mum, but at least he'd had one, to nurture him through adolescence; and until recently an attentive father too. Who knows how I would have turned out, given a bit more emotional security? And who knows how Luke would feel if he realised that, in his absence? I was becoming preoccupied with people whose background was so similar to my own, so very different to his.

5th June 1910 – p.m.

A leaden sky befits my heavy heart as Alice and her mama leave for the railway station. Let it be written: my betrothed leaves Samphire Hall one last time!

The night the King died I had a strange dream: a vision of an exotic red-green bird caged deep in a wood, under a Giotto sky. As if it were a prophecy, the idea came to me at first light: to fell the mammoth cedar where we pledged our troth, in order to fashion, from its august loins, a lair: a marvellous cabin, to stand on the site of the ancient boathouse. Here my love shall dwell for all eternity. And I shall never be alone again.

The passion of this darkly profound and ambiguous confession sent my mind in a spin, and I got up for fresh air. Opening the little lancet window, I glimpsed Samphire Hall through an avenue of silver birch trees, autumnally bare. It was the north wing, by my guess, in clear view. A stained glass window of lofty dimensions stared back at me. Perhaps – since this Gothic kaleidoscope was brightly lit from within, to combat the gathering dusk – Tilly and her fellow conservationists were still hard at work up there.

I started tidying the ledgers away. Imprinted on the front of each was a bold heraldic crest, the corporate logo of the day. A cardinal red shield, an emblematic cedar in green: at its base, a wreath of prickly samphire and a purple ribbon coiling with the family motto, *fortitudine prospero*. 'By endurance I prosper', I reckoned; I'd been one of the few boys in my class who had actually liked Latin. The bold crest hailed from an era of prestige and power, but in fact the once-magnificent ancestral pile had not prospered, and scarcely endured, beyond the days of Lord James Newton-Grey. NHS fund-raising had kick-started its present resurrection.

James's next entry showed him putting his building plan into operation.

16th July 1910

Here at Pater's baronial desk in the Great Library – with anarchy in my heart – I conspire to fell The Boleyn Cedar, which in all its majesty has stood at Samphire Hall so many generations back; a veritable 'family tree', extolled down the Newton-Grey line as our Eighth Wonder of the World. To me, though, as I contemplate its scented boughs, it is the mere vessel whose regal loins will give birth to a cedar cage – a rustic temple divine – to caress my bride.

It was clear to me, from the purple of his language, that Lord James's Edwardian upcycling project was deliciously Gothic in conception. And as I read on I learned how, with the help of an estate manager named Stanley Sellars – who presumably operated out of the Audit House – Lord James had begun to search out the finest master carpenter in Norfolk.

They advertised a prestigious contest: 'County Carpenter of the Year'. The winner would be engaged to build 'a secluded bolthole and romantic retreat' for the future Lady Alice, when she returned. Furthermore, it would be presented as her wedding gift. The diary also revealed that James's champion would be bound by a legal *caveat*, sworn to secrecy regarding the cabin's exact whereabouts. Twenty-five guineas, and a Royal Doulton 'Loving Cup', would be the extent of his prize, along with the prestige accruing to a winning finalist. There was no public mention, I noticed, of James's iconoclastic scheme to transform the famous cedar.

20th July 1910 – p.m.

I met my five finalists today, a most promising coterie of craftsmen, including Skipper Wood, the former athlete of Stiffkey, now residing in Binham, who made a lasting impression. I was thinking in terms of tables and tallboys, but this hearty fellow earnestly told me he plans to sculpt 'a Blakeney seal' from Senegalese ebony, lately arrived in a mercantile shipment into Wells town harbour. Among his rivals one Caleb Bacon – his upturned snout befitting his porky name – plans to create a wader in Scots pine, though he failed to state which particular species.

There it was, a mention of Skipper Wood! But at that point my mobile sang. Boo jumped up and banged his head under the table.

"Bertie, Mam got a cancellation. Hip job by the end of next week."

"Oh Luke! You must be so relieved."

"Aye. Where are you, picking up instantly like that?"

"Samphire Hall. Good connection, eh?"

"What the fuck are you doing up there?"

"Well, I tried to tell you the other day. These dreams I keep having, at the boathouse, it all..."

"Not this dream stuff again, Bertie, I honestly haven't got time for one of your epics."

"Of course, you've got a lot on, but Luke..."

"Uncle Vin wants me to sort the flood insurance, replacing white goods, TV, furniture, soft furnishings, the effing lot. Then a general refurb when it's all dried out. I was knee-deep in paperwork all morning."

"You're sure they'll pay up?"

"Aye, and there's no way she can cope if they don't: her pension is stretched enough, the way prices are going."

"Luke, I need to tell you..."

"Bertie, I've got to shoot: I'm due at the hospital in half an hour." He did sound stressed.

"Give Mum my love."

"Miss you and Boo. Bye."

Damn. Poor Luke was too bogged down with family troubles to listen to my concerns. And here was I reading archaic diaries, when I should have been getting our home together. Yet somehow – even if it sounds like a cliché – I knew I was embarking on an odyssey, its destination shadowy, but its purpose crystal clear: to investigate the tragedy in my home so long ago, which I was convinced would have a substantial bearing on my continued happiness there.

Still no Tilly; Lord James beckoned again.

31st July 1910 midnight

Summer Bank Holiday: Stanley Sellars has been most accommodating with all the arrangements for my mediaeval fête, I shall toast him with a full glass of absinthe.

1st August 1910 – p.m.

The fête fared well. I have my supreme carpenter: Mr Skipper Wood. His 'Blakeney Seal' was indeed a triumph. Truth to tell, he left the other four carpenters standing!

Cocky Caleb Bacon, with his second-rate attempt at a Spotted Redshank, failed to impress, and he lacked sportsmanship, snubbing Skipper without a handshake. Poor show!

Still, Skipper had the crowd at his feet, as he doused himself in champagne from the Loving Cup. His wife Beulah Wood, plain as a pikestaff, scowled at the pretty servant girls, who fought like street-whores over the spoils of his sodden shirt. It was Skipper's day all right!

Lord James – awaiting his true love's return from America – seemed smitten with this talented master carpenter. I closed the window against the evening chill, knowing I was on to something, and then I reached the point when his full intentions became known.

31st August 1910 – p.m.

As my former guardian, Ida Henderson feels she must warn me of dire consequences, should I persist with felling the Cedar, 'the elder statesman of the Estate' as she calls it. Do I not realise, she asks, that such an act will kill Pater? I must admit the idea has crossed my mind.

My bride's cabin will be a testimony to a new epoch at Samphire Hall. And besides, any remaining timber shall be reborn – how sweet the irony – as prosthetic limbs to my own design.

Prosthesis, for whom? Lord James had started to sound like some kind of sociopath: and indeed, as I read on, I learnt how he blithely ignored Ida's warnings, and his own intimations. Assisted by Skipper – and some well-paid farmhands – he did dismember the patriarchal cedar, carefully cutting out, as if it were a heart, the precious part where Anne Boleyn had carved her name. James referred cryptically to a plan he was hatching, to hide the Tudor Queen's signature in the boathouse, not only to preserve it, but also as a ploy to amuse his Virginian bride with a drawn-out game of hide and seek.

It was getting dark: still no Tilly. I had time to think. For me, James's actions spoke of revenge for all the years he had suffered at the hand of his cruel, cold father. But his language was apocalyptic: one entry stood out in this respect:

7th September 1910 – p.m.

My faithful staff crowded every window as Skipper handed me the axe to drive one last fatal blow. A tremendous thunder shook the Hall to its mediaeval foundations, as if Krakatoa had been reawakened. No cheers, no applause, only the sense of a momentous watershed. A creation in the name of my love – Alice – became a task completed.

A few days of sawing and haulage followed before James's 'creation' was followed by an equal and opposite reaction.

12th September 1910 – p.m.
The doctor pronounced Pater dead at noon. I pulled the linen off his withered visage to witness the certainty of his extinction. I pondered, briefly, this consequence of my defiant destruction of the Cedar. But only the superstitious shall judge me my father's executioner.

I took to my bed before sundown, absinthe my only comfort.

I was shocked. I flicked through the next few weeks in the diary. James focussed on practical consequences of the felling: innumerable local kilns were requisitioned to hasten the seasoning of the timber, the boathouse site was levelled, foundations dug. Hunting jaunts and social fixtures continued. There was no further mention of Lord Randolph's death, no funeral or burial. Nor did I find any untoward mention of Skipper, nor any indication of exactly where the Boleyn carving was to be hidden.

Boo tapped me with his nose, broke my concentration. While I'd been lost, sleuthing around in James's world, he'd stayed on duty in ours, monitoring footsteps on the stone steps. Then Tilly burst in, with a delectable smile.

"Bertie, it's gone seven. Terribly sorry to have been so long."

"No probs. Hey Tilly, do you think the Norfolk Heritage Society – the 'NHS' – would let me borrow the diaries? There's so much juicy history in here for your exhibition."

Her eyes widened curiously, and appeared more violet than ever. Her tongue rolled around behind her lips as she imagined research kudos enhancing her employment prospects.

"You realise you're the first person to read them, given that there's no Newton-Grey heir? I think it'll be okay to borrow them, on condition you open them carefully, clean hands, and guard them as if your life depended on it." She lowered her voice. "I'm screwed if my boss finds out. Dr Wulff, he does everything by the book."

"Dr Wulff? Does he bite?"

"I wouldn't put it past him. Cambridge PhD, and he cut his teeth at the History Department in Copenhagen, where he comes from. Karsten Wulff: you can Google him." She sounded awestruck.

"No need, I promise. I'll treat them like gold dust. Cedar dust even."

"And remember, Bertie, I'll need a précis of everything relevant. ASAP," she added.

I got up to give her a hug, and was taken aback as she closed her thick-lashed eyes and projected her lips. An unexpected reminder, of the dubious sexual exploits of my college days, awoke in my jeans. Tilly's fragrance – a seductive, masculine cologne – dizzied my senses. Somehow I contained myself, and planted a single kiss on her cheek, which flushed a deep pink, like a winning camellia at the Chelsea Flower Show.

"Come on, Bertie. I best lock up."

"Good idea. Come Boo, off your arse." I carefully stowed the diaries in my bag, and we all trotted down the Audit House steps into the mews.

"D'you fancy dinner at the local?" I asked.

But Tilly loosened her hipper-than-thou tartan tie, like a St Trinian's schoolgirl, and mischievously suggested a quick sneak round Samphire Hall. Night was drawing in, all the NHS personnel had clocked off: she had a torch and a key.

"Then a well-earned drink afterwards," she said.

"Deal."

She linked her arm with mine, and we ambled up the north drive towards Samphire Hall. The thrill was intoxicating. And apart from the privilege of going off-*piste* in an historic house, I was about to cross the threshold of the fascinating James Newton-Grey. Moreover, as Tilly explained, we could peek inside his private suite of rooms, practically untouched since the late twenties. This would no doubt double my insight into the man himself.

As we approached, I looked up at the shadowy Hall: eighteen windows wide, three storeys high, four in the central block where the impressive, gabled entrance stood. Tilly explained that James had commissioned the main oak doors, embellished with hammered copper, and chased with Arts & Crafts serpents, in 1910, in memory of his father. Lord Randolph would obviously have hated them. Her torchlight danced teasingly over a stone relief, hewn above the entrance, featuring the same crest and motto I had seen embossed on the ledgers. I felt an adrenaline rush: Mother would have been envious of this heady high.

"Bertie, keep close, hold on to Boo. The lighting's atrocious, while the contractors rewire the chandeliers and so on." Tilly unlocked, and we stepped into a gloomy vestibule. I fancied I could smell aniseed.

"Come through," she whispered. Holding my breath, I followed her into a great dark void. And as she shone her torch above us there came a vicious whip-crack sound, followed by a cacophony of terrifying crashes. Something unseen, yet audibly massive, came tumbling down a stairway towards us...

CHAPTER FOUR
SAMPHIRE HALL

Tilly recoiled. Boo yelped. I ducked. A white projectile exploded, with an appalling crash, into a clatter of marble fragments just inches from our feet.

"Everybody okay?" Tilly asked shakily. Her torch swept the shadows.

"Sh-it," I gasped. "That could have killed us." I checked Boo for injuries, but he was more interested in sniffing around the broken remnants of what had evidently been a life-size statue. Tilly knelt at the foot of the sweeping staircase, inspecting the decapitated torso. As for me, I was dazed by the omen: it seemed like a replay of Skipper Wood's death.

"A strange happening..." I began.

"No Bertie; the place is not haunted, if that's what you're thinking." Tilly had read my mind. "Just hope I don't get the sodding blame," she added.

"Why do you say that?"

"This is pretty-boy Antinoüs, and I'd already logged an unstable crack in his heel. He was due for pick-up by some local stonemason, to go and be fixed. The guy was booked for this morning, but he never appeared and, worse still, I forgot to chase it up."

"So it just toppled off its plinth, and plummeted down the staircase?"

"Yah, exactly. So no poltergeists..." She smiled for a brief moment. "Karsten – Dr Wulff, I should say – won't have much trouble finding a living culprit."

"Can you pin the blame on me somehow?"

"Oh, Bertie, not to worry, I'll get round it," she sighed. She turned on a builder's spotlight, shaky on its paint-spattered tripod, then fired off a text to Karsten. Something about her posture told me she would have liked nothing more than a drink to fix her stress.

"Antinoüs, wasn't he the lover of some Roman Emperor?"

"Hadrian. He had an eye for a dishy lad."

We gathered the various limbs into piles, anatomically sorted. The last piece to be shifted, naturally, was his rather weighty member, sheared off in the fall: Tilly seemed to be leaving this to me, doubtless thinking me more experienced in handling such items. I was thinking the same thing about her, as she could tell when our eyes suddenly met. Luckily we both burst out laughing, and shared the chore. The mood lightened.

"Oh, sod it... c'mon, let's have a wander," Tilly suggested, gesturing that we should proceed warily across the damaged floor. She turned on a second site light, and I started to take in the surprisingly avant-garde style of the décor.

"Tilly, I had no idea."

"Fab, isn't it?" She seemed back in control, tilting the light on its tripod for a better look at the ceiling, all intricate carved reliefs and flights of angels on inlaid panels.

"Amazing."

"This entrance hall is known as St Benedict's Foyer, precisely because of this brilliant roof. It's stolen."

With real relish Tilly spoke of a fifteenth-century ancestor, Sir Thomas Newton, who had managed to come home from his Grand Tour with this choice 'boiserie' ceiling in his luggage. Her own research had established how Thomas had promised a Benedictine monastery in northern Italy that their ceiling would go to the Holy Shrine at Walsingham – not so far from its actual destination, his ancestral home. The monks had parted with an exquisite treasure, commissioned by no less a patron than the Duke of Milan, for peanuts.

"This way. There's something that'll really blow your socks off!" She aimed her torch at a pair of ebony doors: inlaid glass eyes winked back from gilt-edged sockets.

"If you think they're creepy, wait till you see the other side."

She carefully opened the great doors, revealing an impossibly long gallery, and switched on a long line of uplighters, newly installed. She wasn't wrong about blowing my mind: two shadowy files of white horses' heads were mounted high on opposing walls – each fitted, by some bonkers taxidermist, with a narwhal tusk, so as to appear like a unicorn.

"Shades of Damien Hirst," I said, though Samphire Hall was a century or so ahead of that particular trend.

"Quite a shock to the system, yah?" At least Tilly was able to reassure me that the NHS had proved these horses had died in the Great War, their heads shipped back to England by a serving officer at the time. "Still gruesome; but at least they weren't murdered for art's sake."

"Let me guess, Tilly: that officer was Lord James?" She nodded.

"You should see some of the stuff we've found – the NHS and I – since we opened up his private quarters. It's going to make one hell of an exhibition."

Tilly led me past the unicorns, across an intricate patchwork of Moorish tiles, and through further ominous doors into a vestibule whose walls and ceiling were padded in dark red leather, like a Chesterfield sofa. The colour alone made me shudder, as I thought back to the dog killer in his oxblood Doc Martens.

One of the padded panels turned out to be a concealed door – impressive from a Panic Room point of view – and through it we passed into darkness. There was that familiar aniseed smell again.

"Lord James's inner sanctum," said my tour guide. "Preserved like a time capsule, thanks to someone called Ida Henderson."

"Aha, James's guardian: just read her name in the diary."

"Brill," said Tilly, as she felt for the light switch. "Exactly the kind of detail I'll need in your notes. We just know Ida as the chatelaine here during World War I, when Samphire Hall was an auxiliary hospital." If sick people had lived here, I thought, then Tilly's acronym habit, which turned Norfolk Heritage Society into 'NHS', helped to join James's world with our own. I liked that kind of connection, whether or not it made sense.

Tilly switched on a chandelier – metallic, iridescent glass – and a high-style Art Nouveau fireplace came into focus. Playfully, like a showgirl, she also flicked on the light above a portrait that hung above the mantelshelf.

"Wow, who's this?" I enquired.

"This, for all his sins, is your man, Lord James Newton-Grey!"

There he was... and now I had a face for the mind whose innermost thoughts I'd started to discover.

"Blimey, so dashing: you could fall in love on the spot!" Thank God Luke wasn't able to hear me.

"Isn't he the last word: so devilishly handsome?" Tilly sighed like a lovelorn groupie. "Why don't they make them like that any more?"

I'd had the impression she quite fancied me; but James was more than merely handsome. Something extraordinary smouldered beyond his portrait, and the brooding swagger in his features was undeniably sensual. His intense black eyes, viscerally hypnotic, exuded a hungry yearning, as if he could leap from the canvas and ravage you. I surveyed his jet-black hair, confidently slicked back with pomade, and gulped.

He was rather casually dressed for a portrait of the period, in an open-necked penny-collared shirt under a linen waistcoat, his sleeves rolled up to reveal sturdy forearms; the background was the colour of well-burnished saddles.

"Hello? Bertie... I'm over here," Tilly chuckled.

"Err, sorry." I felt a strong *déjà vu* creeping over me.

"Sexy, no?" said Tilly, looking quickly from me to the portrait and back again. "But I've only just made his acquaintance, so to speak. These rooms were out of bounds 'til just recently, even to the NHS team."

"Who's the artist?"

"John Singer Sargent... you know, the American? He obviously fell in love with young James too."

"What d'you reckon, Tilly? Mid-twenties when he sat for Sargent?"

The portrait revealed an enigmatic hint of vulnerability, which somehow added to the patrician's soulful appeal. What really struck me was the way the painter had dared to portray a lord as a strapping prole, a 'bit of rough'. It was rather how I imagined Skipper Wood might have looked.

Boo, in a flash of make-yourself-at-home, had jumped up on a velvet sofa – grey, highlighted with peacock blue. I called his name sharply, and he slid down apologetically, parking himself on a Persian rug instead.

"Watch this." Tilly now hinged open a wall panel, exposing some kind of built-in chest for plans.

"How did you know that was there?"

"Well, there was years of dust on this panelling. The cleaner was so apologetic: she polished too hard and it sprang open on her."

"What bad luck!"

"Exactly. So this is where we found James's diaries, in the top drawer. But also these strange drawings."

Tilly slid a black leather folder from one of the eight drawers and opened it, not without hesitation. I was immediately taken by James's masterly-drawn illustrations – human limbs and mechanical substitutes – and must have stayed quiet for a good five minutes: when I finally looked up Tilly was studying my expression with bemusement. Each study was signed – the same inimitable black-inked hand I'd already seen on Lord James's boathouse designs at the Audit House.

"A prosthetics designer!"

"For maimed soldiers in the Great War, we think."

"They look so ahead of their time," I exclaimed. Something about his pencil shading made me think of the carbon-fibre running blades of today, but James's designs corresponded far more faithfully to the human form: I couldn't guess what material he'd intended to use. "What a talent."

"You can almost see the movement in every joint," Tilly began.

"So James was at the Western Front?" I interrupted.

"We believe so, yah; there's a whole box of military regalia – medals and certificates – but we haven't finished cataloguing them yet."

Tilly pulled out another wad of drawings, and we leafed together through more brilliant illustrations. I told her about the big da Vinci exhibition Mother Dearest had dragged me to as a kid, the first time I'd been in the presence of far-sighted genius.

"All without the benefit of CAD," Tilly added. She seemed addicted to acronyms.

"Precisely."

Out from the mass of pristine designs dropped an old, grimy disc of reddish fibreboard on a leather cord, paper clipped to a photograph. I picked them up off the floor.

The elliptical, sepia picture showed a strapping soldier, with an open-face and dark curly hair: the stripes on his uniform suggested he had been a sergeant. On the reverse was scribbled, 'Affectionately yours, Stanley'. The disc was stamped 'S Sellars, 8th Norfolks. No.1208'.

"You know what," I said. "This dog-tag belonged to Stanley Sellars, James's estate manager: he's also mentioned in his diary." It looked like an expensive studio shot, destined to be framed: a pity to hide it away. "But 'affectionately'... he sounds a bit special, would you say?"

"Yah, strange from a mere employee. Soulful eyes too," Tilly mused. "So James hid personal mementos among his design work. Maybe this Stanley was also a friend, not just a servant. Or else he got wounded and James helped him out with an artificial limb or two. God, let's hope you find something about this in the diaries."

"We're building quite an interesting profile of Lord James," I suggested uneasily.

"Yah, and there's lots more bizarre stuff. Who'd have thought he played the harmonica? But I've got something much more amazing to show you." Moving over to the shuttered window bay, Tilly plucked off the dustsheet from a smallish piece of brown furniture.

"Bertie, this is it: the earliest writing desk ever found, now confirmed by the V&A."

"It's so naïve." The modest desk, in dark oak, had a petite kneehole, and two small drawers either side. With its barley-twist legs and bun feet, it could easily have gone unnoticed amid the Art Nouveau riches of James's sitting room.

"Externally, perhaps," said Tilly. "And cleverly so, warding off unwanted attention."

She coolly lifted the writing slope, revealing an inner panel, intricately tooled with gilt patterning that surrounded a miniature of a young girl, painted in profile, with raven hair.

"Tilly, it's exquisite."

"Who do you suppose she is?"

"Well, and I know this might sound crazy, my guess would be Anne Boleyn!"

Tilly's eyes widened, as if I'd hit on something.

"My hunch too, ever since you said her inscription was hidden in your boathouse somewhere. It's been bugging me, so this afternoon I nipped up to the Great Library, hunted out some inventories."

Tilly handed me a photocopy: the archaic handwriting was perplexing, to say the least, but she leant close, her arm resting on my shoulder, half whispering the story as her breath played on my cheek. Master William Newton, and Anne Boleyn, had been childhood sweethearts. Their betrothal must have been approved by both families, because the little desk was recorded as part of an intended dowry. It had been sent over from nearby Blickling Hall.

I imagined the Tudor children, playing catch-me around the great girth of the cedar, and Anne – a notably spirited girl – taking William's dagger to carve her name deep in the trunk, as lovers still do on many a tree.

"Tilly, this ties up so nicely with the story of the boathouse! But... not so well with actual history as we know it..."

"'Fraid it does," she said, producing a second document. "I'm sure you know Anne's story: gap year in France, internship in London, as lady-in-waiting to the first Mrs Henry the Eighth. And just when Henry starts taking an interest – in the Oval Orifice, as it were..."

She pointed out a death entry she'd found in the parish register: *Wm Newton, aged 16, while riding on the estate.*

"Her young paramour? Lucky for the king, eh?"

"Certainly lucky for me." All these stories amounted to major Brownie points for Tilly's NHS career. "And here's what I'm thinking." Her voice trembled. "For Gala Opening purposes, all the PR... do we dare call this desk 'The Boleyn Bureau'?"

"Nice one," I said. But her saying 'we' that surprised me. That and the hug that followed.

"It was fate, Bertie, bumping into you," she declared. She pressed close, a dangerous moment; I kept my cool, trying to avoid eye contact, to think only of flooding, and Tyneside, and Luke. When the door behind us creaked, it was a very timely distraction.

"Who's there?" I asked, moving quickly away.

"Probably Boo," sighed Tilly. "Slipped out and gone walkies."

"Oh no! For a sighthound, he's got an awful sense of direction."

"Don't worry; split up and we'll find him. BFT goes missing here all the time. In fact, I'm going to stop bringing her to work. Thank God she does wander off, though, or you and I would never have met."

As we left James's private quarters, in search for Boo, I told Tilly she was always welcome to drop BFT off at the boathouse.

"Sounds like a plan," she called back, as she disappeared towards the west wing where James's sleeping quarters were being restored.

"Boo, where are you?" I called. But there was no sign of him. "Treat, Boo, good boy!" I felt bad for rebuking him earlier. Back down the gallery into St Benedict's Foyer, where my repeated calls seemed to fade into far distance. Still no reply.

The sweeping staircase invited me. Stopping on a mezzanine landing, I listened carefully into what felt like a cavernous hollow. Far away, Tilly called Boo's name. Then silence. Up again, towards the top landing, in the

73

penumbra of the builders' spotlight as it spilt off the Benedictine ceiling. A wall of family portraits – Geoffrey, Isaac, Roland and many more – looked on impassively: velvety Tudors, silky Stuarts, red-coated Georgians. The last was a dour Victorian, Lord Randolph according to a brass plaque, dated 1880. I hurried under his surly gaze.

The dim screen of my mobile helped me along a passage, down which a cold draft whispered unnervingly. Was there a sudden presence, on the left? I jumped, caught out by my own reflection. Shades of Versailles, a dozen elaborately framed mirrors either side of the long passage. The one at the end had a hinge: my image shifted as it swung ajar. Still only silence.

"C'mon Boo," I called hoarsely. "Sorry I snapped at you."

I held my breath, sidled through the mirrored doorway. The room was ominously dark, windowless, or shuttered. Strange shapes under my mobile's gleam: a collection, an extensive collection, of Victorian automatons. No sign of Boo. Hurrying for the door again, I lurched into something: a jack-in-the-box: a messy-haired face, a life-size clown, jumped up at me.

'*Calma*, Roberto.'

"For God's sake, Boo, where *are* you?" The rug in the corridor tripped me. Another mirror opened: perhaps they were all doors. Moonlight in this room, almost welcoming. A deep breath and in I went.

Another heart-stopper, worse than the clown. Silhouetted in a lofty window, a dark figure with tousled hair. I aimed my phone-screen, which gradually stopped shaking. It was only – only! – a full-sized tailor's mannequin, in World War 1 uniform, a sergeant's stripes on his arm. Its curly hair was a wig, similar to the hair in the photograph James had hidden among his designs: Stanley. Perhaps this uniform was also a personal memento. A great big beautiful doll?

As my eyes tuned in to the moonlight, a wide array of human limbs revealed itself: wood, fabric, various stages of construction. More tailors' dummies with prosthetic arms attached, chillingly incongruous. On the walls, anatomical charts, all along under the windows, maybe twenty feet of steel and glass cabinets, filled with medical instruments. I recoiled, struck my hip on a steel corner – the kind of table they use in a morgue – and the phone clattered to the floor.

I scrambled about, feeling under the table for it, until the hyperventilating started. I was hiding under mother's cold bed again. The notion entered my mind that Lord James might also have been some kind of psycho. '*Calma*, Roberto. There's nobody here but you.'

The *putto* was wrong. Something wet and cold in the dark touched my fumbling hand. I caught my breath. A familiar whiff, which had always reminded me of buttered popcorn...

"Boo... where've you been, boy?" His tail wagged profusely, smacking my side like a whip. Then footsteps, a torch flashing under the table, a blinding beam like the dentist uses. Boo froze.

"What are you doing down there?" laughed Tilly. "I found Boo, Boo found you."

"And I found... my phone," I said, a little embarrassed, as I crawled out and pulled myself together.

"So, here we are in A&E!"

"More like Dennis Nilsen's closet."

"But tell me," she asked, suddenly serious. "James's sitting room: did you lock the door?"

"How could I?"

"Searching for Boo, I couldn't get in again." She sounded baffled.

"Maybe the lock got jammed," I suggested. "More weirdness." Tilly tutted, as if to say that my getting spooked didn't actually mean Samphire Hall was haunted. We headed back down the stairs – it seemed no distance at all, this time – towards the sitting room door.

"Do you think James could have been a psychopath?"

"Bertie, really. Your imagination does run riot."

"Well, that sergeant dummy: a mock-up of Stanley Sellars? Operating tables, medical instruments, artificial limbs? You don't think he was some kind of psychotic surgical tailor, reconstructing his dead victims?"

"One too many horror flicks, Bertie. A moment ago you were raving about far-sighted genius, no? For all we know, he could be an unsung hero of World War One."

That shut me up.

We arrived at Lord James's quarters. One turn of the doorknob and we walked straight in.

"That is a *tad* weird!" Tilly admitted.

"Now do you believe in ghosts?"

"Bertie, the only spirit I believe in is vodka." She sounded as if she could have murdered a shot there and then.

So I'm hypersensitive: my childhood was dotted with supernatural happenings, no doubt backed up by a fertile imagination. But I'm just 'aware', that's all I can say, even if nobody believes me. Tilly had turned out to be a doubter, just like Luke. My worry about Lord James proving to be a serial killer, still haunting his mansion – to them it would just be paranoia.

Once again I surveyed James's powerful portrait: if only paint could reveal the workings of a mind! But ink could, the diaries had already proved that. I was eager to get stuck back in, to piece together more evidence... either way.

After such a long day, Tilly and I were both a little jittery, trying to preserve our cool.

"Thanks so much. An amazing evening."

"Bertie darling, no probs, any time..." She threw me a gorgeous smile, irresistible as ever. I kissed her cheek as innocently as I could. "I'm parched," she declared.

"You've more than earnt a slap-up meal, and a good drink too: let's get out of here..."

Tilly switched off the lights. Boo followed us out. This time it was human hands that locked James's sitting room. As we hurried down the gallery, into St Benedict's Foyer, round the bones of Antinoüs and his dent in the floor, I was thinking about the varnish on Lord James's portrait. It was cracked and crazed in more places than its artist could ever have imagined.

CHAPTER FIVE
KEY CONNECTIONS

A warren of dimly-lit passages. Behind a dark door Boo is keening, his spine broken. Key after key I try out in that lock, but I've got the wrong bunch. A pressing sensation on my heart, I need oxygen. By an effort of will I get my eyes open, but there's no relief. Dark pools of light search my soul, as if James Newton-Grey is paying me back for disturbing his afterlife. Then, a dank swipe lashing across my face, certainly nothing human.

I shrieked, awake at last.

"Boo, for crying out loud..." My sweet whippet was sprawled on my chest: his chocolate-brown eyes peered into mine, enquiring and loving. Everything was okay. "So, no sawing this time? Must be Skipper Wood's night off."

I felt for my mobile in its charging-cradle: 1 a.m. A hazy moon – perfectly framed by the porthole window – peeped in, as it must have done long ago on Alice Fitzgerald, the enigmatic Southern Belle. The diaries I'd read so far painted an idealised picture, the perfect woman: but then, James had been bewitched by her from the outset. A more objective account could make interesting reading. I don't remember making a conscious decision, yet before long Boo and I were out in the campervan, heading for my nearest Wi-Fi hotspot.

The car park was still teeming at the Blakeney Hotel; judging by the dishevelled dinner suits and evening dresses spilling out of the Harbour Room, some big do was just ending. At least the noisy revellers gave hotel security something to think about, as I found my van an inconspicuous parking bay.

I pulled the blinds down and Boo scrambled over to join me in the kitchenette area. Opening my laptop at the little fold-out table, I entered the borrowed password and logged on. As soon as I typed 'Alice Newton-Grey *née* Fitzgerald' in the search bar, a gratifying column of cyber-minutiae loaded.

Clearly the American socialite had had more than her fifteen minutes of fame back in the day. Scrolling down the first page of search-returns, I randomly clicked a newspaper editorial.

The Illustrated London News, 15th April 1911

Announcing the forthcoming marriage of West Virginian redhead, Alice Fitzgerald, to debonair 22-year-old James Newton-Grey of Samphire Hall on the North Norfolk coast, sole scion of the late Lord Randolph Newton-Grey. The wedding will take place on May Day in the renowned St Benedict's Foyer at Samphire Hall. It was Daisy Greville, Countess of Warwick, long a friend of Lord James's late mother Lady Oona, who introduced the happy couple.

All very well, but this data-geek needed something with more substance. A featured advertisement at the top of the search returns took me to something called *Sociopedia*, which came up trumps with a striking photograph that reminded me of the iconic Art Nouveau poster girl; or maybe its creator had modelled that flame-haired beauty on Alice Fitzgerald? The research that followed seemed impressive.

Alice, like James, had been an only child. She was born, of Irish-American stock, on Christmas Eve 1888: her mother, Constance Ogilvy, hailed from one of the oldest middle-class families in Charleston, South

Carolina; her father, George Cornelius Fitzgerald, was from Richmond, Virginia.

There was a lot to take in here, while an endless din of cars left the car park, flashing headlamps and honking horns, mercifully removing their high-spirited occupants. Bloody Londoners, same as I'd been until a couple of months ago.

Alice's Stateside history seemed tangential at first, but its relevance became increasingly apparent: she had inherited the mercurial spirit of her West Virginian forbears – who had opted for the Confederacy, when in reality their allegiance was divided between North and South. Luckily for Constance, Abraham Lincoln had returned the whole state to the Union, making it safe for her to resume her wonted visits to a favourite cousin, Emmie, in her smart Manhattan brownstone.

A sidebar, promising 'Key Connections', spotlighted Emmie's marriage to a railroad magnate whose eminent friends included John Jacob Astor IV. *Sociopedia*'s idea of genealogy evidently included a fair quota of social snobbery.

Nonetheless the biography soon took a fascinating turn, documenting George Fitzgerald's philandering. Constance – the 'ever-faithful wife' as she was recorded – had ignored gossip as it spread like scarlet fever: a senator's wife, housemaids, a trail of prostitutes. It was not just 'the whole of the South talking' now: George's scandalous involvement with a casino-owner, the one-time *Madam* to several senators, became a headline sensation from coast to coast.

A noisy downpour broke my concentration, and dampened the early hours chill in the VW. Few cars now remained, and I didn't want to draw any attention by running the engine, so I unfolded a blanket. Boo, asleep under the table, helped keep my feet warm while I read on.

It seemed Alice had a pretty dysfunctional background, like everyone else I was interested in – except Luke, of course. A newspaper article, linked from *Sociopedia*, described bailiffs turfing the family out of their mansion, which George had lost, one drunken evening aboard a Mississippi steamer, in a single game of poker. Rain from the trees dripped hypnotically on my tin top as I tracked Constance, her marriage finally over, fleeing to her cousin Emmie in New York: it was to be a fresh start for her sixteen-year-old daughter.

My surfing trance was broken when a torch beam, through the windscreen, suddenly lit up the van interior like a stadium. Boo jumped up. I'd finally been rumbled by hotel security. Still wrapped in my blanket, I sheepishly slid open the side door.

"What yer doin', mate?"

"Sorry, couldn't sleep, too much noise... up in my room there. I need Wi-Fi, catching up with my work, but it's pretty weak back in the hotel." The story spun effortlessly from my mouth. "Great signal out here, though!"

A close-cropped, burly chap peered in, his face streaming with rain.

"Yer work with yer dog – whippet, innit?"

"Yeah, Boo goes everywhere with me. That's why I stay at a dog-friendly hotel."

He started asking why my number plate was not logged at Reception, and once again a little fiction came easily.

"Do you hear from Jake at all?"

"You knew Jake?"

"Yeah, client of mine from town," I said airily. "I design interiors. Pity Jake and his lady never settled into the Norfolk life."

"Top geezer, great manager. He's back down the Smoke now; got some bar he's doin' up, know what I mean?" The East Ender softened his stance, and rolled his eyes. "Cor, that totty of 'is!"

My mind raced, but couldn't call up the name of that Barbie-fashionista: I'd only met the couple once. A rapid change of subject was needed.

"So what brought you up to Norfolk?"

"New life for the missus and me. Pukka!"

"I can think of worse places to live, hey..."

"Too right, mate. Sorted. I'll let yer get on – soz for the bovver, know what I mean? Oh, the name's Tel."

"No probs. 'Night, Tel." He wandered off, torch-beam swinging as he pursued his round. While my heart settled down, I watched musicians trundling gear to their Transit through the drizzle, then I returned to my investigations. Boo curled up again with a sigh.

Ah yes, Constance and Alice, penniless but for Cousin Emmie's kindness, lying low in New York. Having been schooled in French – her second language, back in West Virginia – Alice struck a relatively sophisticated note on resuming her ballet classes, at a studio in Manhattan. Amid *Sociopedia*'s many biographical notes there was a reference to her working at Huberman's, on Broadway and Tenth, as a store model – surprising, at a time when society ladies would have looked down on such an occupation. Feisty Alice must have been desperate for independence from Emmie's hospitality and concern.

The teeming metropolis offered all sorts of temptations to an uninhibited teenager. Alice had apparently been engaged – briefly – to a prizefighter she'd met at Luna Park on Coney Island, which must have led to considerable tension with her mother. Yet this was the vital, independent and seemingly restless spirit that James Newton-Grey imagined would prosper, effectively caged, in the remote solitude of 'Woodfields', as the boathouse was known at that time. Mad as it might seem, I began to think of Alice as a murder suspect: if imprisonment in the boathouse had maddened her, might she have plotted the death of its creator? Such speculation was hollow, though, unless I could find more clues as to her psychological makeup.

Now I had hotel security on my side, I fired up the engine a while, to get some warmth blowing into the freezing camper. I pulled another blanket over Boo, on this chilliest of coastal autumn nights.

Mama Constance had never re-married. Now in her mid-fifties, and in sprightly health, according to the New York press of the day. She proudly chaperoned Alice to just about every fashionable 'parlor' in town. Luckily the scandal, 'The Fall of the House of Fitzgerald' was short-lived, pushed off the front pages by the political intrigues that tarnished the USA's Gilded Age in the half-century that ended around 1910.

It was Emmie's connections that provided Constance and her daughter with their *entrée* into the upper echelons of society. Thanks to Alice's great beauty – and acceptance by Caroline Astor, doyenne of the New York scene – the seventeen-year-old became the toast of Manhattan. Before long a telegram arrived at the modest Fitzgerald lodgings: a life-changing invitation to attend a Royal Ball during the coming London season. Reading between the *Sociopedia* lines, I could imagine Constance pawning her remaining jewellery to book passages on the White Star RMS *Oceanic* to Southampton that spring. She must have been eager to escape New York and curtail Alice's unsuitable modelling career, to say nothing of the liaisons with jaunty undesirables who did not befit her lately-established social standing.

Every webpage I read, with increasingly strained and dazzled eyes, contained a further fairy-tale revelation. Alice and her mother found themselves installed in a suite at Claridge's of Mayfair, guests of the beauteous – yet notorious – Daisy Greville, Countess of Warwick.

Cousin Emmie's connections evidently stretched right across the Pond.

"Now I get it..." I whispered to Boo. "This Daisy – the countess – turns up in James's diaries. Maybe she had promised Lady Oona Newton-Grey, her friend, a love-match for her dashing son." Boo sat up, ears pricked, wondering what I was gabbing about. I gave him one of his treats: a reward for an attentive listener.

Certainly Daisy Greville had taken a shine to the young American debutante: further web articles suggested that 'Mama' and Alice soon joined the privileged few to be accepted as intimate chums with the Royals of the Marlborough House set. The Ogilvy-Fitzgeralds were spotted in the Royal Enclosure at Ascot, at Henley Regatta, at Wimbledon, and at various fashionable soirées.

The Illustrated London News: 10th November 1909

American Beauty Miss Alice Ogilvy-Fitzgerald, chaperoned by her 'Mama', Constance Ogilvy-Fitzgerald, were among the guests at a grand ball last night, to celebrate the birthday of His Majesty King Edward VII at Marlborough House.

Ah, it seemed that Constance was using her maiden name in tandem with her now-forgotten husband's 'Fitzgerald': the double-barrel must have sounded a reassuringly classy note among the English nobility. And that was when James entered the frame: Daisy presumably masterminded a meeting between the eligible young lord and the striking American, and a romance flowered in the course of one particular ball. As the editor of *The Lady's Pictorial* wrote:

Alice Ogilvy-Fitzgerald appeared divine, in diaphanous Chantilly lace. The flame-haired Virginian turned the King's head as she made her entrance down the grand stairway. The sartorially urbane Lord James, heir apparent to the Newton-Grey peerage, glided tirelessly around the parquet with the beauteous *débutante*.

James was evidently so besotted that night by Alice's exotic glamour that he filled every space on her dance card with his own name, striking out all rivals. And, the article reported, Alice was deeply flattered by her ardent suitor. The edgy air of vulnerability, the brooding charisma: I reckoned the Southern Belle found the idea of danger pretty seductive. One commentator mentioned 'the Countess of Warwick peering winningly from behind her flickering fan'; flushed, I felt sure, with satisfaction at this piece of social stage-management.

Alice was a hit. And decorous Constance must have been overjoyed when she discovered that James was a scion of English nobility stretching back to the Normans, and about to inherit his dying father's sprawling country estate.

Sociopedia had proved very fruitful with its 'Key Connections'. Clearly 1910 – the year of Halley's comet and Edward VII's death – was to become a portentous year indeed for Alice and her mother. On the third day of June they passed through the gates of an impressive Gothic manor, on the North Norfolk coast: Samphire Hall.

Damnation! In a moment all the remaining lights in the hotel died, in a power cut that also took out the Wi-Fi connection... just as I was hooked on this fascinating and improbable romance. But it was gone 3 a.m., time to close the laptop and rest my long-suffering eyes. I drove slowly home, barely aware of the storm-darkened countryside around me, my thoughts still illuminated by

Alice's shining triumph. In my mind, however, James's flame-haired Virginian was shaping up to be a simmering volcano.

CHAPTER SIX
MY WINNING CARPENTER

My mind was restless as I unlocked the boathouse, still in the early hours. Now that I had learnt so much about Alice – assuming the *Sociopedia* accounts were accurate, of course – I had also become much more curious about whatever lay behind the shining prowess of her possible victim, Skipper Wood. Jud, the carpenter's scruffy great-grandson, was surely my best hope: but how could I pin him down? He was always hurrying away. What's done is done, I needed to tell him, and if a family has a secret, way back up the line, it's nothing to be ashamed of now. Especially where a prominent ancestor died in suspicious circumstances, which ought to be properly investigated.

I crashed out for a couple of hours: again, no dreams of Skipper building the boathouse, despite my growing preoccupation with him. After my porridge – and the seven-o'clock news on the kitchen radio – I put Boo in his scarlet coat for a foray on to the salt marshes: partly for his early-morning constitutional, partly in hope of finding Jud.

All was grey and silent: the birds seemed to be waiting for sunrise proper. I headed west towards Wells: a good thirty minutes' walk, but I was in determined mood. Stopping midway, to remove grit from one boot, I noticed, through a gap in the scrub, a small boat heading down Stonemeal Creek. My binoculars revealed that it was laden with eight or ten men. And suddenly, atop the bank ahead of them, appeared the shaggy form of Jud.

He turned to look landward, in my direction. I ducked again, and attached Boo to his lead. Jud checked the coast was clear and welcomed the men as they hit shore. He'd been waiting for their arrival. My mind raced as a stocky, bearded chap, in a khaki beanie, handed over a brown package, which Jud stashed in his parka. They shook hands, and the group – straight out of Balkan newsreel footage – started to follow Jud across the marshes, closer to Wells. One or two peered around, fearful of being spotted. Their boat purred out, through the creek to the open sea, and now I saw a cruiser anchored in the distance: presumably its mother ship. Clearly they were illegal immigrants: these desolate stretches, uninhabited for the most part, were ideal for a covert landing.

"Jesus, Jud, what have you got yourself into?" I muttered. The route he was taking would eventually bring his shady band in to Wells harbour. I began to follow them, like some kind of Tommy scouting in no-man's-land, holding back to avoid being spotted. Craning from the shrubby ridges that overlook the vastness of Holkham Nature Reserve, I sneaked occasional peeks at their progress. Boo copied me, standing erect like a meerkat. I had to rein him in, though, when a lone rider swept down the coastal path, close by us. And the moment I looked back towards Wells, the foreigners were gone, vanished. All I could see now was Jud himself, picking his lone way along the coastal path.

Boo and I trailed him beyond the quay at Wells, and westward to the pristine sands of Holkham Beach. A maddening hour followed. His thin path led up to a clearing in the pinewoods, where kids occasionally go to build tepees, and Boo and I drew close enough to see Jud, lounging on a fallen log, smoking. Unable to proceed without being spotted, we withdrew a while, back towards the sea; I waited until the sun was over the wind farm before we ventured back, and still he hadn't moved. The breeze had shifted, though, and a waft of weed now met my nostrils. Maybe the brown packet had been full of dope, and Jud – more reckless than I'd imagined – made his living by dealing? Again we withdrew to the beach, where Boo passed a fastidious quarter-hour sitting on a dune, purging traces of saltmarsh from his paws. Back in the woods – the clearing was bright now – we spied Jud counting out banknotes on the log: it appeared the illegals had paid him in cash after all. Only on the fourth repeat did we find he had moved, and, picking up sudden speed, we finally drew close to him the other side of the car park, halfway up Beach Road.

As Jud turned into the holiday park – its name, 'Pinewoods', painted on the side of a long-defunct fishing boat – I ducked behind a static caravan marked 'Reception'. Jud nodded a moment to a fellow resident. Then, pausing outside a shabby mobile home, he rummaged in his pocket for a key. I watched him slip inside.

Instinct told me *not* to go and knock at Jud's caravan: it would be hard to explain knowing where he lived. Boo and I relaxed for a spell, and I unbuckled his coat and stowed it in my bag. Then, while I deliberated our next move, Jud unexpectedly stepped outside again, and instantly noticed us.

"Oh... Jud!"

"Hey man." He looked at me curiously. "You walk the dog up these parts?"

"Yep, a few errands in Wells this morning. Bit brighter now, huh?" Last night's fluent invention seemed to have deserted me.

"Sure is..."

"Err... Jud, about Skipper, I don't suppose you'd wanna... have a chat sometime, would you?" He shook his straggly hair and sniffed violently, pinching his nose to stem the flow of mucus. Then he shrugged.

"Okay man, fancy a brew?"

"Sure!" He could hardly scarper in mid-conversation if we were sitting at his own table.

"I'll lead the way." With no further explanation he turned back on to Beach Road, heading for Wells harbour. Disappointment, and lack of sleep, was making me feel as if I'd just stepped off one of the boats on the dark swell at the quayside. Jud turned, saw me swaying, asked if I was okay. I inhaled the fresh air deeply, told him I was fine. Up the High Street, away from the harbour, among the mid-morning shoppers: still Jud said nothing. Cheery bunting criss-crossed overhead, and the normally appetising aromas from various cafés, only added to my queasiness.

All this time I could not imagine where he was taking me. He finally slowed down at a bland conglomeration of new builds, on the outskirts of Wells town, and we entered a private care home. On drives along the coastal road, I'd seen it going up: it had been named Walnut Court. An affable lady in blue welcomed Jud in the main hall, clearly recognising him immediately.

"How's my nanna today?" he enquired, unzipping his Parka and producing, not the parcel of cash, but a KitKat.

"Pearl's in fine fettle, lookin' forward to her elevenses," sang the matron, broad Norfolk. "Is this one of those 'PAT' dogs?"

"A therapy dog? Well, he's good with people – especially the elderly," I told her.

"Noo problem, bring the little darlin' in."

She handed Jud a small kettle, and he led the way up to the first floor, where the whiff of old age lingered along an Artexed corridor. Knocking gently, he opened a door – marked 'Pearl W' in a bold, institutional typeface – and a gust of lavender added to my nausea.

And there was Jud's nanna, sparsely haired, propped up in a green Draylon wingback armchair with a lace fabric cover, drowsing. The characteristic care-home magnolia was offset by some homely, personal touches: a clutter of mementoes, two clocks – neither telling the right time, and a rustic jug of artificial flowers in the sunshine. Soon she was greeting Jud with a ragged smile that must have seen ninety summers, and then some.

Boo trotted straight to her. She made a fuss of him, and he settled by her knee. As Jud introduced his grandma, I realised this was none other than 'Little Pearl', until now a mere footnote in Skipper's funeral notice. Still little, still alive: I could hardly believe my luck, as I shook hands with the daughter of Skipper and Beulah Wood.

Jud produced the chocolate: Pearl's face lit up like a child's. He leant down and gave her an affectionate kiss, dislodging a cane that was propped by her chair. In an instant Boo retrieved it from the carpet, and returned it to her in his jaws. He can always sense the presence of a good soul. Spindly, crabbed hands stroked his head.

"Three teas?" said Jud, filling the kettle. We started to talk, or in Pearl's case, to prattle. Her conversation trailed off in places – while her mind chased *non sequiturs* of fancy – then she'd be back, as astute as any radio pundit. She reminisced, first about her older brother Archie, killed in 1942 at El Alamein, then her only son, Jud's dad, killed in a plane crash. As I did my best to memorise details, I realised her conversation was curing my nausea. Then she talked about her own father, killed in my boathouse. Despite his short life, Skipper had left behind all kinds of bespoke cabinets, tables and caddies, she said, some inlaid with what she called 'market-work'.

"See what Pa made for my first birthday. My treasure that is!"

I now noticed, on a stand by the bed, an exquisitely proportioned carving.

"What wood is it?"

"I call that my Blakeney Seal – 'seagull ebony', he's made from." She looked as though she longed to hug the animal, as though it were her father himself. I was very touched.

Little Pearl told me how Skipper's craftwork had become well-known. No one in the region could match his skill, so he and his wife, Beulah, had founded a business: 'Wood's Joinery & Crafts'. And that's how Skipper came to the attention of 'Squire Newton', as she put it, winning his contest with the very seal Pearl believed had been made for her. She reminded us of this several times.

Surprisingly, then, Pearl started to sing, '*Oh you beautiful doll...*' I couldn't believe it, the same irksome tune I'd heard in my Skipper dreams. Jud joined in, urging me to do the same. He seemed to guess I would know it. Though I felt a little embarrassed, Pearl clearly enjoyed the sing along. Even Boo contributed, until Pearl's voice died out. She puckered her mouth and made clacking sounds for a while, then her worried expression was refreshed with a warm glow again, as if she'd just come home, to find friendly visitors waiting.

Jud took the opportunity to explain to Pearl that I lived at the boathouse Skipper had built. But the warmth faded, and her face was etched with foreboding: I prepared for the worst.

Pearl had been barely a year old when she had lost her father, so – beyond the lullaby he always sang – she retained few direct memories. She had only her ma's word to rely on: and her pictures. Jud fetched a dog-eared album from the tallboy by the window, and laid it on Pearl's lap. I moved my chair closer.

Pearl's trembling hand, a constellation of liver spots, clawed at the padded cover. A grainy monochrome photograph fell to the floor, and I beat Boo to it. Written across the white sky, in pencil, was the legend '*London Olympics, 1908*'.

"My Pa: handsome devil, ain't he?" she cooed.

Pale-eyed Skipper stood proud and strong in his Olympic costume: a heroic pin-up, a winning smile. His large hands held up a gold medal. Meanwhile Jud had found a similar image in *Penny Pictorial* magazine: the team parade.

As we talked about the victorious tug-o'-war side, Pearl made a pantomime of flexing her biceps, mimicking her strongman father. Laughter filled the room, then Jud fetched the medal itself, from the tallboy drawer, for me to hold. I began to warm to him, worryingly, given his dubious dealings on the beach at dawn, and its criminal ramifications. As I held the medal, we all went silent, as if dust were settling before a spring-cleaning: I fancied myself touched by the charisma that had made women swoon at the sight of its owner. They'd have felt the same, no doubt, about the prizefighter whose entanglement with young Alice had prompted Constance to move her away from New York.

Pearl started telling stories – some admittedly a bit tangled – of Skipper and Squire James. They had got on swimmingly at first, their burgeoning relationship centring on the construction of the boathouse. But things had changed, not least for Mrs Beulah Wood. Pearl's ma, I learnt, had fallen for her pa at a barn dance, where just about every girl in the village had vied for his attention.

"Ma had never been kissed like that before, she told me!" said Pearl with a naughty giggle.

Beulah, apparently no beauty, had won Skipper with her domestic skills, as well as with a thoughtful, educated mind: her father was the respected doctor of the district.

The first few years of married life had been happy and purposeful: making house, building a business together; Archie's arrival, then Little Pearl.

Pearl's voice dropped to a whisper, as her thoughts returned to the boathouse. Work had started after Alice's first visit to Samphire Hall. By the time construction was almost complete, Skipper and his employer had sealed a firm friendship through the daily collaboration. The carpenter was often spotted around the Hall – a social companion, no ordinary employee – or drinking with the squire in The Newton Arms. With the advent of the glamorous Virginian, all three were soon observed enjoying rounds of tennis, genteel croquet, drinks on the terrace. Gregarious Skipper must have been the envy of his former friends and associates, who remained in obsequious thrall to the Edwardian class system.

Then, to my consternation, Jud brought out an architect's folder containing various foxed copies of anatomical drawings; these, he told me, were artificial limbs Skipper had made for the squire. He had never contemplated work of this sort before meeting Lord James, who – one or other of Jud's late parents had told him this – had been 'obsessed by injuries', and ways of crafting replacements for damaged limbs.

"No wonder he took up with a lowly craftsman," said Pearl. Intrigued by the team's complementary skills – Luke's and mine were similarly balanced – I asked Pearl how Alice had felt about this creative partnership. She answered an entirely different question.

"Ma, she got ever so jealous!" she hissed. Homely Beulah would rage at Skipper, it seemed, when he brought home photographs – taken by Squire James's camera – showing the trio's social escapades: picnics, polo matches, hunting jaunts. Beulah eventually destroyed them all, even those taken at Royal Sandringham, where Skipper had once met the King.

Pearl turned more pages in her album, pointing out a snapshot of her parents laughing, arm in arm, and studio portraits showing their pretty-bonneted new arrivals. But despite being the daughter of a professional man, Beulah was – by Pearl's account – unassuming, with simple tastes. Her Olympian husband, meanwhile, grew more and more like Alice who, as she moved up in her own social world, revelled in the newfound limelight. A great wedge began to separate Skipper and his wife.

And then, as Pearl turned the last page, my heart shuddered. James and Skipper were pictured, standing in the doorway of my boathouse, toasting their finished endeavour and smiling with brotherly familiarity. A caption, written across the then-pale veranda decking, said *'Woodfields, 18th March 1911, my winning carpenter'*. The black ink, and the handwriting were unmistakable.

Pearl's hands trembled more vigorously. She appeared lugubrious, melancholy. I poured some tepid tea. Jud asked if she wanted to rest but she responded with a tight-lipped smile. Then, with renewed relish, she started describing the afternoon Squire James had come home to Samphire Hall with cuts and welts to his cheeks and jaw, cradling one painful arm. His nurse – presumably Ida Henderson – had dressed the wounds, but nonetheless found it necessary to summon the family doctor, who, as it happened, was Beulah's father.

Whoever beat James that badly must have been pretty tough; it was no coincidence that Skipper had returned home the same afternoon with a startling 'shiner' to his right eye. It was never proved that the two had been brawling, but the servants' tongues wagged for weeks.

"Now I am telling you in confidence what Ma told me years later: Skipper and Alice were caught..." Pearl paused, searching for a word. "They were caught, smooching, by his lordship the squire." She raised her sparse white brows and sank back with a sigh.

"Which presumably caused the bust-up between James and Skipper?"

"Sounds likely," Jud replied.

A silence enveloped the room, representing the lapse of nearly a hundred years during which wealth had talked, reputations had been preserved, and rumours had been quashed.

"I wish I'd known my pa." Pearl rocked back and forth, her specs falling off her nose, dangling on their sensible chain while she dabbed her eyes. "Still, I had Ma, she did everything for me."

"So, Pearl, what really happened? To your pa?"

I'd just wanted to catch Pearl before her mind wandered off again. Jud shook his head at me: but the difficult question could not be withdrawn.

"Now I know folks called it an accident, but it were murder!" she said, agitatedly. "Pa were killed by..." She felt about, anxiously gripping the arm of the chair, without apparent motive. I'd felt guilty, pressing her for such painful information: but my tenacity was about to be vindicated.

"Killed by...?" I prompted.

"He were killed," she said, her breath catching, "by his stupidity." I should have let it go; but I couldn't.

"So Skipper's murderer... they've got away with it, all this time?" Poor Pearl was becoming more distressed by the minute, blindly groping for her red emergency button. I passed it to her, unsure if she really needed it: and, oh God, she pressed it, aggressively, several times. We heard a bell ringing behind the scenes, the door swung open, and a carer came bustling in. Boo's ears pricked up keenly.

Pearl already couldn't remember why she had panicked.

"I'm right as rain, Bren," she explained. Bren reminded Pearl she'd be only a moment away, if further help were needed. She glared rather coldly at me, and left the room with emphatic briskness. Jud propped his nanna up, to bolster her confidence, and asked if she needed some rest. But Pearl was back and there was no stopping her flow...

"I did my grievin' ninety years back, 'tis done now! But Pa had no business with her."

"With Alice, you mean?" I asked.

"She spoiled everythin', that one; she were the death of him." She pulled her shawl tightly round her shoulders, and gazed emptily into the ether.

"Somebody murdered your pa because he had an affair with Lady Alice Newton-Grey?" Little Pearl chewed a while on an imaginary mouthful, then fell silent. "So why was it covered up?" More silence; then she breathed in resolutely.

"Squire Newton: fancy connections, he had, right up to the top," Pearl stated. "There, I told it: I'm not long for this world now." She sighed and closed her eyes, clasping her hands to her heart. "Yes, my dear old ma, she knew the secret."

I was on the verge of asking if the large payment I'd noticed in the Audit House ledgers had been hush money for Beulah, in the wake of Skipper's death. But Jud gave me another stern look. Pearl was exhausted; so was I. So I told them I was late for meeting a friend, though I kept quiet about Tilly and Samphire Hall.

I gave Little Pearl a kiss. She patted Boo's nose. "Sweet thing," she sighed, heavy-eyed.

Bren came in with a lunch-trolley. Jud saw me to the door.

"Nanna do fantasise 'bout stuff," he whispered on the stairs. "Dementia, gettin' worse. 'Old-timer's disease', she calls it."

"You're still lucky to have her," I said. "But something I don't get: Pearl was born a Wood, but then she married. Didn't you tell me your surname's Wood as well?"

"Deed poll," said Jud. "My twenty-first present, from Nanna. Part of it."

"Unusual?"

"Fresh start," he said quietly.

"I get it," I told him, as we shook hands. But I didn't.

Boo sat by me on the coast-hopper bus, watching calmly as the scenic coastline unwound. My thoughts, though, were running in circles. If the family themselves thought Skipper had died by foul play, they deserved some sort of retrospective enquiry. Pearl's cuttings and photographs would probably stand up in court. But to take her other memories for gospel... I'd be madder than she was.

I pondered why I'd been taken to meet her. Maybe Jud was using me, a pawn to reopen the case of their ancestor's ambiguous death? He'd been lingering about the boathouse ever since Luke and I had arrived, sizing me up, perhaps. But why get Pearl to unearth family traumas, only to tell me she had Alzheimer's?

At least I had something on him; though the more I thought about his boatload of illegals, the more I worried I might have misread the entire episode. Pearl's stories might be equally delusional... except that some elements tallied closely with my diary reading, and my own experience at the boathouse. But how much of that was real? My mind was a time bomb.

And James... he must have felt so betrayed, both by his wife, and by his new best friend. Small wonder if he'd snapped... but that didn't prove he was a killer. Someone was, that's all I knew: and there was bad energy tied up in the boathouse. The poor carpenter, for all his sins, must somehow be laid to rest. I just didn't know where to start.

At some point my reverie – my torment – must have shaded into sleep. A fellow traveller was shaking my shoulder and the driver was shouting the name of the stop: "Samphire Hall!"

CHAPTER SEVEN
THE GIFT

A billboard had been fixed by the imposing iron gates: 'Samphire Hall – Opening Soon'. A banner, slashed across the picture, advertised the 'Preview Gala' on Bonfire Night: the presentation Tilly's team was so hectically preparing. I was not sure Lord James would have approved of the NHS's rather trite slogan, '*Expect the Unexpected!*' – though in fact my brief time under his roof suggested it was quite apt.

Boo and I had walked a good five minutes down the drive when I spotted Tilly by the entrance, tapping her gloved hand on one of the oak and copper doors. I hurried across the forecourt and up the steps to greet her.

"And where have you two been?"

"So sorry, got delayed: masterclass on Skipper Wood, given by his ancient daughter."

"How come?" She sounded sorry to have been left off the guest list.

"Don't worry, Tilly, all revelations will be added to my notes for the NHS." It was a bit of a porky: to date everything was just in my mind, nothing on paper at all.

"Bertie, I am sure it will," she replied. "And I've got something else for your homework. Sadly, it's not me, but you're still going to love it." She whisked me straight into James's private sanctum.

"Close your eyes," she said, gripping my shoulders and turning me around. "Now, look!"

"Wow!" Staring back at me was Alice's portrait, mounted exactly opposite James's: a study in oils, in which every inch of white flesh was beguiling. "And where was *she*, the other evening?"

"A makeover. She certainly scrubbed up well at the restorers," Tilly remarked, with a note of comic jealousy.

Alice had been captured, for all time, in the plunging 'nude' Chantilly lace gown I had read about. She was posed demurely, head offset at a tilt so that the mesmerising emerald eyes, which had so captivated James, appeared to gaze mysteriously beyond the viewer. No wonder, as I'd read, Alice had turned the king's head.

I leant closer to read the artist's signature: as the style had already suggested, it was again the work of John Singer Sargent. A cardboard folder, on a marble-topped table under the portrait, distracted my attention. I picked it up.

"You found it." Tilly clapped her hands.

"Some kind of scrapbook?"

"Not just any scrapbook. That's Alice's commonplace book, and you can take it to reinforce your research."

I turned to face Tilly – who looked pretty pleased with herself – and happened to catch James's eye: his powerful portrait, peering over her shoulder, gave my heart a thump.

"So it's just turned up?"

"Not exactly. The restorers found it in the back of Alice's portrait. There's a kind of hollow slot behind these antique frames. Nobody else knows about it, yet."

"Our secret, eh?"

"Yah, and remember Bertie: notes, notes, the NHS needs notes. For the Gala Opening."

"Of course. Thanks, sweetheart." Christ, I'd called her sweetheart: now she really was going to suspect I was hot on her. A little kiss of thanks, on the cheek.

"A real looker, wasn't she?"

Tilly was one of those women who have absolutely no idea just how gorgeous they are; Alice, on the other hand, was self-evidently aware of her classic beauty. And boy, she used it!

"Looks can fade," I said. Such a pity her workaholic father's rejection had damaged Tilly's confidence. I hoped I could bolster her self-esteem somehow. But when I turned to Tilly, she suddenly appeared blurred. I was giddy; and my muscles – despite all that expensive toning in the gym – felt no stronger than jelly. As I blacked out on the sofa I felt icy air rushing through me, and I smelt aniseed.

"Bertie? Bertie!" was the next thing I remember. As I opened my eyes, Tilly's face turned to relief.

"Err... not sure what that was about," I said.

"You okay? You've turned snow white."

"Yeah, I think so." I felt as though I'd been dosed with hundred per cent proof alcohol, and I was never the best of drinkers. The strong aroma of aniseed had sent my head into a spin.

"Hey Tilly, do you think James is warning me to stay out of his affairs?"

"Nonsense, Bertie, he's long dead, don't be utterly ridiculous. Have you eaten today?"

"A small bowl of porridge, at the crack of dawn." I remembered I had felt nauseous all morning, after following Jud on the marshes, up until my meeting with his nanna.

"That explains it, then. Look, let me lock up, and get back to the cottage to let BFT out. Then as you're on foot today, I'll take you for a fab meal," she suggested. "Early evening, we won't need to book."

It was coming up to 6.30. Boo was probably aching for supper as much as I was, and, eager as I was to get stuck into the new scrapbook, I couldn't think of anything better than sitting opposite Tilly at dinner. After all, Luke had deserted me...

"Where do you fancy?" I asked, tucking Alice's album into my bag.

"The Hoste Arms isn't too far from me."

"Sounds a bit extravagant."

"I'd like to," she said.

"Okay, you're the boss. Thanks! Come, Boo."

Tilly's rented twee cottage didn't suit her at all. I could do wonders with the place if she owned it. Victoria Albertina fox terrier and Boo fed, watered, even toileted together very amicably: they would be fine, left together for the evening. When Tilly had freshened up – that fragrance again! – we set off for snazzy Burnham Market in her pewter-grey four-by-four, the perfect vehicle for visiting the village some called Chelsea-on-Sea.

The Hoste Arms was heaving with off-duty film-techs, chatting about some costume drama they were shooting over at Holkham Hall. We squeezed through the packed bar.

"Little Black Dress," Tilly ordered. I must have looked bemused, but the barman translated with studied deference.

"Vodka, sir, vodka with a twist of black cherry juice."

"Ah, just half a lager, please," I said, conscious of anything remotely containing aniseed.

Despite the crush, the staff found us a table for two in a nook by the fireplace. Tilly removed her chunky cardigan; her plaid shirt had enough buttons open to reveal a tiny ornamental key, on a fine chain, that dangled in her cleavage. She seemed unaware of the ogling film crew, as she downed her vodka, straight. I took my drink a sip at a time, mindful of my rumbling stomach. Maybe it had been hypoglycaemia earlier, in James's sitting room? I was certainly starving now.

Dinner took ages to arrive, and Tilly was downing the booze at an alarming rate. Her childlike vulnerability rose to the surface: the more she drank, the lonelier she appeared.

"Eat up, Tilly," I said. "The sea bass is terrific."

"I am so-oo glad you're on board, dahling," she slurred. "I wish Daddy could see our work at Sham... Samphire Hall, he's not ease... he's not easily im-pressed." She'd started over-enunciating, hoping I wouldn't notice the state she was in. She pecked at her meal as though eating were a chore, and spoke of the stress at work, as new girl at the bottom of the NHS pecking order. It was a solitary life. Granted, Victoria Albertina was a kind of company, but a terrier couldn't save her from herself.

I could see all the symptoms of my mother's final decline, when I'd been too young to rescue her, the cracked record, "Tomorrow I'll quit – I really will – tomorrow I'll..." But the pills had always had the upper hand. And I remembered Tilly, on my sundeck, saying that either the cigarettes or the booze had to go... it was pretty clear now that she was a borderline alcoholic.

It looked as if I'd be driving home. I bundled her into her own slick motor, while she insisted she was 'just Tilly, not tiddly'. Once I'd put her to bed, in a gentlemanly fashion, I decided to stay over, on the downstairs couch, so she wouldn't have to wake in a house empty of human company. I pulled a handy blanket over myself but sleep stayed away. My thoughts strayed back to college girls, affairs and aberrations so long ago. Tilly was an anomaly and I must learn to ignore the long-dormant lust she aroused.

Finally I slipped into an uneasy dream, into a world where I was unattached; but it was too cold to sleep long, and in the early hours I gave in to my curiosity about another parallel world: Alice's book of memories, languishing in my bag by the sofa. I switched on the lamp and examined the album, flimsy, no more than an inch thick, still carrying the faint bouquet of an Edwardian lady's *eau de toilette*.

I flicked through a jumble of names, places, snippets of her Stateside life: sentimental accounts of this and that, green ink jottings in her elongated hand. But the tawdry love-hearts and tokens from various *beaux*, including the prizefighter, soon gave way to pure gold:

James takes my hand, fixing to leave our wedding-guests. Confetti falls like cherry blossom, Maytime on a Charleston Avenue. The orchestra fades as we pass through a old iron gate. Dusk in Lady Oona's rose garden. James stops to light a Davy lamp. He unravels the cream silk bow Mama twined so fancy in my hair. He blindfolds me, beseeches me to have trust. First we stroll, then we tear up the pace, twenty minutes maybe, rough under my supple shoes. Across a highway, the smell of pine forest, the swirl of the ocean yonder. I get chill bumps all over, mighty aroused by my English husband! He hastens me down a scented alley.

I'm with you Alice, that scented alley is where Luke and I park our campervan.

A door unlocks, into some kinda homestead. Strong smells: the wood of the cabin, the absinthe on his breath.

Blimey, James's sitting room at the Hall *still* reeked to this day, the same absinthe I'd smelt on entering St Benedict's Foyer the first time. Tilly would have to believe me now.

His fingers slide down my corsage. I'm hankering to make love with my nouveau Lord for the first time. He grapples the satin buttons all down the back of my bridal gown. It slides so readily to the floor. Then he gorges on my breasts, like Huckleberry pie. My honey picks me up masterly, carries me up a stairway. One particular step creaks like a goddamn pump-handle in the drought. He tells me to remember it, calls it the 'Love Step'. He throws me like a rag doll, I bounce on a mighty grand bed, and tears off my blindfold. Lordy how we rock that cabin, it's like an old English galleon.

She must mean the Baroque bed we'd inherited with the boathouse: some history it carried! Now I considered the matter, it must have been built in the bedroom: nothing that size could have come up the stairs. Skipper's work again, no doubt.

So James had taken 'the Love Step', whatever he meant by that, and snared his bird of paradise. Another green-inked entry, emphatically titled *The Gift*, dealt with her entrapment:

Les beaux jours pass, a sweet honeymoon fantasy. But, mercy me, I soon discover this 'Woodfields', my wedding gift, is set to be my married home, instead of the fine mansion of Samphire Hall. *Naturellement* – thinking it's a lark – I tell James it is sure ridiculous for a English Lady to live in a shack in the woods. His sassy black eyes widen and put the wind up me good and proper. I fairly gallivant round that cabin, looking to skedaddle. But he has a lock on every door, every shutter, like the workhouse.

"You were made for a magical place," says my husband. "This magical place was made for you, just you, from 'The Boleyn Cedar'. Did I not sacrifice eight hundred years of hallowed history for my love, to gather you into the very loins of my family?" This is his fancy explanation of the wedding gift. How could I resist?

But Queen Boleyn of England had her pretty head cut off! Don't you try anything like that on me, I tell him, in the King's plain English. He smiles like a trickster. Then I know it: I love him so, I can't see any harm in his crazy notions! And Mama, she tells me she'll visit no matter where he keeps me. That's my Englishman...

So James had harboured this twisted plan from the get-go. The cruel abuses from his father, and his mother's suicide, had scarred his formative years with a fundamental insecurity. And to annul this bleak inheritance, he had transmuted the great cedar – the family tree, in fact – into a cage, to ensure his precious Alice could never desert him as his mother had done.

I had read somewhere in James's diaries how his parents' marriage was what today's gossip columnists might term a 'showmance', good only for the unification of two noble families, but doomed to personal misery. Tilly's parents came to mind, and I decided it was time to check she was okay. Her bedside clock read almost 3 a.m. as I poked my head round her door. Resisting the temptation to stand and watch the angel sleeping, I crept back down to the cold silence of Tilly's lounge, and settled back into the racy world of Alice's commonplace book.

She'd been content at 'Woodfields'; and James's confidence had grown, as their relationship flourished, until social outings had begun, bending the rule of seclusion he had originally insisted on. Alice wrote that she had 'never known such happiness'.

Until, that is, Skipper Wood turned up one morning to fix that creaking in the second step off the landing, 'the Love-Step'. Up to this point, I gathered, Alice had never met Skipper, perhaps not even known his name:

The boathouse – my precious gift – remains a secret, as my honey trusts the carpenter who built it not to tell its whereabouts. But he keeps him away from our wedding, fearing a tradesman's presence may bring up awkward questions that will give my residence away.

Yet things changed once James reconsidered the isolation of his trophy. A few pages on, and Skipper is a third party in their social lives.

All three of us take supper out on the veranda, now the English weather is as pretty and hot as a June bride in a featherbed. Young devil Skipper comes around to share our sundowners on the veranda. Other times he brings me pretty gifts he's made, like folks in the South do back home. Things he doesn't want James to see.

This hint of secrecy looked like a flaw in a perfect marriage, but it didn't confirm Pearl's account of Skipper and Alice 'smooching', nor did it amount to a motive for a murder.

We took Skipper gallivanting to London. All the swells love his stories of the Olympic Games. James is mighty proud of his man; he talks of setting Skipper up in a fancy enterprise along Bond Street some day. Mighty queer, when Skipper can never even figure why that pesky second step creaks so bad.

The pesky step still creaked like mad to this day: evidently its grand age was not the cause. Why should Norfolk's finest carpenter be unable to repair one lousy tread? So that he always had a reason to call on Alice, perhaps. But that was my last, somnolent thought, as I felt Alice's book of revelations slip through my fingers and on to the floor.

A bright flash, and the sound of Venetian blinds, told me it was morning. A gentle nudge, and Tilly was at my side with tea and toast and honey.

"Morning, sleeping beauty!"

"Oh God, what time is it?" I flexed my freezing legs. Boo and BFT were yapping out in Tilly's garden.

"8.45 and counting..." she said, slipping into a smart blazer.

"I must have conked out reading Alice's memoirs..." I felt the stubble on my jaw.

"Anything interesting?" Tilly was definitely back in control after her bender at The Hoste.

"Very intriguing in fact: Alice caged up at the boathouse, and some kind of bromance brewing between James and Skipper." Tilly's eyes lit up.

"So his lordship was a perv? Kinky threesomes?"

"Well... it's a bit more complicated than that," I said, wondering what could actually be more complicated than two men and one girl – however large my inherited bed might be. "I need to do more research, before we jump to conclusions."

"Thank God you're covering that side of things. Karsten wants to see me at nine, probably a whole morning deciding how to put Antinoüs back together. At least you got *me* home in one piece!"

"No problem, Tilly; you must admit you weren't quite fit to drive."

"When I'm like that I usually grab a cab," she confessed.

"You'll be lucky in Norfolk."

"Can I drop you off at your... sex dungeon?" She grinned.

"You're late as it is. I'll get the coast-hopper later. No worries."

"*Ciao*, call me when you can. Work hard!" she said, sweeping little BFT into her arms, her workmate for the day. Boo whimpered: the canine mentality likes everybody together in a pack.

I hadn't been much company for Tilly that morning, more like a corpse on her sofa. I had a wash, tidied the place, locked up and ambled with Boo down to the bus stop. Just as we were boarding, my mobile sang: Luke.

Reception was too bad for a proper chat. I heard something about delays with his mother's operation, his uncle replastering various walls in her house. Again, no chance to tell him what I'd been up to. Perhaps it was safer to keep it buttoned.

I hopped off the bus not far from the wooded track, Alice's 'scented alley' to her magical assignation at the boathouse. Boo went ahead. With about a hundred yards to go, I could see him sniffing around somebody at the kitchen door. I had the strangest feeling. The closer I got, the more I recognised the posture. When I was just paces away, he stood up to look at me face-on. Oh God, there was no mistaking the megawatt smile that had illuminated Pearl's photograph album. Skipper Wood was standing directly in front of me: Skipper Wood, back from the dead...

CHAPTER EIGHT
ONE SMALL STEP

Boo looked up at the apparition with calm curiosity. I could only stare in shock and foreboding.

'*Calma*, Roberto!'

"I guess you must be a bit surprised..." said Skipper Wood, turning on his power smile.

'A bit surprised' was an understatement. I wished I still had my old therapist on speed-dial. But then, as he lifted his arm to straighten his tie, the sleeve of Wood's jacket pulled back to reveal a familiar tattoo.

"Err, surely this is actually... Jud?" I ventured.

"Yesirree."

"What's with the new look?"

"Job interview. Got a clip at the barber's, and did myself some retail therapy over in Holt."

"For a minute I thought your great-grandpa had come calling."

"I'm a dead ringer for ol' Skipper when I have a good tidy-up, so they say."

He had lost the straggly beard, fit for an Amish elder, and his unruly strawberry-blond hair was now closely cut: the side parting paid homage to his ancestor. He unbuttoned his grey suit jacket, flashing a top-end label on the inside breast pocket, and wiggled one of his tan brogues.

"What d'you think?"

"You look like a million dollars."

"Thanks, man. But I came to let you know, Nanna Pearl has been asking for you. I didn't have your mobile number, see?"

"Really?" As for revealing my number, that could wait.

"Thinks she remembered something, but she ain't telling me."

"Jud, I'll be there in the morning; before elevenses this time, okay?"

"Cool, dude." I hope he drops the surfer-lingo for this interview, I thought.

"So what's this job you're going for?"

"Holkham Hall. Manager at the Bygones Museum. Recession killed my vintage car workshop, so I need the work."

"Sorry to hear that..."

"I trained as a panel beater," he said brightly. "Classic cars, that's my passion." He'd kept this animated side hidden until now, and it was attractive. But the matter of that dubious landing on the marshes still needed explaining. The Home Office would crucify him for assisting illegal immigrants – if that proved to be the case – and I'd be in trouble too, if I didn't report him. I chose my words carefully.

"How long've you been out of work?"

"Must be six months, maybe."

"How've you been living?"

"Dole, man." Jud looked down: clearly state benefits didn't buy designer suits, like the one he was wearing so well. Nor handmade brogues, the kind Luke saves for months to afford.

"But Hugo Boss costs a packet. I have that same suit." Mine was last season's, but he didn't need to know that. His cheeks flushed, and he looked at a non-existent watch.

"Gotta go, or I'll be late for my interview." Once again, he was primed for take-off: I would have to confront him another time.

"Best of British," I called after him.

I started on some mundane household chores, then sat down to doodle up some bookshelves; but I was distracted, rather than inspired, by the play of late October light on an iridescent sea. Too drowsy to read James's diaries, too preoccupied to start on the notes Tilly wanted, I eventually took Boo for a teatime walk on the marshes. On the homeward straight I rang Luke from the jetty hotspot: but he was at the builder's merchant with his uncle, picking up a second dehumidifier to speed up the house-drying; he'd have to call me back.

I did my round with the keys, checking every entry point was secure. Autumn was kicking in with a chilly vengeance and I settled close by the woodburner, in a waking dream, with James's diaries and a notebook on my lap. By the time the powdery embers had burnt out, I'd written nothing more than my name and a title. I'd felt more motivated as a schoolboy. But I'd had more sleep as a schoolboy too, and I reckoned now that a good night's kip – the first in ages – would reset my body clock and restart my mojo.

The bedroom rafters creaked and groaned like the hull of a ship in distress as I drifted off... into a twilit world of whispers and echoes, as old Samphire Hall filled my dreamscape. Flickering images playing out in my head like an old film: a boy pitifully whimpering, his father looming malevolently with a riding crop. The military regalia, the sour demeanour, I recognised from Lord Randolph's surly portrait on the mezzanine landing at the Hall. My heart went out to powerless, adolescent James, his fears and insecurities so familiar to me. But it was a young, fresh Skipper Wood who came to his rescue. Naked as a statue, he posed magnificent at the top of the grand, sweeping staircase. But then a tumbling sensation, a frightful crash, and I choked bolt upright out of a pool of sweat, temples pulsing like drums. Springing from my bed I ran to the cedar stairway, certain to find Skipper Wood at the bottom, bleeding to death once more.

Of course, there was nothing, only the bright smell of cedar, absolutely intoxicating. I sat in my boxer shorts on the edge of the landing, a desolate fool, eyes gritty with sleep, feet gritty with... raw oats? How had I managed to scatter porridge on the stairs, unless I'd been sleepwalking? I bent to sweep some into my hand, and Boo pattered over for a sniff, then gave me a look with his all-knowing luminous eyes. Something was wrong.

"Oh no, Boo, it's sawdust. Fucking sawdust."

No amount of ghostly sawing can produce real sawdust. I stared up into the rafters for a logical explanation: deathwatch beetle perhaps, an infestation of woodworm? Where was it coming from? I went down a few steps to establish where the dust had chiefly fallen, and found it was closely localised, just on the second step. Sudden realisation hit me, like a branch whipping across a window in a storm. The 'pesky step' in Alice's commonplace book, whose creaking still irritated the hell out of me now: the time had come to take it to task.

A lightning dash, still in my boxer shorts, to the outside shed in search of chisels and saws, teeth chattering in time with my heartbeat. Muntjac darting away: even the woods were alive at this godforsaken hour. So was my bloody boathouse.

Back inside, tools and a charged-up LED lantern in my holdall, I paused at the foot of the stairs to compose myself, breathing deeply, counting to ten. Boo was pacing back and forth like a wild dog. I climbed up to the troublesome tread, placing the lantern on the one above, wondering how to proceed. I noted the square-headed nails, tried to work out how it had been installed. And for the first time I spotted tiny indentations around each nail head: Skipper must have needed to pull them out many times as he tried to solve the creaking problem. Now if

Norfolk's champion carpenter couldn't manage it, what chance had a klutz like me? But the creaking was not the whole story: I felt there was something else, and Boo knew too.

Each tread overhung its riser in a bull-nose, and was neatly set, on the left, into the stringer panel that ran the length of wall, down the staircase. At first I tried to be precious, to prise one of the hefty nails out with my pliers, but they wouldn't budge; then I made a little headway by tapping with a fine chisel around each one. Sweating in the cold, I persevered until each nail finally stood proud of the wood. Anxiously tugging at their heads with various tools, twisting and turning them individually with all my strength, I felt the pesky tread eventually start to loosen.

Luke would kill me: I was making a right old mess. James had called this 'the Love Step', the gateway to scenes of Virginian passion in his marital bedroom. For me it was emphatically 'the Hate Step' now. My patience drained away, and with it any attempt at finesse. Crowbar in hand, I started hoicking at the blasted tread. It complained, it screeched, but it was working free, I was winning. One huge, ruthless tug, with both hands, and I finally jerked the wilful plank off its riser and out from its stringer-housing in the wall. Blast: something sharp grazed my forearm, and I lost my balance. As I grabbed the handrail the tread went tumbling out of my hands, bumping down to Skipper's resting place on the floor below. I also heard the clang of something metallic dropping through into the newly-exposed understair cupboard. It must have been my small pair of pliers.

I skipped down to retrieve the Hate Step, which Boo was already snuffling. I pushed his wet nose away to get a closer look. The underside looked rough and unworked, exceedingly aged by contrast with the smoothly-planed topside. No wonder it had creaked, I thought, as I inspected it from every angle. I swivelled it around and held it up to the lantern – and suddenly a series of pale brown lines in the underbark came into focus: carving, letters, the full yard's width. No time to fetch glasses: my fingers did the reading.

"A... something: A, N, N... Anna, then B something. B, O, L... Bol-ina. Bloody hell, Latin: do you hear me, Boo? Anne Boleyn!" His ears pricked up as if he understood that I had really found Lord James's legendary carving, hacked into the flesh of the Newton-Grey Cedar by the doomed Queen, as an amorous child. Then another realisation, spine-chilling, if I could have got any colder. "Hence 'the Love Step', of course," I said. It was a message from James, or Alice, or Skipper even. From the past, at any rate. A message direct to me.

"How about that Boo? Tilly's going to be ecstatic, and as for the NHS, what a tasty relic for their big opening."

But Boo was not being an attentive listener; he was sniffing a trail of dark spots. To my horror I saw that something had drizzled the staircase with blood, all the way down to the last step and across the floor to where I was standing, over that indeterminate cloud-like stain that even Luke's cleaning skills could not remove. Skipper's blood? Some omen of Anne Boleyn's beheading?

Only when Boo jumped up to lick my right arm did I realise how badly I'd gashed myself, wrenching the Love Step free. Blood was still dripping alarmingly. I hurried across the hall, to the kitchen, flicking on the light and rushing to the sink, shifting the tap lever with my elbow, since my left hand was also sore, riddled with splinters. The customary spurt of brown froth quickly gave way to an ice-cold torrent that stung the main wound and several minor cuts, then swirled pink in the plughole.

Once the wastewater was running clear, I wrapped a napkin around my forearm, twisting it tight, all the while thinking about my extraordinary discovery. What were the odds against finding that inscription? I was already starting to doubt that I'd been led there by telltale sawdust... and of course my labours had destroyed that evidence. The historic creaking was gone too, of course. Building an unplaned step into a staircase: obviously it could never lie flat, Skipper would know that. So either his subsequent repair visits were a sham, or James had sent him there for some other purpose. Surely not to 'smooch' with his bride, though!

I wandered back into the lounge and found my cold club chair. I still had nothing on but shorts, and a napkin now tied round my arm with string; but the excitement of finding the 'Bolina' inscription pushed physical discomfort to the back of my thoughts. At last, I had solid evidence that James's diary told the truth, a great result! I'd always wanted to trust him. I still didn't know why, but perhaps I could at least do so without reservation. I noticed Boo was scratching at the understair door.

"Give it a rest, Boo," I murmured. My eyelids flickered as the room blurred; sleep was calling, but he kept clawing at the door, whining now. "Come on, Boo, it's just coats and stuff. No rabbits," I called. Then I saw the pained look on his sweet face, as if to say, 'Take me seriously.'

I dragged myself up, holding my throbbing arm, pulled the door open with a prickly, splintered hand. Boo slipped inside, turned quickly round, and sneezed. He wanted me to follow him in.

"In the morning, Boo. I'm knackered now." He shepherded me with his nose. Perhaps he'd found where my small pliers had fallen. "Okay, I'll get them." I patted his head. "If you insist."

I sidled inside, among the jackets and boots, kneeling down to run my sore, blind hand over the dark floor. The space got smaller, the air staler, as I fumbled around.

Coats brushed my head. I swept my hand deeper, towards the recess where the oval frame had been, and where the discovery of Luke's spare house keys had quelled my insecurity, the first night alone at the boathouse. But the confined space was getting to me. And as I shunted coats away from my head, along the rail, a shaft of light from the landing came down through the gap of the Love Step, illuminating the cupboard like some ancient tomb. A glint on the floor caught my eye, a Howard Carter moment for sure: for this was no boring pair of pliers.

As I picked up the slip of metal, my hand told it me it was a key, and I felt a stab of panic as the Secret Admirer story threatened to replay itself. But the thrill of the chase got me out of that airless cupboard, straight over to my desk. I switched the lamp on for a closer inspection: yes, it really was a key, ornate and very silvery in places, but very old indeed: in fact judging by the three-looped detail hollowed into the broad end, I guessed that it was probably Tudor.

I glanced back at the Love Step, now propped against the newel post; if the Boleyn inscription dated from the same time as this trefoil key, that made a kind of sense. But if this was the thing I'd heard falling, where had it come from exactly?

Boo had pattered back upstairs already. I joined him, and lowered the LED lamp into the open hole. Removing the step had done a lot of damage, and it was pure luck that the crowbar had spared the inscription itself. But in among the mess, my eye was drawn to a perfect, chiselled cavity, precisely tailored to the shape of key. It was recessed into the stringer, an extension of the slot that had supported the creaky tread. Incredible.

So someone had purposefully hidden the key there. Skipper might have crafted the niche at James's behest, but what would this hidden key unlock, and what would be revealed? I had the feeling I'd discovered a midway link in some complex, witty treasure hunt. It was like joining a film halfway through, to be bewildered by motives and incidents that would have made perfect, logical sense if you'd been in at the start.

Bang went another night's sleep, I thought, as a firework show of explosive theories started in my head. Just a few paces, across the Love Hole, and I slipped into the cold bed to think, the key before me on the duvet to focus my contemplation. Her inscription had been built into my house, by James, to emphasise the historic pedigree of his gift for Alice. But why hide it? He'd have made the point more clearly by setting it in pride of place somewhere, above a door for instance.

Where was Luke when I needed a sounding board to help me sort out my thoughts? But God help me if Luke turned up and found the stairway ravaged and dotted with blood. I'd have to hire a carpenter, get a replacement step made, before he came back. No hurry then, I mused ruefully.

My deputy sounding board was already asleep, twitching his way through some doggy dream, no more mysterious, I felt sure, than my waking life these last few weeks. How about Little Pearl? She'd be a good one to discuss my find with. And luckily, we already had a meeting booked in the morning. I felt my mind relax, at last, and the next thing I knew, it was morning.

I arrived at Walnut Court at ten, hoping for a sprightly, definitive session with her this time. But the affable matron said Little Pearl hadn't slept well, and might seem 'a bit drained'. As I opened the door, her moist blue eyes cheered my spirits... until she spoke.

"Dreaming about my pa." No courtesies, no preamble: Her breakfast tray lay untouched, and I noticed there were towels draped over the Blakeney Seal.

"Pearl, this isn't a good time for you?"

"Ma used to say Pa became possessed." Her tone was crotchety. "He became a devil."

"Why did she think that?" We were a long way from the topic I wanted to bring up.

"Obsessed, that's what he were, with status. 'Blooming obsessed', Ma said. In too deep with them Newtons and Greys."

She dozed off, the frail frame shaken by short sharp breaths. I sent Boo over to lick her hand, and she came round.

"Hello sweet thing." She stroked Boo's head with her crusty fingers, and put on her specs, the chain bright against the dark wrinkles of her neck.

"Ah yes, Jud's friend. You put me in mind of them gigolos."

"Pearl, what are you like?" Nobody had said that to me before. Maybe my slimline shirt made me look like an escort. Luke would be in fits.

"Ruddy Valentino. That I-talian. Ma used to take me to all them matinees." She closed her eyes and sighed. "Did you come to fix the TV?"

"No Pearl; Jud said you needed to tell me something. I hope it's about the boathouse?"

"Y-es, y-es, you were curious about Pa, and the Squire, Newton-Grey as he called hisself." She squinted. "Oh, my memory's not what it were." She snuffled into a tissue.

"Did you ever hear them talk about 'the Love Step'?"

"Is it on ITV?"

I'd threaded the Tudor key on some green twine, to keep it safe. Now was the time to produce it, to trigger something more solid from the muddle of Pearl's memory. I dangled it close to her face, but she swatted it aside without a glance.

"Yes, yes, Pa's key. One of two, it were."

My heart was racing and I could scarcely get my words out quick enough.

"Pearl, I found this one, tucked inside a creaky step at the boathouse!"

"That broke step, Pa were always out attendin' to it, Ma told me. Her ladyship, she'd send for him."

"An excuse to smooch?" I prompted.

"You know I met the squire when I were a little 'un? He used to come round to our house after the war. My ma handed over her will, for safekeepin'. I saw them. I think."

"Pearl, Pearl, you said two keys; was one a copy of the other?" But she had dozed off again. She was definitely not on form at all this morning. Her rambling hadn't really confirmed that last night's trophy had been hidden by Skipper. My mobile vibrated in my pocket, and I stepped into Pearl's bathroom to answer it.

"Thank God I got hold of you," Tilly gasped. "We're all going frantic at the Hall this morning."

"What is it? Are you okay?"

"No Bertie, it's chaos: we had a burglary here last night, the place is crawling with CID. It's just awful."

"Oh no, what's been taken?"

"Some paintings, smaller statues, but the worst thing, imagine: they've got the BB."

"BB?"

"The Boleyn Bureau."

"God, Tilly, that's terrible."

"And the Gala Opening a week away. I'm so stressed out, all the work I've put into this. The NHS are running round like lost chickens, all the money they've put into this opening. The Bureau is supposed to be the star attraction." She was starting to cry when I heard Pearl's door click, and someone else come into her room.

"Look, Tilly. It's difficult right now."

"Tell me about it."

"I mean, I'm back at the care home with Skipper Wood's daughter."

"Okay, but don't be surprised if you get a visit from the police later: they want to talk to anyone who's been at the Hall, and Karsten Wulff dropped you in it."

"Don't worry: they need to eliminate suspects, and we've got nothing to hide. Stay strong, Tilly. We'll speak later, okay?"

Pearl's visitor was a shirty male carer I hadn't seen before. He closed her curtains peremptorily, saying Pearl needed her rest, and would I mind leaving. I hooked Boo's lead to his collar – it was all very abrupt – and I found myself outside Walnut Court, disappointed with my Pearl session, shocked to hear Tilly upset. We retraced yesterday's route from the harbour. Grim news, this break-in. I hoped Tilly wouldn't use it as an excuse to hit the bottle. But she'd be toasting me in champagne once she knew I could save her Gala Opening, a knight in shining armour bearing a Queen's autograph – which surely trumped any little brown bureau – and a beautiful key that could nestle between her beautiful breasts as she made the inaugural speech.

This bracing wind blew away some of the tiredness I felt in my face. Boo asked for his coat, still in my bag, as we faced the chilly blast off the North Sea. Down the causeway, alongside the estuary nearly to the beach, I fingered the trefoil key in my pocket the whole way. What would it open? Some room long gone? An old marriage chest – they were popular with the Tudors. Perhaps a secret cupboard somewhere? Someone like this Dr Wulff at the NHS might be able to judge the sort of door it would fit. But I didn't want anyone else handling it, maybe losing it. I felt no shame about this particular paranoia. Even if James had had the precious key copied – an additional sign of its importance – I was not likely to stumble across the duplicate as well.

At length we were back in the campervan, and I popped into a hardware shop at Wells to get a carpenter recommendation. The pasty-faced girl on the till spread out various tradesmen's cards, as if for a Tarot reading, and I chose one that said '*No job too small – give Tiny Tim a call!*' Hoping his carpentry was better than his poetry, I gave him a call, and he said he'd be 'round in a jiffy'. It sounded promising. Normally nothing in Norfolk *ever* happens in a jiffy...

Home for lunch, and with the trefoil key secure in the top drawer of my desk, I went out to the jetty to call Tilly again. The wind was still sharp, but the signal was fair.

"Bertie, it's been a nightmare. CID seem convinced it's an inside job, and now the press are on to it too. I've had to be really cagey with pushy reporters."

"Anything I can do?"

"Meet me for a drink."

"The Ship in Brancaster, say seven?"

"Yah, sweetie, thanks."

I kept it brief, nothing about my discoveries. Those revelations would be so much more effective face-to-face. But I was glad we were meeting soon. She'd sounded so brittle, one more shock could crack her.

No text from Luke, no call back. Naturally his mum was the main concern, but I felt miffed that he didn't want me up North, helping him. I'd give it till teatime, I resolved, then try him again. But nothing works out the way one plans: the minute I was back in the boathouse, Boo cantered to the door, and a powerful knock announced a visitor.

"Clive Massey's the name. Inspector Massey to you!" He flashed his ID and pushed straight past me into the kitchen, then briskly into the hall area. "Going somewhere, are we?" He was looking at the tall boxes I still hadn't unpacked.

"I've not long moved in. This'll be in connection with the burglary at Samphire Hall. Right?"

"Now why would you say that?" he replied, staring at the makeshift bandage around my right hand.

"Tilly Offord rang me about it this morning. She's the curator up at..."

"You two pals, are you?" He let some spittle fly.

"Quite good pals, actually."

He shuffled around the packing boxes, tapping them with chubby hands, his movements exaggerated by the fact that his suit was a size too small. Then he bulldozed over to my desk to pick up the oval frame.

"Perfect for a photo of your pretty friend," he said.

"Oh, Tilly isn't my partner. He's away on business." I emphasised the 'he'.

"Is 'he', indeed?" So did Massey. "Antiques, by any chance?" His insinuating tone made me uncomfortable. Boo went over for a sniff, and recoiled.

"We're interior designers."

"Lot of wealthy clients up here?"

"Actually, we're on a bit of a sabbatical."

"I thought you said your partner was away 'on business'."

"Err... I meant family business. Some tea?"

"Not on the job..." he replied with an irritating sneer. "So – according to your pretty friend's boss, Dr Carson at the Norfolk Heritage Society – you were given access to the Audit House and spent hours there, 'doing your research'?"

"Correct." I guess Tilly had had to inform her boss – not that 'Carson' was actually his name.

"Why?" he barked, staring out over the marshes, absently scratching his scrotum.

"Oh, I'm investigating... I mean, this boathouse belonged to the Samphire Hall estate originally. I'm pretty interested in history." I wished I didn't sound so nervous.

"Convenient, no?" he boomed.

"Is it?" I said, uncomfortable about the direction this interview was taking. But he was already on another tack, glancing up at the hole in the stairs, picking up the Boleyn step at his feet, being the smart-arse detective.

"DIY?"

"As you can tell from this bandage, I'm not that clever at it."

"And this is all your blood, I take it?"

He'll be asking for my DNA next, I thought, to fit me up for the crime at Samphire Hall. I almost wanted to giggle: his hard-boiled cop act was such a cliché; yet the huge physical presence made him seem ruthless and thoroughly frightening. My anxiety grew as he examined the Love Step closely and it soared when he chucked it aside, like firewood. Then he lumbered back towards the kitchen like a foraging grizzly.

"That's all for now. I'll let myself out." But he swung around, just outside the door. "I'm sure you'll oblige and come down to Wells in the morning, put your grubby prints on record?" He glared at me. "Just a formality, you understand." Then he was gone, leaving his innocent suspect feeling as guilty as hell.

Afternoon dragged into evening, while I waited in for Tiny Tim, who didn't show. I sorted out the dressing on my arm, looked out a shopping bag wide enough for the Love Step. I was counting down the time before I could set out for The Ship, a nice homely pub not far from Tilly's cottage. On the drive over there, I remembered I'd forgotten to call Luke.

The moment I stepped through the door, it was clear Tilly had turned up early, and had already downed a couple of cocktails. We ordered some light dinner.

"Bertie, you've had an accident!" She looked at my bandage, alarmed.

"It's nothing really, I'll get to that later. But listen, I had a visit from Inspector Clive Massey this afternoon."

"Bertie, I'm so sorry. He's a brute. He and Karsten pressured me not to withhold any in-for-mation. I have to think of my job, you do understand?"

"No probs, but don't get upset, it's all fine. He didn't frighten me. And it's not your fault there was a robbery..."

"It's just... ru-ined every-thing." She held her head in her hands and slumped into the high settle against the wall. I got up and sat next to her. In an ideal world I'd have put my arm round her.

"Don't take it personally," I said. "You're doing a great job, no matter what."

"Yah, I am trying... fuck I'm trying..."

"Maybe I can cheer you up a bit?" I brought the shopping bag on to my lap. "How would you like Anne Boleyn's autograph?"

"Don't take the piss, Bertie."

"Ta-dah!" I opened the carrier. "Found at the boathouse last night."

Tilly said nothing, but turned the Love Step every which way, holding it up to the light, tapping it, smelling it. Onlookers must have thought she was mad. I thought she was going to cry.

"So... how, where?" she said eventually, her voice low.

"Blood, sweat, tears. Mostly blood. Come up some time and I'll show you the devastation. But the main thing is, it's yours for the Gala Opening. Tell the NHS your own research turned it up, and they'll love you forever."

She lowered her eyes.

"Bertie, you don't know what this means to me."

"I think I do..."

"The lab will want to run all sorts of tests."

"Anything they like. It's the genuine article. Promise!"

The waitress approached with our meal. I went back to my side of the table. Tilly put the step in the bag, leant over the table to kiss me, pretty much on the lips. Then she polished off another vodka, down in one.

"I'm still hoping the BB turns up by Bonfire Night, for the opening," she said.

"Wish we knew Massey's track record... " I began. But she was unstoppable.

"Anne Boleyn's Bureau – and her writing on the ancient cedar – exhibited together – a show-stopper!"

"There, you feel better already, eh?"

"To my dearest, sweetest Bertie!" But her glass was empty.

"No probs, Tilly, don't get up. Same again?"

Her glazed eyes watched me at the bar. Of course she'd had plenty already, but we had prospects to drink to now. And she ate with good appetite, eyes sparkling as I described my day, keeping the trefoil key in reserve for another meeting, another meal. At closing time I paid, and offered to walk her home. It wasn't far, and she really needed the air.

"How about a little harmless... nightcap?" she asked, steadying herself on the gatepost. I fought the temptation to put my arms about that drunken lithe waist, kiss that warm mouth.

"Tilly, get some rest, you need it; I'll call you tomorrow."

BFT jumped up to greet her as she turned on her hall light.

"You're right, you're right. Silly Tilly. Dirty Bertie, not. But thanks so much." She blew me an unsteady kiss, holding up the carrier with its precious contents. "One small step for a man... saves nine."

As I made my lonely way back to the pub, and the van, I wondered how James Newton-Grey would be feeling:

the heart of his accursed cedar tree poised to return, in triumph, to Samphire Hall?

Turning the VW down Alice's 'scented alley', I could already picture Boo, alert and waiting behind the boathouse door with his lively welcome. I turned on every light, quickly checked every room, every cupboard. Nothing amiss. I closed the shutters, attended to the locks, put the precious key in the drawer of my desk. I needed to get back into James's diaries, if I could stay awake. They were still upstairs.

"Come Boo, mind the step, boy."

I lay on the bed, turning pages. I had a gut feeling that the word 'key' – or better, 'second key' – would catch my eye, to help unlock the mystery of Skipper's early death. The bedside lamp shed its glow across an ocean of unfathomable depths. How painful, having sailed this far, if I never uncovered the lock that matched the key. Such a fine line, between hidden treasure and eBay bric-a-brac. I was bidding for it myself, but any price I typed in, unseen rivals promptly topped it. Their names scrolled up: Wulff, Newton-Grey, Wood. I was losing my grip...

Was it Boo's yelp that awakened me, or the footfall below, on the veranda? A heavy step: Muntjac don't come up this far? A crash, something colliding with the deckchair. Then tapping, tapping on the kitchen window. Not muntjac then. 11.30, said my mobile. The tapping grew louder. My pulse ramped up. Boo rose from his basket.

"Shush, Boo."

I crept to the landing, grabbing the weighty Eco-Design pencil from the corner. I found I'd left all the lights on. Stealthily down the staircase, over the ruins of the second step, banister beneath my free, splintery hand.

'*Calma*, Roberto!'

Banging on the French doors, steadily louder. Steps pacing back and forth, round to the kitchen. I creep through the little lobby, listen at the door. A kind of muted curse. A zip being undone. Then, horrors, a key slides into the lock – impossible – I hear the levers fall, watch the knob twist, slow motion, anticlockwise, a full turn. In the dread of the moment, I imagine the Secret Admirer's vile face. How has he found me? He's supposed to be in jail...

'*Calma*, Roberto... *calma, calma...*'

The door creaks slowly open. Barking, Boo lurches forward. I hold my breath, design trophy raised high like a bludgeon.

CHAPTER NINE
NIGHT VISITOR

A shadowy figure stepped into the hallway. I lowered the Eco-Design trophy, like a fool.

"For fucksake!" Standing in the doorway was the light, cheeky, sexy grin of my beloved Luke. I went to embrace him. Boo sprang between us, right into his arms: I welled up at the sight.

"Is that a dildo you're holding, or are you just pleased to see me?" said Luke. I leant the embarrassing pencil against the wall. "And what's the story with your arm?"

"DIY, bit of a mishap, that's all. And the frigging dildo, well I was just unpacking things... wondering where to park it." I hardly expected him to swallow that.

"Aye. Right. Where you're concerned, DIY is best left to the professionals."

"Luke, I thought you were a burglar, honest." Honest? It was less than half the story.

"So burglars have started knocking, before they break in?" He laughed. "I leave you alone, you go to pieces."

"Well, why did you knock? You still live here, don't you?" It came out more quarrelsome than I'd intended.

"You had all the lights on," said Luke quietly, "And me keys were in the bottom of the bag." He plonked it down, to terminate that topic, and came in through the kitchen. "How are you, my little bairn?" He and Boo made a fuss of each other again, while I waited my turn. It came in the form of an almighty hug.

"I couldn't miss our anniversary! You'd not forgotten us?"

"Nooo... I just hadn't expected... you seemed so busy." I hoped he would swallow that one; in truth I'd completely forgotten. "Shall I crack open... some bubbly?"

"Come on, Bertie, you'd prefer a cuppa," he said. As the kettle boiled I heard the tale of his impulsive – yet hardly romantic – trek to see me via National Rail.

"By 'eck I've missed you," he declared. "And I'm famished. Not a buffet car working the whole way down."

I set about making a sandwich, while he walked around, surveying the scene.

"Not a lot of progress, then," he commented, as I brought the tray in. "What have you been up to all this time? In your underpants?"

Before I could reply, he'd taken his jacket into the understair cupboard, and was looking up at the hole in the staircase.

"We had some sawdust, thought it might be woodworm." What if he asked to see the tread I'd removed? "The electrics are diabolical too, so I've gone ahead and drawn up a total rewire. I've designed a new bookcase for the recess, and I'm planning..."

"Aye, I only asked," he interrupted. He sensed my tension all right. I didn't like lying to him, but I just didn't know where to begin with the truth.

"You do like living here?" he suddenly asked, mid-mouthful.

"Ask me that again, come Christmas." Then I tried a new tack. "When's your mum's op, did you say?"

"Tomorrow, she goes in," said Luke. "I'm only down here for the night. You understand." He yawned hugely. "Thanks for the sarnie."

"Tomorrow, that's nice." But his devotion to 'Mam' really pissed me off. Here was me, keeping Tilly at bay, my emotions in turmoil... I wanted him home for good, for the sake of our future.

"Aye, hats off to the NHS."

131

He had no idea what that acronym meant to me now: parallel universes, different languages.

"Poor Mam. It's not just the flooding, it's the stink. Sewage. Everything needs replacing. That three-piece suite she paid for by the bingo – she loved that like some priceless antique." He'd gone over to my desk, and was looking at me through the oval frame. He looked knackered. The talk of antiques might have led naturally to the Boleyn Bureau affair: but there was just too much detail for the state he was in... and it was not exactly anniversary material.

"That frame was under the stairs," I told him. "Left by an earlier occupant."

"What, the boatbuilder?" Of course, what other previous residents did Luke know about?

"We should go up," I suggested, pointing at the clock.

"Come, boy," said Luke. A happy whippet followed him up the stairs.

"Mind the hole," I called. "And the blood."

I locked up. By the time I got upstairs Luke had crashed out, shirtless, on top of the duvet, still with his jeans buckled. He was fit and very appealing, and it had been ages... but by the time I'd bundled Lord James's diaries away, I knew I had missed my chance.

"Happy flipping anniversary," I whispered, sliding under the duvet.

Dawn struck swiftly, and I had to get Luke over to Norwich for the 7.55 train. I took muesli bars, bananas and a flask of tea out to the van for a quick breakfast on the road. The commuter traffic, into the regional capital, was reminiscent of London, and took all my concentration. Staying awake took all Luke's. When my mobile sang, moments away from the station, I nudged him to pick up. He blearily peered at the caller display.

"Do we know someone called Tilly?" he whispered, switching to loudspeaker mode.

"Hello, Bertie sweetheart," came her merry voice. "Any news from the police?" Luke must have seen me blushing.

"Say I'll call her later," I blurted. How was I going to explain Tilly away, with only ten minutes until Luke's train pulled out?

"Tilly, this is Luke. Bertie's partner. He says he can't talk now."

"Hi Luke, nice to meet you, so to speak. No worries, *ciao* for now..."

Driving on to the station forecourt I nearly took out a parking bollard. Luke braced himself against the dashboard as our bumper clipped a ticket machine. I shouted "Sorry!" to the man who was using it.

"You would have been too, if you'd killed him like," said Luke. "What's going on then: the police? Who's this Tilly?" He turned to look me in the eyes, pained and puzzled.

"There's been a burglary, antiques. The police called in... it happened quite near us." Then I added, "Remember my nerves last night, wielding the designer-trophy thingy?" One set of facts, two stories. It was happening more and more.

"And Tilly? You're not going all straight on me, are you?" There was a pause, and he added, "Sweetheart?" I looked, in vain, for a twinkle in his eye.

"Well, when we talked the other day, while I was over at Samphire Hall..." I began.

"That's where she... receives you, does she?"

"Look, she's just a junior curator over at the Hall, helping me sort out some research on our lovely boathouse," I said, hoping to sound dismissive.

"Bertie, it's 7.51, I've got to run. Call me when I'm on the train and we can talk then, okay?"

He grabbed his bag, pecked me and then Boo.

"Bye Luke, love you."

"You better," he replied, but at least with a curious smile this time. And then he jumped out and disappeared among the commuters.

"What a mess, what an utter mess..." I sighed to Boo. Luke was right: left to my own devices I did tend to come unstuck. Boo hunched on the empty seat, saddened by the shortness of Luke's stopover. I sat quietly for a few minutes to calm myself down, people-watching. I should let him settle into his journey, before ringing. So I called Tilly.

"Luke sounds really nice, very masculine," she remarked. "Look forward to meeting him sometime, but guess what?" She sounded excited.

"Go on."

"Do you want the good news or the bad?"

"What do you mean?"

"The police got CCTV footage from an antiques fair, Norwich Showground I think, and you can see the BB on it, being sold. The stallholder's been arrested and they've issued descriptions of the man who bought it. Haven't you had your radio on?"

"No," I said, "there's been enough drama at this end." But Tilly didn't cotton on.

"And there's more."

"What do you mean?"

"Now Bertie, I don't quite know how this has happened, but the *EMA* has reprinted a great shot of you and Luke picking up your award at the BM, the big chunky pencil you showed me. Bertie, are you still there?" My stress levels were soaring.

"The *Eastern Morning Advertiser*, that rag? How the hell?"

"It's a news piece on the burglary. Supposedly. They wanted a snap of the Bureau, and we didn't have one. I suppose they Googled 'Newton-Grey' and found the boathouse, checked out who's living there now? It's stupid, but not too negative, not really."

"God, I hate the media."

"Bertie, don't worry, everything will be fine." Her turn to reassure me, I suppose.

"If you say so..."

"Got to rush: big kissy."

"Yeah, okay." And we signed off.

Luke had hated all the publicity surrounding our award, back in the spring of 2007. He couldn't stand it, felt hounded, unable to work. This wasn't what he'd signed up for, he insisted... so for the sake of our relationship I agreed we should pack up the business and bow out for a while. He would go mental now, if he found out that we were in the limelight again. Or that I'd been asked for my fingerprints.

"I'll be five minutes," I told Boo, as I parked outside Wells police station, recently built, with its striking asymmetric frontage. I gave my name to the desk sergeant, who repeated it into an intercom. Then he took me into a tiny, cell-like room furnished with an insipid blue Formica-topped table.

Clive Massey appeared in the doorway, his serge suit still busting its seams. I should give him the name of a tailor.

"Right, let's begin. Sergeant, switch!" We all sat down at the table and the sidekick activated an antiquated cassette recorder.

"Time: 9.31," he said, then recited all our names. This was not what I'd been expecting at all.

Massey flung an *Eastern Morning Advertiser* on the table. As Tilly had said, they'd used a reasonable photo: Luke and me decked out in hipster suits at the British Museum, for the occasion, collecting our Eco-Designer pencil trophy from the celeb *du jour*. But the *EMA*'s caption – '*Turn On Your Gay-dar*' – was beyond outrageous, a homophobic jibe to sell a total non-story. 'Stupid', Tilly had called it... protecting me with a half-truth, same as I'd been doing to Luke. Reading on, I felt more and more incensed.

'Anne' old Queen lost her head, and now this pair of Pink Panthers have 'designs' on her lost 'Anne teak'!

Pencils out for our well-endowed London Lads, and write in to the *EMA* if there's a Stolen Boleyn in your closet!

"What dickhead would print that, for fucksake?" I exclaimed. "Or buy it?"

Massey paid no attention at all.

"What can you tell me about Charlie Snyder?"

"I know Snyder," I said in surprise, wiping the inspector's spittle from my cheek. "Norwich Showground. He's a clown. Reckons he's an antique dealer, but he doesn't know his dresser from his Davenport."

"So if he's a clown," Massey boomed, "how come CCTV caught you – and your male partner – at Snyder's stall last month?" He slapped a blurry enlargement down on the Formica.

"This is what you spend our taxes on?" I felt angry. "Yes, that was us, browsing tat, basically. It's our trade, re-inventing his kind of crap. A bit of paint, some varnish, and a spot of flair. It's called 'upcycling'."

"Is it indeed? Well Charlie Snyder 'upcycled' a very significant piece of furniture yesterday."

Massey obviously didn't understand what 'upcycling' meant, but I knew exactly what he was talking about.

"A Tudor writing desk, I assume? Not a chance. Snyder couldn't rob his own shed, let alone a stately home."

"I'm not saying he's the robber, though naturally he's being questioned." The hawkish eyes homed in on his prey. "So are you."

"You think I sold it to him?"

"Someone did!" he boomed.

"Well, surely a more important question is, 'Who bought it from him'?"

"So you're the detective now, are you?" Massey yelled. The hand that wasn't fondling his scrotum smacked down on the table. "Funny, I thought it was me."

"You know gay guys love to shop?" I needed to lighten the tone. I also wanted to get back out to Boo: I'd told him five minutes. "You can't build a case on coincidence, Inspector. Your CCTV will show us with loads of different dealers. Are you questioning them as well?"

"I'll have none of your lip," said Massey, wiping evidence of early elevenses from his own. Then I remembered the recording machine.

"This is my statement, for the record. As I believe I told the Inspector yesterday, I was researching the history of my boathouse, thanks to my friend, Tilly Offord, who works at Samphire Hall. I did not steal anything, nor handle anything stolen. Some upstart chancer, working on the local rag, is fishing for a hashtag story, that's all. They got wind of our hideaway, and they think two plus two makes fucking five." I'd kept my cool almost to the end.

"Any more cheek from you and it's a formal caution." Massey's face lit up at the prospect. "To me this smacks of an inside job. And in my book you, plus your pretty friend Tilly, plus a photo of you in cahoots with Snyder – that adds up to a lot more than five. Years." He was fumbling his scrotum again. "That said, someone did smash a window from outside... maybe to put us off the scent." He stared smugly at my bandaged arm.

"I told you I injured myself doing some DIY, didn't I?" I was feeling overheated. "Look, if I'd stolen the Boleyn Bureau, do you think I'd have come here to hand myself in? You asked for my fingerprints, I've come to give them. If you want DNA as well, go for it. I really have nothing to hide."

"Interview ceased 10.10," he said, jerking his head to dismiss me. As I stood up, I spotted my chance.

"I'd get that down to the clinic if I were you," I said, indicating his renewed, shameless engagement with his crotch.

"Go on, get out of here."

On the way out the sergeant took my fingerprints, with a scanner, before I scarpered.

As soon as we were back at the boathouse, unlocking routine over, I unrolled my yoga mat at the foot of the stairs and attempted to find some inner stillness. The first calming insight told me Massey was incompetent, and had let the Boleyn Bureau slip through his fingers. Then an even less Zen-like one: muggins was being set up as his 'patsy', as he would doubtless have put it.

"Tell you what, Boo," I whispered, holding *Savasana*, the corpse pose, "Snyder must know there's CCTV at the antiques fair. If he'd thought the Boleyn Bureau was stolen, he wouldn't have handled it on camera. And it doesn't *look* valuable, so I reckon some local housebreakers, who nick smallish items, flogged it to him cheap; and whoever spotted it on Snyder's stall is the expert. And they're about to make a killing on the international black market. Elementary, my dear Boo!"

Boo came over and licked me, watching with expressive eyes as I uncoiled myself, really trying to tell me something. I stroked his adorable head, and went to get him a 'good listener' treat.

Then I spotted the bananas and our faithful old striped Thermos I'd brought in from the van. Shit, I hadn't called Luke, and it was gone midday. God knows what he'd be thinking, all this time. I went to the jetty in search of a decent signal.

"Hi, how's your journey been?"

"Nowt but tedious. What happened to you?"

"Oh, I got caught up in Norwich, something to eat." A lie, but a white one. "You forgot to take your tea and snacks. In case you're wondering, Tilly is our new friend."

"*Our* friend, is she? How come?" He was right to sound surprised.

"She has an adorable wire fox terrier. Like those old-school toy dogs with wheels. Anyway it got lost, and she knocked at our boathouse."

"Aye, cute. Did she find it?"

"No, actually Boo did."

"Aye. Boo's the smart one."

"Well, Tilly, like I told you, she's working over at Samphire Hall for the NHS..."

"Need a nurse, do you?" he interrupted. I translated. "Uh-huh. So what are you telling us?"

"What better way to find out about our boathouse – you know what I'm like with history stuff. She's the same. So that's... why we clicked." There was no response. "Hey Luke, your accent has got pretty thick since you've been back up North."

"What, proper Geordie like ten years ago? When we met in Soho Square?"

"Just as sexy," I said. But then the reception became dodgy, despite the Indian summer weather.

"I can hardly hear you." I ambled up and down on the deck, but he was fading fast. "Luke, come home as soon as you can. I miss you."

"Aye Bertie, you're breaking up. I'll call you soon as poss. Still love my Essex boy!"

For the moment, now, I did feel at peace with the world. Luke knew about Tilly, and I had nothing to feel guilty about. And that's how it was staying, I decided. No more straight fantasies for this gay boy.

It was time to start writing my notes for Tilly, my digest of James's diaries: it was ages since I'd started reading them. But the yoga endorphins had a different idea: to spend this fine afternoon in the sunshine.

"Come Boo, walkies..."

We strolled down the coastal path towards a favourite spot, Stiffkey Creek. The holiday season was edging into off-peak, and the picturesque creek, when I reached it, languished empty, under a majestic Turner sky.

I gave Boo some water, from the cup of the dog flask, and sat myself down on the edge of a rickety jetty that must have featured in a million amateur watercolours. Despite the physical exhaustion, I began to feel mentally invigorated for the first time in weeks.

Boo larked about with a gang of pink-footed geese, who eventually took to the air. I unzipped my fleece jacket, plumped it up into a pillow, and lay down to lap up the autumnal sun. I inhaled deeply. My eyelids felt heavy; gulls screeched overhead, waders fished the inlet. I squinted for a second, to catch Boo frolicking on a steep bank of gorse scrub. Then, overwhelmed by the sea's whispers, I slipped into siesta, a fire-striped sky for my blanket.

I jolted out of empty dreams into a shock of pitch black. The night-time numerals on my watch glowed an alarming 8 p.m. I shivered, and sat up. Where was Boo?

There was movement nearby. I listened. The water lapping, then the sound of oars along the creek, faint foreign voices, answered by another much nearer at hand. Jud? There was no mistaking his curious lilt. Now was not the moment to call out for Boo.

Torchlight flashed through the darkness. I ducked behind tall reeds near the jetty. A group of men, and maybe a couple of women, jumped ashore close by. Jud called again, 'Victor?' or more probably 'Viktor' judging by the Eastern European accent that answered him. I gathered my things into my bag, wondering how I was going to find Boo and get safely away. Suddenly I could hear arguing.

"Viktor, I've been tellin' you, this is my last time!" Jud's voice was raised in anger.

"*Nie, Nie!*" It clearly meant 'no'. Then the foreigners talked vociferously among themselves, and Jud protested again. With terrifying suddenness the quarrel gave way to sharp punching and kicking: someone was getting a ferocious beating. And then, out of nowhere, Boo barking fiercely, in a voice I had never heard before. Were they attacking him too? Something impelled me to get up, and heard myself shouting, 'Police. Border control!'

The effect was instantaneous. The gang abandoned their victim – it was Jud – who fell down in the mud, moaning. Various women screamed and waded back into the water. The men clambered into the boat and this time a motor started. "British bastards!" somebody shouted. Then they opened the throttle and escaped towards the sea.

Boo stuck his head through the reeds. He was unhurt, thank God: my life without him... it would be impossible. We picked our way over to Jud, and I touched his stone-cold face. My fingers felt blood around his mouth. I found a torch on the ground – still alight, but with broken glass – and shone it on his face. He had taken a hammering.

"Jud. Jud!"

He moaned and slowly rubbed his wretched head. A tooth slid from his mouth, and thick blood oozed as he struggled to speak.

"Jud, can you hear me?"

"Ow..." And he crashed out again.

I laid my jacket over him for warmth, and tried to pour a little water into his mouth from the dog flask. Boo licked his face. The guy needed help fast, but Morston Quay was a good twenty minutes away.

Jud's breathing was shallow, and he was drifting in and out of consciousness. I tilted his head up and held the flask to his battered lips.

"Slowly does it, Jud."

"It's you..." he groaned.

"Do you think you can get up?"

"Don't know."

"Grip my arm."

With terrible effort, slithering for footholds in the mud, we got him standing, all six foot of him. Luckily he was no longer wearing his posh suit... only a gay man would worry about such a thing in a crisis, I thought.

"Easy, Jud, easy. Any chance you could make it to Morston?"

"I give it a go..."

He clutched on to me, for balance. I could feel him shivering. The temperature had plummeted.

"You been followin' me?"

"Jud, believe me, it's a coincidence. I overslept on the jetty, back there, then the fighting woke me. We... we need to talk..." I quivered.

"I know."

We stumbled towards Morston. I was hoping to make it as far as The Anchor Inn, and use their landline; out here there was no chance of a mobile signal. Boo led the way, but progress was pitifully slow. With every painful step Jud's torch flickered and dimmed, then the battery died. The route was hard to find in the hazy moonrise. We staggered round sudden potholes, and Jud flinched in fear as odd-shaped shrubs loomed at us in the desolate terrain.

His terror filled me with pity. He'd brought it on himself, but he'd clearly been trying to get out of the immigration scam. This was my chance to confront him: he wasn't going to rush off anywhere.

"I did it as a one-off. Viktor had kids and I needed the cash. Met him in Norwich."

"A one-off, what, to save your vintage car workshop, was it?"

"I been fundin' my nanna too. But Viktor, he threatened to, threaten me. Trouble, I told him... he's got a syndicate, a mafia." Jud gasped for breath, jumbling his words in pain.

"You wanted out, but he kept you in."

"He do know where I live."

"And so, tonight? They come ashore somewhere different every time, I guess?"

"It works," he said. "But you gotta believe me, man, I were desperate, my workshop were goin' under, which it fuckin' did, so the money all goes up to Walnut Court anyway."

"Jud, don't worry, I believe you."

"Dude, thanks."

Finally, around 10.30 p.m., we limped into Morston quay. I was frozen, and Jud was done for. The cuts to his face were congealing, and the harbour lantern revealed heavy bruising. He held his ribs bravely, making no fuss, and point-blank refused an ambulance. He obviously couldn't involve the authorities. I found a tap, topped up my flask, and he drank again, sprawled on a bench.

"Jud, I'm going into The Anchor, to find us a taxi, okay?" He didn't respond. "Boo, stay." He lay down by Jud's feet.

The lights of the pub quickly came into view: it was just before closing time. I hurried in, squeezed though the steamy bar towards the phone. People shied away as if I were carrying some deadly virus. When someone tapped my shoulder, a stab of fear suggested that the unsavoury Inspector Massey had been trailing me. But, as I swung around, it was an anxious-faced Tilly that greeted me.

"Bertie, what's happened to you?"

"Tilly... you're here!"

"I was just leaving. But look at the state of you!"

I looked myself over. No wonder the drinkers had given me a wide berth: trousers thickly caked with mud, Jud's blood blotching my sweatshirt. My bandaged arm completed the gory picture.

"Tilly, it's urgent: do you have wheels?"

"Yah, why?"

"Can I tell you outside?"

I followed her out of the pub, as did plenty of prying eyes. So she'd been drinking alone, I was thinking. Not even BFT for company.

"You're a godsend, an absolute godsend," I told her, as she started her four-by-four. I directed her down to the quay.

Jud was lying on the ground now, but Boo, bless his white-sock markings, hadn't moved. He stood up to greet Tilly's car.

"Good boy," she told him.

"Jud, I'm back with help: a friend of mine is here to take you home." I nudged his shoulder repeatedly.

Tilly's expression was full of concern, but she kept her cool impressively. Jud squinted through puffy eyes and we both helped him up slowly. He yelped with pain, clutching his ribs again. When I told him Tilly's name, and vice versa, Jud's eyes opened fully for the first time, as he registered her beauty for a second.

"Jud, with one 'd'," he told her.

"Sure you won't need a doctor?" I asked him.

"I'm fine, man; just take me home."

"It's your life."

"A pretty shit one an' all."

The back seat of Tilly's car was wide enough for Jud to lie down. She didn't seem to care about the mud. She just pulled a dog blanket over him, and Boo sprang dutifully into the boot. I thought I should offer to drive, but Tilly got in first, and swiftly accelerated. I prayed.

"A&E in Cromer? Or wherever Jud lives?" she asked as we reached the coastal road.

"The caravan park at Wells. Beach Road."

"He's in shock. He should see someone."

"Let's get him home and look at his wounds." That was my view.

She was driving fast, concentrating on the road. A mile or two further on, I came out with my question.

"So, what took you to The Anchor Inn?"

"I should ask you the same thing. I assume you didn't beat this Jud up yourself?"

"For God's sake! He's Skipper Wood's grandson. Great grandson."

"No, really?" She had no need to whisper. Jud appeared comatose.

"Long story. I'll tell you later."

"Mine's short, so I'll tell you now. I had dinner with Karsten Wulff, my big bad boss, as you know. You must have just missed him. His treat, to clear the air. Things have been pretty strained, what with the break-in, and me letting you raid the Audit House."

"You're in trouble over the diaries, then?"

"He got over himself especially when he heard you were lending us Anna Bolina. He practically swallowed his beard." Her giggle was adorable. "So I wangled it for you to keep all the diaries, almost up to the Gala Opening."

It struck me that Tilly was on excellent form.

"Karsten's excited about your notes. So am I, otherwise I won't have anything to say." Then her voice sparkled and caught at the same time. "I'm giving the keynote speech, apparently."

"Brilliant, well done!" I said, biting my lip in the dark. I had yet to make a start on my homework.

"Bertie... as of tonight, I've quit the booze as well. No more silly Tilly."

"Tilly, that's fantastic... but, all this pressure..." She broke in at once.

"Career-wise that speech – on live telly – will be a dream step. Crucial I don't fuck it up." She braked suddenly to avoid a deer that bounded across her headlights, and for a while we were silent again. I watched her face in the reflected light from the road, trying to guess what she was thinking.

"Massey's a brute," she eventually said. "He thinks you and I are in it together."

"I can handle bullies," I told her. "Specially ones that talk crap."

"And Luke, did he see the 'Gay-dar' crap in the *EMA*?"

"No, God no... he's back up north again, thank goodness, still helping his mum out."

"He sounds... very nice. I don't think I'd realised you guys were *that* famous."

"Infamous, in Massey's eyes. I don't think he can handle gays."

Her left hand slid over mine and gave it a squeeze. I was about to mention the trefoil key, when suddenly she removed her hand again, to work the indicator. We were turning into the Pinewoods caravan park.

"Which one's Jud's?"

"Scruffy one there, with the dead potted tree outside. Just pull up here, okay?" Tilly switched the engine off.

"Jud, you're home."

"Cool, man," he murmured. He tried to slide toward the car door, grimacing with the effort. We helped him out slowly. "Key's in my left pocket."

Tilly obliged as I helped Jud up the sagging steps. I was not altogether surprised by the stench of weed that greeted us as we got his door open.

Tilly and I laid him on his thin bed and set to work, cleaning his facial wounds in the shadows cast by harsh overhead lighting. I found him brandy in a cupboard. We teased him out of his mud-soaked trousers and I tore the ruined shirt off, to spare his ribs the pain of undressing. His gallery of strange inkings then revealed another surprise: an ornate key dangled on his six-pack from a finely tattooed *trompe-l'oeil* neck-chain, which disappeared tantalisingly into his underpants. Was it my imagination, or was this a representation of the key I had found in the Love Step? Were his private parts therefore tattooed with an indication of what it might unlock? The strangeness of the scene, as Tilly tenderly washed him with a damp flannel, struck me forcibly.

"So, what does a Sotheby's grad make of this body art?"

"Not my period," Tilly quipped. So that was that. The geek in me was itching to take a peek below his belt, but decorum prevailed. It would be awkward, but I'd find some way of asking Jud if he had a lock tattoo to match his key, once he was well again. We pulled the bed covers up and turned out the unforgiving light. A couple of days' rest, then some remedial dental work, and I was fairly sure he was going to be okay. In the doorway I remembered something.

"Hey Jud, how did it go at Holkham Hall?"

"I start next month!" I could hear his smile.

Tilly and I stepped outside: I had some explaining to do.

"Aiding illegals you say? Serious stuff," she observed. To my surprise I found myself defending Jud.

"He's just a decent bloke, down on his luck. Thought he could help some stranger with a family, and put a bit towards his grandmother's care place."

"I'm sure you're right, but the law won't see it that way."

"He's back in work, he won't do it again," I said. "But the gang know where he lives. They could still come back for him. I don't know what to do." Naturally, I knew what I ought to do. I just hated the implications.

"If Massey finds out we helped him..." Tilly stood there, vulnerable, detached, shivering in the night air. Skipper's *Beautiful Doll* tune – '*Let me put my arms about you*' – came into my head. I made a real effort to shut it off. Boo's sweet face was peeping out from the back of the four-by-four; his tail was wagging. I owed it to him, I thought, not to break up the nuclear family.

"Thanks for being such a good pal tonight." I went over and kissed Tilly briefly, on the forehead.

"Oh Bertie, the boot's on the other foot. You've made my life bearable out here. To say nothing of my prospects at work. Thank you! Let me drop you and Boo home."

"Jud," I said, "Sure it's okay to leave him?"

"He's a mess, but I think he'll be okay, nothing broken. I'll drop by on the way in to work tomorrow. I drive through Wells anyway."

We were painfully silent most of the way back to the boathouse. Both of us knew what the other must have been thinking, and another word could have destroyed the equilibrium of our restraint. Finally, the end of the track on the coastal road. Boo hopped out. I followed. Tilly blew me a kiss. I responded in kind.

"Goodnight, Bertie."

She drove off to her empty cottage, and I walked down to unlock mine. It was the best way to look after one another: the responsible thing to do.

CHAPTER TEN
DARK PASSENGER

I'd made a key decision last night, not going home with that 'beautiful doll'; but even so, Skipper's music-hall tune was in my mind when I woke the following morning. And who, I started wondering, had been in Skipper's mind, when he sang his Little Pearl to sleep with it? Surely not her mother Beulah, described in James's diary as 'plain as a pikestaff'? Lady Alice Newton-Grey, on the other hand...

Picking my careful way down the cedar stairs I pondered why I hadn't asked Jud to replace the missing step. His panel-beating career presumably meant he'd inherited good craftsmanlike genes. I took my cagoule and called Tilly from the windy jetty; she'd said she might look in on him, on her way to work.

"Jud is doing just fine," she reported. "I made him breakfast, he sat up and chatted a good while. Nice guy; you were right."

"Glad he made it through the night," I said, unable to prevent myself from adding, "What did you chat about?"

"Oh, nothing important; not the illegal landings. I said I'd drop in again on my way home."

"Tilly, you don't have to. I can do that."

"It's no trouble, really. And I've still got my first-aider badge, somewhere."

"Okay, then." Her sudden interest in the people smuggler was making me uncomfortable.

"Catch up soon: the graphics people want me now. Promo-stuff for the opening. *Ciao*."

What's wrong with me, I thought, as I ate my porridge and blueberries. They might as well have been gooseberries, the way I felt about Jud and Tilly sharing sweet nothings on his bed. I pushed the bowl away, and set the Newton-Grey diaries out on the table. The past would be a safer place to spend the morning. Alice's commonplace book: that was the material that needed corroboration now, if my investigations were to proceed.

A Baltic blast had swept in overnight. I wrapped a tartan blanket around me, and Boo slept by the fire, as I rejoined the Lady of Samphire Hall.

Saturday September 30th 1911

My husband has crazy ways in the boudoir, but this last night he goes plain too far. Lordy, he has me tied on that bed, unable to move a single limb. Drunk as a skunk, he's pushing & shoving against my wishes & all as though he's possessed. An' the minute he's done, he skedaddles back to his goddamn mansion!

In the morning he comes on by, begging my forgiveness something bad.

I guessed it was the absinthe that had brought out this shocking side of James. Alice's wording seemed to make light of an episode that our era would class as rape: horrible to realise it had happened in the same bed I'd been laying in an hour ago. At least James had begged forgiveness, and I turned the pages quickly, hoping for further evidence that he'd made it up to her. But the next four months or so were sparsely covered, until I found an entry that spelt out the consequences of that horrifying night.

Samphire Hall. February 17th 1912

Early morning — Mama has been minding me, in my boudoir at the mansion — an' I waken with a mighty awful sensation in my uterus. The linen is drenched – Lordy, blood red – everywhere: my poor baby child is born dead – a miscarriage or a murder – 'cause I do declare my husband has cussed my belly. He deserves to be punished, so help me God. Will this dead son be punishment enough?

Alice sounded wild and superstitious, vengeful. Might she later have seduced Skipper, to get back at James? Though my heart went out to her, I quickly turned to James's 1912 diary, in case there was another side to the story. Initially, it was only workaday jottings, as if James had buried his head in the running of the estate. It was almost a month before he felt able to record his feelings.

10th March 1912

As God is my witness and the devil my advocate I will win Alice back. My remorse for the demonic act of my dark passenger knows no bounds. I will make amends, and Deauville shall be my ruse!

James's inner world came to life in three bold strokes: 'devil', 'demonic', 'dark'. Or maybe 'ruse' was the key? All too soon my own world interrupted: a knock at the door.

"Hang on!" I made myself presentable.

"I come to measure up," said a small voice, as I opened the door. One glance was enough to establish that this must be Tiny Tim. He hadn't exactly turned up in a jiffy, as he had promised, but here he was, with toolbag and samples of timber. I showed him the Love Step hole, made him coffee and excused myself, saying I had work to do. I also picked up the notepad in which I'd failed, thus far, to record any crucial nuggets for Tilly.

18th March 1912, Samphire Hall

A first-class ticket, C66, arrived today for Mama

Constance's passage to New York. We are to see her off from the port of Cherbourg, on a new ocean liner. Little does my wife know that I have also booked the adjoining cabin, so she may accompany her mama, and visit her cousin Emmeline, should she so wish.

For the moment Alice must know nothing of this plan: she will assume Deauville – the Gallic quaintness of the hotel there – to be her holiday destination.

It was fascinating to read of James's machinations, his pleasure in surprises that bordered on deception. It confirmed the nature I'd sensed already in his bizarre collections, behind the secret doors at Samphire Hall.

Damn! Already the tiny carpenter was hovering at my elbow, with a checklist of mundane problems: thirty-three inches was an unusual width for a step; he'd never seen such thick boards in a staircase; he couldn't match the red of the cedar, and would have to 'shop round the sawmills'.

"Understood," I said, shepherding him to the door. "How long will that take?"

"Be done in a jiffy," were his parting words.

I stoked up the woodburner again and returned to work. Soon enough, I found proof that Alice had forgiven James sufficiently to take up his wily offer of a spring holiday.

6th April 1912 – a.m. – Normandy Barrière Hotel, Deauville

Our bedrooms are separated by a commodious parlour. Lady Alice has insisted on such sleeping arrangements ever since that unspeakable night at the boathouse. Constance, it appears, is none the wiser; I applaud my lady for her discretion in the matter. My cloth is cut, but I shall tailor this marriage so as to please my dear Alice in every way.

I tried to come up with some bullet points for Tilly's notes – 'Lord J's plot to save marriage after stillbirth', 'Wife keeps rape secret from mother'. But I struck them out immediately: too much like tabloid straplines, complex family woes reduced to bite-sized scandals.

6th April 1912 – pm. Normandy Barrière Hotel
We dressed for dinner apart, only to meet on the main staircase for the sake of appearances. As we descended for pre-prandial drinks, Alice turned toward me and straightened my tie most fondly. The meeting of our eyes spoke volumes of Byron to my ailing heart.

7th April 1912 – p.m.
Our day at the races hinted at further reconciliation with my dear wife, who smiled when my horse came in at fifty-to-one. I feel my Virginian soften like a ripening peach, although I have much more work to do.

Wednesday, 10th April 1912 – Normandy Barrière Hotel
For two or three hours, we motor west. I shall choose my moment at the port, and present the second ticket so she may accompany her 'Mama' on the American voyage.

10th April 1912. Port of Cherbourg – 3 p.m.
Our automobile arrived, under clement skies, into an immense flurry of quayside activity. I let Alice and her mother weep together at the prospect of a long separation, while I awaited the moment to present my peace offering. The porters collected Constance's luggage – hatboxes enough to sink the damn ship! It was due to sail at 8 p.m. I kept an eye on my wristwatch.

But James's 'sinking' metaphor reminded me uneasily of the frowsy old newspapers from under the stairs, wrapped around the oval frame. I read on with trepidation.

Wednesday, 10th April 1912. Cherbourg

Our last moments with Constance, in the Mercedes. I reached inside my blazer for the additional ticket and handed it to Alice. Mother and daughter hugged one another in beauteous amazement. Constance applauded the timing of 'this thoughtful gift'. Alice thanked me most playfully: "Truly, my dear James, a '*Titanic*' surprise!"

I closed my eyes in dread. So my boathouse, which had already lost one of its characters to an unsolved murder, looked set to sacrifice another to the sinking of RMS *Titanic*. But only if Alice had actually decided to travel?

And as I hastily read on it became clear that James, like a master conjuror, had timed his revelation to coincide with the arrival of the Astors – Constance's dear New York friends – on the train from Paris. John Jacob Astor was returning home from an Egyptian honeymoon with his young wife, Madeleine.

Wednesday, 10th April 1912 – pm. Cherbourg

Much jubilation ensued, with fond greetings and jovial repartee. Constance was utterly delighted. Colonel Astor introduced the new Mrs Astor, who is heavily expectant. The manservant carried her little Airedale dog, named Kitty. Alice took an immediate liking to Madeleine and her terrier. Circumstances could not have fallen out more propitiously.

I felt all the innocent excitement among the travellers – I shared James's pride in his careful planning. Yet my heart sank.

Wednesday, 10th April 1912 – p.m. Cherbourg

Suddenly my beloved turned to bid me farewell. It was a fond display of emotion such as I formerly had from her, until that bestial night at the boathouse – when absinthe indulgence allowed my dark passenger access to realms where the *real* James does not dare to venture!

That 'dark passenger' idea again: what a hideous burden for Lord James, to suppose there was some lurking aspect in his nature, over which he had no control.

Constance and Lady Alice, mother and daughter, descended the gangway to board a tender. As my dearest prepared to stoop beneath its canopy, she turned and smiled up at me most tenderly: a smile to launch a thousand ships. In that instant, I knew my patience and planning had borne their longed-for fruit.

Bon voyage – Godspeed my love – I write no more this long day.

The safety, or otherwise, of Constance and Alice – even if their destiny had actually been sealed almost a century beforehand – now threw me into turmoil. Without Internet passenger lists at my fingertips, James's diary was my only means of ascertaining their fate. Yet what of those doom-filled newspapers, which, it now occurred to me, James must have stashed in the boathouse shortly after the disaster? I fetched them from my desk drawer and examined them under the lamp. Poring through the yellowing pages, however, I was mortified not to find Constance or Alice on any survivor lists.

There was still hope, though. What was the date when Alice and Skipper had been caught 'smooching'? If that happened after the *Titanic* went down, then of necessity Alice had survived. Little Pearl had been my source about the smooching, but of course her memory was no longer dependable, and the story had been hearsay even to her. Thus far James had made no reference of this whatsoever in his diaries: but a hurried search revealed that various pages were missing in his April entries, and some later in the year as well. Had he recorded Alice's infidelity, then later torn it out, in shame, or rage?

I was shocked at how tense this was making me. Could I ever know the truth of these affairs – and what did it matter – I asked myself. But the answer was clear, and it was a matter of procedure: understanding James's distant deeds was going to enable me either to add Alice to my list of suspects in the Skipper Wood murder case, or eliminate her.

With a tap at the door, Tiny Tim was back – his 'jiffy' this time had been inconveniently fast – carrying an armful of timber. He resumed his repairs on the staircase, while I brewed him more coffee, and let Boo out.

I returned to my workstation and stared out across the sea, dark under a shark-grey sky, before immersing myself in James's next stream of entries: a series of Marconi wires sent from RMS *Titanic*, and pasted in his diary, daily, as key events unfolded.

RMS *TITANIC*: Thursday, April 11th 1912

Dear James,

How thoughtful of you to forward Alice's trunk to Ireland. My dear daughter is firm friends with Madeleine Astor already, and all conveniences of this floating Versailles help to heal the painful memories of losing her child. We remain deeply honoured by your kind generosity.

We leave Queenstown at 2 p.m.

Fondly, Constance x
P.S. An Airedale like Madeleine's 'Kitty' might do the trick.

"Well, how about that, Boo?" Constance was oblivious about the root cause of Alice's malaise. She must have taken the chilly marital atmosphere for British reserve, following the loss of a child.

Thursday April 11th 1912 – Normandy Barrière Hotel

Eureka! An Airedale puppy shall await Alice on her return to Norfolk.

Skipper could fashion an amusing kennel in the form of the boathouse.

So at this point James was still collaborating on good terms with his carpenter. Either Skipper's dalliance with Alice had not yet occurred, I reasoned, or James had not yet discovered it.

Still, evidence for a murder enquiry was building up: my bullet-point digest of clues from the diaries now filled a page. Tiny Tim, cursing and sawing on the stairs above me, barely intruded on my senses – as if he were some ghost in a twenty-first century future, and I were embedded in the world of James's Edwardian narrative.

RMS *Titanic*: Friday April 12th 1912

Dear James,

Alice and Madeleine take exercise together in the gymnasium, or in the swimming pool – aboard an ocean liner, whoever heard of such a thing? It's getting mighty raw out on deck. The captain talks proudly of our journey time to New York City, and hopes to break the speed record, God willing. Meanwhile, my dear Alice longs for you.

Constance x

Hotel Normandy Barrière, Deauville: 12th April 1912

Dearest Constance,

What a pleasure to learn that your crossing is so agreeable. In *The Times* newspaper the Head of the White Star Line commends the 'triple screw' that impels *Titanic*. She proves as swift as she is unsinkable. Please convey my deepest affection to Alice.
Bon voyage.

James x

James's outgoing message – in his exacting way, he had preserved all the handwritten forms from which his wires had been prepared – seemed thoroughly upbeat about the success of his scheming. Thoughts of a renewed life with Alice must then have spurred his return from Deauville to Norfolk, since it was his chauffeur, Bailey, who presented him with the next telegram, collected from Holt post office just before teatime on Sunday.

RMS *TITANIC*. Saturday, April 13th 1912

Dearest James,

We glide along, wrapped in blankets on steamer chairs, or warm ourselves with sweet tea on the promenade deck. Tonight we are to dine at the Captain's table, with tennis players Williams and Behr.

Just five days until my dear cousin Emmie will be welcoming us at White Star Pier 59. So long since I saw New York! Alice's bloom has quite returned.

Constance x

Tiny Tim was hammering away on the stairs as I spread out my entire trove of newspapers, grimacing at the bold headlines that had sent such shockwaves through the self-satisfied world of 1912. An artist's impression showed the iceberg striking the 'unsinkable' vessel just before midnight that Sunday. Her lights, said one account, died at 2.18 a.m., and she foundered within a few minutes of that.

Scenes of chaotic desperation filled my thoughts, as complacent passengers dealt with a dire reality: the freezing deck, the ghostly calm of the ocean, and the knowledge that, in barely a few hours, their great ship would have disappeared.

James had dined that Sunday night at the Grand Hotel in Cromer. He sent his last wire to the ship just before sitting down to dinner:

Grand Hotel Cromer, Sunday 14th April 1912 – 7 p.m.

My Dear Constance,

I have wired funds to Chase National Bank for your disposal while in New York. Alice has told me of your cousin Emmeline's extravagant hospitality: you must feel able to match it. I count the days until your safe return to Samphire Hall.

James x

Settling to his meal, James must have congratulated himself on the scope of his foresight. Not even he, however, could have imagined that message, sodden and unread, at the bottom of the Atlantic.

That Monday's diary entry shows James rising at dawn, 'happy as a skylark'. He rides out on his beloved mare Pocahontas, at peace, for once, with the world and himself. Yet his good cheer, as he jauntily gallops home, is to be short-lived. On seeing his sombre-faced guardian, Ida Henderson, awaiting him at the entrance to the Hall – on noting the huge headlines on the early editions she hands him – his world suffers a shuddering change.

Monday, 15th April 1912 – a.m.
As I dismounted, Bailey brought further front pages but I could read nothing. I had seen that word 'unsinkable' too often. On its promise I squandered my gesture of redemption. On its untruth I gambled the lives of my wife and her mother.

I sat, surrounded by the very pages James's staff had brought him, and spoke aloud some of the headlines he'd been unable to digest: *'J. J. Astor lost on* Titanic, *1,500–1,800 Dead'* and *'White Star Liner Sinks in the World's Greatest Marine Disaster'*.

Tiny Tim's racket had stopped: perhaps he'd heard my voice.

It was impossible to imagine James's trauma, his shattered heart. How did he muster the courage to turn the front pages, as I now did, and wade into the oceans of text dramatising the tragedy, the 'ice razor' ravishing *Titanic*'s supposedly watertight compartments? Yet as the liner's last moments ticked away I somehow found myself 'channelling': a phantom bystander, back on board the stricken liner, I watched its beleaguered officers, swamped by helpless passengers, all fleeing the rising havoc below.

This was my world now: the newsprint stories seized control of my thoughts and encaged me in a labyrinth of slanting galleyways, churning ice-water, flickering lights and alarums ringing. My fellow-passengers, rushing this way and that in their terror, groped for companionways to the upper decks. Many, like me, were locked in a nightmare quest to find people they cared about, more than their own safety.

It was as if I were in the grip of some computer game – '*Unthinkable!*' Yet to me this story was not about a sinking ship: at its heart lay Alice, lay the heart of James Newton-Grey.

In a cold wet moment, Boo brought me back to reality. He was licking my face, puzzled to find me on the floor, surrounded by newspaper cuttings, scribbling my impressions manically in a notepad.

"Boo, paws off the papers!" I shouted. But where was he to tread? They stretched from coast to coast across the living room. Somewhere among them the Astors' little Airedale was drowning. I wanted to dive back into that icy ocean, to save their dog as I would my own.

Tiny Tim appeared to my left, as if summoned by my shouts. While I reconciled with Boo, he trotted across my pages himself in his tiny boots, opened the stove and stocked it with offcuts from his apron pocket.

"Firewood," he observed, though we could both see that the stove was cold. Then he named his fee, and I gave him cash; he wrote out a receipt and added it to the sea of papers, and I saw him to the door in relief. There would be time to inspect his efforts when my own work was done.

Back in Norfolk, James had Bailey drive him over to Holt to collect a reply from his wire to the White Star offices. The post office must have obliged him by remaining open after hours.

White Star Offices, Canute Chambers, Southampton
16th April 1912

Dear Lord Newton-Grey,

Every effort is being made to establish survivor lists. It is with regret that we must vouchsafe that we have no knowledge of your family members at the present time.

We understand, and of course share, your grave concern.

Sincerely yours,

Edward Smythe
Communications Officer, White Star Line

James's next entry records how he returned home heavy-hearted, uncertain if he would ever see his beloved again.

Events at Samphire Hall were very upsetting, and I have to admit that James's next entry had my lip trembling. Later that evening a horse-drawn cart drew up outside St Benedict's Foyer and a farm labourer, carrying a puppy, was shown inside. He had heard from Stanley Sellars, the estate manager, that Lord James Newton-Grey was in need of an Airedale terrier.

In his emotion James apologises to the diary for his handwriting. Its wildness heightened my compassion for his distress. He describes how his soul was lightened by the sight of the sweet creature, and he paid the farm worker generously for his trouble. He details how he held the puppy up in the air, and named him Kit, in reference to the Astors' terrier, Kitty, that Alice had so taken to, just before the fateful embarkation at Cherbourg.

Subsequently, he writes that he loaded his leather hunting bag with a couple of bottles of absinthe and, with Kit in his arms, made his way down to Woodfields. The boathouse 'languished in deceitful quietude, shrouded by a sweeping mist' as his shaky scrawl puts it. He bolts the door. In the very place he'd intended to be Alice's haven, he is now consumed by fear for her.

Generous with detail even in his despair, James describes laying on the Baroque bed, clutching Kit – 'my token for Alice' – while tears flood his eyes as never before. Racked with guilt for tricking his wife into sailing with the *Titanic*, his torment surpasses even the harshness he endured as a child from his overbearing father.

The man who appeared to have everything now doses his tortured soul with absinthe unmoderated, a palliative to ward off his demons. As night takes hold, he writes, he sobs himself into the darkest of drunken stupors.

CHAPTER ELEVEN
THE SACRIFICE

I don't have the mania for order that Luke suffers from, but this sea of *Titanic* papers was getting to me, and it had made me snap at Boo. I couldn't face another hour in so tragic a world. In the end I crammed them into my deep drawer unsorted, happy there was no archivist present to disapprove.

With the loss of Alice and Constance, my morale needed a lift from Luke's voice. I went down the glistening jetty just before six and called him a few times, but his mobile was perpetually engaged. I rang Tilly instead.

"Bertie hold on; Jud, excuse me a sec'..." Ah, so she'd kept her promise to return to his static van on her way home.

"You sound harassed."

"Well, Inspector Massey turned up at the Hall and interrupted my high-end graphics session, wanting my fingerprints. Not a proud moment for my CV."

"Is he still banging on about an inside job?"

"You and me and the antiques guy – Schneider, I think? Massey's suspicious because Schneider insists he doesn't know us."

"And we're the best Massey can come up with?"

"He needs a result, any result. Rumour says he's gunning for some top police promotion, coming vacant in the New Year."

"Dream on, I say. So long as the NHS – and your boss Karsten – they don't believe you're involved?"

"No, luckily, it's Karsten who told me the promotion rumour. He's... well connected, you might say. By the way Anna Bolina's up at the lab, and the preliminary results are great: right age of wood for the carving to be authentic."

"There, you've got your fallback for the Gala Opening, assuming Massey won't get the Bureau back in time."

"Oh, don't say that..." Her voice was shaky, and I wondered how her born-again sobriety would stand up to all this pressure.

"Hey, do you want to eat over here later on?"

"Bertie, I'm whacked, but the good news is, Jud's on the mend already. He's asked me to stay on for a takeaway, fish and chips. Such a nice guy..."

"Oh, okay." How cosy, I thought.

"Bertie, I'm planning an early night, so once I'm through here it's bedtime for this city girl."

"Look, thanks for checking up on Jud," I said. I wondered what she saw in him, since his famous Skipper Wood looks were closed for renovation. Maybe a certain kind of girl goes for the injured, motherly look anyway? Or, maybe, he simply isn't gay?

"Sweetie, I'll ring you tomorrow. Have a restful evening."

"You too, and..." I held back.

"Bertie, are you all right?"

"I'm fine," I said. "Bye for now."

I wanted to tell Tilly I missed her, and explain my latest findings, but I guessed that would have to wait. I made myself a snack, while Boo enjoyed a sachet of 'gourmet special', for dogs of a certain age.

Before I resumed my research, I went up to examine my repaired staircase. It was worse than disappointing – Tiny Tim had overlaid two boards to get the tread thickness right, and there was a visible join in the top surface as well. He was no Skipper Wood for sure: so that explained his cheap fee. I needed a word with Tim, when other pressures eased off.

Low cloud had swept in off the sea. I firmed up the shutters, Boo slumped into his basket, and a new fire raged in the woodburner. I anxiously got back into James's diary, to discover what I could of Alice and Constance's fate.

Tuesday 17th April 1912 – p.m.

Skipper was in my bedroom. I finally awoke to a plash of icy water. My head thundered. My first words to this steadfast companion: "Dear God, Alice?"

I could see newspapers that he'd piled on the tallboy. But Skipper pulled a telegraph wire from his pocket and read aloud: '706 survivors'. Then, a winning smile: Alice Newton-Grey was among them, safe and sound. I rose from the bed to hug the good fellow, but he held me off and read again. 'The whereabouts of your mother-in-law, Constance Ogilvy-Fitzgerald, are still unknown.' Such conflict in my soul: I fear Alice will never forgive me.

Kit came scampering across the floor: I held the puppy aloft and told him his mother-to-be would soon be home.

I rejoiced with James that Alice was safe; but of course my trepidation for their marital future extended beyond estrangement to the infidelity Pearl had talked about. The very wire that Skipper had brought was here, pinned to the page in James's diary. A Marconi operator on board RMS *Carpathia*, which had arrived a four full hours after *Titanic* went down, had sent it. Overleaf I found a heartfelt wire from Constance's cousin Emmie in New York.

Then I felt a wretched frustration about my own stupidity. All this worry about whether Alice had drowned: I could just have looked for any post-*Titanic* entries in her scrapbook. This was incompetence of

Massey-like proportions, I told myself. But that didn't make me feel any better.

Flicking through Alice's pages brought a further shock: there was nothing at all after April 1912, when she'd decided to accompany James to Deauville. Obviously the book had not gone with her on the ill-fated crossing, or it could not have been discovered at Samphire Hall this year. But, given that Alice had survived, and she'd never again used it as her *confidant*, I could make one crucial deduction: the Alice rescued by RMS *Carpathia* was hardly the same Alice who had embarked so smilingly at Cherbourg.

I turned the pages, blank and stale, in vain. Yet on reaching the end I noticed the back cover felt thicker than the front one, and inspection revealed that some extra card had been glued to it, making a kind of sagging pouch. One of Luke's kitchen knives soon opened the edge of this blister, and with thumping heart I pulled out two ivory foolscap sheets.

I was holding a stenographer's transcript – in characteristic American typewriter font – that recorded Alice's eyewitness account of the *Titanic*'s final hours. The hearing had been held at New York's Waldorf Astoria Hotel: under the embossed letterhead I found the date, April 19th 1912.

Impossible to imagine the traumatised delivery, as Alice stood in front of the Senate Commerce Committee, still in shock, her mother still missing at sea. A terrifying scenario unfolded as her account transported me – another virtual tour – deep into the disaster zone, from her last supper – shared with handsome tennis stars Karl Behr and Dick Williams at the captain's table – to being jolted awake, when the ship eerily stopped moving, at precisely 11.40 p.m. I saw her check her watch – a wedding present from James – then abandon it in the ensuing panic. And I was there on the deck to witness the fateful scene related on the second page:

Mama and me, in line at the handrails: it's awfully cold. Colonel Astor tells how he put Madeleine aboard Lifeboat 4, through a window from A-deck. Suddenly an officer orders us to board the same lifeboat. 'Women and children!' he insists, and the colonel gallantly stands back. Distress rockets whistle overhead: everyone knows we're sinking. The band plays up on the deck now, the one tune over and over.

A hysterical gentleman begs the officer to let his son board this last lifeboat. Says he's just thirteen but as he looks older the officer refuses. Mama holds out her hand, insists on going back aboard so the boy can take her place. And for the sake of keeping company with the colonel, I'm darn sure. She orders me to stay as nursemaid to Madeleine. And before I know it Mama has disappeared into the bedlam.

I'm sobbing so bad but they tell me to row, all of us, away from the ship's suction. The bow of the *Titanic* is vanishing at a fearsome rate... and that's the last time I see my mama, Constance. Suddenly everyone abandons ship, hollering, folk plunging into the black ocean like a thousand discarded liquor bottles.

I couldn't read on. As dusk fell over the boathouse, night engulfed my inner world too. I'd been transported to the darkest of times, and desperately needed a break. I got up to stretch my legs, but everything felt weak, as if my increasing absorption – my trance-like participation – in these historic accounts was using up a lot of personal battery power. I attempted to recharge by holding Boo close for a while, as Colonel Astor must have held Kitty in the freezing sea.

A change of scene would revive me, I thought. But the only change I wanted was to unfold the rest of the *Titanic* papers, and pore through the survivor lists in later editions, still looking for Constance. Wondering if I could actively induce the trance-like participation – which so far had only come unbidden, like a dream – I went back to the final paragraph of Alice's testament.

I search for Mama and the Colonel and his dog, all over the *Carpathia*, everywhere, just everywhere. Lordy, poor Mama! The moment those lights died on the *Titanic* – a light went out in my own life too.

It worked, in a way. I found myself not so much on board *Carpathia* as embroiled in the nightmare that stalked Alice's soul: a Babel of desperate voices rising from steerage, the towering stern, propellers monstrously exposed, sliding into sub-zero waters. And no sign of Mama. Minutes in that sea would have stopped her heart, frozen her blood, in the most haunting silence imaginable...

When I awoke, realisation struck me again. Alice's commonplace book fizzled out, but James's diaries covered the years to 1918. Reading on through the series, I would surely pick up the fallout of the *Titanic* saga.

14th June 1912 – p.m.

Bailey drove me to Norwich to meet Lady Newton-Grey's train. The ride back to Samphire Hall was indeed sombre, with little said. I offered her a Turkish cigarette, her brand, from the gold Fabergé case she gave me. She inhaled deeply, her face drawn, cheekbones razor-sharp. She is more ravishing than I ever remembered: but alas, her fiery spirit, which I so adored, seems to have been quenched.

I escorted my doubly-estranged wife through St Benedict's Foyer, to prepared rooms upstairs. I am at a loss to know how our marriage can ever be retrieved.

I opened the door to her quarters, and there on her bed was my puppy token, Kit. He jumped up to greet her. Perhaps she believed, for an uncanny moment, that it was the lost Airedale Kitty that she swept into her arms. For the first time, she wept with abandon. I needed to embrace her, there and then, and could scarcely contain the sadness in my heart. But Alice needed time, a good deal of time – and so I withdrew to my studies.

On Sunday 7th July 1912 James wrote poignantly of a memorial service for Alice's mother, officiated by the rector of Stiffkey. Cousin Emmeline had come over from New York. Emmie stayed on for a few days, devoting all her time to Alice's consolation. They walked the grounds arm in arm: James watched them from his father's Great Library, from which they remained in full view, now that he had destroyed the Boleyn Cedar and, as he goes on to admit, 'torn out the heart of Samphire Hall'.

Alice accompanied Emmie to the station, as she set off for New York, and on returning to the Hall she told Ida Henderson that all her personal effects were to be conveyed to the boathouse, as she wished nothing to remain under her husband's roof. Perhaps it was Ida, I thought, who had slipped Alice's abandoned scrapbook behind her portrait?

Alice had chosen seclusion, to help her come to terms with her grief; James was now isolated in turn, to come to terms with his guilt.

12th July 1912 – p.m.

I could not have engineered the annihilation of my tragic marriage more successfully – it appears the house of Newton-Grey is cursed with a Sophoclean propensity for self-destruction.

He evidently busied himself for the next couple of months with affairs of the estate, which he had been neglecting, and with the continuing development of artificial limbs from his designs. Skipper fashioned successful working models 'from remnants of the Boleyn Cedar'. I pored over entries where James hoped Alice's 'time reflecting apart' might still bring about a marital reconciliation. But it was evident to me that he lost himself, most evenings, in his absinthe. Past 10 p.m. or so, his diary ramblings and sloppy handwriting testified to a drunken state of mind.

It was growing late; the squally weather had passed over the boathouse. I let Boo out for his night-time constitutional, wrapped myself up and ambled downstairs to the signal hotspot, hoping for messages. Luke had tried to call, and had texted to say that his mum's hip operation had taken place at three: it was too early to say how it had gone, but she was safely back in her room. And, for the first time, he thanked me 'for my patience', signing off with a smiley-face symbol. Hoping he'd be resting by now, I resolved to call him in the morning.

Locking up, I wondered why the idea that Luke might soon be home had not raised my spirits more. Physically I longed for him. The difficulty was on the mental front. My investigations centred on the idea that an unquiet presence was making it impossible to live happily in the boathouse, but that its influence could perhaps be neutralised by uncovering the hidden details of its story. Luke, however, was vociferously sceptical – worse than Tilly, even – about anything beyond the material world, and dismissed any talk of curses or hauntings, even canine telepathy, as self-delusion. Or 'bollocks', to use his preferred term. Once Luke was back, it would be impossible to devote due time to my enquiries. Whereas now, at last, I had an authoritative ally: James, in his diary, had mentioned that 'the house of Newton-Grey is cursed', and here I was, literally inside the cursed house of his creation. Admittedly I was unsure what he meant by 'Sophoclean propensity for self-destruction': but no doubt it would be possible to find out.

Climbing the stairs to bed, I tested Tiny Tim's handiwork for the first time. The Love Step had creaked, perhaps even screeched, as James had carried Alice into the boudoir where he would later violate her. Its replacement did not creak as I trod on it: it now emitted a sharp click, the sound of bones snapping.

I climbed into bed, holding Lord James's diary up to the bedside lamp; three months in, I came across a pivotal piece of evidence.

29th October 1912 – p.m.

At tennis with my footman, I noticed a solitary Kit mooching about beyond the fencing. Most peculiar, for where the puppy went, Alice normally went too. Abandoning the game, I followed Kit – with unaccountable trepidation – as he headed home in the forbidden direction of Woodfields.

As we grew near, I first heard Caruso singing *La Donna è Mobile* on the gramophone, but then Verdi's melody gave way to that confounded tawdry song that Skipper whistles incessantly. I stole around to the veranda, following the puppy, already a spirited whippersnapper, grown almost level with my knee.

Peering through the glass, I was horrified to espy my darling wife – still so grief-stricken in her mourning – in lascivious embrace with my man, Skipper Wood. I burst through the doors to knock Skipper down.

James, ever the wordsmith, described the scene in such vivid detail that again it played out in my mind like a CGI animation, as if I too had witnessed the event. What strange trick were these diaries playing on my soul? Had I slept so many troubled nights at the boathouse – called 'Wood Feels', in my world – that the paper traces of James's life had the power to draw me in, sapping my mental energies in order to re-animate themselves? I was reliving past events with ever more sensual impact, in the cinema of my helpless skull: no wonder I always felt so tired.

James met Skipper's guilt-ridden face with his bunched fist, and the carpenter staggered back, begging to be heard, proclaiming the innocence of his visit, showing the groceries he'd brought, Binham Blue cheese, late tomatoes. But James had seen what he'd seen, and struck him again. Alice, shrieking hysterically, ripped at his tennis shirt, but James was oblivious, bent on revenge, cursing his betrayers, taunting Skipper to fight, to provide good reason for James to be done with him in an instant. Skipper fought back half-heartedly at first, reluctant to use his Olympian strength against his master and friend. James went for the eyes, the groin, no concessions, until, to preserve himself, Skipper was obliged to wrestle his adversary to the floor, writhing and grappling across the cedar planking, the two of them brawling like guttersnipes.

Alice's pleas go unheard; Kit cowers in some corner, while James, drenched in fury, locks his sinewy arms in a stranglehold around Skipper's windpipe. A trembling Alice brandishes a knife from the scullery, threatening to slash her wrists if the fighting does not stop that instant. James, forced to come to his senses, releases his grip on a groaning Skipper, who humbly repents his disloyalty, sputtering through pummelled lips. He is the spitting image of Jud after his beating at Stiffkey Creek. The disgraced champion drags himself off the floor and, at James's terse direction to leave, grabs his peaked cap, downcast at the ignominious ending of his career on Newton-Grey soil.

The Southern Belle wilts to the floor – speechless with remorse for her weakness – as the weight of infidelity compounds her marital grief. A broken James, his lips tightly compressed, refrains from verbal accusations; he makes an ungracious exit without further ado except – by way of a parting shot – to pull a tennis ball from his pocket and toss it into the room towards his own token of remorse. The puppy ignores it.

As I closed the diary, and inhaled deeply, I wondered why James had taken such pains to catalogue this ignominious episode. It was as if he expected one day to be obliged to produce it as evidence in a court... but surely any counsel would seize on it as providing a motive for the killing of Skipper Wood... by Lord James himself? Perhaps, then, the series of eight diaries constituted an autobiographical account, intended for publication should he be sent to the gallows?

The Boleyn Bureau heist looked like child's play by comparison with this upset. The Edwardian story had left Skipper ostracised, Alice in disloyal turmoil, and James seething, but none of it was reducible to simple bullet points. And it left me aching, mind and body, with an exhaustion I had never known before. I was desperate for sleep, but wary of more debilitating dreams. The rhythm of past intrigues – for all it seemed to chime with the pulse of contemporary affairs around the boathouse – offered maddeningly few hints of how tensions were likely to resolve.

CHAPTER TWELVE
A GOOD WIFE

Downstairs I unlocked the shutters and stepped naked into the sunshine on the veranda. The decking was strewn with broken branches from last night's squall; droplets still blinked in the blinding glare.

Happy birthday, I said to myself. I could never understand the fuss people made over such anniversaries, after a certain age. Still, when I found a signal on my mobile, I was annoyed to find no greeting from Luke. Forty fucking three. Isn't a man's prime supposed to be his early forties? Yet these last few weeks had weakened me: the strange effects of spending so much time in the past, and the revival of insecurities I had hoped never to acknowledge again.

Wait... there was a text, but it was from Tilly: Jud was at Wells Police Station, having turned himself in. I was the only witness who could attest that he'd wanted no more part in the people-smuggling. I dressed at once, apologised to Boo for leaving him behind, and hurried back over to Wells. The desk sergeant again announced me to Clive Massey by intercom, and the Inspector emerged with a typical quip.

"You again?" he boomed. "Watch out, Warren, I think he fancies you."

"Very good, sir," said the sergeant tonelessly.

"I'm here about Jud Wood. With one 'd'."

"And the connection?"

"He was assaulted at Stiffkey Creek the other night. I was there."

The hooded eyelids rose like festoon blinds.

"And you're confessing to that as well?" His laugh was mirthless. "You'd better join us in the interrogation suite. You know the way by now."

Rather unorthodox to sit in on another man's police interview, I thought: but this was Norfolk. Jud's solicitor introduced himself, Lewis Stone. Jud managed a smile, marred by a missing tooth. Sergeant Warren produced a metal-framed chair, and sat me across from Massey. He was uncomfortably close in such an airless room. Warren then announced my name and continued recording the interview. It was 10.25 a.m.

"Let's hear your story," said Massey, adding a gloating "Sonny!" Truly he was the last man on earth – except perhaps the Secret Admirer – that I would want to have as a father.

"I met Jud out on the marshes..."

"A welcome committee for our Iron Curtain friends?" he interrupted.

"We're absolutely not friends..." Lewis Stone held up his hand and Jud's intervention hung in the air ambiguously, and perhaps fortuitously, I thought. Better not to explain my boathouse link with Jud. My own investigations needed to be kept separate from Massey's, for clarity's sake.

"So, if it wasn't the Volga boatmen, what brought you to Stiffkey Creek in the dead of night?" bellowed Massey.

I recounted the events of that evening: my walk, my long sleep, and my chance overhearing of Jud's declaration that he would not be part of any further immigration scams, which had earned him such a savage beating. Lewis Stone jotted down notes, and Jud gave me a bruised thumbs-up. Though every word I said was true – the fiction engine was not needed – Massey's incredulous gaze made me very uncomfortable. I'm sure my body language felt more guilty than I did.

"Your reason for not reporting the incident immediately?" He got up and trundled over to the window grille, using both hands to test its fitness for purpose. My eyes followed him back to his swivel chair.

"I couldn't get a mobile signal, and Jud was in a bad way. I walked him to The Anchor Inn at Morston, and we drove back..."

"What did you drive? You said you were out *walking* your dog." He was a little more astute than I'd given him credit for. Now I would have to bring Tilly into things.

"I met a mate, who drove him to his mobile home – his Winnebago, I should say – outside Wells. We cleaned Jud up, and he seemed well enough not to report it."

"The beating is not the incident that concerns me. As you very well know. You failed to report a border violation. Didn't you think the Home Office might be interested in a horde of illegals...?"

"I hear a foreign voice, I don't instantly ask to see the passport." Once again Massey had me riled. "One keeps an open mind about minorities, eh Inspector?"

"Strange how you always turn up in the wrong place at the right time, isn't it?" Massey, and his body odour, drew closer. Here it comes, I thought, accusations about my supposed involvement in the Boleyn Burglary. I felt uneasy, and nauseous.

"I told him," said Jud thickly, "I were goin' to hand myself in anyways, and there were no need for him to report it."

"Please let me deal with this," Lewis Stone broke in.

"And I'm here anyway," I exclaimed. "What else do you want?"

"Who was this 'friend' you bumped into at The Anchor?" said Massey sharply.

Jud threw me a cautious look – concern for Tilly – and took a sip of water through puffy lips. Oh God, I thought, if I lie now I could be in deeper shit; yet if I say

Tilly drove Jud, Massey will think all three of us are in the burglary business, along with Snyder.

"Inspector," said Stone quietly, "my client is here of his own accord, showing willingness to cooperate: identifying this chap's friend is irrelevant, while we have more pressing issues to deal with."

Massey leant back, staring at me, scratching at his privates – which Stone and Jud pretended not to notice – presumably in hopes of stimulating some juicy legal *aperçu* from his brain. It wasn't long in coming.

"I don't know why I don't throw the book at you this minute. Go!" he barked.

A relief! I'd thought he was going to read me my rights. I went out to wait for Jud in reception. But it was twenty minutes before he appeared, looking ashen; Massey rolled past and disappeared into his office.

"Bail has been set at thirty-five thousand pounds," Lewis Stone informed me.

I really felt for Jud; he had enough financial worries already. He'd also been ordered to surrender his passport, and report to the station weekly, until he was subpoenaed by Norwich Crown Court. He was likely to go to trial early in the New Year, just a few months into his new job too. As he left, Stone did suggest that Jud's voluntary cooperation might earn a little leniency from the Home Office.

I crossed the road with Jud – he was still in a daze – and we found ourselves outside The Globe Inn.

"Fancy a drink?" I asked.

"I could murder a pint."

As he drank, Jud spoke of his fear that he'd have to put up his only material possession, his mobile home, as collateral. Things looked bleak for him, and Stone's notion of Home Office clemency struck me as improbable. If Massey felt the case against Jud needed any reinforcement, one sniffer-dog visit to the 'Winnebago' would do the trick.

I managed to bring the conversation round to Little Pearl, and Jud's mood lightened. He asked if I'd like to pay her a visit, read something more about Skipper Wood. My mood lightened too, at the thought of Pearl's batty twinkle, and the chance of further revelations. Regardless of Jud's rough-and-ready ways, and his strange lingo, I had quite grown to like him.

I picked up some chocolates for Pearl on the walk over to Walnut Court. Fortunately she was in better shape this time. Despite her great age she giggled coquettishly at my gift; and she complimented Jud on his 'new glasses', the shades he had just put on to mask some of his bruising from her.

Pearl began reminiscing about her mother, about whom I knew little except that she'd been a doctor's daughter, and Skipper's unassuming wife, and that her name sounded biblical. Pearl, on the other hand, revealed that Beulah had been the brains behind Skipper's joinery business, managing accounts, filing ledgers, and keeping a tidy inventory of all customer orders.

"And it was Ma came up with the idea of my seal, what won the squire's competition," Pearl said perkily. For all her lack of upwardly mobile graces, it seemed Beulah had played a key part in Skipper's social elevation. "Show your friend the... whatsitsname."

From the tallboy Jud produced a timeworn newspaper, some kind of special commemorative edition devoted to James's 'County Carpenter of the Year' contest; simultaneously the carer, Bren, came in 'to do Pearl's ointment', which required her guests to go elsewhere for fifteen minutes. Jud went out 'to get some air' – the kind he kept in his wallet, wrapped in tinfoil, I imagined. An empty wheelchair languished at the end of the corridor, so I settled there to study Pearl's antique newspaper.

It was something like the Sunday supplements of our own time. The Cromer-based publisher had taken great trouble to impress: an artist had been commissioned to provide Hogarthian illustrations of revellers at a summer fete on the greensward below the knap-flinted walls of Samphire Hall.

As before, my imagination – my fiction engine – transported me beyond the mere details and I mingled in the vivid, rowdy pageant, an unseen visitor from another time. I watched the Silver Band's buttons shimmer in the sunlight. I dodged a rabble of flat-capped lads capitalising on the unlimited supply of Owld Pippin Cider.

Lord James Newton-Grey was grinning devilishly under his panama hat, commanding our attention like a ringmaster. At 2 p.m. he banged a gong, and in my fancy the crowd piped down as the carpenters, stationed at trestle workbenches, took up their tools in readiness for his tournament.

The author of the feature described, with fan-like fervour, how Skipper dominated his rivals from the outset, '... Viking hair tied back, brow sweating profusely as the day grew hotter and hotter. Every sinew was taut – brawny shoulders, bulging biceps, sturdy, veinous forearms – as he worked his Senegalese ebony with supernatural mastery. The crowd followed every chisel stroke, as Wood's poetic hands liberated the soul of a seal from its cumbersome timber tomb.'

The reporter captured the wholesome spirit of the contest, as other finalists abandoned their own work, mostly routine joinery, to watch Skipper at his – all bar one dogged rival, Caleb Bacon, who laboured on to the bitter end. Time was called at precisely 5 p.m., after three hours in which 'Mr Skipper Wood of Binham, Norfolk's

Golden Olympian, had left the county's other craftsmen in the shade'. As Lord James lifted up the Blakeney Seal – 'freshly glistening with oil, in a diving movement that defied gravity itself' – and declared Skipper the winner, 'the crowd hurled their hurrahs, as well as hundreds of caps and boaters, into the flawless sky'.

I was there in the crowd as Skipper mounted the podium, and a smiling Lord James presented him with twenty-five guineas and a Royal Doulton 'Loving Cup', charged with champagne from the Samphire Hall cellars. Skipper merrily splashed handfuls of drink over pretty servant girls, and porcelain beauties in stupendous hats, all gazing up at him in lustful admiration. Meanwhile Beulah, his plain wife, consoled the unhappy runner-up. Skipper's Olympic former glory had been rekindled, as he posed – shaking hands, all smiles – with the dashing Lord James for a commemorative photograph.

A century in the future, I examined this haunting memento. One small, slightly blurred figure caught my eye. I had a feeling it might be the unfortunate Caleb Bacon, 'the only soul at the fair not to share in Skipper Wood's joy' as the reporter had observed. Bacon's 'pig-like snout' had already cropped up in James's diary. His unworthy conduct at this event must have sounded a sour note with the Edwardian revellers. Nonetheless James's quest for a champion carpenter had certainly ended in triumph. Skipper was the perfect man for the project that lay ahead: the building of my boathouse... in which he would meet his mysterious downfall.

Pearl's door opened, and Bren signalled that I was free to continue my visit. Though Jud was not back, I went in, hoping to resume my chat about Beulah. The scent of lavender now mingled with the sting of TCP. Little Pearl was propped up in her wingback chair watching *Loose Women*.

"I see you got your TV fixed," I said.

"I do love the tittle-tattle," she shrilled. Then, fumbling with the remote control, she immediately turned it off.

Pearl promptly resumed her narrative, but from a point long before her own birth, when Beulah had worked as dispenser for her father, and had 'known all them chemicals by name, like they were her friends'. I couldn't see this assisting my enquiries, but in any case Jud now reappeared, evidently refreshed from his 'airing'. Pearl seemed suddenly vexed by his Raybans.

"Too bright for you, my wallpaper?" she asked.

"Bit of a gammy eye," said Jud.

"Looks like you been at the fisticuffs," said Pearl, with a mischievous grin. "Look at your lips too. Who you been kissing?" I came to Jud's rescue.

"It was a stormy night, Pearl. The door of his caravan blew in your face, didn't you say, Jud?"

"I got a mug like a pug," Jud sniggered. When he lifted the sunglasses, Pearl seemed enchanted.

"Ooh, Ma would've made a poultice for that, all right. Time was... damn this memory... I knowed the names of all her magic plants."

Suddenly she lapsed into silence again, standby mode, gazing ahead, chewing on air. I hoped she hadn't exhausted herself relating these peripheral memories. I needed to know how Beulah's marriage had fared in the wake of Skipper's dalliance with Lady Alice. When Pearl slowly came out of hibernation, she pointed at Jud's bruised face.

"That was it," she said. "Pa turned all Jackal and Hythe, after he got involved with them Newton-Greys. Ma told me."

"You mean he had mood swings?" I asked. The phrase puzzled her.

"Moody? It were Squire Newton. He gave him a shiner. In that eye." Judd nodded in agreement. I'd witnessed the event itself, on my mental travels through James's diaries, but it was quite a thrill to hear it confirmed a second time by Pearl.

"And Beulah knew it was Lord James who'd given him that black eye?"

No response.

"You mean she didn't know what they were fighting about?"

"It were probably nothin'," said Pearl, and then, infuriatingly, she closed her eyes. If she really didn't know about her father's adultery, I thought, it was really not up to me enlighten her.

When Pearl again returned to life, the first word she spoke was 'wallpaper'. Some time after the black eye episode, Beulah and Skipper had apparently quarrelled about the décor, in the parlour of the semi-detached Victorian villa she'd had inherited from her physician father, and which had become their marital home. Beulah had protested that the wallpaper in their parlour reminded her of the waiting room it had once been ('all them sick ghosts hangin' around for their treatment'). Skipper, in 'Jackal and Hythe' mode presumably, had said it looked posh, and refused to change it. I noticed Jud nodding: he'd heard this before as well.

"Ma took me away, and my brother Archie, God rest his soul, to Southwold, round in Suffolk. I were about one year old. It weren't a holiday, it were a bargain. She told Pa we'd come back when the walls were fixed. But when we came back it were all bare plaster now. He hadn't been able to finish the job. Ma were so upset."

"Skipper got sick," said Jud. He fetched a hanky from a drawer, and Pearl dabbed her eyes with trembling hands.

"Skipper? He looks pretty strong in the pictures."

"Gastroenteritis weren't it, Nanna?"

"The air were bad in our parlour," said Pearl. "Ma had to take Archie and me away again, down the road this time, to Uncle... Uncle..."

"But Pearl," I broke in, confused by her fixation with this tale, "You were only one. You can't remember this. When did Beulah tell you? And why?"

"Two children, no father? Of course she told us, every year on the day he died. So we would understand how he'd gone." How he'd gone? I wished my mother had been sane enough to explain that sort of thing to her fatherless child.

This was not only the first time I'd heard Pearl sound indignant: it was also the first time I'd heard any mention of Skipper's death that differed from the newspaper story, in which he fell on his saw. Suddenly Pearl's random memories were sounding like part of my case, and I wished I had a tape machine, like Massey used for his interviews.

"So Skipper, you're saying..." I checked myself. "This bad air?"

"Pa got the cramps," she said. "In his belly. Giddy spells an' all."

"And this bad air... from the drains, was it?"

"You never listen," said Pearl, crotchety again. "It were from the walls. A bad smell in the wallpaper."

Wallpaper with a poisonous odour? My mind went back to student days, a morning lecture on period interiors, 'Fads and Fashions'. The nineteenth-century vogue for some wall-covering that had turned out to be toxic. 'Scheele's Green?' 'Paris Green?'

"Pearl, what was this wallpaper like?"

"It were bright, like an emerald. Ma told us."

"And Skipper spent a fortnight stripping it all off, and then got stomach cramps?"

"Like I told you."

"Pearl, I hate to tell you, but that wallpaper contained arsenic. That's what gave it the bright green colour."

"You do talk a lot of nonsense," said Pearl, quite cheerfully. "Ma knew arsenic, she always told Archie and me not to go under the sink where she kept the rat poison. She knew all the chemicals."

"You know Napoleon?" I said.

"The one what killed Beef Wellington?"

"No, the one who got killed... by fancy wallpaper." Both Pearl and Jud stared at me for a moment.

"Dude, you're kiddin'?"

"He was exiled to St Helena, where he complained about 'bad air' in his apartments. They'd been done out in that rich Regency green. Believe me, I went to lectures on this. When they analysed Napoleon's hair, it was riddled with arsenic."

"Arsenic, that's for rats," said Pearl.

"Not for fancy wallpaper," said her grandson.

"Think of asbestos, then," I told them. It was exactly the parallel the lecturer had used twenty-odd years before. "Used for generations in house-building. Turns out to be lethal, deadly, when you disturb it."

"Ma never mentioned anything about asbos," said Pearl. "And I never said Pa died from the bad air. He died from bad guts. He'd taken so many rich meals with the squire. Ma told me. Jud, dear, all this talkin': I need a tinkle."

Jud helped her up and into her bathroom. The minute the door was shut I got out my NHS notebook, and, breathless with the excitement of my runaway thoughts, added Beulah's name to my list of suspects. Then I sketched out a theory. Enraged by rumours of her husband's fling with Alice, which was confirmed by James's black-eye assault on the man who had cuckolded him, Beulah had plotted the subtlest of murders. The wallpaper bargain was of course a smokescreen. Skipper had died from the rat poison Beulah, the attentive wife, had subsequently put in his food. As a doctor's daughter she'd known that arsenic symptoms could be passed off as gastric infection. And the yearly repetitions, by which she indoctrinated her poor children with the tale of the Paris Green paper, were intended to clear her name if any subsequent questions ever arose about arsenic in Skipper's body. They would parrot out the innocent explanation, of the daft marital spat over interior design.

I heard the toilet flush, and quickly put my notepad back in my pocket. I helped Jud convey Pearl to her wingback chair, and we spread the blanket back over her lap.

"That's better," she said, as her marvellous blue eyes twinkled. Jud rested her cane by her chair and then sat on the bed. "I enjoy natters with young company."

She had quite forgotten that we'd been discussing her father's bizarre death. She spent a few minutes clacking a boiled sweet in her mouth. Jud tidied up the selection box I'd brought, from which he'd eaten the entire top layer, then dabbed some saliva from his nanna's lip. The hanky, I noticed, was embroidered with a flowery 'B'.

"Is that your mother's initial?" I asked, to get the family history flowing again.

"Ma liked sewin' – to while away the time after the first war. She never needed to work, you know: Archie and I wanted for naught."

"She didn't remarry?" I asked.

"Ooh no, she were never interested in other gentlemen after Pa died. She were a good wife. There was always money for my schooling, and sensible frocks an' all. Until I were sixteen. Then it all stopped. 1929, that were."

"The Great Crash," I said.

"Is that how Jud hurt his face, you say?"

Jud peered at his non-existent watch.

186

"Nanna, we should let you rest."

He's always in a rush, I thought to myself: but I took the hint.

"I've really enjoyed our talk," I told Pearl. "Would you like me to bring my little dog next time?"

Pearl sank back and closed her eyes, without replying. Jud kissed her, and by the time we'd crept to the door she was asleep. We chatted briefly on the stairs.

"Jud, look, thanks for letting me see that newspaper feature. Really thoughtful, specially with all you've been through."

"Any time, man: thanks for comin' down the station an' all. And..." – he pointed to the welt below his right eye – "The story 'bout my face, for Nanna. You got a high-octane imagination!" He shook my hand, and we seemed to be on the threshold of a buddy relationship, something I would never have foreseen the day I bumped into him out on the marshes.

"Look, I'm dining with Tilly later; would you like to join us?" It was a way of helping him out without openly offering charity.

"Dude, that be cool," he replied, without an instant's hesitation.

"Victoria Inn, Holkham, at seven, then. Where are you off to now?"

He pointed out the new gap in his mouth and tried to say 'dentist' without biting his finger.

"Ah. Good luck," I started. But he was already disappearing through the main doors.

I was euphoric as I drove back to the boathouse, my head full of clues and theories. I imagined a dialogue with Massey, in which I dazzled him with my deductions. But the closer I got to home, the more I realised that my case was about as clever as Massey's nonsense in which I was the Boleyn Burglar. It was one way of looking at the facts, but it didn't mean it was the right way. And what were the facts, in my case? Granted, Beulah had taken her children away while Skipper stripped the wallpaper – it did look as though she wanted to spare them from any toxic effects. But none of this explained Skipper's swan dive on to the jagged edge of his saw at the bottom of my stairs. I'd been helped out once or twice lately by my fiction engine – 'high octane' as Jud had called it – but on this occasion it had run away with me.

I opened up gloomily and gave Boo a cursory greeting. My first task was to demote Beulah from the head of my suspect list. She'd been there about an hour. I also crossed out another late entry, the curmudgeonly rival carpenter Caleb Bacon. A snout-like nose didn't make you a murderer. Shit. I ought to be spending my time on the diaries and Alice's commonplace book, researching the primary sources, not relying on faded newspapers and batty geriatrics. And I didn't have long: the documents had to be back at Samphire Hall by Bonfire Night, the Gala Opening. It was just a week away.

The best of the day was over. I skimped the housework and skipped lunch. I forced myself to read page after page of trivia early on in Alice's book. Even once she got to England, much of what she wrote was typical tourist stuff. Her entries didn't have the poise, the sense of an audience that James's had. But I was brought up short by one piece from 1911, headed 'Audit House'.

I ride Frieda, my bay mare, back to the stable yard. I think I'll surprise my husband at the Estate Office where he works while Stanley Sellars, the manager, is away on leave.

Well I do declare... I peep in the door, only to find James & Skipper larking in there. Quick as a cat chasing a mayfly round the dinner table. Belly-laughing they are, suspenders hanging by their breeches an' all. Mighty peculiar, I'm reckoning, master & servant playing cockfights in a place full of books. But what in blazes am I thinking? Everyone knows the English are crazy.

What in blazes *was* Alice thinking? This seemed to be the only mention in her book of James and Skipper crossing the bounds of a regular friendship. Even when I realised that suspenders, in those days, meant merely trouser braces, the scene was still redolent of something like a 'bromance'. But I cautioned myself, throttled back my racing thoughts. An intimate friendship wasn't necessarily a carnal one: look at Tilly and me.

Seven o'clock was imminent. I reached the Victoria Inn earlier than expected, imagining Jud would be late and I'd have some quality time with Tilly first. But the two of them had evidently been there a while already, close in conversation by the fireplace, where a good blaze allayed the evening chill. They smiled as I approached and offered them refills. Tilly's sober apple-juice was a good sign: but like an addict in withdrawal she seemed to have found a substitute craving in the form of Jud. Or maybe it was playacting, I tried to convince myself, to prod me into jealous action?

It was nice – if bittersweet – to see Tilly enjoying her evening; but her vigorous appetite astonished me. She felt my eyes on her face.

"Yah, I know it's stodge," she said, as she loaded her fork with steak and kidney pie, "But I really am famished."

"Don't worry Tils, you wicked figure can afford it."

So their intimacy had reached the 'Tils' stage already, and 'wicked figure' too. Jud probably didn't realise he was muscling in on my half-baked fantasy. But we both stopped thinking about Tilly when his phone buzzed on the table, and he read the incoming message with a panicky expression. He passed it me.

'Jud my man – hope you feeling better – expect a Home Visit soon if you can't make my next beach party. Viktor.' I showed Tilly.

"Out-and-out intimidation," she said.

"But cleverly worded," I pointed out. "If you don't know the background, you won't see the threat. Show it to your solicitor, Jud; don't go answering this yourself."

"Man, I will in the mornin'," he said. Then he downed his whisky.

"Make sure he shows it to Massey," said Tilly. "Could be a factor in getting you off the hook." Her eyes met his with a sparkle I'd imagined she kept for me. Jud held her glance, then placed his large, calloused hands over hers, across the pine table.

"The thing about a nightmare," said Tilly to Jud, "is that it really can't last." She seemed to be making a promise.

By now we were on sticky puddings. Jud ordered yet another whisky. I cautiously sipped my lager. The logs crackled and spat; Tilly shed a couple of layers. And though Jud rambled on and on about what a good mate I had become, his lecherous eyes never left Tilly's cleavage, where the tiny ornamental key dangled. Then I had an idea, to claw back a little attention.

"Something else for your exhibition," I said to Tilly, unzipping the trouser pocket where the old, trefoil key from the staircase had been hidden all day. I dangled it over the table.

"Pretty," she said, as if it were just another necklace.

"D'you think it's Tudor?"

"We could ask Karsten. His PhD was on keys." She'd scarcely given it a glance, and her hands continued their tabletop foreplay with Jud's. As for him, he didn't even pretend to look at it. 'I've got that key inked on my belly' was what I wanted to hear, but no. The mysterious key, upstaged by frigging lust.

So Tilly had given up on me, as was well within her rights. But she deserved the best: her sophistication, her artistic sensitivities, her inherent fragility – how would these mesh with Jud's stoned, breezy attitude to life?

On the other hand, as I watched them giggling together, it occurred to me that – bleak though it might be – if Tilly were to have sex with Jud later on, under his harsh caravan light, she would be well-placed to discover where his key-chain tattoo led. If so, I might find a tangible lock for my ancient key. And that might lead to the solving of the Skipper Wood affair. It was a sacrifice I should be prepared to make. I zipped the trefoil key away again.

"Come on Mr Wood," Tilly was saying, "someone needs to get you home." Jud chuckled. She put on the various layers of clothing she had discarded.

"Sorry if I got a bit canned," said Jud, as I paid at the door. "I needed to chill." He patted my shoulder.

"No need to apologise. Look guys, have a good night, and I'll... I'll be in touch."

"Bye, Bertie dear. And thanks."

The Chelsea tractor purred away. As her lights reached the coast road, I noticed, Tilly turned west towards her own place, the opposite direction from Jud's. Ah: there was a good chance of some progress on the matter of the intimate tattoo, then. I just wondered how on earth I was going to broach the subject with Tilly next time we spoke.

CHAPTER THIRTEEN
BOO

As I awoke next morning I was already rewriting my suspect list: James, Alice, Beulah, even this shadowy Caleb Bacon, didn't they all have possible motives for ending the life of Skipper Wood? But I was not cut out to be the solitary detective – who does so well in *noir* fiction – ruminating alone. A sounding board was what I needed, and the only listener available, in Luke's absence, was Boo.

"So sorry about yesterday," I told him as we unlocked and stepped out to inspect the day. A salty wind swept the veranda. It didn't look like a good morning for a walk, though I owed him one. Boo isn't one to hold a grudge, after a day of neglect, but he was behaving quite oddly, pacing up and down, clacking his nails on the boards. Luke is the family manicurist, not me: he'd probably be happy setting up a posh pets' parlour.

I wanted to get Boo up-to-date with all my recent discoveries. Principal among these was how Tilly had ended up with Jud and his tattoos in her bed, but I didn't want to talk about that. Boo came up to me, head down, whining and pawing by my boots, then repeatedly tapping his nose against the leg of my combats.

"Hey, enough!" I said to him. He seemed to be nipping at my mobile now, in the zipped pocket. I wrested my trousers from him, and he stared intently up at me. His long, curvy tail lapped his rump, where a little dash of white gave the impression he had been signed by his creator. Then he began teasing at my pocket again.

"Ah, you want a treat, boy?" It might have helped put him in 'good listener' mood, but I was pretty sure there were no treats in there. I unzipped the pocket and showed its only contents: my mobile, and the trefoil key. He cocked his head at it with interest – more interest than Tilly had shown, or Jud. I dangled it on its string a moment, like a hypnotist: and Boo sat up, sniffing it as it caught the sunlight.

"What does this unlock?" I said to him. "That is the question." A dark cloud, louring over the marshes, plunged the boathouse into shadow. Boo sat firm like an ancient statue, his gaze searching my eyes, and mine his, for once as inscrutable as hieroglyphs.

"No treats, boy. Maybe later. Sorry." I zipped key and mobile away, but before I had a chance to pat him, Boo jumped down on the jetty, then leapt like a springbok on to the saltmarshes below.

"Where are you off to?" I shouted. I followed him down the steps, but he was already haring along the coastal path in the direction of Stiffkey Creek. When he reached the jetty walkway where Jud had had his fracas with the illegals, he sat and monitored my jogging approach. Then he turned again and ran, on towards Morston. Across the marshlands I followed him, a fawn dot; he finally settled to wait for me by some beached boats on a prominent mudbank.

"What's got into that whippety brain of yours?" I panted as I drew closer. "Who's the sidekick here, me or you?" Boo's answer was simple: he got up again and ran on, effortlessly, in the direction of Blakeney Point. This excursion had initially seemed like a kind of mischievous revenge for yesterday's neglect, but I now worried that in fact he might be running away from home. The day was going off. Luckily the lowest of tides was still way out, but I was uneasy, not having consulted my tide-tables – the habit that so irritated Luke – before the outing. I hoped Boo would come to his senses soon.

But on he trotted, with me lagging ever further behind, over great swathes of desolate saltmarsh, my neighbourhood no-man's-land. His sleek silhouette, against a slate sky, cantered along ridges; he skirted the Blakeney Channel, and waited again by a wrecked hulk. Panting like a racehorse, slithering and skidding in the mud, I almost got my fingers under his collar. Boo just wagged his tail and set off again, further north and east, descending into a waterless creek, with gnarled roots jutting from its sides.

After a good hour on this madcap trail Boo headed, still at full pelt, across another dried-out inlet, and up a bank, thick with marram grass, pierced by a bleached jetty, where a derelict sloop was moored. A few paces further, and a lonely redbrick cottage revealed itself.

"The Watch House, Boo?" I wheezed, as he led me down towards the weathered blue door of this erstwhile coastguard station. Expensive hours at the gym in Hampstead had made me pretty fit for my age; but I had a full-blown stitch as I crouched on the three stone steps. Boo looked at me and sat down firmly, as if to indicate that the trail ended here.

He scratched at the door, then looked up at me, then started to worry at my combats again, the same zipped pocket. As I checked that the trefoil key was still safe, I suddenly got a flash of what had been going on in his tiny mind, and the question he'd been trying to answer.

"You dotty pooch," I told him, slightly sharply, as I noticed the ominous grumbling clouds. He seemed crestfallen.

"This little key, look –"I dangled it in front of him again "– is a good four hundred years old. That huge lock..." I indicated the chunky Yale job with which the National Trust had secured The Watch House, pending renovations, "...was made about six months ago. Draw your own conclusions!" I felt a bit like Clive Massey.

The cool eyes gave me another look. Boo turned and scrabbled at the door again, with fresh vigour. It seemed to flex; it rattled, and it wasn't just the wind. Now I noticed that someone had jemmied the locking bar clean off the jamb. They'd banged in a few nails, though, and that was all that stopped the door from blowing clean open.

Moments later the clouds burst, and to my dismay I'd become a housebreaker. We were standing in the main room: grey, dull, abandoned.

"Anybody here?"

I stood still for a moment. Of course, the nails, having been banged in from outside, answered my question. But someone had been here: I could smell tobacco. Panic mode, just a nanosecond – I curtly reminded myself that the Secret Admirer was in jail – but the adrenaline would be with me for hours.

We were alone: Boo would have barked, otherwise. He was snuffling around the fusty space: the gritty boards were vaguely imprinted by trainers, and cigarette butts were stamped out everywhere. A towel on a nail was still drying; firelighter wrappings, spent matches and kindling were strewn in the hearth. A smutty magazine lay on a farmhouse table, under a cracked window.

Madly, it all felt unreal, like a scene in a diary I'd slipped into, as a mental trespasser. Whose eyes was I seeing through, then? Opening the door into a basic kitchen, I found a kettle and a camping stove, damp biscuits and a bowl of sugar. All seemed solid again. You're using your own eyes, I assured myself. And this stuff must belong to builders. No mystery.

Yet Boo had now started to whimper: not a danger sign exactly, but still with a sense of urgency. He'd found a folded camp bed in the third room, and a ladder up to a loft hatch. Why would anyone have spent the night here?

"Hello, hello?" I called again, looking up to the attic. Still no reply, just Boo growling at some object behind me, under a tatty dust sheet. He was tugging at the fabric, teeth tearing it.

"Leave that, Boo, good boy."

It was just like an episode of *Lassie* come to life. The cloth slid away, revealing a naïve-looking brown desk, no taller than four feet and possibly just three feet wide. I could not believe what I was seeing, had to lift its writing slope to make sure. But there she was, the young girl with the raven hair. Boo – by some trick of clairvoyance – had actually led me to the Boleyn Bureau. He ran around excitedly, tail wagging. My heart was thumping. If ever a dog-treat had been needed, it was now. I wanted to call Tilly. No signal, of course. I looked at the trefoil key. The adrenaline did the thinking.

"Boo, bloody hell, it's been staring us in the face. Anne's name, hidden under the Love Step; her picture, inside the Bureau... this key, this hidden key is the link!" Lord James had plotted this treasure hunt with typical ingenuity. He'd known someone would solve it, one day. He just hadn't known who.

My hands tingled at the prospect of finding the hole where the key belonged: no need, now, to wait for Tilly to decipher the map of Jud's privates. But I gauged the bureau from top to bottom. No suitable hole presented itself. Let's try to stay rational, I thought. I re-opened the lid and felt around inside for any canny mechanisms. The musty smell was mingled with beeswax from a recent NHS cleaning. Apart from the knobbly corners by its nailed-in joints, all was flush.

The Boleyn Bureau was eluding me, or I was deluding myself. But Boo's pure instinct – unclouded by ego, or sleuthing ambition – how could that be wrong? Down on my knees, I pulled out each side drawer by its plain, pewter handle. No false compartments, no hidden keyholes. Finally I groped round the kneehole, up in the cavity. Nothing.

But what's this?

"Feels like a lever," I whispered to Boo. To start with it was stubborn, wouldn't shift. I repeatedly urged it, shoving until the metal grooved my thumb, and cramp gripped my bandaged wrist. The blasted thing was jammed, seized. Damn. So near, and yet... and yet I could be pushing it the wrong way? Changing hands, I slid it to the right, and it instantly yielded, with a dry click, and the muted twang of an unseen spring. A small, hinged panel of wood dropped, a two-inch square trapdoor.

What if someone was watching me now? I slipped to the window. Grey rain was lashing down. I crouched under the Bureau – it would have been easier to flip it on to its back, but that did not occur to me until later – and ran my fingers along the vacant space, into a deep recess. The dim light of my phone-screen helped a bit. Bending my head unnaturally up into the dark cavity, I glimpsed a keyhole – yes! – set within an ornate iron escutcheon plate. It was engraved with the same trefoil design as my key. To the left, stamped deep in the metal, an initial 'A', to the right, 'B'.

"Praise be... " My heart pounds. I finger the trefoil key. Reach up. Slide in. Turn, click. A second trapdoor opens, and I am mere moments from the end of my treasure hunt.

The trail had been set in playful times, by James, for Alice: I was sure of that. But following her betrayal of him, he would have used his duplicate key to remove the hidden love-token – necklace, brooch, whatever – and insert something altogether darker: a murder weapon, someone's confession, some testament for posterity? I was praying, oh praying, that the light this would shed on Skipper Wood's death might finally exorcise him from my boathouse, and from my dreams.

But, I told myself, 'Be careful for what you wish for'. There were several murder suspects. What if it the killer had somehow been James himself? Various diary entries, corroborated elsewhere, had until now proved him a man worthy of my trust. How mortifying, now, if the second truly-significant key in my life were further to blacken my trust in mankind.

My prying fingertips could feel the edge of some rolled-up document, a tube pushed deep into the long, narrow cavity. My whole arm shook, as I gripped the coarse paper with a couple of fingers, ready to slide it out.

But wait, the sounds of an engine: some vehicle was pulling up nearby, presumably having driven all the way up the shingle spit from Cley. Boo's keen ears pricked up; I heard a door slam. I crept from under the Bureau, shuffling along the boards to a spot below the window. Peeping up, I glimpsed a white Range Rover, unmarked, and plain-clothes figures hurrying through the rain towards The Watch House. CID? The Boleyn Bureau might be their business, but the secret space was certainly not. I snapped it shut again, fumbled the drawers back into place. The dustsheet was back over the bureau, and the connecting door was closed, just as – with the blow of a boot – The Watch House portal burst open.

Chairs scraped, lighters rasped: tobacco fumes, the whiff of hashish? Possibly not the police, then; probably not builders. Whoever these men were, it certainly wasn't safe to reveal my presence. The window hadn't opened in a hundred years, and there was no other way out. I grabbed Boo by his scruff, and somehow got him up the ladder, into the attic. Through the crack of the silently-closing hatch, I saw the door opening below. I held my breath, muzzling Boo with my hand.

'Okay, good boy,' I mouthed to him. '*Calma*, Roberto!' echoed the *putto*.

The attic was surprisingly bright: it had a kind of belvedere window with wide views of the gathering storm, hence 'Watch House', of course. But my watching interest was downwards. Through a floorboard knothole I could see two hats and a close crop, just a metre or so below me. I wondered for a crazy second if this was the perspective Skipper's spirit had on my boathouse, from his roost somewhere in the cupola.

The red-tweed cap was lifting the dust sheet, showing the Bureau to the baseball hat and the shaven skull.

"You boys, tell your boss, it's exactly the piece I sent in the photos."

"Sick innit!" Fingers clicked the air.

"Bruvs, here's to my new yard in Marbs."

The first voice spoke local English, the Londoners favoured 'Jafaican'. I'd wondered a moment if the red-cap were Charlie Snyder; but I now realised this must be the more savvy operator – with his wealthy, international connections – who had picked up the Bureau as a bargain from Snyder's stall. Its final owner was paying these posers to retrieve it for him: enough, the minions believed, to buy them a place in Marbella. I gripped Boo, absolutely still. With the salary they commanded, I could expect a merciless beating, or worse, if any sound above them gave us away.

Wind noise was doing its bit to mask any suspicious noises from the attic, but it also obscured the conversation downstairs. Through my peephole I saw a tarpaulin unfurled. The Bureau was leaving now! In an ideal world, of course, Massey would by now have identified red-cap from the Norwich Showground CCTV, and would intercept his Range Rover as it drove off the shingle-bank into Cley. But that would deny me any second stab at opening James's secret cavity. And – even less ideal, now I thought about it – CID would find my fingerprints all over the Bureau, and I'd be nailed as an accomplice. But in the real world – in which Massey was a lazy, self-serving slob – the Bureau would in fact enjoy a trouble-free ride to Heathrow tonight, and Anne Boleyn would wake up somewhere in the Middle East tomorrow, where not even Boo could sniff her out.

"Cautious. Da booty Jurassic, innit."

My nerves were so stretched; I feared I might spontaneously combust. Even the rumble of my unfed stomach was ready to give me away. I held Boo close, he looked frightened, too, at the turn his innocent adventure had taken.

Oh Boo, if only I could see inside that canine-stein mind of yours. So many of a dog's regular senses exceed the reach of a human's: had some extrasensory perception led you to The Watch House? If so, why only this morning? The Bureau had surely been guarded here at least one night. But then again, perhaps Boo could have brought me here yesterday, if I hadn't left him alone in the boathouse. Or – just as unlikely – maybe he'd just run randomly, after a day caged up, and we were here by coincidence. Had Boo tuned in to Skipper's presence, somehow, back at the boathouse? Not that Skipper could tell him where the Bureau was. Boo had seen the Bureau himself at Samphire Hall... but that wasn't much of an explanation either. I caressed his noble head. There were no easy answers where dogs were concerned.

The sky framed by the dormer window was whirling with black clouds; these were northerly winds, the kind to whip up a tidal surge. Maybe the Range Rover's route home would be cut off? I could hear them now, manoeuvring the Bureau towards the door below me.

"Yo, easy."

"Safe!"

Boo began to wriggle, and I muzzled him ever tighter. He looked at me, in puzzlement, and whimpered. Movement stopped downstairs. My eye, at the knothole, looked straight down into another face, staring up. My body went clammy in my hooded fleece. Silence below, while they listened, while I counted the pulse in my head... twenty-two, twenty-three.

"Pigeons, boss."

Another hiatus, while red-cap weighed things up.

"We're out of here," he said. I exhaled, very slowly.

I followed the kerfuffle of the Bureau's progress through the tight doorway into the front room and then out into the storm.

Phew. I carefully peeped out to get my first proper glimpse of the gang. The Jafaicans were of course white-skinned: one in a red tracksuit, the other in a Spurs shirt, they were struggling along with the Bureau, behind the local man in his waxed jacket. As I watched, the gale snatched the red-tweed cap from his head and flung it in the waves. Why were they going so close to the sea?

Only then did I notice a substantial motor-cruiser, perhaps six or eight berth, moored at the jetty. How had I not heard its approach? Figures appeared on deck, and I ducked for a second as the Spurs man pointed back to The Watch House. By the time I stealthily looked over the ledge again, the Bureau was being loaded aboard, and the Range Rover was pulling away: no chance of reading its number plate. Soon the boat was under way too, but I did manage to clock the name on its bow as it crossed my line of view.

I had to think quickly. The Bureau was going by sea then; and it could be Interpol who found my prints all over it. To cover myself I had to let Massey know what I'd seen. Snyder clearly wasn't in the gang – not least since he'd have hidden the Bureau from the antique fair's CCTV if he'd known its provenance or worth – so the heat would be off Luke and me for consorting with him earlier. But Massey would want to know why I'd been at The Watch House. And I couldn't explain that, even to myself.

I got down the ladder, carrying Boo tight against my chest. He didn't try to run away again, but sniffed where the Bureau wasn't. Bizarre how its transit station, so rarely-visited, had nonetheless been visible on the horizon from Wood Feels. But we needed to get closer to civilisation: there was no phone signal here.

I wondered if I should take something to enable Massey to lift the gang's prints. They'd left traces in the small room, remains of the Jafaicans' joints and the local man's sandwiches. No, CID could come here and search the place properly, I thought, assuming The Watch House wasn't washed away in the next few hours. It had barely survived the Great Flood of 1953, and this storm was shaping up to be a monster as well. So I took the greasy cling film from the kitchen table and snap-wrapped my mobile in it. There was a chance it would survive the rain.

Boo and I stood in the open doorway. It seemed reckless to venture out into such relentless wind, which was driving a perilous tide closer by the minute. But to stay here was to risk being cut off, even drowned. No tide-tables, no shipping forecast: but I knew the moon was right for a high tide; the sea spray smelt fishier than ever, and the distant wind turbines were spinning manically. Rising water would very soon bar my way home across the marshes, and likewise the route the Range Rover had taken, back down the shingle to Cley.

I zipped up my sweat jacket and stepped out on to the coarse, grassy scrub, leaving The Watch House door open to the driving rain. Even on the lee side of the building I was soaked in a moment. Noisy waves came crashing over the shingle ridge, only feet away.

"Got to chance it, Boo!" He looked up at me fearfully, eyes streaming in the wind, ears too. Then we started to run for home.

The first few minutes seemed pretty successful, and we sloshed across the first creek, up a high bank. The wind was merciless through my soaking clothes, and doubtless worse for Boo, but we wound along the ridge southwards until there was no choice but to climb down into another deep gulley. I picked Boo up, to save him from getting stuck in the doughy mud; several waves came washing along it, each one higher than the last. We'd made about forty yards' headway when, to my surprise, the surge brought the red-checked cap close by us. I parked Boo a moment, and made a grab for the evidence. All at once an immense wave came over the top, knocking me sideways, right into the swiftly-moving, freezing torrent.

From there on, nightmare. The snakelike gully had filled so fast, seething and frothing as if the Kraken of Nordic myth had been awakened, that I was carried along in its writhing current, scarcely able to breathe as I was tumbled from one side to another. Somewhere in the roaring tumult Boo yelped, and leapt in to rescue me. I saw his head bobbing up and down in the murk.

It was impossible to swim towards him, almost impossible to cry out. He doggy-paddled bravely, but the heavy swell was swirling him ever further out of reach. '*Calma*, Roberto,' called the little *putto* in my head. I cursed it. Who could be calm in such circumstances?

The current dragged me down, and I came up gasping. My own *Titanic* drama had washed Boo from my sight. I fished blindly in the water, flailing for a feel of my beloved companion, surfacing only to scream his name with every gulp. But it was hopeless: the torrent took over, sucking me out to sea like flotsam, crashing me brutally against the banks of the creek along the way.

So this was how I was going to die. I snorted in bitter salt water, felt its cold drain deep into my core. Fleeting thoughts started to flicker... drowning passengers, a valiant violin... then Luke's bright smile as we lay in our Muswell Hill garden, Sunday brunch with Ella Fitzgerald, Boo catching sunbeams on the lawn. Dancing with Lauren Porter at the college disco, trying to be straight. Rugby at school, mates hugging me after my first try... falling off my red bike, my bleeding knee... nicking sherbet from Mrs Bloom's shop... listening to my beautiful mother read Bible stories at bedtime... that girly drawl jingling sweet serenity through my sun-dazzled body...

Abruptly the chilly current flung me against some embedded branch: jolted to life, winded, I began to rise rapidly. Blasting back into air, I gulped the oxygen for dear life. A pulling sensation lifted my head as if the *putto* from childhood were rescuing me once again. I scrabbled desperately up an embankment.

'*Calma*, Roberto!' This time I didn't curse him.

I crawled in stinking sludge, coughing and spluttering lung water; for miles around all was dark sea, and above an even darker sky, an afternoon deserted by the sun. Painful images of Boo, fighting the tide, flooded my mind. I shouted his name until I was hoarse with sobbing. Teeth chattered, limbs quaked; brain decided to shut me down.

When I awoke, the rage of the storm was spent, the rain abated. But I had never been so cold. I crept stiffly up into the sanctuary of the pinewoods to survey the twilight. That undercurrent had carried me a mile or more; I was not too far from home. I checked for my watch but it was gone, torn from my wrist by the surge. Bandages too. I felt crushed by the loss of Boo. What words could I find to share this heartbreak with Luke?

I set out, desolate, for the boathouse, sopping and heavy under the rising moon. Here was the boathouse, still standing; Lord James had done well to site it higher than the former structure, to spare it from cataclysms. Only the handrail had been torn away as I climbed to the veranda. Trivial. Shivering mercilessly, I felt my sodden pockets for the house keys. Only the trefoil key and the snap-wrapped phone. Oh God, all kinds of nightmares awoke in my mind. But worse still, here was my boathouse door, swinging open. It could have stood open nine hours, since I'd dashed after Boo, before breakfast, without looking back. There was no saying who could have got in.

I stood a minute, sopping on the threshold, straining my ears in the stillness, sniffing, as Boo would have done, for any telltale odours. The Secret Admirer? My keys were there on the dresser, van keys too. I should have been relieved.

Suddenly, I was panting outside the boathouse again, locking up so any intruder would stay trapped in the cedar cage. The van would be my refuge: its cupboards were far too small for the Secret Admirer to hide in. I pulled off my sodden clothes and let them fall to the ground, climbed into the driving seat, sobbing, freezing. I fumbled with the ignition – grabbing a picnic blanket to allay the shell-shocked shaking – and turned the heater on, high. The VW didn't let me down. I slumped into the seat and closed my eyes, weeping over poor Boo. I don't remember falling asleep.

But when I awoke it was bitterly cold again. The engine had stopped running – perhaps I'd been wakened by the diesel running out? At least there was life in the battery, and I caught the tail end of a news bulletin. Oh God: some kind of row about sex-offenders being released, before their time was up, to ease prison overcrowding. I snapped the headlamps on, to light the ground down to the jetty. Nothing moving, at least, nothing visible. The boathouse loomed in darkness.

Skipping stations... same story, different slant... the names of the criminals who'd been freed. I knew what was coming: yet the one inevitable name still struck me with shocking force, a name I hadn't heard for over thirty years. Panic hovered close by. For a while I tried reason. The Secret Admirer wasn't jailed solely for what he'd done, or longed to do, to me. So if he now set about stalking the people who'd effectively sent him down, I wouldn't necessarily be top of his list. Panic receded, just a few paces.

But this shattering news couldn't have come at a worse time, when I was low, and dogless. I groped for something positive in life. Maybe call the coastguards? Boo might have somehow been found, in living form. I jumped out into the night, wrapped in my blanket. No point struggling back into clammy combats. My phone was still dry in its snap-wrap. The ancient key... I chucked it into the van. Nothing mattered *less* now than raising the alarm for the bloody Bureau: it was those detective fantasies, my evidence-gathering games, that had killed Boo. I was being eaten up by remorse...

Around to the deck side of the boathouse. The campervan lit my way. Slipping down the veranda stairs, the jetty slimy from the tempest. It would be spilling calamity on some other part of the coast by now. I waded along the walkway, waist-high in cold water, grabbing each post along the way until I could anchor myself to the end one for safety. Amazingly, there was network coverage. The coastguard was in my contacts. Someone told me to hold on while they checked. I waited impatiently, jangled my keys to keep... something... at bay; I'd never been so cold.

"Ah, no whippet dogs..." I replied. With desolation in my throat I described beautiful Boo, his tan collar, brass dog-tag. "Yes, he's microchipped," I confirmed. "Of course, yes, missing people are the priority. But you will check, won't you?"

The call centre said they'd check all the dog rescue centres, they'd try local police stations too. I was faintly heartened. Inspector Scrotum could come knocking for all I cared, so long as he was bringing my Boo, whose companionship was the key to my sanity, with Luke so unexpectedly away.

This was no night to be out of doors – not for me, not for some vile sex-offender on the loose from a nearby prison. But I had the keys, not him. I had to brave it, venture back into the boathouse. Warm, dry clothes. Discard the dripping blanket. Step through the French doors, timorous, naked.

Two hands gripping the hefty Design Award. Thwacking the coffin-like removal cartons, fit to rouse the dead. Rushing up the cedar stairway – death click on the second step – shouting with the intensity of mad revenge.

"If you're up here, motherfucker, come out and get it!" The Secret Admirer was dealing with the man, now, not the little boy he had terrorised in another lifetime. I'd give him something to admire.

And then, only silence... until the little plump angel in my head replied, 'There's nobody here but you.'

Little Oscar, my black dog was gone with my childhood, strangled, spine-broken, but I was damned if I was going to lose Boo that easily. I flung open the wardrobe door: still no red-booted bastard leaped out at me. Into my sweatpants, shirt, cagoule, trainers... I stamped down through the kitchen, grabbing a torch on the way.

I roved for ages in the thicket, aiming my flashlight down endless irregular avenues of trees and relentlessly calling for my dog until my voice could barely croak his name.

I don't know how many hours passed, but my despair for lost Boo became unbearable. I sobbed intermittently. Depression is a black dog; it preys on the weak, the hungry. When had I last eaten, or drunk fresh water? Hypoglycaemia? Shock? I was amazed to be still standing.

I was desperate to speak to Luke, but terrified of telling him the bleakest news he would ever hear. Shared memories flooded me: adopting Boo the puppy, eight Junes back, rescued from his first few terrible months of beating, starving, chains. His hop, skip and jump, from our old jeep straight into his basket by the fireside, the sweet glue to meld us forever.

Strong tea, bread and cheese, puny fire, slump in my chair. I had never hated the boathouse more. Woodfields, Wood Feels – or whatever it might be called – jinxed in every way. Its occupants endured only misery. I was living proof. And I wanted out.

But the only way out was sleep, where the black dog could not follow, where Skipper's pathetic song and his endless sawing would mean nothing. Good riddance to the Boleyn Bureau, and good luck to its thieving new owner: he was surely going to need it.

When sleep finally took me in its tide, Boo's cold body spun, helpless, in the depths far beneath me.

CHAPTER FOURTEEN
WHITE RUSSIAN

I woke up unrefreshed and aching. I had slept patchily in my chair, calling out for Boo each time the boathouse creaked. My first action was to call again, from the jetty. He had not returned. The kettle whistled on the range, and as I filled my coffee mug, emblazoned with Boo's handsome image, I welled up. I was going to have to tell Luke, and soon. And worst of all I felt completely to blame.

I slumped in my club chair with a bowl of cereal I really couldn't stomach. I felt a nudge at my side... but it was only Boo's favourite toy bear. I buried my nose in its fur. The whiff of buttered popcorn – so redolent of Boo – made me sob and sob, just as James Newton-Grey must have done the night *Titanic* sank, as he locked himself away with Kit, the Airedale pup, in this cursed place. Was I reliving James's nightmare? A man could go mad pondering parallels between past and present. And thinking over Boo's tragic end, I felt closer to madness than ever before, and began to curse the *putto* for saving me, and not sparing my hound.

On my way to the jetty hotspot a zombie image stared back at me from the hall mirror. The face, caked in dried mud, spoke of trench warfare, as if I were an escapee from James's 1914 diary – which I had so little time, and so little inclination, to read. And the helpful coastguard was no help at all.

"Just a spaniel? I'm sorry," I told him. "But any other dogs, drowned, or injured, you'll let me know?" The tide was receding: just a metre or so of seawater lapped the embankment at the foot of the woods. I had time for a bath. Boo had always loved a good soapy massage too. I couldn't give up hope, I thought, as I hurriedly washed myself: surely he was out there somewhere, and I was going to find him.

Only when I unlocked the VW did I remember I'd run the fuel dry in an effort to get warm last night. In the shed we kept a reserve can of diesel; but someone had forgotten to refill it, and I listened despairingly as a mere cupful of fuel trickled into the tank. I slammed the empty container to the ground; and when I turned the ignition key my agitation intensified.

"Come on, come on!" I twisted and turned it repeatedly: not even the slightest click. Of course, I had left the headlamps blazing half the night. No wonder the battery was stone-cold dead. Banging the dashboard in frustration, I jumped out and rushed inside for my bus schedule. Checking the time reminded me I'd lost my classic watch – my Civil Partnership gift from Luke – out on the marshes. Everything was falling apart.

By the clock on my old mobile I reckoned I had fifteen minutes before the next coast-hopper service into Wells – time enough to contact some breakdown garages. But, as I dialled forlornly from the jetty, the response was unvarying: there'd been a storm; there were already dozens of breakdowns, associated with Sunday's upcoming vintage car rally. All their call-outs were booked up till the weekend.

I was on the point of calling Jud – no longer worried about giving him my number – to see if his classic car expertise extended to VW vans. My phone died in my hand. With no further options available, I locked up and stiffly ran the length of the scented alley, just in time to catch the yellow-and-blue bus.

The coast road in to Wells was strewn with storm debris. The bus picked its slow way around fallen trees, and the sirens of emergency vehicles sounded just like a normal day back in London. Yet judging by the cheery prattle of my fellow passengers, very few homes had actually been flooded. A shift in wind direction had spared the coast an even bigger catastrophe. It was ironic, I grimly thought, that at least Luke and I were back in synch now: him sorting out his mum's flood damage up in Tyneside, me sorting out our own right on our doorstep. I wondered if he'd heard anything on the news?

Sergeant Warren's phone rang incessantly as I waited at the front desk. Inspector Massey appeared with his usual good cheer.

"Rough night?" The consummate professional had spotted my pallid appearance.

"Somewhat," I began.

"Enjoy it, did you?"

Here we go again, I thought: any mention of a missing pet will just sound like a whingeing poofter, and if he attempts any of his typical wit about Boo I'll just sob. Better to keep him guessing, I thought, make him do some detective work.

"I got a little snippet... something else you might like to know."

"Be my guest." He gestured once again towards the interrogation chamber.

"If I'm a guest this time, how about a coffee?"

To my great surprise, Massey clamped his hand over Warren's ringing phone, and nodded him over to the drinks machine by the entrance. I went in first, brushing some flakes of pastry off the blue Formica-topped table with an attempt at proprietorial confidence.

"I notice you're trembling," said Massey, following me in. "Am I expecting a confession?"

"Not at all. Listen and I'll tell you. My dog and I ran over to The Watch House yesterday, just before the tidal surge."

"That was stupid."

"Not when you know the whole story," I told him. Then I paused.

"So, go on?" Good: he was asking me for information. I made him wait. He leant close, and I inhaled a good deal of garlic. Sergeant Warren arrived with the coffees. I desperately wanted to cut straight to the question about canine casualties that might have been reported; but toying with Massey was a giving me a kind of pain relief.

"I have the name of a boat that may interest you," I said finally. I knew that if I said it straight out – 'White Russian' – he'd start teasing me about cocktails.

"I'm not interested in boats."

"I thought you were interested in the whereabouts of the Bureau that was stolen from Samphire Hall."

Massey slurped his coffee and recoiled

"Hot, Sergeant!" he shouted. Warren came in.

"No milk or sugar, sir: you said you were on a diet." Massey's crimson glare sent him back to his post.

"So let me get this straight: you're claiming you saw the Tudor Bureau on a boat off Blakeney Point?"

"Very good."

"And was your friend Snyder with it?"

"Several men were handling it. I can give you descriptions. None of them were friends of mine, any more than Snyder is."

"You know making a false statement is perjury?"

"If I make a false statement, I'll let you know." I left my mouth open to vent the coffee's sour aftertaste.

"Too many coincidences if you ask me: first you're caught on camera dealing with Snyder, then you're out on the marshes with illegals, and now you've witnessed stolen goods being shipped overseas." Then he shouted, "You're going to tell me you're not involved?"

"Perhaps you'd like me to leave now?"

"I'll tell you when you can leave." Making it difficult for Massey was definitely working: the glint in his eye confirmed that he relished extracting information, even from a witness who'd come expressly to give it to him. But my breathing tightened. All I really cared about was Boo.

Massey got up and lumbered about the interview room. He rummaged in his pockets, removing a variety of sweet wrappers, which he unselfconsciously threw on the table.

"So these men you say you saw, you can describe them?"

"You must understand the weather was terrible. The local man had a red-tweed cap..."

Suddenly I couldn't go on. If I hadn't tried to retrieve that as evidence, Boo would not have been washed away by the sea. Massey saw my turmoil; and he didn't sneer.

"Take your time."

"One was wearing a Tottenham shirt."

"My team," he said.

"Well the other one could have been a Man U supporter, judging by his tracksuit," I replied. "So it's not all bad." Massey permitted himself a slight smile. "They were speaking 'Jafaican'."

"What the hell's that?"

"Fake Jamaican, new slang. All the rage with white twenty-somethings down in London. You've been stuck out in the sticks too long, Inspector," I said, aiming for a nerve.

Massey said nothing, picked up one of the chocolate wrappers, and sniffed it as if it were a fine wine.

"Anyway," I said, "their prints will be all over The Watch House. The Bureau had been stashed inside."

Massey got up and left, remarkably quickly. I saw him outside talking on the phone, and took the opportunity to plug my own mobile and charger into a grimy socket by my chair. When he came back into the room, his tone was almost reasonable.

"Your man with the red-cap, we may have him on the Norfolk Showground CCTV. And the fake Jamaicans, you think they work for some well-heeled collector overseas?"

He was almost asking my opinion now.

"Not necessarily overseas. But wealthy enough to run a fair-size cruiser."

"Name?"

"I read 'Russian'. It was during the storm."

"Not a very likely name for a boat."

"There was another word. You're the detective." I could have been more helpful, but it was nice to see him doing some work. Immediately he was out of the room again, giving Warren some instructions.

My mobile rattled on the floor: a text from Luke: 'Mam doing well – home next Wed. Hope U + Boo didn't get 2 wet Xx.' He sounded infuriatingly blasé, given that news of our tidal emergency had obviously reached him. But I shivered: what was I going to tell him? I just had to be sure about Boo, either way, before we spoke. The police calendar on the wall said Wednesday was Bonfire Night, and that was the Gala Opening at Samphire Hall. Today was Halloween. So Tilly's big event was suddenly just a few days away, and my research deadline, in the diaries, was even more imminent. She was going to kill me if the only notes I produced weren't up to scratch.

Massey was back in the room. The look he was giving me was practically human. His hand havered over his crotch, decided against a scrotal visit, and moved up to toy with his lower lip, as if I had whetted his appetite. I decided to go all the way, not mentioning Skipper's ghost – Halloween or no Halloween, Massey was the last man in the world to have any truck with the spirit world – but spelling out the bodily mechanics of my unsolved murder mystery.

"There's more," I told him.

Tilly had told me Massey was desperate for kudos: to uncover the fate of a regional Olympic hero would be just the high-profile success he needed to earn the coveted promotion she'd hinted at. Suddenly I felt empowered.

"It's a cold case." I'd heard the phrase in a film.

"How cold?"

"Red hot. Olympic athlete, Norfolk man. Unexplained death, 1913."

"Don't tell me, you witnessed it yourself?" But this verbal sniping was just a defensive reflex. He was obviously interested.

"Well... Clive... you saw me at the crime scene."

That had him hooked. And so I found myself spending twenty minutes with the man who'd seemed to be my nemesis, talking him through the Skipper Wood mystery, two detectives pooling their talents.

Massey listened intently, twiddling a foil wrapper around some ostentatious ring on his visible hand. His eyes widened, and the unseen hand, below the table, went into overdrive at my revelations. He didn't particularly try to intimidate me, and I didn't particularly warm to him. But somehow I felt myself crossing the line from suspect to... well, colleague.

"But what makes you think there's a document stashed away in that Bureau that resolves any of this?"

Of course this was an impossible question to answer. Just as I'd kept any supernatural angle out of my story, I'd also failed so far to mention the trefoil key.

"A lot of people are interested in this case, glory hunters looking to restore the reputation of a home-grown Olympian." Thanks, fiction engine. "I cannot reveal my sources at present."

I could sense Massey's greed. I just hoped to God I was right. I had no Plan B if the document in the Bureau turned out to be a dud.

Massey invited me to 'take five', and condescended to explain that he had some calls to make – tracing the full name of the 'Russian' cruiser, I guessed. When he found my story was true, he might buy fully into the Edwardian part of our conversation. While he trundled out to his own office, I stepped out to reception, into the fresh air.

"Sergeant, I don't suppose anyone's reported finding a fawn whippet?" I asked. I gave him enough detail – the two-tone head, the white neck-blaze and socks, the striking double-diamond markings on the upper back – for an APB, as Jud might have called it, or Tilly too.

Warren couldn't have been more helpful. He offered to phone round other stations in the area. I went back into the small room, and smelt the garlic. It felt like lunchtime, but of course my watch had gone, the same way Boo had. I felt terrible. This play-acting with Massey was taking me beyond exhaustion. He mustn't catch me crying. I leant down towards the floor to check my mobile. It was getting on for noon.

Massey made his entry, with all the grace of a hippo. I blew my nose and looked up: my moist eyes met his smug smile.

"'White Russian' ring any bells?" I nodded. "The Cromer coastguard logged her. Port of London gave us the berth, and the owner's name is on its way. That's a professional line of enquiry opened. Doesn't pay to hang around," he said.

"You'll give Skipper Wood some thought?"

"We're done for today. Get some rest: you look like shit." As I retrieved my charger and phone from the socket, he added, "Oh, we'll keep an eye out for your dog."

He didn't wait to show me out. I waited until I'd stopped blubbing – his kindness, albeit tiny, was so unexpected – before leaving the room. Sergeant Warren told me Holt police had not found any whippets, but he had other calls to try. He shook my hand and told me to stay positive. How things had changed.

I rang Tilly from the bus stop, told her all about finding the BB, and the terrors of the flood that followed. Okay, she was with Jud now; but she couldn't have been sweeter to me.

"Stay calm, Bertie; Boo probably sheltered in someone's shed. They're probably looking for you." Kind of her, but it wasn't working. I was so tense it was hard not to bawl.

"And now my campervan is buggered, I'm stranded out in that frigging hellhole."

"Get Jud on to it. I had a flat and he pumped me up in no time."

She could hear the silence as I struggled to keep control.

"Look, I'll drop everything at the Hall, I'll come and pick you up right now."

"No, Tilly, you've got a lot on. Here's the bus anyway. But why don't you both swing by after work? Bring some jump leads too."

I could stand only a few minutes at home: the place didn't make sense without Boo. Luke's binoculars hung by the kitchen door, and I took them out on the saltmarshes, locking up carefully this time. Yesterday replayed. I traipsed through marine sludge, retracing our route to the spot where, as best I could judge, Boo had been snatched by the torrent. All was flotsam, odd shapes of driftwood, plastic crates, orphan shoes, blue and orange clumps of knotted rope. I trained the glasses over the inlets towards The Watch House, all along the south side of the shingle ridge, to the North Sea. All in vain.

I found myself desperately shouting Boo's name over and over, into the vastness, up to the flocks of migrating birds. I staggered west. Skipper Wood started to sing. '*Let me put my arms about you*'. And that's when I spotted it, a little corpse in the distance, washed high on the shingle: the size, the colour... of a whippet. My heart raced.

"Boo. Boo!" I cried, and set off, running straight towards it across the squelching shallows of muddy creeks, my hopes jangling, my breathing short. On the pebbly shoreline I sank to the ground and cradled the heavy, waterlogged carcass to my heart. So this was it. Acid tears stung my eyes: was this really better than not knowing what had happened? 'Boo, sweet Boo,' I heard myself crying, hoping he might respond: but the body was cold, malformed, and utterly lifeless. My right hand was slimy from clutching his flank, and I tried to blink my eyes clear enough to discover what kind of wound had ended his life. There was a kind of rip in his fur, a patch of bloated, purpling, torn-back flesh where maggots had already started feasting. Oh, God! I howled again, and, standing and turning in a single gesture, was shocked to find myself confronted by a walker, sprung from nowhere over the shingle ridge, who asked if he could do anything.

"Oh, my lovely little dog, look! Worse than a child..." I fell to the ground again, knees deep in sharp gravel, and sobbed over the corpse, the sleek pelt. The faceless person prodded my shoulder with his stick.

"Looks like a newborn seal pup to me, mate. It's certainly nobody's dog, I'll tell you that for nothing."

"What have I done," I snapped at him, "to deserve this... this torture?" The walker, the twitcher, or whoever he was, hurried away from the madman. Was I in such a delusional state that a Blakeney Seal – the same image bloody Skipper Wood had carved into my mind – could supplant my beloved Boo?

Activity, I needed activity, to keep the black dog at bay. Back on the jetty I called up the coastguard. Once I'd made myself understood, between panting and sobbing – there was still no news of Boo. I went up to the bedroom, where James had deadened his own abject desolation with drink. Had there been absinthe, I'd have copied him. The people-smugglers came into my mind, the violent Viktor. Then the Baroque bed claimed me.

I awoke around five in the afternoon. A few hours' sleep had taken the edge off my wretchedness. I sat up, determined not to retreat into misery... and James's diary of 1913, on my bedside table, was open where I had left off.

18th March 1913

Riding into Binham today I happened to pass Beulah Wood on her errands: an opportune moment to question her about the wretch Skipper. I found Mrs Wood to be more subdued even than usual, unkempt and suffering with melancholia. She vouchsafed that she was shortly to take her 'nippers' on a seaside holiday to Southwold. She mentioned her adulterous husband only to tell me he was redecorating their parlour while she was away. Strange that she found fit to burden me with so pedestrian a detail. It did little to banish my loathsome preoccupation with Skipper, and his treacherous defilement of my wife.

So James's account verified what Pearl had said: her mother, Beulah, had taken the children away while Skipper stripped the toxic paper from their living room. It also reiterated his hostility towards his former champion and friend. But hadn't I discounted Beulah? Unless Massey was able to get Skipper's body exhumed, to test for arsenic traces in his hair, as had happened with Napoleon?

I needed to eat, so I amassed a few meagre leftovers on the refectory table, which had seen so many boisterous dinner parties in London, back when Luke and I were the golden couple who seemed blessed with everything. Our mates would be shocked to see what I had become, and where I seemed to be heading. A knock at the door dispelled my useless self-pity, as the Secret Admirer rose up in my thoughts. But it was Tilly who stepped into the kitchen. I'd forgotten she was due.

"Any news of Boo?" she said, giving me an emotional hug. Before I could register the complex sensation of her lithe body pressing tight to mine, Jud appeared behind her. Tilly and I declinched, and Jud gave me a second hug, equally well-meaning, infinitely less appetising. Meanwhile Bertie fox terrier ran through my legs looking for her friend. It made my heart weep.

"Man, I'm so sorry about Boo," said Jud sweetly. "And the VW an' all. But there's not an automobile built that I can't fix, you know that."

"Cheers Jud." I tossed him the keys. "Guys, I was about to make some dinner, so you'll join me, won't you?" God, I needed the company.

"I could slaughter a bronco burger!" Jud called as he went out to the campervan.

Tilly mucked in, helping me rustle up a simple dinner. As I rinsed a few salad leaves over the Belfast sink, I caught sight of my reflection in the window: my youthful looks were fading, not with age, but with grief. Those hollow eyes, overwritten with pain, belonged not to me but to some unknown forebear. If we truly pay for the sins of our fathers, as Tilly had once claimed, mine must have committed some pretty hideous crime to have bequeathed such misery on me. Then we heard the roar of the VW revving up.

"Jud knows what he's doing with that toolbox." Tilly grinned, as she drained the pasta. I made no comment.

"All done, an' enough diesel to get you to the truckstop," said Jud, coming in to wipe his oily hands on a pristine towel.

We ate round the woodburner, trays on our knees. The scene reminded me of my mother's wake, when everything had tasted of nothing. But Tilly and Jud were wolfing it down. For a workaholic who'd lost a priceless Tudor treasure Tilly seemed remarkably cheerful; for a beaten-up man on police bail Jud seemed positively insouciant. So this was love, the painkiller: and not a spoonful for me.

Tilly maintained her sobriety, but Jud and I made short work of the remaining cooking wine, from back of the dresser. I talked them through my Watch House trauma, and Clive Massey's response to my evidence. I can't pinpoint exactly when it happened, but eventually the pleasure of their company overtook me: I loosened up, felt a glimmer of my old self again.

"Bertie, there's a twinkle in your eye; what are you thinking?" said Tilly.

"Like I said, that fat bastard Massey: my tip-off about the BB has gained his confidence a bit. Big kudos for him if he finds it of course. But what if he could also shut down an illegal immigration scam as well? What's the big promotion? He'd be straight into it, surely."

"Super superintendent for the whole region," according to Karsten Wulff," said Tilly.

"How does he know?" I asked.

"How do you think?" she said, then corrected herself. "Of course, you haven't met him, have you?"

"What does that mean?"

"Special ring. Same as Massey's," she said, tapping the side of her nose with a conspiratorial finger.

"You mean they're Masons? God! Another reason to dangle the carrot then. A deal with Massey, to get Jud off."

"Dude, how you gonna do that?"

"Listen, do the police know about Viktor threatening you with a 'home visit'?"

"I gave the whole SIM card to my attorney," said Jud. I rolled my eyes at the Americanism. "But as for the home visit... well, I'm not stayin' in the Winnebago at the moment..."

He gulped some more wine, beaming unabashed at Tilly. She crossed her legs seductively, and looked demurely down at her coffee. Happy families, then. Company for Albertina fox terrier during the day. I noticed she was keeping Boo's basket warm now, out of loyalty.

"So what's this cunning plan?" Tilly enquired.

"Just a trap for Viktor. If we can find out where the next illegals are going to land."

Jud's face lit up with boyish enthusiasm.

"Dude! There's this Slavonic couple, layin' low in Fakenham. They'd be clued up for sure."

"Why's that?"

"Viktor sends the new arrivals over to them, to get naturalised – however he does it, I dunno."

"And you have their *add*ress?" I even pronounced the word the Stateside way.

"Yessiree..."

"So there's a plan then. Jud tips Massey off, who catches Viktor and his operation red-handed. Massey gets loads of good press, clinches his promotion: and he lets Jud off – a plea bargain, or something – with only a slapped wrist."

"Risky, yah?" Tilly looked over at Jud with fond concern. "Why would Massey play ball?" I was on the point of saying that Massey never stopped playing ball, in his trouser pocket, when Jud chipped in.

"Why not just shop the couple in Fakenham?"

"What, and let Viktor get clean away?"

"But if I ask when the landin' is... what if they tell Viktor I'm sniffin' around?"

"Give me a minute, guys?" Tilly went out to the bathroom.

"Top up, Jud? Seeing as you're not driving?"

"Thanks man; you been such a good mate lately." I had indeed, handing him the beauteous Tilly on a plate. I wondered if she'd mentioned how much I'd fancied her as well, told him about my old-fashioned marital fidelity, such as it was? He pulled his mobile out of his pocket, and started thumbing in a text.

"That won't work here: the signal is hopeless." He was trying to text Tilly already I was sure, anxious in case she'd flushed herself down the loo. She was certainly taking her time. Jud shoved his phone away, and slumped back into the chair. I felt my own in my pocket: I was dreading further messages from Luke; but itching to call the coastguard again, in case there was dog news.

In a moment our stupor was broken by an apparition, mincing in from the kitchen: it was as if Jud had succeeded in phoning to order some sort of horrendous escort, from the 'trailer trash' end of the range.

"What the hell?" I began, jumping out of my seat. Tilly's sobriety had given her a slatternly chutzpah I would never have imagined. Her fine eyes and mouth were lost under a garish scrawl of make-up. With towels packed up her sweater to inflate her boobs, she sashayed round the floor, toasting us from the bathroom tooth-mug.

"*Darlink*. Come up and see me some time." Bracelets hung over her ears like hoops, and her slick hair was dishevelled, the shower sponge somehow fixed on the top, as a bun. Jud and I applauded.

"Guys, you didn't know I was into amateur dramatics, did you?"

"We sure do now," Jud said.

"I was the lead in *Streetcar*, back at Roedean."

"Which part?" I asked.

"Brando, of course."

"That figures..."

"Yah, so here's the plan: I pose as some kind of foreign national... *darlink*!"

It was a brilliant offer from Tilly, but did she have the time, I asked, with the Gala Opening just round the corner?

"Yah, it's stupidly hectic right now, but I reckon I've earned a morning off. You're doing the donkey work on the diaries, don't forget," she replied, starting to divest herself of the gruesome get-up.

"Yes, of course," I said, a bit too quickly given how little work I'd put in so far. "So how about Sunday? Then Dr Wulff won't even know you've been away from your desk."

Jud's crystal blue eyes gleamed.

"Sunday, it's the classic car meet in Fakenham. Morris Minor meet an' all. I been looking forward to that," he said.

"The place will be crawling," I added.

"So nobody will notice me!" said Tilly. It sounded like a done deal.

As I stacked up their plates and trays and took them out into the kitchen, Tilly and Jud excitedly started planning operational details, why her White Russian – another meaningless coincidence, I thought to myself – couldn't leave the country legally, and needed to know where Viktor's gang was landing. Their laughter reached my ears over the sound of the tap running. A lapping sound came from Boo's bowl behind me – BFT of course – and misery flooded my eyes again.

By the time I'd made coffee and sorted out my red eyes, the lovebirds were looking very cosy on my sofa.

"There's load of other details, Tils. I'll fill you in later."

"I'm counting on it," she said. They laughed, and I felt like an unseen intruder. I spoke up loudly.

"Look, why don't I take BFT for her late constitutional?" They both started upright, and Tilly unwrapped Jud's arm from her waist.

"I can go," said Tilly.

Besides giving them some space, I wanted to end up on the jetty one last time that night to call the coastguard: I just didn't fancy going on my own.

"Relax, I won't be long. I just need some air. Be good..."

I whistled to Victoria Albertina, and we hurried out through the kitchen and up the track. The crisp air rushed to my head, and I felt giddy. I had really, definitely, lost the lovely Tilly Offord now. My loyalty to Luke had been paramount – or else to blame. But I felt doubly empty as BFT, not my beloved Boo, scampered ahead of me through the fallen leaves.

A couple of hundred yards up from the boathouse, in swirling mist, little Bertie stopped suddenly and growled. I shone my torch about, but she had already vanished into the undergrowth. Oh for God's sake, how could I face Tilly if I lost this one as well? With my heart pounding, I ventured a few steps into the unknown. My cropped hair was bristling; something was there, whether the brutal Viktor, or my red-haired psychopath... I would shortly discover. I listened. A crackling of branches. BFT yelped, a muffled cry. A frantic scrabbling. I could see nothing except the torch beam, so I masked it with my fingers for a moment.

The scene turned red. In my mind, great warty hands reached out from the darkness, groping to break the terrier's delicate spine.

CHAPTER FIFTEEN
MESSAGE FROM THE SKUNK

"Bertie? Bertie, sweetheart, where are you?"

"Dude? What the fuck?"

"Here," I wailed.

"My God," said Tilly. "What's happened?"

I had brought up my supper, true, after screaming a thousand-yard scream. But inside my heart, all my Christmas wishes were coming true at once.

"Listen!" I said. Deep in the bushes there was barking... there was whimpering... both at one time... both real.

We all three grappled with the thorny shrubbery. I flicked the torch beam through the gnarled branches, desperate for an opening. Jud forced a way in, where the undergrowth was sparse. BFT found Tilly. Tilly found a lighter. We followed. Tilly crouched down. A heavily soiled creature. Hollow eyes glaring at the flame. It tried to get up, limped a second, yelped, collapsed again. BFT licked it affectionately.

"Boo, you made it back..." My stomach revolted again, with sheer exhilaration.

I took off my puffer jacket. Bending low, Jud and I slid Boo's mud-caked form on to it, and I dragged it out into the open, a makeshift cradle. Jud lit our haphazard way through the misty bushes, BFT scampering around our feet, and – once we emerged on the clear track – Tilly and I lifted the stretcher and carried Boo back into the light, the warmth.

He looked around, eyes already gleaming. We laid him carefully by the woodburner. Every limb was shivering, surely a sign that his back was intact. He tried to bark, but his exhaustion could produce only a gut-wrenching rasp that broke me up.

The strangeness of the scene, as Tilly tenderly washed him with a damp flannel, struck me forcibly. Encrusted mud peeled away from his flanks. I inspected him thoroughly. There didn't seem to be any broken bones, nor obvious gashes. No colonies of maggots feasting.

"Fatigue, dehydration," said Tilly.

"Pain an' all."

Jud found it, an inch-long splinter lodged in the pad of one front paw. No wonder his journey home had been hampered. We held a water bowl to his mouth and I wept to hear him lapping. He chewed gamely on an anti-inflammatory tablet from the canine first aid box. And then we undertook some surgery – a good team, Tilly definitely in charge – and the jagged fragment came out, stubbornly, with much flinching and a fair bit of blood. Tilly declared that he would not need stitches and applied antiseptic: she bandaged his paw as if she'd known another career – another life – tending the wounded in some field hospital.

Victoria Albertina rubbed affectionately against Boo's side, and I plied her with well-earned treats and grateful petting. Jud went out to make coffee – he was surprisingly good in a crisis – and I took Tilly in my trembling arms.

"Thank you," I said.

"Darling," she whispered. So it wasn't over. Maybe this crisis had reset the clock? Jud came in with the tray. He didn't seem troubled that I was hugging Tilly, and she didn't disengage. There was no brawling, no re-run of Skipper and James and Alice. I thought about the dog – the Airedale, Kit – that led James to that adulterous scene, and at the same moment Tilly remarked that it was funny how BFT had led her to me, she'd led me to the NHS, and Boo, having found the BB, had been found by BFT. It was acronyms all round. Jud said we should contact the BBC.

Tilly and I lifted Boo into his basket by the fire. I covered him with a blanket, kissed his sweet head, gave him his toy bear. Victoria Albertina climbed in as well and they snuggled down together. I'd monitor Boo, to see if he'd need a vet in the morning.

Within an hour Tilly and Jud were gone, and I was clearing up. Having Boo back made me light-headed with optimism. No more dread of Luke calling me. There was still a spark with Tilly, though: who knew how that would play out? As I plumped up a cushion on my club chair, something wrapped in shiny Cellophane caught my eye. Lying where Jud had sat all evening was a nugget of tightly-packed herbs. I gave it a good sniff: skunk!

"Shit!" The freaking junkie... it was one thing to use it himself, but another to plant it in my house, even by accident, while rummaging his phone in and out of a pocket. What if Massey called? I stowed it in my desk drawer, ready to confront Jud with his carelessness next time we met.

I gently carried Boo and his basket upstairs, and turned in around eleven. The sea fret must have cleared: looking up from my pillow I noticed – through the roof lantern above the bed – how the night sky was clear as crystal. The bright pattern we call the Plough: you could join those dots any number of ways, fashion other forms just as valid. One reality, many stories. In my twenties this was the sort of stoner wisdom we'd mumble all night, laying by a fire, in a field, at a festival. But it was over ten years since I'd had even a puff. And now there was some in my drawer. Tossing and turning, I couldn't dismiss the thrilling possibility. Christ knows, I'd been through enough these last days. Didn't I deserve a guilty pleasure?

Out of bed, across the landing, down the dark stairs, skipping the step with the death click. All was silent, nothing lurked in the shadows, I told myself: yet I still checked over my shoulder as I guiltily switched on the lamp. In the old tea caddy – among the coins and watchstraps, trinkets and badges – I found a packet of Rizla and a lighter, still working. Did I dare? My pulse raced. Luke would never need to know. Just one sneaky joint.

My fingers knew the routine. I watched them crumbling weed into paper, rolling a whopper, ripping a roach, choosing the music, sparking the spark. Blimey Jud, this stuff's a lot stronger than it used to be. Or I'm a lot weaker.

And it took effect a lot quicker. Within minutes, every slight inflection of the swing band, every melisma of Ella Fitzgerald's miraculous delivery, tingled constellations of pleasure. I exhaled slowly: the smoke sank around me and the habitual aromas of cedar, and Tilly's lingering cologne, began to fade into the background. The membrane that keeps now from when, real from uncertain, became porous, and images came seeping through. My trance-sensitive iPod morphed Ella into some otherworldly, light fandango: acoustic guitar, a dash of tambourine, spilling their Italian ambience as the ceiling flew away.

Over on a table, the other side of the café, my mother Miranda was dancing, naked but for a sheer lacy cardigan, a floral miniskirt. Go-go hips, shameless legs, jet-black bouncing hair. A rasp of passing Vespas, and the fluid scene became an open-air bar – orange and lime, colours of the sixties. Miranda high in a window: an erotic dance for the drunken Latin youths who egged her on: 'Randi! *Bona* Randi!' I turned away – taboo, taboo – but there she was again, languorously flirting with some debonair silver fox, perhaps an Italian count, his hungry eyes pinned fast to hers. And suddenly her hair was hanging on my own shoulder, her lips close to my ear.

'Little lost Robert: time to tell you a secret.' That innocent sing-song voice I had never forgotten. She knelt down on my table, took my face in her hands, reading it closely.

'I don't like secrets.' I couldn't look her in the eye.

'Your real papa... did you never want to know?'

'By the time I knew the facts of life, you were too far gone. I couldn't get through to you.'

'But I'm getting through now.' She giggled. 'The stoned leading the stoned.'

'Decades too late. Forty years and no role model, to look up to and admire.'

'Admire, Robert?' She spoke so gently. 'Real papas can do things their sons won't admire. Sons do the same: where d'you think your nature comes from?' Wherever she was going with this, instinct said I could not afford to hear it. 'But face the facts, Robert: he's been with you, he grows closer all the time.' I tore my face from her grasp, and she was singing as I forced her to fade. *'Someone to admire at last, face a secret from your past...'*

"Oh my God, oh my God!"

Shaking. Sweating. Panicking: I banged my head to dispel the hallucination.

'*Calma*, Roberto!'

Secret, she'd said, *Admirer*. Both words winningly emphasised. And 'Miranda' means 'fit for admiration'. It all made ghastly sense. Closer, he's getting, could be hiding now, anywhere in the boathouse. My father? So Miranda – the reckless 'Randi' – had really been his lover? The man who wanted to rape me! Who broke my poodle's back? What kind of genes have I inherited? And I wonder why my life feels cursed?

I picked up the rest of Jud's dope – God knows what else was cut in with it – and staggered to the bathroom, watched it spin away down the toilet. I shivered. My circulation seemed to have stopped. The boathouse hit an iceberg. All the doors fell open at once, cupboards, chests, secret panels... all empty. Was this supposed to reassure me? If my mother's Secret Admirer – my childhood stalker, my father – was not behind any of these doors, then where was he? Up above, snapping Boo's spine? I ran for the stairs, but all was in slow motion. I found myself crawling, unhinging each tread, reading the names hidden under them, lingering inordinately over the Death Step, where the new fake timbers clicked their warning, the sound of vertebrae snapping. How long before Jud's skunk would leave me alone?

Boo watched my uncertain progress from his basket, as I made it to the *en suite* bathroom.

'*Calma*, Roberto. There's nobody here but you!' said the voice of the *putto*.

But it lied. No matter how much security I installed, and no matter how many times I checked the locks... according to my mother's revelation, her Secret Admirer would always be in my house... living in my genes. What Lord James had called his 'dark passenger'. I knew what he meant now: where I went, they went. It would always be that way. That's when I held my head over the bowl and was very, very, sick.

The next thing I knew was Saturday morning, and I found myself in bed. But what a godsend to be awoken – as if from a hideous dream – by Boo, still alive, back unbroken, a slight whimper alerting me to let him out for his business. I would never smoke another joint as long as I lived, I swore.

I had a severe case of the munchies, but I carried Boo downstairs and fed him before seeing to my own needs.

Finishing off last night's garlicky pasta, my thoughts turned to Inspector Massey, and the scheme to get Jud off the hook. But I also had to get Boo to the vet's and have him thoroughly checked over.

On the drive inland into Holt all was business as usual, with no evidence of a near disaster in the locale. The whole landscape felt different, though, in light of my mother's revelation. As I queued to pay for diesel, I had a shivering realisation: her words rang so true precisely because of the way I'd found James's diaries coming to life in my mind. I was by nature a watcher, an observer, peripheral to the action, a secret admirer myself.

This chill hung on me all through the vet's session. In a blur I watched the dog nurse inspect him thoroughly, prescribing muscle-relaxants, and adding a hefty sum to our account. As I stepped out – Boo walking quite confidently already – I wondered how Luke could be prevented from seeing that bill. Then my phone rang.

"Luke!"

"You sound surprised. Where are you?"

"Holt."

"Shopping?"

"Taking care of business, you know," I said.

"How's Boo?" It was as if he knew what I was hiding.

"Doing great," came my quivering reply.

"You're so lucky, not to have been flooded: me Mam's been through hell."

"Oh God, Luke..." I began. But I couldn't tell him.

"Bertie, something wrong?"

"No, no, just worried about your mum."

"All tucked up at Uncle Vin's, resting. So I'm still aiming to be home Wednesday. The early train: gets to Norwich about one."

"We've never been apart this long," I said.

"Aye, it's been awful this end, all the worry."

"Of course, no blame: you've only got one mother."

"And you, you've missed me?"

"Luke, you have no idea... how much this break has affected me."

"We'll be back to normal in no time, hey? Chilling out in the boathouse? Some seal-spotting?"

What could I say?

"Love to Mum. See ya Wednesday."

"Bring Boo to meet us, won't you?" he added.

"We'll be there, on the dot." Something else I'd have to explain, losing the watch he'd given me. We signed off.

I walked on into town. It began to feel good to be out and about, with Boo at my side, albeit not quite himself yet. In a window I glimpsed myself smiling, like a man returning from the brink of madness. Luke would be home very soon: I absolutely needed to have everything resolved, worries buried and laid to rest, so we could get 'back to normal' as he had prophesied.

Passing the post office I could almost see Lord James's uniformed chauffeur, Bailey, waiting in the Rolls for news of Alice and Constance, via the marvel of the Marconi wireless. My business now was a modern marvel, in the gadget showroom nearby, where I'd once thought about upgrading my mobile phone. The glass cabinet was labelled 'Monitors'; sleek, miniature gizmos more suited to the world of surveillance than to household use. With Sunday's daring mission in mind, I was visualising ways by which Jud and I might follow Tilly's conversation with the Slavonic couple, and mount a rescue if things started to go wrong. A blue-shirted assistant broke into my thoughts.

"Looking for a baby monitor, sir?"

So I looked the fatherly type.

"Ah. Yes, could be..." I looked down at Boo.

"A great feature of this range, sir, is how they link to a mobile. It won't even look like it's switched on." It was as if Q were briefing Bond for a babysitting mission.

"I see," I nodded slowly.

He laid out three contenders on the glass, and I picked one up at random.

"You've got a good eye," came the sales spiel. "The C23C, excellent battery life, and a 3G interface to connect to your laptop... as a remote bugging tool." Our eyes met for a moment. "You can use it for live recording, even view texts and e-mails, as required."

I brought out my mobile, and he laughed. Within five minutes I'd signed for a long-overdue, shiny update. It took my existing SIM card. He downloaded the bugging app, and gave me a demonstration. The geek in me was getting excited.

On the drive home, despite my upbeat mood, I felt my father's dark genes hinting that, if I left the C23C with Tilly, I could monitor her activities with Jud. No! said my higher nature. This MI5-style purchase was solely to be used for her protection, at the illegals' flat in Fakenham, in our ploy to set up Viktor's arrest.

It was still fairly early when Boo and I got back to the boathouse. I had a good search around the place, still unable – even in unstoned, broad daylight – to dismiss the fear that my one-time stalker, now my father, might be somewhere close at hand. Boo settled happily in his basket, and I settled seriously to research the diaries, determined to make best use of the few days before they were needed back at Samphire Hall for the Gala Opening.

I surveyed my notepad, surprised by the extensive tracts of speculation about the Skipper Wood case, where I fancied I'd listed objective historical data. So little time to put this right: I must not let Tilly down. I sank into my chair, and began my journey back into the world of Lord James.

20th March 1913

Skipper Wood, directly descended from illustrious boat-builders: Norsemen mariners, endowed with God-given skills. Caleb Bacon, his clumsy-handed brother-in-law, good only for fence-posts and pick-handles. Bacon can never compete with Wood's legacy, and in his envy, dear diary, I espy a foolproof tool for my vengeance on the Viking.

Brother-in-law? So Caleb was Beulah's brother, and the uncle whose name Pearl had vainly tried to recall at Walnut Court? This much was new to me, but I had read plenty about his envy, in particular his failing to congratulate Skipper on winning the 'County Carpenter' prize. And now James was planning to use Bacon, somehow, to get back at Skipper for his dalliance with Alice.

20th March 1913 (continued)
In happier times Skipper would regale me with colourful tales of his rivalry with Caleb Bacon, which has festered since their schooldays. It amuses me to think of Bacon's self-pitying, drunken rage, in the Newton Arms, when the Diving Seal trounced his Hobbling Redshank. Yes, Caleb is the perfect agent for my machination!

I checked on Boo: sound asleep. But I had never felt more awake, as the history of my boathouse unfolded into a new, disturbing phase.

21st March 1913
A visit to Caleb Bacon's frugal workshop this morning. Blind to his own inadequacy as a craftsman, he protests that 'Wood's Crafts & Joinery' is poaching his proper clientele because of Skipper's social prestige. In his desperation, the odious fellow can ill afford to reject the pieces of silver with which I purpose to tempt him.

Caleb a hired assassin? And what kind of man plots to kill his former friend, just over a few kisses stolen from his wife? But I can't expect to think like an aristocrat, I told myself.

26th March 1913
Bacon is shameless: he dares to demand an additional ten guineas, over and above my more than generous offer. However, I have conceded, and a date has been set for Skipper's comeuppance, while Alice sojourns with Countess Daisy, no doubt repenting her carnal involvement with my man.

Carnal involvement? During my *tête-à-tête* with Massey, over this 'cold case', I'd called it 'a surreptitious snog'. Just as I was embarking on this significant revision of my evidence, there came a vigorous knock at the door. Fearing the inspector, I opened up gingerly; but the visitor was altogether more appealing.

"Hi there, sorry to bother you." He flashed an identity pass. "Perry Tatlock, *News of the World.* Saw you in the *Eastern Morning Advertiser,* you and your king-size pencil!" He grinned provocatively. They probably thought they could send a blue-eyed cutie and I'd tell-all. "Look, I won't beat about the bush. We're offering forty grand for the right dope on this Anne Boleyn Bureau heist. Seems plenty of big players are interested in it."

"Forty grand!" I swallowed deeply. Thirty-five of that would cover Jud's bail.

"Upfront – direct bank transfer to your account first thing – just needs your autograph, here." I stared at the contract he'd shoved into my hand.

"Um..." I was taken aback. Boo came out and yawned pointedly.

"Call me Perry." He winked and produced a digital recorder from his man bag. "And I'll get some cool photos: you and your lurcher – something atmospheric – out there on the deck, what d'you reckon?"

Boo turned up his nose at the 'lurcher' slur and pattered back indoors. Tempting though his offer seemed, Luke would go bonkers. I thought back to his reaction when we won the Eco-Designer award and woke to find press in our front garden.

"Perry, thanks, but it's no. Okay?"

"If you change your mind, I'm at The Blakeney Hotel. Until three tomorrow," he added, cocksure in his pretty-boy charm. He receded up the track, all athletic in his slim-fit jeans. My mind went back to Tilly. The new phone, disappointingly, worked only in the same spot as its predecessor: out in the cold.

"Er, Tilly, our hug last night..."

"Best not go there," she replied, uneasily.

"Okay... well why I rang... I've had a visit. A reporter."

"Yah, probably the same one who was here – cute and full of himself? I'm under strict orders from Karsten, all the NHS are. No interviews while the thefts at the Hall are under investigation."

"But Tilly – forty grand would see Jud nice, no?"

"Forty? He offered me thirty! But it's just too risky, sweetie."

She was right of course, and surprisingly objective, given her carnal involvement with Jud. Though her lingering embrace with me last night made me wonder just how deep that involvement went.

"I've been *workink* on my accent for tomorrow," said Tilly, suddenly full of Eastern promise.

"Very *convincink*," I said. "But can you really spare the time?"

"It's 24/7 here, but I'm taking three hours out or I'll go mad. It's a hell of an exhibition but I've had enough of dreaming about Newton-Grey inventories." I know the feeling. "Oh before I forget," Tilly added, "Jud's set everything up with the Slavonics. Yurik and Katya they're called. I'm due there at eleven tomorrow."

"Great," I said. Astonishing Jud could think straight at all, given the strength of his smoking mixture.

"Just remember your deadline for the diary notes, Bertie: I'm counting on you."

"Yeah, no probs..."

I could procrastinate no longer. Back up in the boathouse, I closed all the shutters, in case further Perry Tatlocks came snooping. With anglepoise, teapot, sandwiches and notebook in place, I settled – finally – to my promised analysis of James's diaries.

10th April 1913 – 5 p.m.

God knows I had struggle enough, getting the perfidious Skipper back into the boathouse. My messages were unanswered, my intermediaries rebuffed. Some claimed he was unwell. Or perhaps he was poleaxed with shame at his betrayal of my intimacy and trust.

In the end, an appeal to his pride prevailed, as I knew it must. In a note I declared that the secret step at Woodfields must be cured of its creaking once and for all, and that he is the only man in England able to do it. Since he had ignored all promises of payment, I declared I would reward this labour with the gift of his prize-winning sculpture, the Diving Seal from St Benedict's Foyer. Truth to tell, I can no longer bear to look upon it.

He has agreed to attend the boathouse at the specified hour. Sellars will ensure it is unlocked. And once Wood is about his labours on the stair, my hireling Bacon will make his move. I had him parrot his text several times: he is word perfect.

Skipper Wood shall be removed from my life!

There were crumbs of social history here for Tilly, but there was a bellyful of distress for me. James was painting himself in a very dark light and, though I wanted to give him the benefit of the doubt, I felt too sick, too excited, to imagine any extenuating interpretation for these startling disclosures.

Thankfully, his next entry provided one:

11th April 1913 – 9 a.m.

Breakfast in my study was rudely interrupted by an hysterical Caleb Bacon. He did attend Woodfields, purposing to discharge Skipper Wood from his work there, but did not deliver my letter nor recite his damning lines, informing Skipper that 'by this I annul our recent contract, and instruct you to cede this most delicate task to Mr Bacon'.

He claims, on the contrary, that he found Wood dead, and now accuses me of a ploy to frame him for murder, a murder he says I had already committed 'in revenge for Skipper's dalliance with Lady Alice'. Lies, lies!

And then the weasel had the gall to threaten me. He would smear my reputation, he says, alleging an indecent relationship between Skipper and myself. I am mortified by Bacon's about-turn, and the private information he appears to have gathered. I sent the liar packing and burnt his script.

But within minutes an ashen-faced Sellars arrived, and verified part, at least, of Bacon's story: Skipper Wood lies dead – Skipper, dead! – at the foot of my boathouse stairs, his neck slashed.

'Lies, lies!' James had written. But would I be able to work out exactly *who* was lying? The whole diary could be a fiction, whitewash for some very black deeds. As I excitedly re-read the entry, my newfound voyeur's genes came into play. Lurking within eyeshot of James's unfolding crisis, I found myself visualising his account of the police enquiry, point by point.

Inspector Douglas Colman arrives promptly at the crime scene. He invites Lord James to wait in the scullery, now my kitchen. James's cool exterior conceals mighty alarm. And I'm hoping against hope that my faith in his integrity will not be shattered by any upcoming revelations.

According to James's account Colman was a friend of his late father, Lord Randolph. This link notwithstanding, he follows procedure. In shaky handwriting he later records how Colman picks up a red-dogtooth cap, inspects it, sees it's far too small to have been worn by Skipper. As the diary points out, James quickly realises Caleb Bacon has made a 'monumental blunder'.

James is seized by panic – smoking furiously as he spies the scene – from behind the louvered doors. If Skipper was not alone when he died, there will be very awkward questions.

Skipper's toolbox lies, swamped in congealed arterial blood, by the bottom step. Colman directs his men to roll the body on to its back, which reveals 'a Sheffield crosscut and a compass saw' – James's precision is unsettling – in their sodden cardboard sleeves. A 'sturdy sixteen-inch brass-backed tenon saw' is wedged among the others, blade-up, unsheathed. This is the one that apparently took its owner's life. James initially speculates that Bacon killed Wood, then 'arranged the body athwart the sharpest tool in Skipper's possession': he concludes that the corpse is too heavy, the blood-spill too localised, to warrant such an interpretation. He must trust that Colman will come to a similar verdict.

James composes himself, perhaps rehearsing a response to the inevitable questions about the rogue headgear.

11th April 1913 – 4 p.m.
Colman maddeningly twiddled the peaked cap, red with Skipper's blood, but his speech made no mention of it.

Inwardly I cursed the swine Bacon for not keeping it on his ugly head.

Then Colman asked, courteously enough, after Lady Alice Newton-Grey. If he has been attentive to the same rumours Bacon claims to know, might his forensically schooled mind consider my wife's transgressions as motive enough for a wronged husband's revenge?

Colman peered through his magnifying glass at banisters, handles and tools, before finding prints on them with his squirrel-hair brush and canister of inky powder. All of this clearly left James in a neurotic state of anticipation, and perhaps powered up his own fiction-engine: the bloody cap, he eventually told Colman, belonged to his manager Stanley Sellars, who had presumably doffed it on discovering the body.

Colman, as he prepared to leave, offered to drop the cap off at the Audit House – where he no doubt planned to establish whether Sellars recognised it. When James informed the detective that he was himself going to the Audit House – to sign off bills that Sellars had prepared – the inspector 'touched his forelock and left the evidence with me'. This deference left me baffled.

I checked on Boo, and refreshed the teapot, and put my detective mettle to the test by trying to divine what would happen next, before reading James's account. I imagined myself at the blue Formica table, chewing the case over with Massey.

'Well, Clive, two suspects in the frame: Lord James and Caleb Bacon, both with motives for killing Skipper.'

'Sexual jealousy, professional jealousy?'

'Exactly. Yet James's diary makes it clear: he wants only to humiliate the carpenter.'

'Well, he would say that. Why should we trust him?'

'It rings true, given what we know of his devious thought processes. Tactically sending a useless carpenter to sack the master craftsman. Totally mortifying.'

'Nah, you're thinking like a poofter. When the pizza boy shags Bruce Willis's tart, does he get revenge by teasing him? He blows his fucking head off!'

'So you think Caleb's hunch is right, then? Does James think like a... in a pink manner... because he's that way inclined with Skipper?'

'If Bacon can prove Skipper and James are shirt-lifters – pardon my French – he's better off blackmailing them, not killing one of them.'

'Nah, you're thinking like a fat bully. The little man, the nobody: he finds his rival weakened – by gastroenteritis or arsenic – and seizes the moment to slash at his throat.'

'Then leaves his own hat to marinade in the toolbox?'

'Well, you tell me, if that's such a big clue, how come the inspector doesn't take it with him?'

'Looking after the squire. The old-school tie. Maybe they're Freemasons?'

'If class sides with class, Caleb's not our killer, then.'

'Your words not mine, sunshine. And I thought you fancied the bum bandit...'

Oh God, I'd drifted off: the dream-Massey had shed no useful light on my investigation, and I had dribbled on James's diary. I dabbed the words with a tissue: 'Not Guilty'. Though, to judge by his scrawl, James had been pretty wasted on absinthe by the end of that day's writing.

My own writing for Tilly was still painfully meagre. I sipped cold tea and returned to the diaries. News of Skipper's death had spread quickly. Lady Alice had cut short her sojourn with Daisy Greville and returned: presumably a troubled night's sleep at the murder scene. The Samphire Estate was awash with all sorts of unsettled speculation, until the coroner's verdict – the 'accidental death' I had read online at the start of my investigations – dispelled any unsavoury rumours for Lord and Lady Newton-Grey.

James's account of Skipper's funeral, some days later, showed a welcome degree of remorse at a second humiliation for his winning carpenter:

20th April 1913 – p.m.
From Binham to Stiffkey the lanes were lined with mourners, as if a great warrior had passed away. Thank heaven for dear Stanley Sellars who punctiliously, at my behest, put everything in place *per* the Wood family wishes. How grim the irony, though, to see Skipper's Tug-O'-War team as pallbearers, carrying their Olympic captain in a primitive pinewood box, from the workshop of Caleb Bacon. This was a world more humiliation than I had planned for the dear fellow.

I was intrigued by his gratitude to Sellars. It reminded me of the sepia photograph I'd found among James's prosthetic designs up at Samphire Hall, with 'affectionately yours, Stanley' scribbled on the back. Lord James certainly seemed to rely a great deal on this discreetly efficient estate manager.

I took the diary into the lounge now, as it was chilly and Boo deserved some company. James's response to the coroner's verdict was jubilant:

20th April 1913 late
Old man Colman came up trumps, and Caleb's cap has not been mentioned. Woe betide Bacon now if he thinks he can frame me as a murderer. Tonight I celebrate alone, but for *La Fée Verte*, whose juice is my perpetual comfort.

But his absinthe high was short-lived. A brief, transactional note from Lady Alice, brought by his morning valet, was pinned in the diary, and followed by a desolate entry.

23rd April 1913 Midday

The Rolls throbbed on the forecourt, as Alice prepared to decamp for New York. Divorce without chattels. She claims she is still 'in love' with me, but that our relationship is irretrievably broken down. My last glimpse of her Titian hair, blazing through the rear window, as my rare bird takes her flight to freedom.

Oh dear God, bereft of Skipper, and now my dearest Alice. How will this grief end? The green fairy, my blessed absinthe, beckons me to madness.

I was glad to see such natural humanity from James: after he'd shown no trace of emotion following his father's death. But I was sad to see Alice departing: the spirited social climber had brought an exotic touch to the story of my boathouse, as well as to James's circle. But if she was 'still in love' with James, her flight to New York after Skipper's funeral raised obvious questions. Was she looking for a fresh start following an adulterous liaison, a broken marriage, a rape, and the loss of her mother? Or was she a fugitive, decamping before the law caught up with her? Fourteen months earlier she had written of her son's stillbirth as 'miscarriage or murder' and noted that James 'deserved to be punished'. What if she'd sneaked back to the boathouse from her London sojourn, and punished James by despatching his Olympian lover?

"What do you think?" I asked Boo. "Am I raving?" He looked at me with all-knowing whippet eyes, and had the good grace to pass no comment at all.

2nd May 1913

True to my word, I had the Diving Seal delivered to Skipper Wood's family. Beulah, sombre still in widow's weeds, cradled tiny Pearl, while Archibald ran amok in their freshly-papered parlour.

I also informed her of a deposit fund in the sum of £600, which I have advanced to the London & Provincial Bank in Norwich. This is by way of a pension for Skipper, which she accepted most graciously.

Ah! The 1913 payment to Beulah I'd seen in the Audit House ledgers. It would be worth a thousand times more in today's money: a bequest large enough to spell guilt as much as compassion. Pearl had told me her mother had never needed to work again, and she and Archie had benefited from a good education. But they'd also had good indoctrination, every year on the anniversary of Skipper's death, with Beulah's saga of the poisonous wallpaper. Beulah had destroyed photographs of Skipper's innocent escapades with the aristocrats; once again I began to wonder if his less-innocent escapades had impelled her to destroy more than his mere image? A former dispenser, she could have dosed him progressively with rat poison, knowing that if any coroner found arsenic in the body, it could be blamed on the wallpaper. Granted, Skipper had bled to death: but he could have fallen down the stairs under the effects of his good wife's recipes.

As I read on, James's entries for that summer became threadbare, with just a few engagements, mostly cancelled. I wanted to believe this represented a respectable period of mourning, but entries later in the year gave the lie to that.

25th September 1913

I hear that Bacon's workshop now enjoys a roaring trade. Our covenant has made him prosperous beyond any dream; but his greed becomes insufferable. Stanley grows suspicious of my frequent disbursements to so tawdry a craftsman.

10th October 1913

The vulgar Bacon swaggers his newfound riches in every eye: gaudy pinstripes, garish checks, a ludicrous feather in his brown bowler, showy tiepins, flashy rings. And yet I sign another banker's cheque – for fear of scandal – as he threatens me with the gallows. How can I prove things otherwise?

It was galling for me to see how badly James had fared at the hands of his homophobic hireling. Yet this grim turn of events added several lines to a good afternoon's work on my part: I had pages of bullet points now, and I read the last few back to Boo. He sat up in his basket, ears poised, surely convinced I was doing something worthwhile. When he limped over to me for a cuddle, I read the next entry to him aloud.

12th December 1913

The wastrel will bleed me dry. A rented mansion, a motorcar with white-walled tyres, extravagant wardrobe for 'Madame Bacon' as his wife now likes to be addressed; apparel for his five brats; joints of meat; rugs, lamps, an endless roster of indulgence with which to entertain his fair-weather friends… I am at my wits' end!

Bills stack up on Sellars's desk. And yet my loyal Stanley knows his place, and my nature; he cannot question such folly. But unless I make another fortune, with my prosthetic devices – now, with Christmas almost upon us – I fear Bacon may render me bankrupt.

Boo jumped down, needing to go out, so I took a breather down by the deck. With renewed appetite for my mission, I began to feel I could solve the mystery of Skipper Wood's death myself, even without the help of the Boleyn Bureau, or of Inspector Massey. It was only

Saturday, mid-afternoon, and 1914 was fast approaching in the diaries. As Caleb's demands mounted exponentially, something had to give.

And of course it did. Archduke Franz Ferdinand, of the Austro-Hungarian Empire, was suddenly assassinated in Sarajevo, triggering the first Great War, and plunging Lord James's world into another orbit of untold nightmares.

CHAPTER SIXTEEN
CHRISTMAS ROSE

Perhaps I was mad to suppose that tomorrow's scam in Fakenham, by which we hoped to tip off Inspector Massey with the people smugglers' schedule, might help to earn a reprieve for Jud. I needed to drive out in the van, get online somewhere, and Google up a whole backstory for Tilly first. But James's diaries, the key to my research into Skipper's death, were all I could think about. And my time with these precious documents was almost up.

I sped through week after week when James lived at his London Club, assuaging his loneliness with visits to teaching hospitals, medical suppliers and mortuaries. But I found nothing specific to Samphire Hall – nor to Tilly's exhibition – until midway through the year.

2nd August 1914 – a.m.
Going back will be painful. But I must pay a visit to Woodfields on a matter Stanley has brought to my attention. Apparently locals – and other staff – are starting to gossip of strange happenings.

3rd August 1914 – a.m.
Caleb Bacon toys with my emotions: the weasel shall be damned for the replacement nameplate he has nailed up at the entrance: 'Wood Feels' is an outrage.

And yet, truth to tell, whispers of Skipper's maddening song did seem to intrude on my thoughts. I fancied also that I heard him sawing, with demonic relish, as night crossed swords with dawn. It mortifies me that Bacon's mocking plaque is in truth a most fitting house-name for this cedar mausoleum.

So the name 'Wood Feels', which so unsettled me, was Caleb Bacon's sardonic commentary; I was not the only soul to have heard Skipper perpetually rebuilding the boathouse, in the soundtrack of my dreams.

"You too, Boo, we've both been plagued by Skipper, eh? What's he trying to tell us?" I gave him a hug, my ally, my second sensitive soul. By the sound of it, Lord James was a third. 'Tell Tils about Skip Wood ghost ref 3 Aug. entry', I jotted in my notes. I'd make a believer of her yet. And if I could exorcise Skipper's trapped spirit from this place, I told myself, it would not only justify all the shit I'd been going through, it might even redeem the guilt of the Secret Admirer's genes that I was obliged to carry. I wondered when James would next refer to his own 'dark passenger'.

Unable to quash the haunting rumours, James simply instructed Stanley Sellars to have the boathouse boarded up, 'to frustrate ghoulish trespassers' as he put it. Clearly the 'Wood Feels' sign was never removed.

4th August 1914 – p.m.
Caleb Bacon had the gall to taunt me with yet another stunt. In The Newton Arms he was whistling Skipper's tune as I privately slipped him his envelope of banknotes.

As Bacon was leaving the snug, a dayboy from Gresham's School sped over from Cromer on his bicycle with the most alarming news, that England has declared war on the Hun!

Later, as I made my way out through the smoke, I spotted Inspector Colman, who tilted his Homburg in my direction. Unnervingly, though, he had been engrossed in private talk with Caleb at the bar, ignoring the patriotic fervour pouring in from the street, the jaunty cheers and a call to bring down the Kaiser.

James had good reason to be unnerved. Colman had chosen not to act on any suspicion about the cap he'd found by Skipper's body. But if the inspector discovered James had succumbed to blackmail, which works only on the guilty, he might feel obliged to dig a little deeper.

"You see, Boo, even if I was a paid-up detective, things wouldn't seem any more clear-cut."

As I read on, the situation between Lord James Newton-Grey and Caleb Bacon grew more intricate still. They found themselves together, conscripted into the battalion of the 8th Norfolks. And fate, or the inequitable class system, dealt Caleb another cruel card: at twenty-nine years old, he must have felt sorely piqued to discover – in September, at the Colchester training camp – that Lord James Newton-Grey, just twenty-four, was to be his commanding officer, by entitlement alone. The loyal Stanley Sellars, at thirty, had been drafted as colour sergeant into the same battalion. Luke liked to deride my mathematical capabilities: but these ages were easily deduced from James's detailed reports.

I could imagine tensions mounting all along the Samphire Coast, as people faced the ever-growing possibility of being shipped to France, the Western Front. But for Lord James – who lived in perpetual fear of Caleb blabbing, or of Sellars's loyalty wavering if he learnt too much – it was already a hotbed of torment.

A flame-red sky signalled dusk, and the midges began their hazy flurry, as chaotic as the turmoil in my head. I stood on the jetty tapping in Tilly's number.

"Still at the Hall," she told me. "On my own, doing a bit of prep for tomorrow. The story is, I want to get out of the UK, home to the Ukraine. But I haven't got a passport so I need to meet up with Viktor's next landing."

"Good. But what stops you applying for a passport?"

"I came in illegally too. Anyway it's urgent. My *matir* is dying."

"Matir?"

"Ukrainian for mother. Though I came to the UK so young that I don't really speak my mother tongue as such."

"Brilliant. And you haven't seen your mother in years."

"Never a truer word, sweetie."

"Sorry, you know what I mean. Anyway, you'll need a moniker."

"Okay, 'Monika' it is." Then we laughed and said "Great minds..." at the same time.

"I did mean to work out some background for you..."

"Been there, done that," Tilly interrupted. "I'm from Kerch. I know more about the Crimea than its own inhabitants do."

"Tomorrow, I'll give you a gadget I've picked up, looks like a mobile, but it's a bugging device. So once you're in with the Slavonics... I'm in there with you."

"Bertie, you think of everything."

"Well I try. And I... I still care about you. Something rotten."

"I know it." She paused. "Thanks, Bertie. But I wonder: it's nice and everything, but why are you doing all this for Jud?"

"Jud's really helped me, helped my investigations. And don't laugh, but I feel I owe it to Skipper."

Tilly did laugh, quite a snort.

"Same old supernatural bullshit. Living on your own, you've got obsessed. Don't you ever stop?"

"Well, what if I told you there's black and white evidence, right here in James's diary. I marked the page for you: he spends a night in the boathouse, and he hears Skipper singing and sawing away... a year after the murder."

"So that's where you got it from!"

"You're impossible."

"And you'll bring your notes tomorrow, for my presentation? Can't wait to see what you've done."

"Fakenham will be insanely busy. How about we leave it and get together properly on Monday?"

"Okay, but that's the real, dead deadline. We're talking *rigor mortis* after that."

"Trust me," I said. Will she ever make sense of my scrawl, I thought.

"Oh I do: and nobody else really..."

"Not Jud?"

"Well he trusts you too. Think about last night, when we were... after Boo came back."

"Oh God... I didn't mean to complicate things." I really wanted her to believe that. "Look... I've been meaning to ask you something pretty *off-piste*..." This was going to be tricky, but over the phone was probably easier than face-to-face. "Tilly, remember when we got Jud home after his beating, and washed him up? Well, he's got a key tattooed on him, and I can't help wondering if there's another inking, a clue... down below... as to what that key opens?"

She went silent, and I held my breath. I didn't know who was more embarrassed. Eventually Tilly giggled.

"Bertie, you're totally obsessed! That key... the shaft's a lot longer than you might expect, but I don't think there's anything for it to unlock. At least, not until I came along..."

"Jesus, Tilly," I thought, or did I say it out loud? "Don't say you're a walking gallery as well?" In a moment I was overwhelmed by a vision of Jud, stiff key at the ready, discovering that Tilly's intimate flesh was decorated as a keyhole, no common inking, but a vajazzle picked out in Swarovski diamonds, and winged like an angel.

"Bertie?"

"Never mind. Forget it!"

"I'd best get on," said Tilly, suddenly businesslike. "See you in the morning."

I gave Boo some dinner before resuming my research. Looking at the stack of diaries still unopened, I felt like a schoolboy on the eve of a major deadline for homework I'd barely started. 'There's nobody here but you,' I said to myself, acting as my own *putto*, 'and the work's not going to do itself.' So I knuckled down to speed-read the whole of World War I: otherwise, I'd be answering to the head of history – in this case Tilly's redoubtable boss, Dr Wulff.

As I skipped from November through December to Christmas Eve, so Samphire Hall gradually became an auxiliary war hospital. Thanks to her nursing background Ida Henderson, James's former guardian, was appointed head matron by the War Office, in addition to her duties as caretaker of the Hall during Lord James's tour of duty.

James vividly depicted his trip home for a couple of days' Christmas leave. Norfolk had responded magnificently to the great 'call'. Most animals, as well as men, had gone to the Front, including Lord James's beloved black mare, Pocahontas. 'An Eden without Adam,' he wrote, noting how 'my homeward path is shovelled clear by womenfolk'. He described Zeppelins, in 'whale-like formations' over his white estate, portents of darkness. But all this was as nothing compared with the shock of seeing, the suffering of casualties from the trenches he was yet to visit. St Benedict's Foyer, a chaos of iron bedsteads, was home to dozens wounded at Ypres.

Christmas Eve 1914

In timeworn tradition, a blue Scots pine from the Estate graces St Benedict's Foyer for Yuletide. Loyal Ida saw to it as always. Beulah Wood, wearing her Red Cross brassard, has become a nurse under Ida's watch. Solemn when I encountered her, she eventually managed a greeting of sorts, not quite a smile. We must find a moment to converse privately.

James's detailed narrative engaged my overwrought imagination, once again drawing me into familiar surroundings, now transformed by war.

A new arrival in St Benedict's Foyer, howling with pain. Ida and Beulah, among other nurses, pull a canvas screen around the wounded Tommy's bed. Driven by congenital curiosity, James sidles in to join them. As at the teaching hospitals he frequented, he takes stock of the surgical instruments, laid out 'as it were the finest cutlery'. He suspects the Red Cross may have raided 'my own collection', presumably the arsenal of medical implements I'd found while searching the Hall the night Boo got lost.

Christmas Eve 1914 – p.m.
A brisk surgeon in freshly laundered whites appeared at the bedside. The poor Tommy's incalculable agony provides my most salutary instruction. I shall ensure that he is equipped with a cedar-wood leg and foot from my cabinet of prototypes.

Here was heartening proof that James intended his artfully-articulated prostheses to replace the Captain Hook-like relics that were War Office standard issue at that time.

James observes how the surgeon's whites are blooded with 'the finest scarlet threads': finer than the red twine that portrays bleeding on his life-size mannequins upstairs. I recalled the dummy dressed in WW1 uniform, with the curly wig, and wondered if the enigmatic Stanley Sellars had also come home this Christmas.

As the soldier's anaesthetic wears off, Lord James retires to his private quarters in the west wing, which Ida has managed to preserve from War Office requisition. Just as providently, she has laid on James's painkiller of choice: a carafe filled with *La Fée Verte* – The Green Fairy' – sparkles in the lamplight.

On Christmas morning James pays a wistful visit to his late mother's rose garden.

Christmas Day 1914
Deep in reverie, I spotted, scarcely visible against the snow, a sublime white flower. One solitary 'Lady Oona' rose had sprung forth, my solace, even in this bleak midwinter.

James sprints back to the Hall to share this miraculous news with Ida – like the child he once was, with the guardian she still sometimes seems. Entering from the kitchen garden, he finds no sign of staff below stairs. The stove has been stoked, and pans steam... as they still did in his childhood memories of fraternising with the servants – much to the disgust of Lord Randolph – especially with the affable Stanley Sellars, then just a young clerk on the estate.

Bounding up the servants' steps into St Benedict's Foyer, James throws open the Gothic door and emerges at the scene of last night's operation. His impetuosity – ill-befitting a captain – earns censorious glances from nurses and patients alike. He looks around in dreadful surmise, sees Ida weeping silently by the Tommy's bed. The youth, whose blind howling had torn all hearts the previous evening, has not survived the night.

James departs. He returns, not with a wooden limb as he'd intended, but with Lady Oona's Christmas rose, and places that quiet miracle on the young Tommy's breast.

I broke off reading, to weep; perhaps in sadness for the death of the soldier, perhaps in gratitude that the diary's meticulous author did again appear to have a heart.

That night Lord James is back on the bottle. But Boxing Day finds him on the train back to Colchester Barracks, without having had the chance to meet Beulah Wood privately – unless a meeting occurred that for some reason he didn't mention in his diary.

Within a few months James's battalion of the 8th Norfolks was shipped to a new base camp, the support trenches at Flesselles in northern France. Once again I passed through the trance-portal that Jud's smoking-mixture had helped to open, and witnessed the continued training, the mounting tensions.

25th July 1915
My good Colour-Sgt Sellars ordered the lads to fix bayonets, and they vented their harrowing battle cries, as is essential for a dry run. Bacon was the last to charge at the swinging hessian sack, and as he twisted his blade the weasel glared back at me, insinuating the prospect of my own body hanging lifeless from a scaffold. He tries my patience beyond endurance.

Despite Caleb's financial demands, and his obnoxious attitude, James maintained an outward cool, befitting the responsibility of his rank; meanwhile the stench of war dominated their holding bay outside the gates of hell.

The one upbeat piece of news – 'a spiffing development' as James put it – came in a telegram from the War Office. The Office was convinced by his prosthetic design patents, and – in a new artificial limb unit at St Mary's Hospital Roehampton – 'hemispherical joints of Bakelite and nickel, in skin-like stretchable sheaths' were about to go into production.

James read this wire aloud to his trusty Sellars; they discussed the alchemy by which Boleyn Cedar off-cuts had been transformed into elegant prototype limbs. Like brothers in arms, they toasted Skipper's craft legacy 'most fondly', their tin cups charged with 'absinthe acquired from the local brothel'.

It was to be another full year before James's battalion was called to duty on the trenches at the Western Front. And on the eve of his brigade's baptism by fire, a barely coherent entry mentions a letter he plans to send to Alice in New York:

Friday 30th June 1916
And so be it – if I am to be the last of my dynasty – sacrifice for King and Country shall be my salvation. Should I not return from my impending duties, my testimony, baring my soul without reservation, as if under oath in a Court of Law, shall assure the world that, in the final analysis, I am a man of honour.

Was this troubling entry the fruit of terror, or intoxication? It suggested that James, faced with his own mortality, had penned some kind of confession that cleared him of the taint of dishonour. But what dishonour? Homicide, homosexuality? Had this 'testimony' – of which no specifics were divulged – really been sent to his beloved ex-wife in America? Was it the same document I had fleetingly felt in the depths of the Boleyn Bureau? Or was the whole thing a hoax, a lie, to make posterity believe that Lord Newton-Grey's innocence – of something – had at one time been provable?

1st July 1916 – p.m.

Today was indeed a date with destiny: The Battle of the Somme. I write by candlelight in my sodden, verminous dugout, just north of Carnoy. Fatigued from combat, I cannot find words to depict this spectacle of utter carnage.

By the grace of God I still have reliable Stanley by my side: in view of all that came to light after Pater's death, I must treat him as one of my own.

'One of my own?' This Stanley must have been a bit of a crutch for James, both now and during his difficult childhood under a tyrannical father. Why else preserve both the uniformed photo and the curly-mopped mannequin at the Hall? There could well have been something more to their camaraderie, maybe an intimacy initiated in adolescence, perhaps contributing to the failure of James's ill-starred marriage. A pink angle to James's background – bringing into focus the likelihood of a sexual relationship with Skipper too – would help explain James's inner turmoil, and preoccupation with dishonour. And now I wondered if at thirty, this Stanley Sellars was indeed married, or just considered in polite Edwardian terms, a 'confirmed bachelor'.

It was getting late; my shutters had been closed most of the day, and my eyes now begged for permission to follow suit. I saw to Boo's needs before turning in. The glow of the bedside lamp offered no relief from the fears James's reports had awakened in me. The creaking boathouse cracked its whip, to marshal the nightly circus of dreams; but, like the men of the 8th Norfolks, I found sleep slow to come. Skipper's manifestations, waiting in the wings, were no longer my primary fear. A long-dead intruder in the building seemed a somewhat pallid threat next to the flesh-and-blood possibility of waking to find mother's Secret Admirer towering at the foot of my bed.

But there could be no waking, until I'd slept. Holed up on the edge of no-man's-land, I worried over our imminent sortie into Fakenham, the target in my immediate sights, just beyond tomorrow's horizon.

CHAPTER SEVENTEEN
FAKENHAM

I'd never seen Fakenham – often dubbed 'the most boring town in Norfolk' – so lively. A chaos of Morris Minors had descended on the centre like a plague of ladybirds, and my campervan was hard-pressed to find a parking space. Minor mania had seized the crowds, who milled in the autumn sunshine, goggling at authentic renovations and customised curiosities. My VW had definitely turned up at the wrong party.

"Bertie, over here!" Monika from the Ukraine caught my attention, and I picked my way towards the bright red lips, false eyelashes, and jacked-up cleavage.

"You certainly look the part," I told her.

"I put the 'fake' in Fakenham, *darlink*," came the reply, moreish as Russian layer-cake.

'More like the 'ham',' I thought to myself: thank God she had toned it down somewhat for daytime realism.

"Cute huh?" said Jud absently. Was it Tilly he meant, or the nearby stall selling fluorescent Morris Minor hats and inflatable strap-on gear sticks: a garish kitschfest alongside which Monika's stretchy tracksuit and Day-Glo pink trainers would raise no eyebrows at all.

"No Boo?"

"He's resting up for the morning, wants to be in good shape for Wednesday."

"For the Gala Opening?"

"That too. But specially for when Luke gets back. He doesn't know what's been happening." Was it my imagination, or did Tilly show a moment's disappointment that my partner was heading home? I asked if she really had time for the illegals' stunt.

"I've ticked all the T&Cs in my head: let's do it!"

I steered them both back to my van and slid the side door open. Tilly got in, but Jud remained outside, gazing around as if he'd ascended into BMC porn heaven.

"This is the C23C spy-phone, so don't tamper with the settings. Just casually stick it on a coffee table or whatever. The range is excellent so we'll hear what everyone's saying."

"So I just press this for 'on'?" Tilly's hand brushed mine.

"Yes, and it pretends to be on standby, no lights, no beeps. If we hear trouble, we'll be in that door before you can say Action Man."

"Real SAS stuff. Thanks." She zipped the device into her pocket, touched my hand again, and we were back out in the sunshine.

"Take care, Tils." Jud pecked her affectionately, though his eyes were glued to a heavy metal Moggie, revving and sounding its klaxon.

"Guys, wish me luck," said Tilly. We walked her to Market Place, where I hugged her carefully, so as not to displace her enhanced boobs. We watched her disappear, straight-backed and confident, into the throng.

As we threaded through the car-stalls back to the van I was telling Jud how my nerves were jangling, when I noticed he was no longer with me. I found him deep in shouted conversation with two Morris Minor geeks and their souped-up creation.

"If you ever need another pair of hands," said Jud, "I've done loads of work in this line." He put a card in a man's hand, planning, I guessed, for a fall-back job in case Holkham Bygones Museum didn't work out for him.

"Cheers, but we gotta go," I said, digging Jud in the ribs. Why was he not fretting over Tilly, as I was? Just as I finally got him into my van, my new mobile rang.

"Shush, it's Tilly!"

"Just passing down the passage off Bridge Street from Market Place. Yah, I got it now, a yellow street-door, redbrick building."

"You're loud and clear this end," I said, plugging in dual earphones and a trailing mic so Jud and I could both be connected.

"Go upstairs, Tils," Jud said. "The blue door in front of you on the first-floor landin'."

"Yah, outside blue door," she whispered. "Here goes..."

She knocked twice, and we heard foreign voices. A door opened and we could hear a blaring telly being switched off.

"Hi, Yurik; this my wife, Katya."

"Hello. Please sit," came Katya's voice.

"Coffee, or little stronger? Yes, I think vodka," said Yurik.

I looked at Jud, shocked at the prospect of Tilly's hard-won sobriety being tested under this kind of pressure. He gave the thumbs-down.

"Oh, coffee. Black no sugar. *Spa-see-ba*." Tilly did sound Ukrainian, up to a point.

"So, you know Viktor?" Yurik said.

"From friend," Tilly replied.

"What friend?" asked Katya.

"Er... Jud. Car-mender. Norfolk boy. Months back."

Then came the fluent rigmarole of her birth in the ancient city of Kerch, her mother's terminal illness, and her need to find a passage home ASAP.

"How you come here... so many years... without passport?" Katya broke in.

"I was dancer, come to England with ballet, very young... but never go home to Ukraine. Long story. English boy, first love. He-he..." Tilly chuckled like a teenager. "He fix visa. Ah, con-nec-tions! But the big

262

break-up – my man unfaithful with fucking teen bitch-whore understudy slut. So I come to you for help. Yes?"

I eavesdropped intently; Jud's eyes grew wider and wider. Tilly was well-rehearsed, her accent seemed consistent, and was living the part: it was going as well as we could have hoped. But a mighty bang on the campervan door made us both jump. I could see a familiar, balding head tried to peer in, but my van had come with tinted one-way windows, just the thing for surveillance work.

"Shit!" It was Tel, my tame car park warden from the Blakeney Hotel, which was so unwittingly generous with its Wi-Fi signal. I gestured to Jud that I'd get rid of him pronto, then slid open the door. Chaotic sounds, and a tasty aroma, swam into the van.

"Wotcher!" said Tel, through a mouthful of pastry. "I 'ad a 'unch it was you. Fancy a Danish?" He offered a paper bag, close to my face. I covered the mic and pulled out my earphones.

"Look, Tel mate, you're too kind, but I'm a little bit busy at the mo." I jumped down on the tarmac. Tel backed away, still looking in at Jud – wired into the phone on the kitchenette table – and understandably trying to figure out what we were up to.

"Okay, no probs. See ya mate, back at the hotel sometime, eh?"

"Cheers, Tel."

I got back in the van, fearing I'd missed something crucial.

"Houston, we have a problem," said Jud. "Katya's got an uncle in Kerch."

"What you miss most about Kerch?" Katya was asking, as I rejoined their meeting. Turning my thoughts inward, I summoned my fly-on-the-wall mode, and envisaged Tilly's self-imposed ordeal. Outwardly poised, she was inwardly scrabbling through her web-trawlings for convincing details about a place she'd never visited in her life. All this, I thought, to prove to herself what she could do without a drink.

"Ah, so many things... more coffee please?" She was stalling, in need of a caffeine hit. A filter-coffee machine gurgled in the background, then a cup was placed right by the spy-phone, on a pound shop side-table. After a few moments' polite tittle-tattle, Yurik changed tack abruptly.

"I speak with Katya in kitchen!" A sound of folding doors followed: my CGI ghost, frustrated at merely following the proceedings, wished it could somehow influence events in Tilly's favour. Yurik seemed suspicious, and I feared things were about to get nasty.

Tilly was gasping, perhaps starting a panic attack under the alarming pressure. The sounds from the kitchen reminded me of foreign relatives murmuring at my mother's funeral. Tilly's increasingly restless movements, creaking against the *faux*-leather sofa, began to obscure the voices. She pulled a zip, indicating she must be getting hot. My own scalp was prickling.

"We got to go in." Jud jumped up, forgetting to remove his earphones. My new mobile swung down and cracked against the floor.

"Bloody moron! You've lost the connection!" I shouted.

Jud picked the phone up. It had shut off. I fumbled around, trying to reconnect with the Slavonic flat.

"Dude, this whole stupid thing's your fault!" Jud yelled. I kept pressing the power button.

"Well fuck that. I'm doing this for you!" I told him.

"If anythin' happens to Tils, it's you I'm gonna blame!"

"For fucksake, Jud, shut it!"

We dashed out, across the road towards Market Place, jostling through a cacophony that would have made Tilly inaudible even if I'd managed to retrieve the connection.

I don't know how many people cursed me as I bumped into them, while skunked-up Jud went on hollering at me like an idiot. But finally we reached the relative silence of the passage off Bridge Street, and stood panting outside the yellow door.

"Right Jud, shut the fuck up, while I try and hear what's going on up there." I shoved him, he shoved me back: a couple of squabbling yobs. But when I put my earphones in, the voices were clearer even than before. I raised my hand. Jud plugged as well, and we listened silently, standing tight in the entrance.

Disconcertingly, another mobile phone started ringing in the flat upstairs.

"Yes, Viktor!" Yurik shouted.

Not one word made any sense to me, except 'Monika' a couple of times. I imagined Tilly's craving for drink was reaching breaking point. Yurik rang off.

"You okay?" he asked her.

"Flushes – hot time of month," Tilly responded, a quiver in her voice. I fancied I saw Yurik gauging her like a horse he might put money on.

"Okay. Viktor happy. Bring five thousand cash to next pickup, and you have place on boat."

"Next landing, *vere* and *ven*?" Tilly's drifting accent reflected the Colditz-like tensions of the moment. I saw an exuberant glint in Jud's eye as we held our breath to hear the all-important details.

"Kelling Hard – tomorrow 5 a.m. – is too soon for you?"

"Absolutely super!" said Tilly, adrift again. "No problems, I know this place," she added, hoping to bury her brief burst of posh SW1. It seemed to work on Yurik: we heard him hug her as if she were a comrade-in-arms. Jud and I high-fived: a couple of *happy* yobs.

Our Mata Hari slipped out of the door and trotted downstairs. We greeted her in exuberant silence.

"Quick, back on to the main road," she whispered. "Katya likes looking out the window."

We emerged on Bridge Street, where the crowds were thinning: everybody seemed to be hurrying to the town centre, anticipating a drive-past.

"Guys, I could have murdered a stiff drink up there." Jud wrapped his tattooed arms around her.

"Never mind the stiff *drink*." He winked. "They don't call me 'Woody' for nothing."

Tilly blushed, and quickly changed the subject.

"So, Bertie, you heard everything, I take it? Landing 5 a.m. tomorrow, timing couldn't be better." She was visibly trembling.

"Let me get you a coffee?"

"I'd love to!" she shouted, over the cheering for the drive-past. "But there's nobody up at the Hall now and I've still got heaps of exhibits to label. I'll change and clean up there."

A surge in the crowd parted us.

"Diaries and notes, don't forget," she called, over the roar of engines and motor-horns as the Morris Minor cavalcade swept past us.

"Tuesday night okay?" I shouted.

"Yah, but sweetie..."

"Sorry, can't hear you."

Spectators were hollering madly, waving flags and sounding air-horns. The crush became claustrophobic. A fifty-something woman, bulging in a black PVC bikini and Hammer Horror cloak leftover from Halloween, screamed in my ear to sell raffle tickets. St John's Ambulance were rescuing a pensioner in a lilac raincoat, overcome by the throng.

"Call you," I gestured to Tilly, as I was borne further along the pavement, which scuppered any plan to get back to the car park with her. A side alley presented a sudden shortcut, and within moments Jud and I were escaping the human tide.

"Man, I owe you an apology," he panted as we approached my VW.

"No worries," I told him. "Get in."

I called ahead to the police station, where good old Sergeant Warren picked up. Massey was expected shortly, he said, to collect his mail before a lunch engagement: I'd have to be quick if I wanted to catch him. Though Wells was only a short hop from Fakenham, the traffic leaving town was a nightmare. It was a good fifteen minutes before we were clear of the classic car maelstrom.

"Brilliant operation, no?" I said to Jud, once the Wells road opened up ahead of us.

"Just one thing I regret," he said. "First time in years I haven't checked out all the motors."

Bloody redneck, I said to myself. Here I am straining to reach Massey, all for Jud's sake, and he just wants to prattle about classic cars. I didn't want another argument, but I didn't reply, and he stayed quiet, which suggested he'd understood my disapproval, my disappointment at his shallowness. Knowing the strength of his weed, I wondered if habitual use had warped his judgment, damped the heroic DNA he ought to have inherited from his Olympian ancestor. And so, when he suddenly spoke again, his choice of subject came as quite a shock.

'So, you believe in life after death, then?"

"Blimey, Jud, what makes you say that?"

"Tils tells me you're always windin' her up about ghosts and hauntin' and that."

"I'll tell you what I think," I started, with no idea what I was going to come out with. "Maybe ghosts and hauntings, in the old days, correspond to DNA and genetics in our time. Maybe something..."

"Somethin' gets passed on, you think?" said Jud. "Memories an' that, as well as what we look like?"

"Well I couldn't help noticing your tattoos," I said. "Aren't they like memories, of Skipper's history?"

"Not my memories, though. My nanna, Pearl, she paid for all that ink, for my twenty-first: she were the one that suggested it."

"As well as changing your name to Wood?"

"Better than a borin' old key to the door."

That remark made me very uncomfortable. But so did the idea of being gifted with indelible body art depicting my ancestors – whoever they might have been – or being obliged to use some forebear's name. Maybe this was just what they call 'Normal for Norfolk'.

"So, you look like Skipper, you wear his history on your skin – but nothing was passed on mentally. Is that what you're saying?"

"Don't be daft," said Jud, but not unkindly. "Do you have the same thoughts as your dad?"

Another uncomfortable remark: and for a moment the Secret Admirer's awful face filled my vision. Simultaneously, though, we reached Wells police station, and Massey's grey Audi was pulling up beside the campervan: so that difficult conversation died a welcome death.

"Inspector, could you spare us a moment?"

"What is it? I'm pushed for time already." I was dismayed by his curtness, given that we were now on first-name terms, and effectively sharing case notes. He must have been gagging for his lunch, of course; perhaps he was entitled to be moody. We followed him into the station.

"Jud, you tell the inspector..."

"Tell me what?" Massey barked, checking his watch, as Warren nodded to us and handed Massey a bundle of letters.

"I've got some inside information for you," Jud began.

"Have you really?" He surveyed Jud – and me for that matter – with contempt.

Jud hesitated, looking at me, then at the inspector, even over to the sergeant.

"Come on, come on, I've got work to do," Massey snapped.

"Viktor, who beat me up is landin' more illegals tomorrow," Jud eventually blurted. "Kellin' Hard. 5 a.m."

"Really?" Massey glared at Jud warily. "And he tipped you off to say sorry for the missing teeth?"

"It's a long story," I interjected, "a tricky set-up involving Viktor's agents in Fakenham. Jud arranged the whole thing."

I signalled Jud to stay quiet, fearing he was about to contradict me.

"His plan was to let the authorities – that's you, Inspector, catch Viktor red-handed on the beach, tomorrow morning."

Massey chucked his mail back on the reception desk. While his eyes widened, his hand dived for his groin. Nothing could have signalled his appetite for promotion more succinctly.

"Sergeant Warren, cancel my lunch meeting at The Blakeney Hotel and order some fish and chips."

"Your diet, sir..."

"Starts next week," said Massey, grinning at Jud and me. "Make that cod twice, double chips and mushy peas, bottle of ketchup, Coke two litres, buttered white four rounds." As his sidekick began ringing the order through, Massey boomed an afterthought, "Saveloy, Sergeant. Three!"

Christ, we were joining him for lunch! Jud and I exchanged glances: surely it was a sign we were off the 'most wanted' list in his mind, and becoming a valued part of his operation.

"You're not giving me much notice," said Massey, "but if your information's true – as it happened to be on the 'White Russian' case..."

"Any news on that?" I interrupted.

"There might be..." he said. "But first things first, if I'm to nail these Gyppos at dawn. Fakenham contacts: Sarge, take down the particulars."

Sergeant Warren took out a notepad, and Jud played Judas somewhat hesitantly: perhaps he was mindful of the oppressive regimes these illegals were fleeing from. And while they talked I thought of my own case. My mother had been a migrant – driven not by necessity but by pure whimsy – and the Secret Admirer, who knows where he sprang from. Luckily I possessed a British passport: but in other times, under other regimes, our family might have been the 'Gyppos' about to be 'nailed' as Yurik and Katya were now.

Massey leant his backside against the reception counter, supporting himself with both elbows on the polished wood, his belly rumbling, his eye on the clock above the door. I noticed, for the first time, an ornate onyx ring choking a chubby finger on his right hand. He was indeed a Freemason, as Tilly had intimated. There would be no end to the strings he could pull.

"One thing, Inspector... this will bode well for Jud, won't it?" I asked.

"One good turn deserves another," he said. "Is that what you mean? Sarge, get me the chief super on the blower?"

Jud at last was looking excited at the prospect of his good turn buying him some leniency. I only hoped Massey would keep his word.

"Thanks, Clive, we really value your help," I said. Relations might be warming up, but I assumed the man could still appreciate flattery. Massey registered only the arrival of the delivery boy, relieved him of the two bulging carrier bags, and started trundling towards his office. I signalled to Jud that we should follow and again asked about the Boleyn Bureau investigation. The aroma of the upcoming lunch was good: but without a further word the inspector slammed his door and pulled down the blind. Surely he couldn't scoff the lot by himself?

Jud and I stood outside, nonplussed. Massey's nameplate had claimed my attention on several occasions: reading it backwards, I'd tried to make sense of 'Yessam' and 'Evilc', without success. This time, though, I said it out loud: "'Yes, am Evil C'," just about summed the bastard up. So much for my integration into the fraternity of investigators.

"Did you ever find your dog?" the sergeant enquired as we turned to leave. I thanked him and reported that Boo was doing well.

A burst of anxiety swept up from my bowels. I looked up at the clock. I'd left Boo for hours. The sicko Admirer might have seized the opportunity of my being away.

"Look, I gotta go..."

"You okay?" Jud asked, following me out.

"Got to dash."

"Cool, I can walk it from here. Oh man, thanks: you're a star!"

"No worries. Fingers crossed Massey nails Viktor," I called to him as I unlocked the van, dizzy with worry.

Trees flashed by the corners of my twitching eyes. My breath shortened, horrors filled my thoughts. What would I find when I got home? I continually felt for the boathouse keys in my pocket.

"Oh God, God!" I yelled, banging the steering wheel. The whole journey back to 'Wood Feels' – careless of speed limits – I had Boo's winsome face hanging constantly before my swimming eyes.

CHAPTER EIGHTEEN
TIPPING POINT

My 'cedar mausoleum' – as James had described it – felt stale and empty the moment I unlocked.

"Boo?" I whispered, sniffing the woody air for traces of my loathsome father. No response. My right eyelid flickered like a paparazzo's shutter. Up the stairs – death click before the landing – and I was stooping over Boo's basket in the bedroom. One clean swipe removed the blanket. He was gone.

'*Calma*, Roberto.'

I opened the circular shutters to the porthole window, the better to search the room. Childlike fears flooded my mind, of mother's Secret Admirer ripping out my dog's windpipe. To survive the tidal surge, only to die like this? My adult self tried to rationalise: how could the Admirer possibly have got in when I had checked countless times before leaving the boathouse in lockdown? Obviously, the sick bastard must have a key.

"Come out, you cowardly fucker!" I yelled, whipping away the throw and peering under the Baroque bed, reversing our positions the day I'd hidden from him in my dead mother's room. The space was bare. But as my breathing subsided, I fancied I could hear Boo whimpering. Once again armed with my Eco-Designer trophy, brandishing it like a baseball bat, I approached the *en suite* bathroom.

"One hair harmed and you die, father or no father!" I bellowed. Boo managed a faint bark, but there was nothing from his assailant. Careless of consequence, I aimed a punch-kick at the door, right by the old lock. The jamb ripped apart, the dark bathroom gaped. I reached for the light switch.

Boo was cowering under the washstand. I advanced toward the freestanding copper bath, high on its plinth. If the Admirer was lying in its depths, like a stowaway in a lifeboat, he would be invisible from the doorway. I raised the hardwood club above my head, and brought it down with my full force into the bathtub. The hollow echo sent Boo scampering.

'There's nobody here but you!' said the *putto* in my head. I sank to my knees. My torment, at the imaginary hands of this historic nemesis, seemed relentless. Boo was scratching to get out. The door had shut, as was its habit. He must have got trapped on a visit to drink from his bathroom bowl. Nobody had broken in. When would these mind games end?

It took me a long while to settle down and Boo watched me warily for further inexplicable violence. I thought about Luke coming home to a partner who, in a matter of weeks, had turned into a quivering paranoiac. All the more reason, I realised, to get on with the diaries, and find the Skipper Wood clues that might allay his ghost and allow me to sleep at nights.

I coaxed Boo downstairs, and let him out to do his business. By the time I'd reactivated the woodburner, I saw him waiting patiently – back to his normal gentlemanly ways – beyond the glass of the doors. I let him in and settled into my club chair – a symbolic anchor to happier, London days – to return to World War One.

18th July 1916

Sgt Sellars, during his last round, had happened upon Caleb Bacon on night watch. Over a cigarette, the subject of Skipper Wood having come up, Bacon had suggested that Skipper's services to me extended 'beyond his remit, into impropriety'. I told Sellars to go back and order the Private to remain on his fire-step, devoting his full attention to watching the Hun, and nothing else.

Now I get it, I thought: Stanley Sellars and James had some kind of understanding, by which Skipper Wood was accepted without question as his lordship's companion. Might Sellars therefore have had knowledge of something more substantial than a 'bromance' between master and servant? It would have mirrored the intimacy that – assuming my hunch was right – had existed many years earlier, between himself and Lord James.

Sellars, I remembered reading, had risen from a young clerk, under the auspices of Lord Randolph, to become James's trusted estate accountant. James's regular disbursements to the second-rate carpenter went through the Audit House ledgers. Sellars would have suspected blackmail: but perhaps he knew his place, not to question? Or did some other duty – a bond of admiration, or even love – still bind him to James?

I walked through the trenches of Captain James's war as if I were an avatar, watching campaign after campaign unfold as the longhand on his harrowing pages sprang into life. Personal tensions seethed and simmered, climaxing in the aftermath of his battalion's battle at the Somme village of Longueval.

19th July 1916
Men fell like skittles under a stultifying barrage, but onwards the gallant company drove. We succeeded in recapturing part of Delville Wood, although at bitter cost: three hundred lost at last count, as streams of stretcher-bearers brought the dead home.

Following this terrible battering the 8th Norfolks were sent back to the support trenches to recuperate.

Billeted in roofless farm buildings surrounding a *château* smashed by crossfire, James felt a stark omen of what might befall Samphire Hall should Great Britain lose this war.

On a brighter note his friend Countess Daisy had, exploiting influential connections, arranged a shipment of luxury goods from home: chocolate, biscuits, Scotch and tobacco for the troops; and, for James personally, two dozen bottles of his beloved absinthe.

20th July 1916 – p.m.
My good Sellars played his harmonica: the homesick soldiers sang spiritedly, in barns open to the night sky. Yet my lightened mood was short-lived. Cocky Bacon brushed by the officers' table, whispering 'You beautiful doll!' in my ear. He treads dangerously close to the mark.

Caleb swaggers off toward his sleeping quarters, his parting shot a vile sneer. A fellow officer comments on James's ashen visage, as if he has 'seen a ghost'. Was this a sign that he'd sensed my presence, a witness from the future monitoring his crisis as it unfolded? James excuses himself to retire early.

Back in what passes for an officers' mess he broaches a fresh bottle of absinthe, spitting out the cork. First he toasts Countess Daisy's largesse, and then he curses Private Bacon for persecuting him 'like a trench rat'. He lights a cigarette – dragonlike smoke gushes from his nostrils – and pours out frustration to his one true *confidant*: his diary.

20th July 1916 – p.m.
Death rains down upon us, like a Great Plague on the Egyptians – and this little serpent is proving one plague too many.

He lies on his unyielding War Office bed, listening to distant mortar fire, fuelling his dream of revenge with drink until he can stand it no longer. Has he not kept his part of the bargain, ensuring that the pestilential Bacon's family shall want for nothing? His indignation boils over into rage, and he jumps to the ground, ties his boots, hastily buttoning a woollen coat. Then, by the faint light of a new moon, he picks his menacing way across the night-still camp towards Caleb's open-air quarters.

The battle-weary lads lie stupefied, thanks to Countess Daisy's largesse. James seeks out Caleb's makeshift bed: just to be sure, he flips his paraffin lighter for a second. He stoops to pull a jute cord from his pocket, wraps it round the soldier's scrawny neck. He slowly tightens the ligature. My eyes widen. Bacon squirms, little eyes bulging. James's face looms so close that his bristles scrape Caleb's pale cheeks. A soldier in the next bed groans, momentarily awakened. James holds Caleb stone-still until the neighbour rolls over, back to sleep.

21st July 1916 – 2 a.m.
"Hush… Private Bacon 1369!" He gasped for mercy, frantically grappling to free the grip of my slipknot. "Take heed, filthy toerag! These threats will cease, or your funds will be paid no more." He nodded his pathetic head in desperate agreement. I let go – tantalisingly on the *very* brink – having overcome my visceral desire to snuff out his rotten existence.

It was astounding. James – or his 'dark passenger' – had come perilously close to murdering one of his own Tommies. Yet in the battalion's eyes young Captain James, their aristocratic role model, could do no wrong.

25th September 1916
I am unworthy of the adulation of my men. Sellars, moved and proud, claims Pater would have applauded my courage.

Truth to tell, I do risk life and limb in nightly sorties to reconnoitre fresh avenues into enemy lines, part of the Big Push. But pigs would fly, the day Pater congratulated this unworthy scion!

Lord James, for all his vicious foibles, continued to beguile me. As I read on in his troubled diaries I was filled with admiration for his modest bravery, at a place named Schwaben Redoubt, on 4th October 1916, which earned him one of the highest awards for gallantry: the Military Cross, and some time recuperating in a field hospital, having suffered a fractured rib.

A telegram is brought to his bed by Sergeant Sellars. James beams at Sellars. The heartening message, sent by a professor at the Royal College of Surgeons, commends his prosthetic models – 0A16 to 0A20 are now in production – for their 'outstanding contribution to the quality of life for soldiers maimed in the European war'. The College, he learns, wishes to honour him with a special presentation when he is next on leave.

James must feel tormented by the knowledge that the income from his patents will largely end up in Bacon's coffers. But the salons of London society know and care only about the dashing captain's heroism.

And James's glittering reputation meant he had more than ever to lose if one particular Tommy – now crippled with jealousy, as he'd once been by Skipper's celebrity – dared to make the revelations he'd been threatening. I closed the diary, puzzled, energy sapped by my psychic involvement. After all this reading – sore eyes, aching back – the core of James's nature remained uncertain. Was his patriotic courage just reckless penance for crimes past, or was he *genuinely* the man of honour who filled me with instinctive awe? My notes might seem inconclusive, but at least they were fulfilling my obligation to Tilly... assuming she could decipher the scrawl.

Boo whined, and I looked at the clock: almost six already. I headed for the kitchen – diary in hand – and scrambled some eggs, one of his favourite human foods. Boo's helping soon vanished and I sat down at the kitchen table in front of my own. But my mind was filled with the impact of shells, and maddening rainwater dripping into tin cups from a bunker roof. The evidence I needed, to restore peace and sanity to my own life, was surely somewhere in James's pages. I found I'd brought the volume dated 1917 to the table.

20th January 1917

The weasel now informs me he keeps a floozy, a dancer from the Pavilion Theatre on Cromer Pier, and requires a double disbursement to keep both mistress and wife in the style to which they have grown accustomed. I acquiesce *pro tem*, although news has come in that will shift the balance of power: old Inspector Colman has died from the influenza. Checkmate Bacon!

'Checkmate Bacon!'? James's strange words opened a sudden vista, in my mind, in which the Edwardian boathouse scene presented like a chessboard, crowded with pieces poised for a denouement, an endgame in which the subtle equilibrium of their positions and powers would reach a tipping point, beyond which devastation lay.

But for whom? As if I'd been endowed with a moment's crystal clarity, logic illuminated a path through the tangled evidence at my disposal.

Inspector Colman was gone, taking with him the knowledge that Caleb Bacon's blood-spattered cap had been found near the corpse. That simple anomaly was the difference between a mere mortal accident and a scene of foul play. Hence James's relief. But why had he ever wished the cap hidden from the police? To prevent anyone knowing he'd used Caleb as his messenger, thereby enhancing the humiliation of Skipper's dismissal? A weak motive, but it proved lucky. Since nothing could now prove Bacon had been at the boathouse, his blackmailing power would be seriously weakened. His lowly word against that of the aristocrat, the war hero? If James flatly denied that Bacon had been his pawn – and he'd fortuitously burnt the letter containing Caleb's instructions – people would instinctively believe him. Nobody knew about Skipper's dalliance with Alice... so nobody would imagine James had a motive to kill Skipper, or to attempt to frame Bacon for doing that same job. Hell, nobody even thought Skipper had been murdered!

Then, a qualm. James must have known Caleb would never blab: the minute he did, his income-stream would dry up. And James could easily prove he'd been blackmailed: his bank could provide details of myriad payments. But if you pay a blackmailer, aren't you admitting guilt? So... and my heart thumped afresh when I reached this conclusion... either James really was guilty of murder (and I loathed the prospect of believing that) or the blackmail was not about Skipper's death, but his sexuality. Which was I to believe?

To my modern sensibility, one choice was still a hateful crime: the other was positively endearing. But the Edwardian world would have seen things very differently. Maybe James believed that Bacon could really prove that he and Skipper had been more than friends. And if that scandal broke, people would swallow it, thinking it made sense of his puzzling estrangement from Alice, which was no doubt apparent way beyond the flinted confines of Samphire Hall. Poor Beulah Wood would have been shamed by association... and by her own brother's revelations. So that meant... what did it mean? Why was James so preoccupied with Sellars?

As quickly as it had arisen this lucid dream, this hallucinatory clarity, came to an end: it was as if a flare, sent up on a battlefield, had fallen back to earth and been doused in the swamp of my speculations. I left my cold supper, wandered back through the hallway, unlocking shutters and French doors in hopes that some evening air would refresh my puzzled mind. I had to get to the bottom of this saga before the night was through.

The kitchen radio had reminded me that the clocks were due to go back: I had an extra hour! Boo followed me back into the lounge, and I resumed my speed-reading, holding the diary up as I paced around. It was not enough to have glimpsed the endgame. I had to see the fall of the pieces, and applaud the last man standing. I scarcely dared to acknowledge what I was hoping as I found myself back at the Western Front, among the smouldering craters of the Somme, awaiting a showdown between the adversaries.

James arises from his coarse bed – sacking filled with horsehair – long before dawn. An oil lamp throws shadows round his dank dugout as he devotes his habitual few moments to noting the day's schedule.

17th February 1917 – a.m.
Objective South Miraumont Trench and Boom Ravine: my 8th Norfolks, 18th Eastern Division, 53rd Brigade, are to be deployed at 'Oxford Circus' between Grandcourt Trench and The Gully. Curious how homesick soldiers name posts – neither familiar nor friendly – after favourite London landmarks.

A mirror hangs above a pitcher. James douses his face with icy water and then, catching sight of his cracked reflection, runs a hand across many days' growth of bristles. He stares at himself so long that I grow concerned. Is he somehow seeing me in that reflection, photobombing him, as it were, from another century, through the intensity of my involvement in his writings?

He combs his thick black hair – with the last of his pomade – into a glossy side parting that foreshadows the matinee idol archetype of war films to come. At last he stops gazing, at whatever he's been seeing in that fragment of mirror, and writes again.

17th February 1917 – a.m.

Five years to the day – bleakest France, the blackest of anniversaries – my son Robbie, stillborn, a curse not only on my kin, but on Anne Boleyn's head too – had I not felled her sacred cedar, I might have a son and heir today. Joy that cannot be.

This reference to a sentimental anniversary surely showed that the man I so longed to trust could not be a monster, like my own father.

"Good God, Boo: he even called his son 'Robbie'!" I took to the comfort of my special chair, shaken to have come across my namesake – short-lived though the poor child was – in the story of Lord James's life.

Back in the bunker, James raises the lantern to inspect the stain of German blood on his breast pocket: not a good look for an officer leading his troops into battle. His quarters offer no means to erase the blemish, so he pins his Military Cross over it, though he knows it will mark him as a target. Is this a sign that he's already contemplating suicide, I wondered, a way out of his manifold troubles? The seed of a self-destructive impulse to which he will finally succumb, in 1929, on the veranda of my own boathouse? James dresses in his full khakis, fills his hip flask with absinthe, and steps out of his bunker into the war-torn trench.

Tommies are queuing in dark mist by the latrines, in the civilised fashion only the English can muster. Hurrying past, James is greeted with the respect due to his rank, except by Private Bacon, who whistles a snatch of Skipper Wood's maddening song. Even nearly a hundred years ahead, I have a bad feeling in the pit of my stomach...

James and his company make slow progress initially. A thaw has set in, making the ground sodden. A dense fog, reminding him of the sea frets over the saltmarshes of his homeland, blights their vision. Its saving grace, though, is that it shields his battalion from the enemy.

'A' Company, and the sappers from 'C' Company, disperse down the face of a treacherous gorge, through the barbed-wire entanglements of Grandcourt Trench, slipping and sliding through the darkness into the ravine. Painful cries tell of twisted limbs, ankles fractured. The men lie still each time shells burst overhead, their orange detonations the only hints of light at this hour in an unforgiving winter.

And as fate would have it, the next blast of mortar fire reveals to James that he has been trailing Caleb Bacon in the darkness. They are separated from their company, both panting heavily. James hears Bacon trip, slipping down the gully. He halts, listening to the silence. Then a yell of pain: the private has injured himself in the fall. Captain James's duty is to help a fellow soldier in need, but this is no ordinary Tommy...

17th February 1917 – p.m.

Bacon had crossed my path – the King of Darkness shrouded us in His cloak of isolation – my fallen prey, stranded in the mud-flow, his leg buckled.

Bacon hears James scrambling down the scree, calls out nervously, "Friend or foe?" Another shell explodes overhead – Roman candles at a gala opening – starkly revealing their faces. Caleb gasps.

"Foe!" James's black eyes glare as he pulls his dagger from its sheath.

"No!" I shout. Boo jumps up in shock.

'*Calma*, Roberto.'

James, an agitated animal, sweeps his quick gaze all around. *There's nobody here but me.* He plunges his blade deep into Caleb's gut. He twists it like a key in a lock, until blood spills from the private's lips. Bacon's body convulses, and one last gasp – "Sellars!" – escapes him before he goes still, sinking back into the reddening sludge.

I drop the diary, devastated by this terrible turn of events. So much for that elusive, soul-bearing 'testimony' James had promised to write. Nothing could prove him 'a man of honour' now.

Boo comes by to comfort me as I slide from the sanctuary of my chair to the cedar-planked floor, weak with despair and the mental exertions of my time-travelling. My eyes are sore and wet with pitiful disillusion. The one, key character I have grown to trust has let me down – just like everybody else in my life.

It was as if I had awoken from a nightmare, and it was going to take all my investigative powers – my psychic CGI – to get back into the moment. Yet this was one bad dream I just had to revisit, to discover what happened next.

James falls to his knees in the mire, murmuring how he is paying for the sins of his forefathers, crying his poor Robbie's name, as if killing Bacon was some kind of sacrificial atonement. Sobbing with shame, he rips the medal from his uniform and flings it deep into the ravine.

Sobbing 'with shame', he wrote, 'not satisfaction'. Was this a psychopathic diarist covering his traces? Had he also sobbed on killing Skipper? For it surely seemed probable – if any of the diary was true – that both victims had died by the one, vengeful hand. As I feverishly found my place, once again immersed in the stench of no-man's-land, I found James hastily purging the bloody traces from his dagger, as a fast patrol approached.

17th February 1917 – p.m.
Caleb Bacon was no more of this world. His corpse, half-sunken in muck, looked like an enemy killing. Over his face I placed his bloodied cap – sickeningly reminiscent of the portentous cap Colman found by Skipper's body.

Further down the line James encounters another detachment, soldiers from the 10th Essex, in a bad way, laying amid dozens of Allied and German bodies peppered across the broken terrain. Sniper fire makes him duck for cover: he sees the face of Caleb in every dead soldier illuminated by the rockets. Despite being rid of his accuser and blackmailer, he is still tortured... by whatever Caleb might have imparted to the loyal Sellars.

A Tommy moans in dreadful pain, distracting James from harrowing thoughts. He crawls along the freezing ground to comfort him. The soldier's head is bandaged with a torn shirt, his teeth chatter in the charred vestiges of a dawn so grim it might as well have been a nuclear winter. Captain James Newton-Grey removes his own jacket and lays it over the soldier's chest: sitting cross-legged, he lifts the boy's head on to his lap. He lets the lad swig from his silver flask, precious absinthe to numb his suffering. My failing spirits are lifted by James's compassion. He listens to the lad's quiet tales: his upbringing on a farm near Epping Forest, with his collie, in 'the greenest countryside you ever did see'; his couple of years as a footman, then his big break, landing a job as steward on a White Star Liner, the RMS *Titanic*.

James tells the young Tommy how his own wife survived the sinking, how he longs for her now. Equally quietly he talks of the brief life they shared, how he wishes one could travel back in time and put things right. He talks about Robbie, and how he never knew the love of his own son. But the boy soldier on his lap starts convulsing, gasping, and without warning he passes away in James's arms. James sobs, I sob too. He recites as much of the Lord's Prayer as he can manage, then covers the boy's face with his jacket.

Harsh shreds of morning reveal a number of felled soldiers clasping photos and letters from loved ones. James pulls his own wallet out, his face overwritten with heartache as he contemplates a photograph. As he tilts his paraffin lighter, hot tears blur his vision; I lean over his shoulder for a closer look, but he snaps the lighter shut and speedily closes the wallet. His diary does not mention whose image he carries so close to his heart. My avatar feels cheated, bewildered.

James's gritty eyes widen with a wild glare, as if he's possessed by more than the adrenaline of assassinating his countryman: and before he can come to his senses, he's screaming at the Hun, "Come on, do your worst, shoot!" I am truly watching a man bent on suicide now.

But a platoon of the 8th Norfolks hears his cry through the morning mist, atop the parapet overlooking the ravine. They take James's raving as an incitement to patriotic valour. Wielding bayonets, inspired to heroism by his extreme passion, they descend into the valley of death, hollering some undecipherable battle cry. I turn away with fear like a man facing a firing squad.

As the gunfire dies down I hear James's voice, close by me in the smoke, muttering "By George!" in disbelief. To my astonishment white flags appear, as hundreds of Germans clamber out of their funk holes, at every point of the compass, to surrender.

17th February 1917 – p.m.

Boom Ravine was won – alas with a heavy toll of casualties – worst of all, from my selfish perspective, my colour sergeant, the good Stanley Sellars: missing at roll call. To my chagrin nobody has seen him since we left Grandcourt Trench.

21st February 1917 – a.m.

It is said that I single-handedly brought the Boche to their knees, forcing their retreat right to the Hindenburg Line. No, no! I am to be awarded the Victoria Cross, and promoted to the rank of major, both honours of which I am wholly unworthy. A white feather is more fitting for my buttonhole, as my secret rots undiscovered in no-man's-land.

Yet there, pinned in James's diary, was the telegram from his Royal Highness King George V, praising Captain James Newton-Grey for outstanding valour in the field of battle: a must for Tilly's exhibition, surely. But James himself, the tormented soul inside the hollow hero, was not only mortified by this misconception of his bravery – citing his brigade as the real heroes – but was avidly monitoring every stretcher that came back from the Front, in an increasingly desperate search for his sergeant. It seemed the enigmatic Stanley Sellars had vanished.

And just as I was about to take a shower, by way of a breather, I heard a car in the scented alley, quick footsteps, and a tap on the glass of the French doors.

Boo pattered over to investigate.

CHAPTER NINETEEN
SOWING SEED

"It's me."

"Tilly!" I opened up. "Come in, you're soaking." Something was wrong: even in the low light I could see her eyes were bloodshot.

"I had to see you," she said. "Sorry I didn't call first."

"What's wrong?" I took her sodden reefer coat and showed her through.

"I'm at my wits' end, that's what," she croaked.

"What d'you mean?"

"Just that Jud is getting too heavy, really. And most of the time he's stoned and he knows I'm trying my best to stay sober." She rubbed her wet hair; black ringlets cascaded on to her forehead. I fetched her a warm towel from the downstairs loo rail.

"Do you want me to have a word?"

"Oh Bertie, I am so damn confused."

"I thought you two were... well... into each other?"

"He's eye candy... but he's not exactly the catch of the century." Her tears welled up.

I tightened the cord of my sweatpants and straightened my V-neck jumper, suddenly conscious of my slovenly appearance.

"You're saying there's something missing?" I knew what was missing: a hug. But I didn't dare.

"I'm making such a fool of myself..." she whimpered, wiping her eyes with one hand, digging with the other in her jeans pocket. She found a dog treat for Boo, who gobbled it down then sat by her like some living sculpture, willing her on.

"No, but you're being a bit hard on yourself; this sober routine, it's still so new, it's screwing with your emotions."

"It's all getting too much," said Tilly, fresh tears streaming.

"Fakenham this morning... has the strain caught up a bit?" I fought the urge to take her in my arms.

"I was desperate not to let the side down."

"I was so worried about you. And Jud owes you. I'll put the kettle on, okay?" She followed me into the kitchen.

"Where's Victoria Albertina? Boo's missing her: look how he follows you round."

"Back at the cottage. Jud-sitting."

Our eyes met, then dropped. We listened to the angry winds. Sea spray drenched the windows, like a car wash. Debris clipped the veranda, and the whole boathouse seemed to shudder. When the kettle whistled like a steam train, I came over all *Brief Encounter*.

"Another tough storm," I observed, to stop myself blurting anything more heartfelt. I handed Tilly a spare cardigan from the back of a chair.

"Thanks, it is a bit draughty."

"Let's take the coffee in by the fire," I suggested.

"Oh, no!"

"Typical Norfolk: first sign of a storm and the power goes down. Hang on, we've got candles." I felt around, shuffling towards the dresser.

"I think I've got a light." As Tilly fished in her pocket I dropped a candle into a jar. Her matches were damp, but when she eventually struck flame she smiled up at me, through the glow, with boyish charm. We touched foreheads. Disconcertingly, I was already turned on at half-mast.

Back in the lounge, side by side on the sofa, we listened to the cacophony for a while: the pinewoods dancing hip-hop style to the wind's rap, while gyrating flames threw a disco lightshow over the walls. Tilly had never looked sexier. It would have been the perfect seduction scenario, in a world where we were both unattached.

"Don't worry," I offered. "Everything will turn out okay."

"Nice of you to say so," she said, with a wry smile. "But you know the real problem?"

"What?"

"It's you."

"Me?"

"I've adored you since the day we met, on your veranda. Jud is sweet, but he just doesn't have... your sensitivity." My ego was stoked, her vulnerability smouldered. Time to play the martyr.

"Go with the flow: by Christmas you'll probably be besotted with him. But you know what my predicament is." I reached for a cushion to lie across my sweatpants, where a second predicament was growing more and more obvious. "Luke comes home on Wednesday."

"Shush, no more. I've never been a home wrecker." But she closed her eyes and dropped her head on my shoulder. I put my arm around her, just a brotherly gesture. Our silence spoke volumes, of a story stillborn, too sad for comment. I broached a more businesslike topic.

"If this weather carries on there'll be no immigrants in the morning for Massey to nab." But Tilly was already asleep. The firelight, playing over her shirt, highlighted the delicious rise and fall of her pert breasts. I teased the sofa throw over her a bit, before lying back to try and rest my head.

The warmth, and Tilly's Mediterranean fragrance, transported me into another surreal dreamscape. Major James Newton-Grey, former matinee idol and war hero, was now a faded, silver fox figure – notwithstanding his suicide here on my veranda. In his lap he was cradling a healthy baby – notwithstanding the stillbirth I'd so lately seen commemorated in his diary. He was whispering into the child's little ear as if both their lives depended on the transmission of some particular secret. But pealing bells – the carillon from some Italianate bell-tower, or the chime of my new mobile asking to be charged – summoned me home.

Tilly and I awoke to mere embers in the woodburner, and the solitary glimmer of the candle, now swollen with veins of hot wax. We shivered closer under the throw – my lust now past hiding – and kissed gently, passionately. I felt Tilly's hand sliding down, below the Plimsoll line of our fidelities. But just as my own trembling fingers were setting out into no-man's-land, she bottled out.

"Bertie, I best get home," she whispered. "BFT will be missing me." Not Jud, I noticed.

"We've got a spare room," I said softly. "You need some proper rest. Don't risk driving now: we don't want a tree falling on your car." This grim detail was my attempt to banish any sexual thoughts, so I could dare to stand up in my flimsy sweatpants.

"I don't want to encroach." She yawned.

I wanted to assure her she could never encroach, to thank her for coming over, to beg forgiveness for leading her on: but that would all have been far too Am Dram even for Tilly. Going to the other end of the subtlety spectrum, I simply told her she was too knackered to leave. Then I dragged her to her feet, took her hand, and the little stump of candle, and led her to the downstairs bedroom.

"Ooh, Bertie."

"That's a wind-up LED lantern on the bedside table. Extra blankets in the under-drawer. Loo's through there, and a spare dressing gown behind the door. Make yourself at home."

"Goodnight, then." Tilly sounded a little disappointed, or so I told myself. "You think of everything. As usual."

"Sleep well." I sighed and closed her door.

Boo was snoring in his basket: not much of a sentry for the sleeping beauty. I felt my way upstairs and into the big bed, shifting across for once to lie on Luke's side, some kind of statement of loyalty. But it was unearthly cold, as if I'd lain down in his grave. As I set about relieving myself, to purge erotic tension, the potency of the bed itself overwhelmed me. This had been James and Alice's honeymoon suite... where some absinthe-driven sex game had destroyed their relationship. Which side of the bed was James's, which Alice's? My wank was guilty, brief, joyless. I can't write down whose face was hovering over me as I came, but, on lapsing into nightmare, I found myself giving birth to his dead child.

God knows, I was never happier to wake when morning showed its face. The stillbirth was Boo, curled up on the bed, alive and well. The power was back on. I freshened up, dressed, went downstairs: I could hear Tilly showering. I lit the woodburner and put some coffee on. It was just eight o'clock as I turned on the radio.

"And now some breaking news: in a dawn operation this morning at Kelling Hard Norfolk police arrested thirteen illegal immigrants." I stopped buttering, mid-toast. "Organised criminals who brought them ashore are also in custody. Details are sketchy at present: stay tuned for a full report." I suddenly sat down, weak with relief.

"Good morning," said Tilly, smiling in the doorway.

"Did you catch that? Sounds as if Massey's got Viktor."

"You sound surprised?"

"Well Monika did a great job, no question. Nice to know Massey's not completely useless. Best of all, Jud should be okay now. Massey's virtually agreed to drop charges."

"Lucky Jud, I'll call him from the Hall," Tilly exclaimed. I was thrilled to see her so animated, after last night's miseries. "Bertie, it's all been down to you."

"Teamwork," I told her.

"One less thing to worry about, anyway?" she replied, not entirely convincingly.

"We should try and count our blessings."

"We should," she said. "You're one of mine." She sipped her coffee and nibbled the toast, but she was soon on her feet. "Bertie, I'll take your notes and the diaries with me now, please."

"Look," I began, "I'm up to 1917 now: can I just give you the earlier ones, to be getting on with? I'll bring the rest – and masses of notes – up to the Hall tomorrow morning first thing?" Tilly looked doubtful. "Promise," I added, with my breeziest smile.

"Of course *I* trust you," she said slowly. "But Dr Wulff, I don't think he trusts anyone. We'll have to hope 1910 to 1916 – is that right? – will keep him happy." Then she brightened. "Bertie, I can't wait to show you what I've been doing, presenting Lord James's personal effects, and related artefacts. It's going to be really fab!"

"Can't wait; and fingers still crossed for the Boleyn Bureau, eh?" I was sure Massey had been about to reveal some news, before the saveloys swallowed his attention. But I had news for Tilly too. "Before you get to work, there's something I've been wanting to tell you."

She gave me a wary look, as if I were about to start analysing last night's indiscretions – putdowns from her about Jud, hard-ons from me about her.

"I really can't cope with any more stress right now."

"It's just... that key Jud's got tattooed on his..."

"For heaven's sake..." she interrupted.

"Can I tell you why I'm so interested in it?"

"For God's sake, Bertie..." Her cheeks flushed. She buttoned up her reefer coat and glanced pointedly at her watch.

"Just hear me out?" She was halfway to the door. "You know I showed you that old, ornate key?"

"Sorry," she said immediately. "I meant to tell Karsten all about that. I'll catch him today, promise. Keys are his baby."

"Then he'll want to know where I found it. Right there, in the second step. Hidden by Skipper Wood. Instructed by Lord James."

She put on a stripy scarf and gave me a quizzical look.

"It fits a secret door in the Boleyn Bureau. I was so close to opening it, but the thieves turned up at The Watch House. The day Boo and I nearly drowned."

Tilly pulled a beanie hat from her bag and continued to eye me sceptically.

"Behind the secret door is a document, a confession. The name of the killer!"

She could keep quiet no longer.

"What killer?"

"Skipper's killer, of course."

She let out an exasperated laugh.

"Bertie, you're losing the plot. What's Skipper Wood to Anne Boleyn, for crying out loud?" She pulled the hat down her forehead deliberately, challengingly.

"Think of your exhibition! James's treasure hunt: the engraved name on the Boleyn step, leads to a key, leads to Anne's bureau. What a story!"

"I'm a professional historian, not Enid fucking Blyton."

"Look, it makes sense. Trust me. James hides it in case he gets accused of the murder himself – because of his close relationship with Skipper."

"You're about to tell me James and Skipper were gay lovers, aren't you?" she said sternly.

"Well you're the one who says I'm so sensitive…"

"Bertie, that's enough, I'm really off…" I followed her to the threshold, very anxious that she seemed so tense. But halfway to her four-by-four, she ran back to give me a kiss. "Thanks for everything!" she whispered in my ear. "You're quite mad, but I still wish…"

"You wish I could get the BB back for your Gala Opening?"

"That too."

"And if I do, here's an idea – a mad idea, if you like – to crown your whole presentation. We get Massey along to open up the secret compartment, and he solves Skipper's murder in front of all the TV cameras!"

"No, Bertie, absolutely not, okay. Save that for the Agatha Christie convention," she said. "Now look, I'm running very late…" She turned sharply around.

"Of course. I'll ring you later," I called, as her jeep disappeared up the scented alley. Was I conning myself, or had I sown a useful seed? There was still a way to go, of course.

The storm seemed to have passed without a great trail of damage. I sniffed the crisp air.

"Come Boo: a lot to do today…"

I locked up with care, a little more at ease than I had felt in weeks. Maybe Tilly had done something for my confidence. Or maybe it was the fact that Luke was due home so very soon.

I crunched out across the saltmarshes, nose dripping in the chill, breath condensing all around. Boo scouted ahead, his handsome scarlet coat a dash of exotic colour in a monochrome coastscape. It gladdened my heart to see him strong and happy after all the threats, real and imaginary, he'd had to face.

We rambled a good forty minutes without seeing a soul: this really was a no-man's-land. The moment we got home, I sat at the kitchen table to list my Monday tasks: 'Diary 1917', 'Call Massey re: BB and Jud', 'Diary 1918', 'Tilly's notes (urgent!)'. 'Get bathroom door fixed.' And I'm done.

But nothing is ever simple. Just as I opened James's diary, ready to rejoin him in the trenches, a loud knock made me spring up, like a private soldier coming to attention in the presence of his commanding officer.

"Friend or foe?" I called.

CHAPTER TWENTY
AN INSPECTOR CALLS

Massey rolled in, momentous as a tank. Boo took cover under the kitchen table, while I trailed the inspector into the lounge.

"Friend, today," he grunted. "I've got news for you."

"Really. Some tea?"

"Two sugars. I'll sit here." He came to rest in my special chair; the castors protested, but nothing snapped.

The kettle whistled, and soon I was bringing tea and biscuits to the trunk table. Boo came out to sit by him, anticipating crumbs.

"Look," said Massey, crumbs spilling from his lips. "Conditions were atrocious but I took Viktor and his illegals into custody. It'll be all over the news today."

"On your own?" I asked. "Incredible." But Massey was impervious to irony.

"A tricky operation. Three key units in the field, crack Norfolk Blues. All controlled from my vantage on the ridge. The illegals sweep in on a huge breaker, precisely as my informant predicted. I give the command, and we rush them from all sides." He paused to inhale to give his megalomania some air.

"Total surprise, then, thanks to the tip-off? Jud's tip-off, let's not forget."

"They all panicked – the riot shields, the batons, the coshing. We took out a few with Tasers." Massey sounded positively Churchillian.

"Led from the front, surely," I interjected. Massey nodded his big head.

"Viktor and his thugs, cuffed, and slammed into our vans."

"Bravo," I crowed, forcing my sycophantic pantomime to record depths. "And Jud?" I asked.

"Yes, yes, I'm coming to that. I'm going out live on Radio Norfolk today, the afternoon slot: 'The Battle of Kelling Hard', I'm calling it, for PR purposes."

"Can't wait!" I replied. At least it would be brilliant to hear Jud's exoneration, from the Home Office, live on air.

"But there's more...!" Massey boomed. "Traced your cruiser to a white Russian oligarch with a very fancy London address. Paid him a little visit. Turns out his basement complex is choc-a-bloc with black market goodies."

This was surely what he'd wanted to boast about the other day at the station. I guessed he'd had kept schtum for operational reasons at the time.

"It was practically the pissing Pentagon down there, iris-recognition sensors, vaults of steel." There was a manic look in Massey's eye. "Called in a few favours at the Yard, went in with a search warrant."

"Scotland Yard must be pretty impressed with your information," I said, heaping more biscuits on his plate. "You told them where the tip-off came from?"

"Yes, quite a catch. Number fifteen on the Forbes List." He rubbed his plump hands, unleashing a hail of crumbs on the kilim rug. Boo hovered up.

"Pardon my curiosity, Inspector." I didn't risk 'Clive' on this occasion. "What exactly was in this vault?" I knew he wanted to tell me.

"Missing masterworks that will send the art-world ponces gaga." I trusted he was going to tone down his language somewhat for his radio spot later on. But, I must admit, he had me riveted... on Tilly's behalf.

"Any Tudor writing desks?" I asked. I could hear the tension in my voice, and I'm sure he could too.

"Yes, yes, I'm coming to that..." Massey evidently planned to milk his tale for maximum praise, so I buttered him up.

"Do please go on."

"As I was saying: a couple of Van Dicks; a Remembrandt; a saucy Rudens – tasty little angels! And a remarkable Vermicelli."

I didn't know where to look, as this Van-Dickhead with the inflamed ego brazenly scratched his scrotum. I was dangerously tempted to dampen his ego by supplying the real names of the Old Masters he thought he'd memorised.

"And why was the Vermicelli so remarkable?" I asked.

"Why? Because I spotted that its frame was hinged, and it opened up another vault, his secret Panic Room. The boys at the Yard don't call me Norfolk's '*Holmes-next-the-Sea*' for nothing."

Sherlock probably turned in his fictional grave. But Massey's phrase, 'Panic Room', had me on tenterhooks.

"And inside?"

"One prize portrait, but here, take a look at this..." He produced a high-end smartphone from his suit pocket, but didn't hold it up. I had to go over from the sofa to take a look.

"A selfie?"

"Closer!" he roared. I fetched my glasses.

"The Boleyn Bureau!"

"Precisely."

"Fantastic!" But as I peered at the image of Massey posing by the ancient desk, I noticed a shadowy figure behind him. "Who's the lady in fancy dress?" I asked.

"No females present at this scene."

I took off my glasses and peered closer. Some kind of apparition was staring over Massey's shoulder. Though faint, it had dark hair. It honestly looked... like Anne Boleyn.

"This is to hype up police publicity, I take it?" I ventured. It was fair enough for me to obsess about Anne, in connection with my boathouse ordeals: but photoshopping her into a forensic picture, that seemed a step too far.

"I'm not interested in publicity," he retorted. "What are you talking about?" He snatched the phone and peered at it. "That's Queen Bess, another stolen portrait. We're contacting the gallery concerned."

"No, no... that fainter figure just over your shoulder. It's obviously the Boleyn girl: she was known for that French headdress," I insisted.

"Listen, sonny, that's a reflection. Of the Queen Bess painting. Nothing queer 'bout it."

"Elizabeth was a redhead. She wore her hair in pearls, not heavy headdresses like this. Trust me, I know my fashion history." But my reasoning was lost on Massey.

"Bah... seen one *queen*, seen them all!" He gave me a contemptuous glare, but that wasn't the cause of the cold shudder that travelled up my spine. Unless he was winding me up, this was freakier than anything I'd experienced in this haunted boathouse: a digital image of Anne Boleyn photobombing Massey's selfie. Sensational, to imagine that her royal avatar might be monitoring my case, as mine had once spied on James's, over his shoulder while he shaved in the trenches. Tilly thought I was mad, she'd said so: but what if I could show her this picture?

"I'll tell you what, would you do me a favour and e-mail this snap to me, when you get a mo?"

"Ah... for you to share on Facebook, show your fashionista pals a shot of a real man, finding the famous treasure?"

"Absolutely." He really was a conceited, homophobic prick. But I had to keep him sweet: this photo was evidence, in a way, of my sanity.

"Now listen. Your tomboy-friend has instructions to call me the minute this Bureau reaches her. She needs it for an opening ceremony."

"She's going to be delighted. Her and the whole Norfolk Heritage Society. More tea, Inspector?"

"Don't mind if I do. Long night doing God's work." It's a thin line between Masonic and Messianic.

In the kitchen I heaped fresh biscuits and teacakes on to a plate, as generous to Massey as he'd been mean to me, with his fish-and-chip lunch. My plan, a mere seed last night, was already growing sturdily. The BB had been found in time; Massey's appetite for flattery was clearly bottomless. All I had to do was dangle an invitation.

"Inspector," I called as I refreshed the teapot. "I know your in-tray must be full of urgent cases, but I'm sure the Norfolk Heritage Society would be seriously honoured if you'd honour their upcoming Gala Opening at Samphire Hall, by unlocking the secret compartment in the Boleyn Bureau?"

"Hmm..." I could hear his vanity coming to the boil. I set the tray down in front of him.

"As we discussed the other day: there's a document hidden in there, a confession, I'm certain. Imagine yourself, solving the mystery of Skipper Wood's death, in front of the world's press!"

"What, and look a prat if you're wrong?"

He had a point.

"Well, Inspector, allow me to remind you about 'White Russian' and Kelling Hard. I haven't let you down yet."

He offered a grudging grunt, but his mind was on the teacakes.

"And I've actually felt an old document, deep inside it." His greedy eyes looked up now. "In The Watch House I got the secret compartment open. But I was interrupted by the oligarch's henchmen. Otherwise I'd have read it. It's obviously something important, hidden for so long, and with such care."

"So, you possess a key," he deduced – to his credit, I suppose. "Show!"

As I bent to unzip the pocket in my combats I had a cold feeling in my stomach, which turned into a numbing panic when I realised the trefoil key was not there. I tried to think back. When had I last handled it? I had no idea.

"Some problem?" Massey asked.

"I think we'll wait before I show you the key," said my fiction-engine. "That's my security, after all. Found in *my* house, up there in the second step: possession is nine-tenths of the law, I believe?"

"Sounds like bullshit to me," said Massey. "It's what we call 'evidence'. I don't proceed without it."

God no, I needed to make him believe me. Opening the Bureau wasn't just going to clinch his promotion; it would crown the Gala Opening, and make openings for Tilly too.

"I've shown you evidence," I said, pointing tremblingly at the foot of the stairs. "Remember, this is the very spot where the murdered man fell. Skipper Wood. The Olympic hero."

Massey's hand started to creep back across the acreage of trouser towards his groin. It surely realised, even if its master was slower on the uptake, that solving the Skipper Wood murder was a first-class ticket to Thin Blue Line stardom.

"And it's easy to prove that the Bureau belonged to Skipper's employer. He hid the key, but kept a copy. It's a treasure hunt he set up. And you're in the frame to solve it!"

"Mind-blowing," Massey mumbled, imagining how his policing skills would dazzle the Worshipful Brothers in whatever Lodge he belonged to.

"Leave it to me," I said. "We'll have a gilt-edged invitation delivered to your office later." I hoped it sounded suave, but inside I was churning. Somehow, I had to access the Bureau before the opening ceremony, to make sure what was in it, or the whole episode might be a terrible disaster. I also had to find the trefoil key. And somehow I had to persuade Tilly to persuade the NHS to make the hidden trapdoor part of their presentation programme? At least Dr Wulff was apparently a fellow Mason. It might not be completely impossible.

Massey levered himself out of my chair, sweeping a clatter of crumbs from his crotch on to the floorboards. Boo was no longer tempted.

"Look, I might. I'm not saying 'no'. That's my best offer."

"You're very kind, Inspector," I said. "You won't regret it. There's just one more thing."

"Not now," he said. "I'm very busy."

"It won't take a moment. It's just... about Jud's discharge."

"For what?" He trundled towards me, boards creaking, and backed me – somewhat pungently – against the French doors. Boo growled, and Massey eyeballed me unsettlingly.

"Jud tipped you off. That's how you caught Viktor, no?" I eventually replied, my mouth dry with apprehension.

"Listen, chummy, I call the shots here, not you. If you want a reward, you've got that crummy little cabinet back, to impress your bit on the side." His lower lip brimmed with dribble as he manoeuvred ever closer, like an angry bulldog. I could scarcely move. Boo growled again.

"Yes, we're all so grateful," I stuttered, not daring to remind him that the Bureau and Viktor were two quite different matters. "But only yesterday you were kind enough to say, if I remember correctly, 'one good turn deserves another'."

"Exactly. Yesterday. And this is today. Just you get that fancy invite over to the station PDQ or I'll see that your pal – Mr Flaky Jud – gets an even heftier sentence."

"Okay..." I replied, my voice all breathy agreement, my eyes a disbelieving glare.

As Massey left he slammed the French doors so hard that the draught lifted papers off my desk. His duplicity left me seething and pretty shaken: Boo sensed my anxiety, mooching around with his tail between his legs.

After a couple of minutes trying to pull my thoughts together, I went out to call Tilly. The minute I reached the jetty hotspot the phone vibrated in my hand: 'Norwich Station = 1pm Wednesday. Luv U + Boo. Luke x.' The butterflies in my stomach started looping the loop. Calling Tilly, I guiltily realised, was the only way to bring them back to earth.

"Hi: just had Inspector Massey here."

"Marvellous, yah?" Tilly was shrilly exuberant. "Everyone's so excited... everyone except you, by the sound of it."

"I had a bust-up with Massey."

"But he brought you the BB news, no?"

"He did, but... Look, I've done another deal with him, but I need your help again."

"Uh-huh?"

"It's all on Jud's behalf. By the way, was he okay about... your night away?"

"Probably didn't notice," she said. I decided not to respond to that.

"Anyway, can you get a gala invitation over to Wells, posh letterhead job, addressed to Inspector Clive Massey? I know you weren't that keen. But Karsten might like to suck up to another Mason."

"The boot's probably on the other foot. But Massey got the BB back, that's all the reason we need. Great idea, we'll make it über-posh. The Bureau's getting a police escort, and the NHS will be massed on the front steps. Like royalty coming home."

I stared at The Watch House in the distance, thinking how Boo and I almost lost our lives over that crummy little cabinet, and nobody had thanked us, not even Tilly. What am I, the Invisible Man?

"Seeing as Massey's such a hero..." – I tried not to let my anger show – "... don't you think the NHS, as part of the entertainment, could actually let him show off the BB's secret compartment?"

I'd soon know if my little seed had fallen on stony ground or not.

"Look Bertie... I'm sorry I called you Agatha Christie or whatever. I never thought we'd see the Bureau again. But now, everyone's so much more relaxed, and I can see it playing out brilliantly for the TV cameras. A neat little stunt. Massey's been a real star, hasn't he?"

"Thanks..." I said, kicking one of the jetty-posts to ease my tension.

"I'll talk Karsten through it. But Bertie, promise me: Massey just shows the little panel. None of this 'confession' malarkey, and keep Skipper Wood's accident out of it, yah?"

She thinks it's a bloody sideshow! She has no idea how my peace of mind hangs in the same balance as Lord James's guilt or innocence. Glaring out across the marshes, to the scene of Boo's near drowning, I struggled to keep my emotions in check.

"Let me call you back when I've checked out the Massey manoeuvre with the powers that be."

I climbed the stairs to the boathouse, fretting that even if Karsten Wulff gave the thumbs-up I still had to find the trefoil key, and I still had a year and more of the

Newton-Grey diaries to read. All this stress, how could it possibly be worth it? My loyalty was divided between the two treasure hunts. The missing key – crucial though it was – would have to take second place to James's War journals for now, and my notes for Tilly.

Tense as I felt, the vivid magic of James's narrative started to work on me the moment I settled to work, allowing me to join him, back in the moment.

10th March 1917 – p.m.

Operations continue – mopping up pockets of resistance from the Hun. As yet no sign of Sellars – dreadful fear that he is dead in action – or taken prisoner.

Something still obliged James to be *sure* whether his *aide-de-camp* was dead or alive... perhaps to establish whether Caleb had indeed poisoned his mind with gossip. I sincerely hoped Sellars would be found: he seemed like an arbitrator in this mystery, enduring and robust like his curly-haired dummy in James's apartments. All the more reason – with the Gala Opening forty-eight short hours away – to find out when and how Sellars came home from the War...

21st June 1917 – p.m.

Dreamt of Caleb as an innocent little child – not the scheming viper he became as a man. If Alice could know all this! And Mater, dearest Mater – I hear your voice crying in every soldier on these killing fields.

The War is taking its toll, dragging on so much longer than anyone has foreseen. James wrestles a deeply-troubled conscience, more harrowing even than the outward misery of trench life. Daily my avatar works alongside him, checking the roll call of soldiers. We scan the list, focusing on the letter 'S', but 'Sellars' never registers.

The summer months turn increasingly wet as autumn approaches and I see, on the table in James's dugout, deployment orders for another objective east of Poelcappelle: it's scheduled for 22 October 1917.

We are on the march across the dreaded no-man's-land. James's field glasses spy Poelcappelle church in the distance: it's in ruins.

It was hard to keep up, as James's diary entries spilt so fast across the pages, his scrawl joining bunker to bunker, punctuated with emphatic dashes like bullet scars on stone. I envision the enemy, winkled out in their dozens each time he pauses. German sniper fire becomes more sporadic, the shelling less assured; despite the heavy casualties on both sides, we finish the paragraph, at the foot of one page, with an abrupt full stop to the hostilities.

Finally, Major James and his patrol come across a half-buried concrete shelter, covered in camouflage netting. Brandishing his bayonet, he kicks the door in. A dust cloud blurs his vision momentarily; mine too. He coughs, and then, to our intense surprise, he espies heavily-wounded English soldiers, captured during counter-attacks, lying in shackles.

23rd October 1917 – 6 a.m.

I called a medical orderly over – before long my men were leading our desperate prisoners from the bunker.

The handwriting was erratic, but James's exhausted excitement was clear.

The last man out – a stooping wretch with head heavily bandaged – breaks file, grabbing my own arm instead. I try to shrug him off – he paws at me – groaning some insistent words I am unable to interpret. He is trembling pathetically – I try to explain that I cannot understand him – he is suffering from shell shock – the Jack Wagon will convey him to the field hospital. To my alarm he drops to his knees – tears open his shirt, bearing his chest – then rips off his fibreboard identity-tags. With a piteous groan he impresses them into the palm of my hand – the soulful eyes, staring up, want no more part in this ruddy war!

The next page was blotched and spattered, as if it had been written in the rain.

I left the fellow and scrabbled up scree, hoping to call for stretchers – the Jack Wagon was already grinding past me – by its fleeting light, I scraped the dirt from the identity-tags, and with thumping heart read the soldier's name. By George – I had found Sellars, my Sellars! This was a godsend – an absolute godsend.

I sprang to my feet in relief. I threw the diary aside, shouting "Stanley, alive!" Boo moseyed around me, sensing the intensity of my relief.

"Calls for a celebration, eh Boo?" Breaking my usual habit, I headed for the drinks cupboard, and poured a glass of port, a tipple I usually indulge only at Christmas.

I switched on the radio, suddenly in the mood for music. Boo gobbled down a treat and then – though never a dog for mindless games – joined in the holiday spirit, playing catch-me around the boathouse.

"You know what, Boo, I should have a drink more often!" I licked my lips. So dear old Stanley would be able to return – 'a godsend' indeed, in the diary's words! He must have been badly disfigured, unrecognisable even to James, who presumably – later entries would surely confirm this – went back to the bunker to refix the ID-tags round the faithful servant's neck. And I wondered:

in his present state, would Stanley still be able to remember whatever Caleb Bacon might have told him about James, and Skipper, and Skipper's death?

The music gave way to the three o'clock news. Then, following a weekly pattern, the spotlight fell on a local celebrity.

"Welcome to *Live at Three-Oh-Five*, where today's guest is Inspector Clive Massey."

"Good afternoon, Helena; a pleasure being back in my favourite studio." Here we go, I thought...

"I believe congratulations are in order, Inspector," she said.

"All part of the job. Wells Police Station may not be the largest in the land, but I am second to none when it comes to protecting the realm of Her Majesty."

"Oh please!" I shouted at the radio.

"So, do tell our listeners about your triumphant operation in the early hours of this morning," said the presenter, with suitable gravity.

"You mean the Battle of Kelling Hard?"

"Yes, and what first alerted you to people-smugglers operating on Norfolk's shores?"

"Well as I'm sure you'd expect, I've been keeping tabs on these undesirables, and their novel slant on our border policies, for months."

"Your unit actively seeks out illegal immigrants living under the radar, seeking to assimilate into the Norfolk way of life?"

"Top of my agenda, Helena; and the county can sleep easier in their beds tonight knowing my surveillance has paid off." I wanted to puke.

"Organised crime where you'd least expect it," she observed.

"That's certainly what the Home Office said, about my performance this morning." There was going to be no mention of Jud, of course...

"Before you go – Clive – breaking news, in my ear, suggests you've also been responsible for recovering a unique stolen treasure."

"Yes, a desk, dating back to the Tudor dynasty, made for Anne of Cleveland." Thank God he's not on *Mastermind*. An audible smirk, as the presenter asked for some operational detail, suggested she was not fooled by Massey's preposterous façade.

"Can't say too much, Helena, not even to you. Just one of many historical cases I'm supervising at present: I've been invited to solve another age-old mystery this coming Wednesday: it's the Bonfire Night Gala Opening at Samphire Hall, and I'm the special guest."

My little seed continued to grow.

"What would our county do without you, Clive?" Helena asked archly.

"Your listeners don't call me '*Sherlock-on-Sea*' for nothing, you know!" Massey chortled. I'd had enough, and went down to the jetty once again to call Tilly. She'd already sent a text: 'Karsten gung-ho 4 Massey manoeuvre – good thinking Bertie. x.'

Massey was becoming everyone's darling – except mine. I fired a text back: 'GR8 and CU 2morrow morning. x.'

I climbed back up to the boathouse, ready to travel back into 1917, and unravel Sellars's enigmatic part in the Newton-Grey plot. Back in the lounge I expectantly retrieved the 1917 diary, where I'd flung it in my jubilation at finding Sellars alive. But to my alarm the next page was empty. I flicked through the subsequent autumn – all blank too – and on into December. Nothing. My throat tightened and my mouth became desert dry. This was definitely not a godsend.

But at least I had 1918 still to come. From my desk drawer I fetched the last unread diary, cached so long behind the panelling in James's private quarters. On went the desk lamp, and Boo came and flopped by my feet, a spectator in the stalls waiting for the show to start. My keen hands tingled with anticipation, as I finally broached the final, revelatory chapters of James's autobiographical account.

"Here goes, Boo..." I unpicked the knotted tapes that had sewn it shut for so long.

The first page was empty but for the outline of a shield, sketched with dotted lines. Under this James had written his family motto, *fortitudine prospero.* Unfinished, but brimming with promise. I thumbed eagerly to the next page.

1st January 1918

It was foxed, travel-worn, but empty. A thump in my heart. I leafed through more pages, all unused, then flicked unbelievingly through the entire, blank diary. So all he'd written, in a year, was effectively 'By endurance I prosper'. I could imagine what he'd endured, but it was difficult to see the prosperity: just disturbing emptiness. As for me, I felt myself fighting back a tide of stress, rising with the growing certainty that I'd never now know what Caleb had imparted to Sellars.

'*Calma*, Roberto!'

"No!" I had run out of material, without discovering the truth of Skipper Wood's end. James had not delivered any answer to my long quest. Such was his cruelty, not only shattering my trust in him after murdering Caleb Bacon, but now he was denying even me the knowledge of what happened after the 'godsend' of finding Sellars.

My lips quivered. My eye twitched. I was hanging on the precipice of a revelation that for some reason James had not wanted to record in writing. A dead end, then? No hearsay account, no family lore, no living descendant to track down for stories. James's body had been washed out to sea in the wake of his suicide, supposedly in 1929. Sellars, I now guessed, must finally have been buried somewhere in France as an 'unknown soldier', though it was hard to see how his army identity-tag had ended up in Lord James's design folder at Samphire Hall. But no amount of speculation could really explain why James had made no further entries in the winter months of his 1917 diary, nor in a 1918 diary purchased in false hope.

Surely this can't be the end, I thought, tipping back in my desk chair, deeply hurt by the withdrawal of James's written guidance, without which I was unable to place myself back into his world. My hungry avatar – my ghost from his future – starved to death!

My only hope of a resolution now lay in the Boleyn Bureau, in that secret compartment. For which I'd mislaid the key.

CHAPTER TWENTY-ONE
INSURANCE

I suffered the kind of night that typically precedes a fever: nonsensical dreams in disconnected snatches, each one a torment. I awoke sapped of energy – my head ringing – to face all the pressures associated with my partner's homecoming. Yet before I could attend to any tidying or cleaning, I needed to find the trefoil key.

All the pockets of all the coats, every cranny of the understair cupboard; all the unwashed trousers piled by the machine: nothing. I tried not to panic. Where had I last seen it? It had survived The Watch House and the flood surge, on its green garden twine, tied around my old mobile in its cling film. So it must be in the boathouse somewhere. Every bag I'd used, every cupboard I'd opened: nothing. All round the veranda, underneath it: nothing. I was going mad. In and under the Baroque bed; by the loo, the bath. Window ledges, bins: nothing. So I started turfing everything out of my desk.

The top left-hand drawer was so stuffed with research material that I had to wrench it open. I pulled the drawer off its runners, rested it in my lap. Yellowing newspapers, the oval frame from the understair cupboard. Piles of clippings relating to the *Titanic*, and forewarnings of war in Europe: events I now felt I'd lived through, not just read about. One yellow slip escaped, spiralling to the floor.

I picked it up: how did that get in here, Tiny Tim's bill for carpentry repairs? Still, a godsend finding it! He might have botched the Love Step, but he could surely fix my damage to the bathroom door, before Luke got home.

As I tried to focus on it, though, a significant surname caught my eye.

"*Bacon*, for heaven's sake, Boo!" Surely a descendant of Caleb? Tiny Tim, then, despite his inherited shoddiness, might have family stories that could flesh out the empty pages in James's diary?

Boo and I were soon on the road, heading for the old Nissen huts outside Wells. 'Shed 2', said Bacon's faint invoice: so we parked the VW by the second of three rundown, corrugated buildings. 'Danger: No Entry', read a mouldy sign, which crumbled from its fixings as I pushed the door open. Just a few moody pigeons, no Tiny Tim: clearly nobody had worked here for many years.

'No signal' said my new mobile. Despair welled up, immediately countered by clear thinking. The family-run DIY store that had recommended Tim in the first place: it was only ten minutes away, so Boo and I hit the road.

The pasty-faced girl who had served me before was at her till, counting washers into a paper bag for a customer.

"Sorry to interrupt," I said, "but do you remember, a while back, you gave me a business card for a carpenter?" She looked bemused. "Tiny Tim. I got the impression you knew him."

"If I knew someone called 'Tiny Tim', I'd keep quiet about it." Her customer laughed as he paid.

"But I've got his receipt," I said, shoving it across the counter. She picked it up.

"Don't say nowt about 'Tiny Tim'," she observed. "Granddad will know, he's the boss." She hollered up a stairwell.

Something was wrong, and I already felt humiliated and embarrassed. On the counter lay a freshly-sharpened saw, awaiting collection, and I glimpsed my dim reflection in the blade. I looked like a crazy man. If Tilly's right and I'm really going mad, I thought, a weapon like this could finish it all pretty quickly. But as my heart went out to Boo – whimpering in the cold camper, his master never to return – a spry, thin voice made me jump.

"I hate to tell you," said the granddad, "but this old stub – for 'works carried out at your boathouse' – is dated '1914' and signed by 'C Bacon'. Nothing to do with 'Tim'."

"Impossible," I insisted, twisting the receipt awkwardly out of his hand, as if one or other of us was dreaming. The old man was right: 'C Bacon'. Yet it made no sense at all. Tim had handed me his receipt while I was searching the *Titanic* survivor lists; I remembered shoving it in the drawer without glancing at it. What a bloody irony, if the great researcher had mixed up parallel dockets from two different centuries?

'Okay, just 'cos it's a coincidence, it doesn't have to be meaningless,' I thought. 'Dated 3 August, just before the Great War... this old chit is that fucker Caleb charging for the 'Wood Feels' sign he made to taunt Lord James. And now the bastard's taunting me!'

"I'll have to ask you to mind your language," said the granddad, his surprisingly firm arm steering me away from the gaggle of concerned customers to the door. I'd been thinking out loud.

He held out his hand in the doorway, and I shook it, to find he was only giving me a replacement card for Tiny Tim. Unwilling to apologise, unable to explain, I simply bolted to the safety of my van, spooked by the whole ordeal. How could I have got things so wrong? Boo was in the passenger seat and I cuddled him close.

"I'm completely losing my grip," I sobbed into his warm ear, like a child. There was a pattern here, there must be: two second-rate carpenters, they had to be related? But it was a fair while before I was sufficiently composed to check for a phone signal, and call the number on the card.

"Is that Tim Bacon?" I began.

"What? This is Tiny Tim Thomas, the carpenter."

Right voice, wrong name. Shit. I cancelled the call. And I'd forgotten to ask Tim to come round and fix the bathroom door. Fuck. I banged my head against the campervan window a few times. Boo cocked his ears in alarm.

"Don't worry, Boo, we haven't come all this way for nothing," I said, wondering if it was mad to justify oneself to a whippet. "Little Pearl's only a few streets away, and Caleb was her uncle. She'll dish some dirt." I didn't tell Boo, but I just needed a grandmotherly hug. I blew my nose, and started the engine.

There were no legal spaces left outside Walnut Court, so I double-parked and nipped in. My luck had definitely run out. The matron wouldn't let me see Pearl, something about keeping her strength up for a planned outing. As I tried to argue my case, distant barking reached my ears, and from her office window I saw Boo, jumping about agitatedly in the front seat of the VW. I made my quick excuses.

As I ran across the road I could see the poor creature pawing at his mouth. Something green was hanging out... not wallpaper? But as I unlocked, I realised Boo was chewing garden twine. Then dangling metal caught my eye.

"The key, the Tudor key!" It all came flooding back, how I'd chucked it in the VW's footwell, the night I stripped off my storm-drenched clothes.

"You're a godsend," I told Boo as I hugged him. A godsend, with an affinity for the Boleyn Bureau and its accessories.

Before long I'd peeled the parking ticket off the windscreen – now I knew what he'd been barking about – and we were passing under the Gala Opening banners, and down the broad drive to Samphire Hall, a little late for my meeting with Tilly.

The forecourt was busy with delivery vehicles and scurrying tradesmen, but chiefly with signs of heavy security: the Bureau had arrived home. I parked up next to a police van; its occupants watched impassively as I checked, in the driving mirror, that my eyes and cheeks were dry.

"Shan't be long, Boo!"

It was turning nippy. I buttoned my coat as I paced across the forecourt – where the Boleyn Cedar had once grown – and up the steps to security control. Tilly had left me a pass.

An ebullient hum filled St Benedict's Foyer. Norfolk Heritage Society people in their brown coats were pottering about, with vases of lilies and potted palms, with paintings and antiques, preparing a scene that looked like a film set. Cables dangled from the mezzanine, and electricians clambered up and down ladders, busy with spotlights and sound equipment.

And then – a little leap in my unsteady heart – I noticed Tilly, in mannish blazer and skinny jeans – arranging memorabilia in a bank of vitrines. Over one cabinet a sign read 'Major James Newton-Grey (8th Norfolks)'. Sensing my gaze, Tilly turned around. She was wearing a flame-red roll-neck, stylish as hell even on a frantic workday: I wondered what she had in store for the Gala Opening itself. She came over, all smiles, and we air-kissed, given the presence of so many of her colleagues.

"It's like some amazing Christmas shopping mall," I said.

"It out-Harrods Harrods." She smiled. I raised my eyebrows. "*Hamlet*," she explained. None the wiser, I moved on.

We skirted a cordoned area where tilers were still fixing the floor where the statue of Antinoüs had shattered.

"We'll have our meeting in Lord James's sitting room." Tilly was in work mode: I liked it. She closed James's door behind us, and there we were, the two of us with his portrait, and Alice's: part of their louche, exclusive circle.

It was James's turn to stare at me, just as I'd monitored his progress through the War diaries. The sensual black-eyed gaze fixed me with unnerving knowing: it was hard to look away. Tilly was fetching the diaries I'd already given back, from the console table under Alice's portrait. For a moment she mimicked Alice's coy pose, and winked coquettishly. I sat in James's wingback hide chair, by the cast iron fireplace, and let out a sigh.

"You look flustered," said Tilly, pulling up a footstool.

"Not a particularly good morning; but I'm here with my notes, as promised." I fumbled my bag open.

"Ooh, at last!"

"No big deal..." I tried to act as if nothing was up.

"Let's see what we've got." She laid out the 1917 diary and the totally blank 1918 tease. The short black hair, the ducktail, the delicate neck. Our fingers touched as I passed her my notes. If she and I struck a match, the rest of the world could go to blazes.

"Okay: so James and Alice, at Countess Daisy's invitation, took tea at the Ritz with Edward VII. That's the starting point for my presentation."

"Yeah, all royal mentions are bookmarked with Post-its," I began.

"Great... but..." Tilly was flicking through my notepad. "Bertie, all I'm seeing is pages of – well, scribble – about Skipper Wood: where's the history of the Hall start?" she asked.

I took a long breath.

"It's kind of implied: remember Skipper is a huge part of the history too."

She held the notepad close to her face, deciphering my scrawl.

"Isn't he just? It says here that you dreamt about the carpenter sawing and singing his crap song again. And here it says Beulah, Skipper's wife, a doctor's daughter, had a parlour decorated in 'Sheele's Green', and down here you write 'probably toxic'. This is speculation, not history." She went silent, and brusquely flicked ahead.

"Err..." I hoped my fiction-engine would help me out.

"Caleb's bloody cap equals prime suspect!" She scowled; her face went taut and flushed. She got up and paced around the room with my notes. She was getting really wound up.

"Tilly..."

"Shush," her hands were trembling. "And you write here that Constance went down in the *Titanic*, so she's no longer a suspect! Who the fuck is Constance? And what the hell's the *Titanic* got to do with Samphire Hall?"

"Everything!" I replied.

She stomped across the room and then, in a sudden spasm of rage, flung my notepad at me, really hard.

"Bertie, you're a fruitcake! You've let me down big time: all you care about is this bloody house-builder!" she shouted. "I am sick to death of Skipper this and Skipper that... who the hell cares about a fucking carpenter falling downstairs?"

"Tilly, calm down, let me explain... please!"

"What's to explain? I've got to make *the* presentation of my life in twenty-four hours, and you've gone and fucked it all up!"

"Look, I know how important that is, but I don't think you realise how detectives operate – we have to follow hunches. But the payoff, what they bring to Samphire

Hall, it's more than any straight historian could hope to do. You just need to trust me!"

Tilly slumped on to the sofa, looking defeated.

"If Dr Wulff sees me like this, I'll get my introduction slot pulled from the event."

"Dr Wulff and the NHS have a lot to thank you for, and from what I've seen, it's all going to be sensational." I sat nearby and handed her a tissue.

"OMG, I need a drink!" she yelled, smacking both hands on the velvet sofa, so hard they left imprints.

"That won't solve anything."

"For fucksake, Bertie, what's got into you?"

"Tilly, look at me." She raised her head. "This is precisely why you've got to let me look inside the Boleyn Bureau before I leave today, just to check there really is a written confession in there."

"Why d'you keep obsessing over that when Jud, the dead man's actual descendant, doesn't give a shit?"

"He does, you know: all that body art is a homage to his ancestor. Don't you find that odd?"

"The whole of Norfolk is full of weirdoes, including you – and you've not even been here that long."

"Well, that makes two of us then," I said, looking right into her eyes.

"Bertie, what the fuck am I going to do?" She sighed.

I stood up, pulled the trefoil key from my pocket, and held it up to the pendant light.

"This is the answer to all our problems!"

"You really do think so, don't you...?" she said incredulously. "Your whole Massey manoeuvre is just a sideshow as far as the NHS is concerned."

"I think not. What the BB contains is going to set the world alight!"

I was overstating my case a bit. As I spoke, I was thinking that – if there really wasn't anything of consequence in the Tudor desk – I might somehow make use of Massey's selfie, with Anne Boleyn photobombing his recovery of her precious desk. Even if it turned out to be fake, it would keep the audience entertained. It just needed Massey to e-mail me the photo: and he wasn't good at keeping promises.

"Where's the BB now?" I asked.

"Upstairs in one of James's holding rooms. Guard on the door. The insurers are due at two: Goldberg Sage, from Canary Wharf. Specialists. Oceans of terms and conditions."

"Can't you get me in that holding room, just a couple of minutes, for a bit of insurance myself?" Tilly looked dubious. "If we know exactly what's in the compartment, you'll know how much time the Massey manoeuvre needs. And you can shorten your own presentation accordingly."

Suddenly she clicked her fingers, and sat upright. A bracket clock chimed on the mantelpiece, quarter to the hour.

"Bertie, you're incorrigible! The place is swarming with NHS staff and the insurance people are staying overnight. It's all arranged." She looked up at the dark-eyed portrait, as if weighing up what Lord James would have wanted. "Look, give me five minutes." And she was out of the door.

Though I was relieved Tilly hadn't been even more angry about the fiasco of my notes, I felt absolutely exhausted. I returned to James's spot by the fireside and tilted my head back, caressed by his high-backed chair. Staring up at his brooding portrait, my eyes began to feel heavy.

The fire crackled in his grate. I heard an antique motorcar pull up outside; the chauffeur sounded the horn. I could smell Turkish cigarettes, the familiar whiff of aniseed. China rattled on a tray nearby: teatime. I slipped over to the bay window and opened the shutters:

the whole landscape was winter white. James, back in his captain's uniform, stood in the snow with his mother's single white rose, looking up at my window. Our eyes met. I experienced a startling, bodily jolt.

"Soz to wake yer, mate, but that Offord bird sent me." He jogged my shoulder again.

"Tel, what the..."

"XL-Guard security services!" He pointed to the embroidered logo on his overall. "I was trying to tell you in Fakenham the other day, but you were getting busy with your friend in the back of the van, know what I mean."

"But Tel... this is a step up from car parking at The Blakeney Hotel!"

"Pukka gig! I've brought me ol' Mile End mob in. Now, let's get yer upstairs."

Shivering, still half asleep, I slung my bag around my shoulder. Tel's voice boomed down the long gallery until we reached St Benedict's Foyer, which was still buzzing. We waited at the foot of the sweeping staircase, while workmen in hard hats winched a marble statue up to the mezzanine. Antinoüs was coming home. You could tell he'd been in the wars, but at least he'd pulled himself together. I tried to do the same.

Someone gave the all clear and Tel pointed up the stairs as we climbed.

"Geezer, that's where we're plonking the famous wossname tomorrow." A presentation platform, with floodlights built into its base, had been prepared so the Boleyn Bureau would stand proud of the balustrade, visible to the crowd below.

"Wait here a sec'," Tel instructed.

There was no need to ask which holding room housed the Bureau. The XL security man listened as Tel whispered something and then strode past me.

Further along the corridor Tilly was pacing anxiously, talking into her phone while she awaited the Goldberg Sage team. She came along to where Tel and I were waiting.

"Guarded round the clock," she was telling someone. "A condition of the insurance. Otherwise we can't exhibit it."

Behind me, the holding room door opened, and a very tall black-skinned workman came out, wearing the NHS brown overalls. He didn't acknowledge Tilly but passed by her, then stopped to straighten a painting.

"How come that bloke's allowed in with the Bureau?" I asked. Tilly shushed me with frantic gestures. The black man turned and stared at me, then walked haughtily away.

"For fucksake, Bertie. That was Karsten."

"Karsten Wulff? I thought you said he was Danish?"

Tilly gave me a savage glare that made me feel knee-high.

"Get in there, if you're going," she hissed.

"Yer got ten, max!" said Tel, looking at his watch. He held up both hands, to confirm the time allowance. One-and-a-half fingers were missing, thanks to an Alsatian at a scrapyard, he was telling me, as I sidled into the room. He pulled the door to, not quite clicking it shut. No windows. I turned on the dim overhead light.

There it was again, the Boleyn Bureau, dressed this time in cardinal red calico. I sank to my knees, not in prayer, but to lift its swaddling, as if I were violating an old priest's habit. I slid my hand underneath the little kneehole. Apart from a whiff of oil that I didn't recall, it was a replay of that distant day at The Watch House, when the oligarch's men had forestalled me.

"Well, Skipper old chum: now we find out who cut short your charmed life," I muttered. Maybe it *was* a prayer.

The secret catch, which had seemed pretty stiff before, now yielded easily. My hands trembled apprehensively, my breathing tightened, and the room felt very stuffy.

"Psst!" Tel was whispering through the gap in the door. "Al' wight?"

"Yeah," I replied breathily.

'*Calma*, Roberto.'

My hand started to shake uncontrollably. The catch gave under my fingers and I heard the click of the ancient mechanism: the miniature trapdoor sprang open. Tel's head poked in again.

"Six mins!"

"Okay, okay," I replied, wishing I hadn't lost my wristwatch on the marshes.

I slipped the trefoil key in its ornate escutcheon, turned it anti-clockwise. Another confident click. I could smell my own sweat now. My fingers, at full stretch, rummaged around inside the secret cavity. Nothing there! Oh God. I squeezed them further in. There was something. Perhaps it had shifted in transit: surely I hadn't pushed it that far back.

My clammy fingertips slowly teased the leading edge of rolled paper from the hidden compartment. My bladder weakened with anticipation. The coiled scroll was out in the open at last. I untied the silky ribbon, blood-red and vivid as the day it was dyed, untouched by harsh daylight. I tried to swallow as I unrolled the document; it quivered in my hands, like the sail of some galleon foretelling a coming tempest, then coiled up again.

I felt for my glasses in my bag, first one pocket then another, then in the zipped pouch. Nothing, no time. I screwed up my eyes and unrolled the page again. *'15th April 1920'* said the top right-hand corner, and I read it again and again, amazed by this confirmation of all my hopes after such a run of bad luck. *'To whom it may concern...'*, the text began; yet suddenly Tel was rapping on the door again. My struggling eyes darted around the page: naïve childlike handwriting, possibly James's hurried scrawl, but not the familiar, italic longhand I'd been expecting. My God, who wrote this? I scanned unseeing down the page, in search of the signature...

"Game over mate! Goldberg Sage are early!" Tel shouted. Then, for reasons of his own, he flicked the light off.

"Shit! I can't see a thing...!" I yelled, but he was beyond earshot.

If they found me here, and withdrew the insurance, the BB would not go on show, and it might as well have stayed stolen. I felt the bile rise from my gut, seasick on a high tide. Bitter fluid burnt my windpipe as I tried to swallow.

'*Calma*, Roberto!'

I blindly tried to tie the ribbon back round the scroll, slipping it into the mouth of the secret cavity, groping round the lock in its recessed panel, shakily inserting my key, turning clockwise, snapping the little trapdoor back into place, all in the remaining moments before I was discovered. I've had a bellyful of keys, I thought.

I jumped up, felt my way across the room, and stepped out into the mirrored gallery – far from composed without the evidence we so desperately needed – just as Karsten brought the Goldberg Sage team to the top of stairs. I was coughing, trying to clear my bitter throat; Tel clapped me on the back as the two insurers shook hands with Tilly.

"Good afternoon, gentlemen."

"David Stein, and my colleague Gordon Pennyworth: Goldberg Sage of London." High-gloss security passes glinted from the lapels of their sober grey suits.

Pennyworth appraised Tel's overalls and logo. Tilly shot an exasperated glance at my continued coughing.

"Norfolk Heritage received your e-mail last night. The Boleyn Bureau, as we're calling it, has been stowed in this holding bay. No window – *per* your terms and conditions. Late tomorrow, it moves to its podium on the mezzanine, for presentation to the public. It will be attended at all times."

"Very good, madam."

"Not so formal, please, Tilly."

"Very well, Tilly." I noticed a tiny silver camera in the palm of his hand.

"I'll 'op it then?" said Tel.

"Oh, this is our man Tel – XL-Guard security services – doing a marvellous job. And this is Bertie... an associate... researcher." I nodded, desperately stifling my acid cough, tears dropping from my eyes.

"Nice to meet you gents," Tel declared. "Safe as 'ouses, innit?"

"No house is safe," sniffed Pennyworth, busy with his clipboard.

"Tel and his team are the best up here on the coast." I'd got my voice back, but it came out foggy and insubstantial. Pennyworth straightened his tie.

"We'll just make our inspection, if you don't mind," said Stein, stepping immediately towards the door.

"I'll be off now, Tilly," I croaked. "See you tomorrow. Thanks ever so much."

"Yah, tomorrow..." she said, in an ominous tone.

Tel accompanied me down the stairs.

"Blimey, they're a 'appy pair of tossers!"

"Yeah," I nodded. Wait till Massey crosses his path tomorrow, I thought.

"None of my biz, I know, but you're sweet with wo'ever you needed in that bleedin' desk?"

"All cool, Tel, thanks for your help," was all I could muster. I felt numbed by defeat, and by my own slew of mistakes.

"Cheers mate." He made for a trestle table, where tea and sandwiches awaited the workers. The Gothic door behind it led down to the kitchens; I'd seen it in James's 1914 diary, when the foyer had been an operating theatre, back before the NHS – in either sense of the acronym – had been thought of.

At the main entrance I turned for one last look into St Benedict's Foyer. Antinoüs was back on his plinth at the top of the sweeping staircase. 'Next time I'm here,' I thought, 'in about twenty-four hours, I'll be listening to Evil C Massey telling the world, on live telly, who it was that murdered Skipper Wood!'

'Or something else entirely,' came my own reply, 'if that scroll isn't what you want it to be.'

As Boo and I drove back to the boathouse, my mobile vibrated. I pulled over, to find an urgent text from Tilly, instructing me to call her.

"I'm worried," she said. "You've put my head in a spin and not in a good way."

"Anything in particular?"

"For fucksake, Bertie, it's everything: first I was really pissed off with your Secret Squirrel notes, then that hideous *faux pas* with Dr Wulff, then your coughing all over the Goldberg Sage reps. And now... to be honest, I can't see how you're in a fit state to attend the Gala Opening at all."

"No, no, I'll be fine," I told her, crossing my fingers. "But you know how it is: the stress of everything piling up these last few weeks, and Luke coming home tomorrow. A lot of explaining to do, you do understand..."

"This is such a big deal for me. My future with the NHS... my whole career in curating... it's all in the balance tomorrow..."

"That's why this particular detective" – I couldn't resist – "says you *have* to build Skipper Wood into your presentation. The NHS will wonder what they ever did without you. Trust me!" Tilly went silent.

"So you'll really be okay for the ceremony?"

"Promise. How could I let my Tilly down?" And as I said that, I truly believed I would somehow handle it all, that adrenaline would save me from mental collapse.

"Bertie, get some good rest, and don't be late. It'll be nice to meet Luke tomorrow. *Ciao...*"

Part of me wanted to drive straight back to the Hall and hold her close, to reassure her, but also – to be honest – to stabilise myself. With my head on the steering wheel, and shivering with a cold sweat, I pondered tomorrow's potential for success and disaster, wondering if I'd feel fit enough to face either.

CHAPTER TWENTY-TWO
PROOF OF PATERNITY

I awoke with the bedding all wrapped round my body, as if tossing and turning had mummified me during the night. I hadn't dreamt about Skipper, but of course he was my first thought on waking. Like him I felt inextricably wound up in the history of Wood Feels. The bedclothes, at least, I could untangle.

Boo paced around, sensing the importance of the coming day, watching me rifling through the cupboards at the gable end of the bedroom. Here was Luke's iridescent dinner suit, not worn since our Eco-Designer bash, when the media fallout had catalysed our escape to Norfolk. Ten years together, sealed by a Civil Partnership back in 2005: but hell, this first lengthy break in our 'marriage' had been unbelievably trying. I pressed Luke's suit back to life, and his dress shirt and silk tie, remembering how handsome he'd looked, my Geordie Daniel Craig. Then it was time to think about Boo's outfit.

"Red or black?" I asked. Only the dog of a gay couple would have choice of bow ties, I guessed. "Definitely red, for Tilly's big night," we agreed.

The five coffin-like crates still stood in our main hall, scarcely touched since the day Luke left for the North. He'd need to realise I'd had more urgent priorities. The mess in the kitchen, though: how would his cleaning mania receive that?

I spilt Boo's dried breakfast into his water bowl. Damn: still groggy from Temazepam. This was how Mother had been: now my Milanese roots were showing. Poor thing... when did her *vita* stop being *dolce*? About the time she hooked up with a pervert and had to hide him from his own son, I guess. I needed to get a grip, clear the fuzz from my head. Boo quivered, sensing my distress.

"Walkies?" I dressed him in his scarlet coat, and found myself a jacket. Just the usual delay, locking up as if I were leaving for a month. What a fucking nightmare.

Crunching over frosty marshes often worked as a tonic, but the landscape seemed nondescript today: my thoughts kept returning to the Boleyn Bureau. The document it concealed had eluded me twice, but surely – I clung to the comfort of the cliché – it would be third time lucky. My pawns, Massey and Wulff, just needed to play their parts. Time was ticking fast, so I turned for home early, lost in worry until we neared the network hotspot and a text alert sounded: 'Leaves on line – 1 hour delay, meet 2. x'.

So I had time to check under all the beds, in all the cupboards, for dread of any unwanted visitor. After a troubled soak I dressed in my smart suit, but refrained from shaving: I didn't want to see what the mirror might show me.

On the road to Norwich I was rehearsing in my head: explanations for the posh outfits, the planned diversion to Samphire Hall. It was not going to be easy. Two o'clock at the station, no Luke. 'Stuck Peterborough, due 3' came his message. My anxiety rocketed: at three the NHS would open Samphire Hall, a full hour's drive away. To forestall Tilly's fury, I fired off an apologetic text: 'ETA 4pm'. She fired back: 'Presentation 5 sharp. Get here ASAP. Need U on stage to present Massey.'

Onstage – the two detectives! A sudden change of plan. So I'd need a few words to say before handing the key over to Massey. Was Tilly putting me on the spot, a mischievous payback for the useless notes I'd provided for her speech? The only paper in the van was fuel receipts: I started jotting one-liners, designed to defuse the stress of the occasion, deflate Massey's ego. But nothing worked. I closed my eyes, hoping for inspiration.

A tap on the window: a blue-eyed, cheeky smile, topped with trademark horn-rims, made my stomach flutter. Boo jumped up, tail flailing like a tiller in a gale, as Luke opened the passenger door.

"Here goes," I muttered to myself, broadening my smile to get us off to a good start. Luke chucked his rucksack in the back. I shoved the scribble-covered receipts under my seat.

"Hiya, bonny lads..." He leant over to hug me, then scooped Boo into his lap. They made a huge fuss of each other. I started the engine.

"I know I'm special, but you didn't have to dress up! And what's with the beard, you going all Muslim cleric like?" he asked.

"Bear-faced cheek," I retorted, and Luke laughed.

"Aye, very *Italiano*!" We went quiet, then spoke at the same moment.

"You first," I said.

"Me Mam is okay, should be back in her house by Christmas. Uncle Vin and my cousins worked like Trojans. But the stress..."

"I can imagine. And her hip?" I asked, inwardly cursing a red traffic light on the ring road.

"It'll take a while. She's planning a trip down here when she's well. I've not stopped talking about the boathouse." He stroked Boo's head. They seemed so happy to have the pack reunited. Myself, I still felt short of a few aces.

"How's the home-making? Enjoying the busman's holiday, I expect."

The word 'holiday' really riled me: did he imagine I'd sat on my arse these last weeks, gawping at the sea and scattering the occasional cushion?

"Don't know where to begin..."

"An hour 'til we get home: I'm all ears," said Luke, tipping his head back, ready for the low-down on my grand designs.

"Bit of a detour first, actually. Samphire Hall," I said.

"Why's that then?"

"Luke, keep an open mind, right, but I've tried telling you – quite a few times – about these weird dreams I've been having." I swerved to avoid a cyclist.

"Too much cheese at bedtime!" he said. "No, you've been longing for us, I can tell." He lifted his hand from Boo and ran it up the back of my neck: pretty stimulating, and pretty reassuring. So I did it: I started my unlikely narrative from the top, when the sawing dreams started. Chapter by chapter spilt out as we drove into the dusk. Luke did listen; but his occasional questions suggested he thought I was just pitching the plot of some novel I wanted to write.

"A bestseller!" he said at one point.

"Luke, you're not listening. It's all true." I heard my voice cracking with emotion. "This is what I've actually been going through. While you've been fannying about, draining floodwater, hanging around in hospitals."

He sat silently, digesting my angst.

"And Tilly?" he said, eventually.

"You'll meet her in half an hour," I said. "If this fucking traffic lightens up a bit."

"Chill pill..." he warned.

Somewhere before Holt I pulled into a lay-by and told Luke it was time to change.

"You want me to drive?"

"Change. Into your Armani."

"I am knackered," he groaned.

"Join the club. I haven't slept properly in weeks."

He squeezed grudgingly into the back and found his suit bag hanging up.

"You know I hate a black tie do."

As he stepped out to dress in the chilly twilight, a sports car slowed down and a couple of old queens whistled at his buff chest.

"Up yours too!" Luke shouted. I watched him zip his trousers, meticulously button his dress shirt, tilt the wing mirror to tie a painstaking Windsor knot. He was not happy with this palaver – especially on top of his complicated day's travelling – and was visibly taking his time.

"Luke, I don't want to hurry you..."

"But it's really important, aye?" he asked, pained. He climbed in the front, slammed the door, and I accelerated away. Then he spent some time checking his mobile – presumably for messages from up North – before making a disconcerting observation.

"Bertie, you've an air about you, that's... different... like."

"Been catching up with my past," I began. Not what I'd meant to say. Damn. Now he'd start thinking I wanted out.

"'Free and single' again?" he asked. "You fancy that? Shame you can't do 'young' as well."

"Miaow. Nobody loves a fairy when she's forty-something. Thanks for reminding me."

"Too sensitive, that's your trouble, always has been. But everything's cool: I'm back, for keeps. Look what you've been missing!" He flexed his biceps, and gave me a flirty grin.

He did seem happy to see me. I half-smiled across at him, then concentrated on the road. Physically he had it all going on, but the spell apart had distanced us mentally. We both knew it.

Luke went quiet, looking out of the window, while my stomach churned on spin-cycle. Tilly and the NHS and Massey swirled in an adrenaline whirlpool as I fretted about the Bureau confession – so soon to see the light – and how sickened I'd feel if it didn't get Lord James off the hook for Skipper's murder.

Fifteen minutes' silence more, and we turned off the coastal road, into the grounds of Samphire Hall.

"*Expect the Unexpected* eh?" Luke parroted the slogan off the billboard at the gates, voice filled with scepticism. A warden ushered the VW into a freshly-designated parking area. As we stepped out, the chapel bell was ringing four. The Hall's imposing façade was floodlit like a stage set and backlit by a mauve evening sky. Stained-glass windows glowed with the Newton-Grey family crest. Luke's not the type to get nervous, but he seemed pretty subdued as we joined the smartly-dressed queue for the main doors. A pair of flaming sconces blazed invitingly.

"Imagine the bills for this place," he mumbled.

"Wait till you step inside..."

Luke straightened Boo's bow, then his own tie. I couldn't imagine how he was going to react to Tilly. We picked up our tickets at the door.

"Sorry, no dogs," said the dashing, *faux*-Edwardian footman.

"Great. Off home!" was Luke's response.

"Please call Miss Tilly Offord," I told the footman. He addressed a walkie-talkie, and a crackling cockney voice gave us the all-clear. Good old Tel, I thought.

"My mistake, gents: your little friend, it seems, is a VIP."

"Very Important Pet," said Luke, not smiling. And in we went.

I watched his face as the buzz of St Benedict's Foyer assailed us: the myriad flickering candle bulbs, the great hearth roaring with devilish flames. A jazzy clarinettist led her team –'cello, two fiddles and a piano – through a ragtime medley by the sweeping staircase. The paintings, the hangings, the sculptures, the photo exhibits: Luke could hardly fail to be impressed. Tilly and her team had pulled everything off with élan.

I looked up, and there on the mezzanine was the Boleyn Bureau, spotlit, enigmatic, and mouse-brown, the unassuming troublemaker, the dowdy prodigy who dominates the party.

We mingled with guests from the arts, the media, county officialdom, the leisure industry: Samphire Hall was certain to become a major tourist attraction. A dapper old gent in World War I uniform approached us with a basket from which we bought two poppies. I pinned Luke's on his lapel like a bloodstain, thinking of Caleb Bacon's last moments. My own, I wore for Skipper.

The NHS guest list evidently reached wider into the local community: I spotted Bren, Pearl's carer from Walnut Court, pointing out something on the mezzanine. Oddly, it was Skipper's Blakeney Seal, occupying the marble plinth where Antinoüs had been stationed the previous evening. Pearl must have lent it for the ceremony.

"A gorgeous piece," Luke conceded. It struck me that the Diving Seal was another covert troublemaker: a poised, elegant masterpiece that had arguably been the beginning of the end for all concerned. "And who are these?" he asked. I followed his gaze.

"The ghosts of our hosts, Lord James Newton-Grey and his wife, Lady Alice," I told him. A life-size banner presented them as smouldering silent movie stars, welcoming their guests at the foot of the sweeping staircase. "And that athlete, in the background, is our very own Skipper Wood." Nice that Tilly had finally acknowledged Skipper's place in the story.

"Aye, the hunk you've had these wet dreams about. I've been away too long," he said. "Mind you, his lordship is seriously hot." I didn't dare reply.

A period butler glided past with flutes of bubbly on a silver tray; a waitress, attired as a parlourmaid, swished by with canapés. Tilly had hired the staff from a London agency: money well spent.

"I'm parched," said Luke, downing his first champagne.

The foyer was filling so fast that we found ourselves pressed tightly against one of three large vitrines – dazzlingly filled with orphaned heirlooms – that lined the long wall beneath the mezzanine. As a drinks party the Gala Opening was already a raving success: I hoped Tilly's curatorial work would be equally enjoyed. She had each case themed to epitomise particular aspects of Newton-Grey history.

Tilly's neat notices described James's tortoiseshell fountain pens, his pocket watch, trophies from various sports his Cambridge team had excelled in. Incongruously there was also a harmonica, such as Stanley Sellars had played to soothe the troops in 1916. Some pieces were showier: the gold Fabergé cigarette case – engraved '*Forever Yours*' – that Alice had given James at their wedding. Wartime memorabilia included James's VC, and a medal from the Royal College of Surgeons commemorating his 'outstanding contribution to advances in prosthetics'.

I tried to interest Luke in James's wartime diaries, but he remained engrossed with a red-nosed colonel – a living Christmas tree of military decorations – hearing all about the exploits of a marvellous whippet the old cove had owned between the wars.

Despite the sketchiness of my notes, Tilly had managed to showcase fascinating entries from each diary: James with royalty at The Ritz in 1910; his marriage in 1911; *Titanic* in 1912, and so on. Heroic episodes were highlighted in the wartime years. Yet when I craned close to examine the 1917 diary, I saw she'd opened it at

James's final, highly-charged entry, the rain-spattered page that ended with the miraculous finding of Sellars, 'a godsend'.

And something horrible immediately struck me. What did 'godsend' really mean? A godsend to have found his loyal man, or a godsend that Sellars had torn off and rejected his own ID? The diary entries... they stopped at that point: had James done something unspeakable? What if the rain-splattering were tears of remorse?

For all I knew, Sellars's army ID-tags were on display upstairs, hanging round the neck of Stanley's lookalike mannequin: dozens of guests could have seen them already. I surveyed the crowded foyer. What if those people then read this diary, which so clearly suggested – to me at any rate – that James had brought back *only* the dog-tags, and left their shell-shocked owner – and the blackmail secrets he probably harboured – to rot anonymously in France?

Some madness seized me. That page could not be permitted to remain visible. I covertly tested the lid: the vitrine was not locked, but it was not going to lift up, because some fellow-guest in a deerstalker was resting his tweedy backside on it, further along, apparently overcome by the heating.

I caught his eye, and tapped the VIP pass on my lapel. He took the hint and shifted his weight off the glass. I looked around. Well-masked by the crowd, I hinged the top up just enough to get my right hand under the glass, and tugged at the incriminating leaf. The stitching gave way: a fold of four pages came loose in my hand. In a swift move, which any sleight-of-hand magician would have envied, I slipped them into the inside breast pocket of my tux, dropped the lid and turned round again.

Not a moment too soon. Tilly came sashaying on tall heels through the parting crowd in a vintage midnight-blue cocktail number, all tiered silk and tulle, with matching pillbox hat and veil. Heads turned.

"Don't you two look scrumptious?" she said, unpinning her headgear and pecking me chastely on the cheek. "The famous Luke, I assume?" she added, not quite as steadily.

"Infamous," Luke riposted.

"Luke, meet Tilly," I said, watching as my partner eyed up the competition.

She nervously held out her silky-gloved hand, which Luke touched gallantly with his lips, following up with a full-blooded kiss to her blushing cheek. We all laughed, and the ice was broken, between Tilly and Luke at any rate. Meanwhile I was already cursing myself for vandalising the diary. What crazy impulse had possessed me to pull pages out when I could so easily have just turned to another, less incriminating entry? And why was I trying to protect Lord James anyway?

"Love the vintage poster," I said to Tilly.

"Same picture as the souvenir pamphlets: they're on the table in the vestibule. Have mine."

"A brilliant image," I said. I was trying to keep my eyes off her beauty, though I noticed Luke continued to observe her admiringly. The cocktail dress displayed a lot of cleavage, yet this evening her little ornamental key, on its neck-chain, was completely out of sight. What a girl! I thought. A girl whose handiwork I'd just violated? I needed to find a moment to slip my stolen pages back into the diary display.

"Unbelievable graphics bill," Tilly was saying. "Luckily Karsten signed it off."

"Karsten is Dr Wulff, Tilly's boss," I told Luke.

"And little Boo, so dapper in his wing collar!"

Luke had Boo in his arms, fearing he'd be trampled in such a crowd. Boo's luminous eyes gazed aloof around the room, adoring the attention.

"No BFT?" I asked Tilly.

"Dropped her off when I went home to change."

"Tilly's fox terrier," I explained to Luke. "The 'B' is for Bertie." His face darkened, and he coughed into his drink. "Just a coincidence, honest! Your pet name for me, Tilly's pet name for Victoria Albertina. A smart pooch," I added, knowing I still had to find a way of telling Luke how BFT had found Boo half-dead in the woods.

"And what's happened to Antinoüs?" I said.

"Had to lie down," Tilly replied. "His new ankle lasted just hours," she added.

"Antinoüs?" said Luke, forever left out. He winced aside as a roving photographer snapped us.

"A beautiful young man," said Tilly. "When he saw Bertie, he went to pieces. And now he's legless again." Her mischief did nothing for Luke. I put him in the picture.

Suddenly Tilly clicked her fingers.

"Before I forget, you got my text, I hope?"

"I'm ready with the key." I pulled it out and dangled it.

"Snap!" said Tilly, teasing on her neck-chain. To my amazement what rose up between those peachy breasts was not her habitual ornamental key, but a perfect copy of the one I'd found, trefoil pattern and all. Pearl had told me it was 'one of two': here was the duplicate! I felt instantly disorientated, somewhere between dream and *déjà vu.*

"How the hell?" I breathed.

"Karsten gave it to me. Belt and braces, he said. He found it somewhere in James's stuff. Told me you would understand."

I didn't. I struggled to find any meaning in it at all. Wulff might be a world authority on locks, but how could he possibly have recognised this key as a copy when he'd never seen the original? Luke was glaring, as if matching keys were lovers' tokens. I put my hand on his shoulder, as if to signify my true allegiance. I really needed to steady myself.

"Where's *your* man?" I asked, raising my eyebrows at Tilly. She took my cue.

"Jud? Oh, he's looking very dishy tonight. He's got Pearl in tow, though: I parked them in the secretary's office."

"Pearl's here?" Another surprise.

"Resting, before the show at five," Tilly explained, suddenly shifting into business mode. "You'll wait on the bottom step, by James and Alice. Karsten talks first, then me. When I call, you walk up, introduce Massey with a few words, then hand him the key."

"My big moment!" I said. In fact, I couldn't have felt smaller. The duplicate key made my astonishing find seem redundant. Tilly turned aside, buttonholed by some Sloaney friend, tall as an ostrich, with a fuchsia fascinator.

"So you'll be on TV," said Luke grimly.

"Yeah, not what I wanted, but... given the circumstances, I have to really..."

"Bertie, you know what publicity did to me before, after we got the Dildo like."

"Please, not now: talk about it at home, okay?" I retorted.

"Too right," said Luke. He gave me a searing look, and returned to his champagne.

As Tilly got rid of the ostrich, a familiar form in mucky grey raincoat came barging through the elegant guests towards us, like a rubber dinghy among swans.

"Good evening, Inspector," she called.

Massey grabbed a canapé off a passing tray, and stared Luke up and down.

"The other half?" he asked, through a mulch of goats' cheese.

"Aye," said Luke, with stony Northern boldness.

"Some joint, hey?"

"You like a joint, Inspector?" I quipped. Massey looked up at the warmly-lit Renaissance ceiling and changed the subject.

"Bet that cost a pretty packet."

"The Newton-Greys conned that ceiling out of some gullible Benedictine monks," said Tilly.

"Art theft?" said Massey, snatching another nibble. "Leave it with me."

Tilly asked if he'd digested her timetable for the presentation.

"Nothing I couldn't have guessed," he scoffed. Luke turned away.

"Pompous git," I heard him say.

Tilly drew a deep breath. This tension, without a drink, must have been killing her.

"Five sharp, but wait 'til Bertie calls you. Introductions first," she snapped.

"He'll want to list my recent cases."

"Natch, Inspector. Why else are we here?" Her professional smile lasted slightly too long.

I drew Tilly's attention to Karsten Wulff, who was surveying us from the mezzanine, magisterial in his academic gown and hood.

"Excuse me, guys: my Higher Power calls," she said, glad of the excuse. Massey and his infected groin promptly lumbered off, foraging. Luke and I looked vacantly at each other, until our silence was broken by a gaggle of London fashionistas, the kind of media crowd that had driven us up here into the wilderness. Their conversation – mostly screeching sound bites – suggested the eye-popping tastes of Lord James Newton-Grey were contagious.

"Grey is the Art Nouveau black," said the editor of an interiors magazine, known to us from our 'Designed in

London' days. She favoured us with a fleeting emoticon of a smile. Her eye then fell on Boo. "Oh, no price tag? Does it come in other shades?"

"This little fella is an edition of one," Luke deadpanned.

"Shame, dahling: whippets are the new pugs!" she shrilled, as her gang moved on.

The party was in full swing now: the house tours, groups of twenty, had mostly returned and the foyer was packed. But the crowd parted again as Jud approached, propelling a wheelchair in which Little Pearl was propped up on cushions, tinier and frailer than ever. She gaped about in cheerful bewilderment, chewing on the air. Her cornflower blue-eyed smile almost made me relax for a moment. I told Jud he'd just missed Massey.

"Thank God," he said. Luke eyed him – his Hugo Boss suit marred by an awful veteran car tie – as if he was a bit of rough, while Jud smiled winningly back. I bent for a grandmotherly kiss from Pearl.

"You look grander than a duchess," I declared.

"Go on with your lordship," she chuckled.

"Lordship?" said Luke, fathoms out of his depth. I tried to signal that Pearl wasn't all there, and also whispered that he should go easy on the champers. I was a bit dizzy with it myself.

"I had to be here for Pa," Pearl was croaking, with a cheeky twinkle. "Like I told you, the treasure hunt ends at Semaphore Hall." She'd said nothing of the kind, but it was interesting that she was expecting some announcement about her father's killer. I just worried about her frailty, as the weighty moment drew closer.

Luke knelt down and prattled a while with Pearl: maybe she reminded him of his mum. I needed a moment with her myself, to establish why she'd paid for Jud's new surname and extensive tattoos. But she was in full spate, about Jud's parents and their fatal air crash in the nineties.

"Hey man, any news from the inspector about droppin' my charges?" Jud's eyes flickered with anxiety.

"I'm working on it, honest," I replied.

Jud wasn't listening, but gazing around in awe. The serious kit for live telecasting was in place: crews with cameras shouldered at the ready, and behind them the sound engineers and vision mixers with pre-recorded vox pops cued up on multiple monitors. For a disconcerting second I saw my own face fill the largest screen, as zoom lenses panned the foyer. Luke ducked for cover behind his souvenir booklet.

Karsten had chosen to allow all this gear indoors, to heighten the sense of occasion, and minimise the impact of outside-broadcast trucks on the Hall's imposing façade. The foyer felt like a studio set. Wannabees jostled their way into shots like latter-day Anne Boleyns photobombing, and scenesters were marshalled by floor managers into flamboyant tableaux. It was as if we were about to shoot a stylish TV commercial, but for what? Absinthe?

The Tannoy crackled into life: the presentation was imminent. The ragtime musicians wound down. The windows were dark now, but St Benedict's Foyer glimmered like a Venetian palazzo during a masked ball: and tonight a real killer would be unmasked. The hum in the Hall simmered into silence, save a few excited, reverential whispers.

Karsten Wulff, tall and commanding at the microphone, began by talking about his own background, which was all news to me. As an Eritrean orphan, adopted by missionaries, and living in the UK as an immigrant, he held Norfolk's native culture in such high esteem 'precisely because I have none of my own'.

I glanced at Luke: he seemed to have regained some sparkle, his curmudgeonly mood thawed by Little Pearl's daft banter. My twitching eyelid was also growing livelier, as the fateful hour approached.

In annoyingly faultless English, Karsten outlined the Mediaeval origins of the Samphire Estate, its Tudor heyday and downfall, its Jacobean revival, Georgian upsets with the South Sea Bubble and Victorian prosperity under Lord Randolph. Then the Great War, eradicating dynasties of estate workers: new managers, heavy mortgages, the Great Crash and Lord James's suicide. Then decades of scraping by, a skeleton staff gradually selling land to keep a roof on the building. Finally, the NHS fundraising to preserve the house, and the collections, for the nation.

Karsten enjoyed his applause, then handed over 'for the interesting part, to my star curator, Ms Ottilie Offord'. I was doubly jealous that he knew Tilly's exotic name in full. '*The Story of O*', I said to myself, 'O, O, how lovely that face would look in Skipper's O-shaped frame.' Luke would hardly approve, though, and it was his as much as mine.

I was not alone in focusing on Tilly. Every camera, every monitor, followed the svelte figure to the microphone, beside the Boleyn Bureau. Her beauty was about to go viral.

"Dr Wulff has outlined the various stages in the Estate's development," Tilly began. "We know all this from research, of course: we're historians, archivists, we weren't actually there. But there *was* one living witness to all those events, across the centuries: a huge tree that grew outside Samphire Hall, right where your cars are parked now. A Cedar of Lebanon: like Dr Wulff, a precious immigrant." This raised a titter. Tilly glanced along at the NHS bigwigs: this was an important moment for all of them, and they looked pretty serious. Only Karsten was relaxed, beaming hugely.

"Cedars are considered a symbol of peace," Tilly continued, her cut-glass voice quivering slightly. "But around this particular specimen we could arguably construct a contrary narrative of violence."

She expertly drew out her theme: how Anne Boleyn violated the tree with her lover's dagger – and died; Lord James cut it down – and died; Skipper Wood transformed it into a boathouse – and died. Presenting the sequence of deaths as a refrain, she had the crowd chiming in by the third. Her showmanship surprised me; but more surprising still was the way her speech was drawn straight from my tangled notes, which she'd originally rejected, angrily flinging them back in my face. It was most perplexing. So many smartphones were trained on her – and I could see people tweeting – the Cedar Curse was about to go viral too.

But then Tilly spoilt it.

"As I said, we're historians, dealers in facts and data, not superstition. I certainly don't want you thinking these deaths are really connected: but the fact that some people *believe* them to be, that clearly is true; and their beliefs are also part of the history of this place.

"Yes, beliefs. All around you in this glorious and important building – open to the public the first time this evening – is evidence of the tastes, outré for their day, of Lord James, last of the Newton-Greys. The pamphlet refers you to highlights of his collection.

"Lord James was an inventor whose beliefs – like those of his distant forebear Sir Isaac Newton – were far ahead of his time. So far ahead, in fact, that in a real sense they are active, here, among us tonight."

There was a stir in the crowd, and a real tremor of surprise from me. Wulff looked even more delighted.

"Let me explain," Tilly continued. "As you've heard, Lord James died in 1929 – what we now call 'tragic circumstances' – at the boathouse he had commissioned. Commentators see that boathouse as a romantic present for his beautiful American bride, Alice Fitzgerald. Our publicity posters play up the glamour and romance of that liaison. But I would urge you to regard it rather as a *test* – a design challenge – for James's employee, and friend, the former Olympic athlete, Skipper Wood.

"To build a whole dwelling-house from a single tree! And what the aptly-named Wood designed, and built almost single-handedly, is a structure of consummate elegance. It stands unspoilt today – a magical cabin – at the coastal perimeter of the Samphire Hall Estate. I urge you to go and visit."

"Great, Tilly," I muttered to myself. I glanced at my partner: his face was flushed not only from the champagne, but also at the prospect of snoopers' cameras probing his newfound retreat.

"Well, *Robert*," he hissed – like an angry parent Luke reserves my full name for reprimands – "That's us out the frying pan and right into the fire." I wondered how much more of this ordeal he would be able to tolerate.

"I say 'unspoilt,'" Tilly was saying. "In fact, the boathouse has one blemish, a creaky step, which became the *bête noire* of its present occupiers, also distinguished designers." She pointed down at me, and aimed her next words straight at my heart. "For one of them," she said, "Glamour and romance were not enough." I felt myself blush.

"Our hero, there, reasoned that Skipper Wood, had he not fallen and died on his own staircase, would have become a nationally-known figure in the decorative arts." The intensity in Tilly's voice was eye-watering.

"Why did this one step creak so badly? Taking a chisel to the site of the problem, he discovered – against all odds – the doomed Queen's carved teenage signature, which you see under glass over there." Her gloved hand gestured, but not a single head turned to follow it. The monitors showed that every vision-mixer had zoomed in, focusing tightly on the one androgynously-glamorous headshot.

"As well as that very significant discovery, the same spot concealed a unique key, which experts have identified as Tudor." 'Steady on,' I thought. 'It's not unique – your cleavage holds the evidence – and no expert's yet seen the one in my pocket.' Our hero believed he'd decoded the thought processes of a man he'd never known, Lord James, and that the hidden key had a secret purpose."

Tilly was following my 'Enid Blyton' notes – the ravings of 'a fruitcake' as she'd called me – so closely that my guilt about letting her down suddenly seemed groundless. I was amazed she was prepared to go this far: I had underestimated her capacity for mischief.

"I'll come back to that secret key. Perhaps we should now turn our attention to this little writing desk – and thank the thieves who recently stole it from the Hall?" The NHS drones stirred in consternation. Only Karsten looked calm, his big smile egging Tilly on. "Why? Its theft and recovery have given such welcome publicity to our work here!"

Tilly explained that it was the earliest-ever writing desk on record, destined to rewrite history books and antique furniture guides. She likened it to the boathouse: two national treasures. And as she opened it up, to reveal the portrait inside the lid, she told how the Bureau had been gifted by the young Boleyn girl, from her one-time family home at Blickling Hall, to her Samphire Hall sweetheart, Master William Newton-Grey. Tilly stopped, to sip some water, then her speech changed up a gear.

"When our hero there heard this desk being called 'the Boleyn Bureau', he conceived that he'd stumbled on an Edwardian treasure hunt. His belief was that James had hidden the key right by the carved 'Boleyn' signature in the boathouse, so someone – who shared his thought patterns – would be drawn to investigate the Bureau more thoroughly." 'Treasure hunt' had been Pearl's expression; sadly she was sitting too low in her wheelchair for me to detect if she recognised it.

"Now our hero became convinced the key would open a hidden door in this little escritoire, a theory that its theft denied him the chance of proving." Another white lie from Tilly, all in the cause of showmanship, I realised. The same with 'our hero', which I wished she wouldn't keep saying. I touched Luke's hand for support, but he coldly flinched away.

"Not only that, but he insists James concealed, in that cavity, a document that would prove Skipper Wood died, not accidentally, but by foul play." The crowd had been silent, but for the click of cameras: now there was excited chatter. "I know it sounds like fiction, ladies and gentlemen. But I am more than excited to announce that tonight we witness, with the world's eyes on us, the unlocking of a century-old mystery, the solution of an unsuspected crime."

Was Tilly mad? She had explicitly said we weren't mentioning the Agatha Christie stuff! All the pressure now rested on me. Nightmare. My shirt felt clammy; I had to loosen my tie. Shivering, I found my way to the foot of the sweeping staircase, steadying myself against the newel post as Tilly announced my name.

"Will you welcome the man who made that extraordinary connection, and whose beliefs we're now going to test?"

To test? I knew from the Monika charade that Tilly liked a bit of drama, and throve on pressure. But this was ridiculous. '*Calma*, Roberto!' my little *putto* reminded me.

Can applause be sceptical? That's how mine seemed, as I trotted up the stairs, as if to my own trial. The air smelt strongly of champagne. I stationed myself by Skipper's seal, feeling horribly unprepared, as in a dream. Speaking without notes wasn't just risky: I needed the prop of a script in my hand. My pocket contained only James's diary pages: it would be a catastrophe to bring those out. No, I told myself, just be natural be calm – *calma* – and let the fiction-engine do the work.

"Ladies and gentlemen," I began, biting back the words 'of the jury'. My amplified voice echoed round the foyer, and died away. Then nothing. I felt as fragile as Antinoüs, the last man to stand in this spotlight. Logs spat in the great hearth below, crystal droplets clinked above as the chandeliers shimmered in the heat from the TV lights. Tilly, a few yards along the mezzanine, gave a little gasp of concern.

My function was simply to praise Inspector Massey. I knew – so did he – that the big boys at Scotland Yard, and his Masonic associates, and the oligarch's underworld rivals, would all see this broadcast in one form or another. No pressure, then. I reached in my pocket, let my fingertips touch James's diary pages. Only then did I feel a current rising, and the fiction-engine starting to perform.

"Ladies and gentlemen, the lovely Ottilie Offord" – the words flew from my throat, I couldn't help myself – "gives me too much credit. I think we know who's the star this evening: she should be presenting her own history programme, don't you think?" The crowd erupted in cheers and whistles. I saw Luke peering up at me, face overwritten with puzzled hurt: our eyes briefly met as he turned towards the great doors. I didn't watch him. My dark passenger had other plans.

"But we have another star here tonight. My own investigations are the merest shadow of this great detective's work. Whether or not we find a confession in this bureau, the credit must all be his, not mine. Let me introduce a true local hero, a man gifted beyond measure in his field: Chief Inspector Clive Massey..."

Massey lumbered up the sweeping staircase. Applause more muted even than mine greeted the appearance of his bulging brown suit on the stairs. At least he had shed the grubby mackintosh.

The rest of my talk was almost entirely lies. I praised Massey's clear-sighted analysis of the Newton-Grey diaries; his shrewd network of informers; the way a single glimpse of the 'White Russian' cruiser had led him to London, the recovery of the 'stolen Boleyn', and the arrest of a shadowy oligarch. I mentioned the illegals, and Massey's Home Office commendation for securing our national border. I even heard myself talking about the New Year's Honours list.

Massey chuckled, unabashed, in the rumble of applause that ensued. I clapped, myself. "Hear! Hear!" came a voice. Naturally it was his own. But if he was really too conceited to appreciate the extent of my flattery, this speech wasn't really buying Jud's reprieve as planned. Tilly, following every word, knew just what I was trying to do. She nodded encouragement; I guessed she realised that, though I didn't want fame and fortune for myself, it was tough ceding them to a slobbish oaf who so blatantly deserved neither. Down below I spotted Pearl and Jud, the latter looking up at me, his wan expression still full of hope. So... out came the trefoil key.

"And so, to the moment we've all been waiting for..."

But, in that very moment, I glimpsed Luke, and Boo, disappearing into the darkness outside, through the great portal of St Benedict's Foyer, which Tel's XL Security guards slammed shut behind them.

The doors were open only a moment, surely? Yet the gust that swept through the Hall seemed to flurry chandeliers, billow tapestries, tilt paintings. Potted palms swayed, candles flickered. The commotion drew gasps from an anxious audience, or was it just the sudden darkness that alarmed them? For the power had failed as well: of that there could be no doubt.

I felt the sudden rush of some kind of vortex, up the sweeping staircase, on to the mezzanine, eddying round the very point where I stood beside the Blakeney Seal, on Antinoüs's plinth. The room dramatically chilled, and the hackles on my neck stood to attention as though a visiting dignitary had entered the room. I gasped for air, and an aroma of aniseed filled my nostrils. Good God, I suddenly understood! This electric presence... Lord James had come to my aid.

Lights blinked on again. Uncertain laughter. Then a rising swell of applause from the crowd, supposing these disturbances were part of the poster's promise, '*Expect the Unexpected*'.

I noticed Massey, striking a pose for the BBC crew as they raced to reboot their camera. And a devilish wit, inhaled with the aniseed – by which Lord James had become a 'dark passenger' inside me – began urging me towards some kind of vengeance I did not yet understand.

"Inspector, indulge us if you would be so kind – your smartphone?" I held my hand out, across the Boleyn Bureau that separated us on its podium. "Please, that amazing 'selfie' you took in the oligarch's treasure room? To set up the climax of the evening? After all, this is really your night."

Massey seemed flummoxed. But, sensing no option, he fished the phone from his pocket, unlocking the passcode, and bringing up the curious selfie before passing it gingerly over to me.

I leant over to the mic.

"One moment, ladies and gentleman," I said. I scrolled the screen this way and that, in case there was a clearer image, but found only workaday shots, vehicles, locations. "Let's hope there's nothing naughty on the DI's phone!" I stage-whispered, to cover the delay. The audience giggled edgily. Massey lurched forward, snarling "No," in the guise of a cough. I still didn't know where this was all heading.

The tipsy audience roared. Nobody really supposed I'd find anything objectionable on Massey's phone, but they loved the teasing. Each time I glanced up, Massey was trying some new version of his 'what a good sport I am' face. His agony was delicious. My pulse was hammering in my temple. Whispering from the foyer below ramped up the tension. I hadn't felt this alive in years.

But then... I got lost in Massey's phone files. I couldn't find my way back to the Tudor selfie. Unexpectedly, I did click on a directory containing dodgy downloads: full-frontal shots of young girls, barely legal. 'Filthy old bastard,' I thought. The crowd was sounding impatient. A camera tech, ducking low to keep out of shot, reached up and passed me a video cable with the right connector for the monitors.

I played up the pantomime of searching the phone. Massey dabbed his forehead with a tired-looking hankie. My own discomfort verged on panic, as my fingers frantically tried to find a way out of his labyrinth of directories, only to delve accidentally deeper, and stumble into a cellar of much darker porn... repugnant images of younger children, some dressed as *putti* –'tasty little angels' as he'd once said – flying, spread-eagled, from abuser to abuser.

'Evil C' – his backwards name now sickeningly apt – must have been caning himself for not e-mailing the one selfie photo over to me, as he'd promised. What I'd found here put his whole professional life, not just the anticipated promotion, in jeopardy. As he leaned ever closer across the Bureau – desperate to grab the smartphone – his muddy eyes bulged with fear. Should I plug it in now, display his depravity to the world? I brought the phone in my left hand close to the TV feed in my right. A wave of uncomfortable murmurs rose up from the foyer. Then I understood how Lord James – no stranger to sexual blackmail himself – was planning for me to help Jud, making up for Skipper's final humiliation. I suddenly understood what I had to do.

"And, just to detain you a moment longer, ladies and gentlemen," I resumed. "The inspector has pledged a pardon for a young chap, here with us tonight, who unwittingly got caught up in the illegal immigration scam. The informant I mentioned earlier, whose crucial info led the inspector to capture the ringleader. Jud Wood, will you step up here, please?"

My hand was poised to connect the phone to the monitor feed. Massey was swallowing hard, quaking in his disgusting suit, moments away from public humiliation as his perverted turn-ons – I'd settled on a graphically vile shot involving a young boy and a dog – appeared in sickening close-up on every plasma screen in the building, in every living room across the county. Our eyes locked in a clash of wills.

Jud had found his way up the stairs. Massey, having dabbed his face and forehead dry, leaned close to the microphone and shook Jud's hand with sour-faced deliberation.

"Congratulations, son – the force is indebted to you for your courage and cooperation in coming forward. My pledge: you are categorically absolved of any charges."

The viewers would not have realised that Massey's gaze was fastened on my own face as he spoke: never a glance at Jud. The Samphire Hall crowd all applauded his apparent graciousness; Massey, drenched in private humiliation, took a bow; Jud beamed and punched the air with a gleeful fist.

But the roof was about to blow-off Samphire Hall: in a blind impulse of revenge – the reckless instinct James had felt when he defied honourable expectation and extinguished Caleb Bacon – I jammed the cable into the phone socket and clenched my eyes tight shut. Total silence told of the crowd's revulsion as the bestial image shattered the spell of a magical evening. How could I have failed to foresee how this moment's vengeance on the hated Massey would humiliate the NHS as well? Darling Tilly, what have I done to you?

Yet the silence persisted. Someone was trying to prise the phone from my hand. I opened one eye. It was the young technician, some kind of additional adaptor clenched in his teeth. The monitor screens had been showing only a jerking zigzag of grey and white. Just like the Gunpowder Plot, my bombshell had failed. And in a moment the problem with the video-feed would be resolved.

'*Calma, calma*!' I felt another moment of clarity, and the 'back' arrow on Massey's phone snapped into focus for the first time. Ten or so stabs at this button, retreading my steps through his virtual sex-dungeon, and I was home where I'd started. In went the adaptor-cable. Up came the Boleyn selfie. Out poured the applause.

There it was, in dazzling High Definition – Massey with the Boleyn Bureau, and, behind both, the unmistakable manifestation of the Queen herself. The audience went wild at this extraordinary apparition, raising their glasses in a deafening ovation, stamping their feet on the parquet. Massey basked in his own glorification, as Karsten and his associates from the NHS – mystified though they undoubtedly were – toasted the wonderful showman. As for me, I knew I had come closer to disaster than ever before, and it was a profoundly uncomfortable feeling. I braced myself weakly, letting the Antinoüs plinth take my weight.

The inspector was gesticulating to the technician to hand him the phone: he would never let that device out of his fat hand again. The applause bore home to me how I had effectively collaborated with this paedophile. The hypocritical bastard had got away with it all. It was I who was left wounded, by the sudden certainty that it had not been the calming voice of the *putto* that had rescued me from the sex-dungeon, but the call of my own hated genes – the genes of the Secret Admirer, the child molester, the dog-abuser – through whose influence I had now opened the doors of promotion for this equally invidious pervert.

It was the proof of paternity I had been dreading, I realised in a moment. But there was no time to evaluate the revelation: the main event was upon me, as the media glare turned towards the star attraction, the Boleyn Bureau, that little time bomb of a writing desk. This too could go 'bang', or prove to be a hopeless fizzle.

Despite my inner turmoil, I reached for the microphone, and managed to speak as suavely as Lord James, hosting one of his lavish parties.

"Where was I, before our royal star guest interrupted?" At a signal from Tilly, the musicians struck up a showy refrain of *Greensleeves*, their token burst of Tudor music. I scanned the crowd below, searching briefly for Jud and Pearl, and to see if Luke and Boo had returned to the proceedings; but a bout of vertigo, induced by the hallucinatory absinthe, made me sway with nausea.

"Please, Inspector, will you do us the honour of revealing the document you say is hidden in the Boleyn Bureau?" I quivered. Massey hesitated. "Go on,

Inspector: without your genius, you Sherlocksmith, this treasure would have been lost forever."

"Of course," he agreed, stepping over to swipe the precious key from my hand.

'*Calma*, Roberto!' I closed my eyes, to pray for Skipper's deliverance and Lord James's vindication. When they opened, Karsten had the Bureau on its back, and Massey was on his knees, squeezing his chubby fist tight into the innards of the secret compartment, gasping with the contortion as he retrieved... what? The long-overdue confession... I felt my life depended on it.

Tilly was sitting on the edge of her seat, but Karsten Wulff seemed insolently relaxed. Huge white teeth smiled at me, eyes laughing. In a lucid flash, like a flare going up, I saw the connections, the hot Masonic power lines glowing under the surface of it all. My God. Wulff had found the duplicate key, he'd been in the BB before me, knew what the scroll actually said. That was why Massey had been invited. He wouldn't look a fool: he'd solve Skipper's murder, earn his ill-deserved promotion. And why did Wulff want such a corrupt copper ruling all of Norfolk? So he could get away with... what? Had he stolen the BB himself? The 'inside job'? My fiction-engine was overheating. I could feel it pulsing in my temple.

"Aha. As I suspected." Massey beamed, standing erect to strip off the red ribbon and unfurl the ivory paper. His hooded eyes widened with orgasmic relish as he began to read.

"15th April 1920
To whom it may concern..."

Nothing could puncture his glory, his apotheosis even – except my swaying, my gasping for air, and the frenzied stir in the crowd as people leapt forward to try and catch me... before my fainting head struck the top step of the sweeping staircase, and I started to fall.

CHAPTER TWENTY-THREE
FIREWORK NIGHT

I was strapped to a stretcher of some kind, my head throbbing. Something had struck me above the eye, good and hard, but I couldn't get my hands free to feel the wound. Consciousness... it came and went.

Tall in front of me, motionless as a hedge, stood the backs of a richly-dressed crowd, whose clothes suggested some period other than my own. They were listening intently as, above the hissing in my mind, a woman's clear voice spoke about "... this good and faithful friend to Samphire Hall, and to me, whose tireless work has taken its toll."

Christ! Surely Skipper Wood was being described, presumably to a courtroom. 'A good and faithful friend...' But if this was Lady Alice, where was her Virginian accent?

I needed to glimpse her in the flesh, but when I tried to move an orderly, in green uniform with black epaulettes, pressed me down again, re-fixing a breathing mask over my nose and mouth. So that explained the hissing. But why keep me prisoner? What were they gassing me with?

It was hard to keep my mind on track. This event had clearly been running a while: I needed to work out whose testimonies I had missed. Closing my eyes, I saw Lord James up front in a chalk-stripe suit, sombre at a mahogany table, his hair already greying at the temples. His spirits must have risen as witness followed witness: Bailey, the chauffeur, commending his employer's steadiness; Countess Daisy with a glowing testimonial to her lifelong friend; the still-comely Ida Henderson, James's latter-day guardian, describing Lord Randolph as an ogre of a father, someone she was terrified of encountering in the cellars and passages. But James's devoted estate manager, Stanley Sellars... what would he have revealed? Perhaps I haven't missed him: he could be called next?

Despite my physical predicament, my mood was optimistic, certain James's trial was going well. Yet some darker part of my mind warned me to see things differently. Why was I here, out of my own time? This time it was no spectral excursion of my CGI avatar: I was in my physical body, wounded, restrained and struggling to think straight despite under the influence of whatever I was inhaling.

Was I to be called to the stand too? I was least appropriate character witness James could hope for: my verdict would depend on something... what...? concealed in the Boleyn Bureau. The Bureau? How and when had Tilly's Gala Evening ended? I racked my muddled brain. Surely we'd never got as far as hearing the fateful scroll read aloud. What date were we, now? I blinked my eyes open for a moment. Formal attire all around me: 1920s perhaps? The long-hidden scroll had been dated April of that year, as I recalled.

Yet if this is really James's trial, I reasoned with myself, he will have brought that scroll with him. He locked it safe for just such an eventuality! And if my testimony won't be needed, what am I actually here for? 'Christ!' I said to myself, 'I'm a prisoner, a guilty man.' But guilty of what? Of concealing how James had murdered Caleb, his blackmailer, in 1917? Or would they make me empty my pockets, display the stolen diary pages recording the 'godsend' – when Stanley Sellars had lost his name, never to be mentioned again? Lord James would not thank me for that.

I opened my eyes again: above me, seraphim were crossing a ceiling... so this hearing was happening back in St Benedict's Foyer? I needed a proper view, tried to get up; my orderly pressed me down again. His voice, muffled, not unkind, said I needed to rest.

I tried to think back to that future time, when Tilly's display of Newton-Grey mementoes had graced the Gala Evening. But in my thoughts her vitrines now displayed court evidence: Exhibit A, Caleb Bacon's blood-spattered cap; Exhibit B, a carpenter's saw; Exhibit C, a swatch of vivid green paper. Each reminder brought a wave of nausea, obliging me to close my eyes again, lie back on my hard stretcher.

Suddenly, a stir in the crowd: the woman's voice again. Surely Alice, her hair fashionably bobbed, was back in the witness stand. Cloche hat, black velvet wrap-coat, Astrakhan collar upturned: the 'silent movie' poster – commissioned by Tilly for the Gala Opening – had been spot-on. James's coal-black eyes dilate: Alice has indeed changed since he last saw her. Or is he gazing, with animal lust, at my beautiful Tilly? It sounds so like her voice.

The hissing fuse in my head tells me time is running out. Lord James jumps from his seat: his counsel restrains him from rash accusations about her adultery with Skipper Wood. A chaos of whispers surrounds me: murmurs sweep the chamber. Again, the grip of a hand holding me down, as if I'm the one who's delirious. A clock ticks portentously, a time bomb.

Surely Lord James will take the stand himself? If I listen carefully I may find out what happened in the year of his empty diary. Just one thing is certain: James may have cheated death in the Somme, but he cannot sidestep scandal at home. If his sexual relationship with Skipper Wood is mentioned, homophobic heckles – 'queer', 'deviant' – will rain from the gallery, a never-ending torrent.

And then I hear a banging – either doors slamming, or the rap of a judge's gavel – and a cry for 'Order!' But when the witness is called, it's not my name. Emotion surges as she's sworn in, Mrs Beulah Wood, Skipper's widow. Once steely and robust, with an abundance of wiry dark hair, the doctor's unassuming daughter seems meek and sallow and pitiful as she feebly steps into the dock.

Straining again to see, I focus on a gas cylinder. So it's oxygen they're pumping into me; no wonder my thoughts are racing. Lying down, I shut my eyes, and James frowns, feels for the absinthe flask in his pocket. Exhibit C – emerald like Alice's eyes – gives the green light: Beulah passes a letter to her counsel, who reads:

"*15th April 1920*
"To whom it may concern.
"When my husband Mr Wood married me, we lived on together in the house where I grew up. My late father was a physician there, and he warned me never to disturb the parlour walls. He understood chemistry, and said there was a strong toxin in their green colour."

A frail voice gasps. Court reporters head up their pads – **WOOD'S WIDOW CONFESSES.**

"After my husband's infidelity with Lady Alice Newton-Grey, revenge was my only salvation. I asked Skipper to strip off that deadly wallpaper, while I went off for a seaside break, taking our children Archie and Little Pearl, to be out of harm's way."

At this revelation a cry rises up from the audience, men and women together. A quick hand removes my oxygen mask, loosens the straps that secure me to my stretcher, and turfs me onto a chair. My warden – I now see he was a St John Ambulance orderly – leaves my side abruptly and pushes the stretcher trolley into the seething crowd.

The gavel raps again, the voice calls once more for 'Order!'

"I saw this coming, all along," it adds. "They don't call me *'The Poirot of the Fens'* for nothing." Jesus, this is fucking Massey! They've made him a judge as well?

"Under cover of the symptoms of copper arsenide poisoning, from the brilliant green pigment, I gradually dosed Skipper's meals with the ratsbane I kept under my sink. His friends assumed he was suffering from gastroenteritis, the symptoms being so similar. My thinking was, even if a coroner discovered poison in his bloodstream, the green wall-coverings, whose toxic properties were known to educated men, would be judged the true culprit.

"I, Beulah Coral Wood, on this day of our Lord 15th April 1920, make this sworn statement in hopes that Jesus Christ our saviour will have mercy upon my wretched soul."

As my head cleared I dizzily rose to my feet, but of course Mrs Beulah Wood was nowhere to be seen: the caterwauling was not in fact her crying mercy, for her children's sake, as she was taken down to the cells. Yet even if the trial had been a delirious oxygen-fuelled illusion, something very real was making the present crowd mill in consternation.

The gavel sounded a third time, demanding 'Order!' But this time it was not Massey who appealed for calm. High on the mezzanine I saw the imperious Dr Wulff taking the mic, informing the crowd that 'a second medical emergency' had occurred, and instructing us to proceed outside and 'quietly enjoy the fireworks'.

I felt weak with foolish relief at emerging unscathed from this nightmare of a trial, and especially at James's exoneration too, in respect of Skipper's murder at least. The Gala Opening was ending; I was relieved to see Massey dithering about on the mezzanine like a leaking barrage balloon, cheated – by someone else fainting, perhaps – of the adulation he'd expected as his reading of Beulah's confession reached its climax.

Outside the Hall the first volleys of fireworks could already be heard. And through the thinning crowd I could see the wheeled stretcher coming back to its station at the back of the foyer.

Wait, what's this... dear God, the hunched form, tiny on the long stretcher trolley, was Pearl's. An orderly held oxygen – my former mask – to her face. Another squinted at a handheld unit whose wires ran under Pearl's blanket. As the little screen approached I glimpsed numbers winking in descending sequence: 64, 60, 56. Jud was white-faced; Bren, the carer, looked grim. Christ, what has happened?

'*Calma*, Roberto,' said the little *putto*. The room swayed a moment as if I were being tossed in a tempest. As my sea legs returned I offered my assistance, but someone had already phoned for an air ambulance. Little Pearl, Bren told me, had had 'a turn'.

Feeling the contusion above my eye, I started to recall how I'd fallen, by Antinoüs's plinth, as Massey was poised to read the long-hidden confession. The screens of scrolling stills brought home the evening's main events – especially those involving the photogenic Tilly, whom the camera must have been following. She'd played an unexpectedly positive part in bringing Skipper's murderer to light: but suddenly that achievement seemed pointless, lightweight, compared with helping Pearl.

Tilly herself appeared, trying like many others to get near the stretcher. Freezing air streamed in through the open doors, and the grandest fireworks detonated in a cacophonous finale. Who would notice, now, if I slipped the stolen diary pages from my pocket back into the vitrine? I took a few paces... but was hauled up short by seeing my own picture appear on the exhibition monitors, suddenly switched to a slide show of photographic poses taken during the evening, alongside Tilly, our pose an eerie echo of James and Alice in the poster at the foot of the stairs. But in the background, rather than Skipper Wood, was Luke: caught in the act of turning away from the camera, his expression was wretchedly pained and unhappy.

Everything came into focus. How very stupid I'd been in my isolation these past weeks, burrowing compulsively into the past, fuelling senseless obsessions, when all I really wanted, all I'd ever wanted, was the northern soul of my cocky partner Luke, and a normal life in the present with our beloved Boo. They were the glue that held me together. And I hadn't seen them for hours.

Blinking tears of exhausted emotion, I made for the main doors, calling to Jud that I'd be back shortly: I don't suppose anyone heard. I had to dodge among the cars that were already leaving; drivers shouted as I brushed their bonnets in my headlong rush, praying Luke hadn't already left me, sharing a taxi with some loathed London fashion diva back to Norwich Station.

There was the campervan, looming over a sea of sports cars. As I zigzagged towards it my heart thumped for Luke, as it had done the first time we'd met, on a blind date ten years earlier. I banged on the VW's tinted window, and banged again. My teeth were chattering, partly from nerves, partly from the chill of the night.

Behind the dark glass a light blinked on. I glimpsed Boo, springing from under a tartan blanket, and then, to my relief, a bleary-eyed Luke throwing a second covering back. He had crashed out in the slide-away bed.

"Luke, open up, please!" I knocked on the door repeatedly.

He stuck a V-sign up, his fingers in front of the light so I couldn't miss them.

"Let me in, I need to talk..."

"Fuck off, Bertie!" he shouted.

"Please Luke, it's urgent."

"Need a bed, 'our hero'? Hasn't 'the lovely Miss Offord' offered?"

"This is serious. Pearl's had a turn. I need to get back to the Hall!"

Luke's face changed; he unlocked the door, and I climbed in, swiftly sliding it shut to keep the cold air out.

"You'd better not be joking."

"Little Pearl heard her mother's confession. What a shock: she's so frail..."

"Her mam owned up to killing her dad?"

"Yeah."

"Jesus... Pearl's a honey, the best in there. What a pity..." Seeing my distress he put an affectionate arm around me, but soon withdrew it. "So if you hadn't got so obsessed with your mission, you think Pearl wouldn't be dying. Right?"

"I feel so bad..."

"You look bad and all. What have you done to your head?"

"It's nothing. I fell. Just tension, lack of sleep..."

"I leave you alone a few weeks, and look at the bloody mess I come back to," he said quietly. "Now I've got two head cases, me mam and you!"

"Fuck, Luke, you've no idea have you... I thought I lost you tonight..." And just as I was going to explain how much I really loved and needed him, the clatter of helicopter rotors interrupted. "The air ambulance, for Pearl. I best get back to the Hall."

"Boo, stay," Luke commanded, pulling a parka over his dress shirt. "I'm coming with you."

The helicopter was settling on the grass across the forecourt from Samphire Hall. The closer we got, the more I sensed something was seriously wrong. Bren was wheeling the stretcher up to the fuselage hatch, but a blanket covered Pearl entirely: no sign of oxygen. Jud was crouched beside her, holding an exposed hand, bawling. The rotors slowed as the engine whistled down, as if the urgency had gone out of the situation. A paramedic packed away a defibrillator.

"What's happened?" I called as we approached.

"Heart failure," Tilly croaked.

"No!" I yelped. "Jud. I'm *so* sorry." I put my arm round Pearl's devoted grandson, and welled up. Luke looked on helplessly.

"Man, I'd've done years in jail, rather than losin' my nanna," he howled. Tilly put a sympathetic hand on my arm. Luke looked very uncomfortable, which made me feel worse.

"We tried our best," the paramedic told us. "Her heart just gave out. Is there anyone you want us to call? There's a radio-phone in the 'copter."

"Nooo thanks..." Jud trembled, wiping his eyes with a handkerchief that was already wringing wet. "I've only got..." The poor soul glanced at me, then at Tilly, and then at his grandmother under the blanket. There was a harrowing pause while he struggled, then failed, to complete the sentence. It was heartbreaking.

"Look, sorry to hassle you folks, but there's another emergency coming through, so we need to get going," the pilot shouted down from his door.

"Yah, of course," said Tilly, drying her eyes. The engines screamed back into life, whipping the night around us.

"Guys, I'll go with Jud and Pearl!" Tilly yelled above the racket. "You get home. You need to see to that bang on your head, Bertie."

"We're coming too!" I shouted.

"Sorry, no room," another medic called, as Pearl's stretcher was lifted aboard.

"Where are you taking her?"

"King's Lynn. Hospital mortuary," he added.

"I'll take Luke home, then drive over to King's Lynn," I offered Tilly, close to her ear to beat the din. She broke away and hauled herself up into the aircraft.

"No need, Bertie. Nothing anyone can do!" she shouted, her face still dripping compassion for Jud.

"I'll call you!" I shouted to the closing door. Luke and I were ushered away, and the crew bundled in for take-off. Our clothes puckered in the downdraught. For some reason we gazed at the yellow shape until its lights vanished completely over the roof of the Hall, carrying Little Pearl away into the dark sky, a plucky survivor from a former world now joining the cast of the departed.

"I guess that's that, then," said Luke, with a quiver.

"Let's get home. We're both done in."

Arm in arm, we walked back to the van over grass churned up like a battlefield by the traffic. A warlike pall of sulphurous smoke still hung over the grounds from the fireworks. I pondered what Skipper would have made of that bombshell confession from his wife – his murderer – which had also, almost a century later, killed his Little Pearl, so close to the spot where James had ordered him to fell the fateful cedar.

Our VW took its place at the end of a long queue, a thousand tail lights winding their slow way down the drive to the bottleneck at the main road. Luke broke the silence just once, as we passed through the floodlit portal and out of the grounds.

"What time is it?"

"No idea. Probably getting on for..."

"Where's the gorgeous watch, Bertie?"

"You noticed?"

"Of course I bloody notice, when someone stops wearing my wedding present."

"Luke, it's a long story. Can we discuss this another time?"

"It better be good," he muttered. A moment later he was either asleep or sulking silently.

I drove home down the dark country lanes, wondering where and how I could explain. A watch was replaceable; and material items seemed a low priority while the guilt from Pearl's death thumped in my chest. Every heartbeat reminded me of the ripped-out diary pages in my pocket. Returning them to the Hall was a problem for another time.

The next few days were a bit of a blur – except for unpacking the five tall boxes in our hall, conducting repairs, and giving the entire boathouse a premature spring clean. Luke accepted the rest of my story; he carefully tended the wound to my head. Staying busy was the only cure for the terrible sense of anticlimax that engulfed me.

Of course, I did my best to be supportive to Jud; Luke was kind to him too. Tilly and Jud came over several times: we told stories of Little Pearl and drank endless coffee, surrounded by the haze of Jud's weed. How often – as I tortured myself over what I'd done to Pearl, and what I'd yet to do to Massey – I longed to join him in hash-fuelled oblivion. But that way I'd only lose Luke as well.

Was it a week, was it two? One chilly winter's morning found the four of us idling, in pale sunshine, on the calmest of waters off Blakeney Point, watched from the shingly spit by hundreds of grey seals, and occasional snowy pups. Moist-eyed Tilly pressed 'play', on Jud's tinny ghetto blaster, and the irksome song from my Skipper dreams – Pearl's lullaby in earliest childhood – shrilled out over the seal sanctuary.

"*Oh, you beautiful doll*," Jud sang under his breath, while he slowly scattered his nanna's ashes, on the whisper of a southerly breeze; spreading like suds, they glistened as pearls do, then slowly sank in the depths of a fathomless grave.

About the time my head wound stopped troubling me, I realised I'd stopped suffering dreams of Skipper Wood at work in the boathouse; he'd been quiet since the Gala Opening. In the here-and-now we all felt damaged, listless, drained: yet it really did seem that Skipper's spirit had been released from the cedar cage by the publication of his wife's confession. One thing was for sure: yet another branch of the Boleyn Cedar curse had come crashing down on dear Pearl. But nobody blamed me for her death, as if they could see no link between consequence and cause. Nor did they credit anything I tried to explain about paranormal interventions at the boathouse and Samphire Hall: not even those I tried to pass off as having happened in dreams.

"So that's it. Game over. Back to normality like..." Luke remarked at the breakfast table, over porridge.

"Yeah... I guess so..."

"You still sound deflated."

"I just expected... something more from the whole ordeal."

"You know who dunnit: is that not enough?" said Luke, taking his bowl to the sink.

"Well... it dragged up some stuff from my past."

"What have you got to worry about?" He took my bowl as well, though I hadn't quite finished. That's Luke.

"Nothing, really..." I replied. I'd only identified my psychotic birth father, and lived with the nightly dread of being murdered by him. Since Luke had been back, that fear had diminished, its place taken by the worry that Massey could be looking for ways of shutting me up. I would not be the first sexual blackmailer in the Samphire saga to meet a sorry end.

"Great; so let's enjoy this place, get some real living and loving done." Luke's cheeky grin was always a tonic. Suddenly we were hugging again, by the sink, and his strong body felt good close to mine. But a knock at the kitchen door interrupted us.

"I'll go," he said. Moments later I heard him shout, "Haven't you scumbags heard? We are not doing any interviews!"

"We're turning away good money, you know," I said as he slammed the door.

"Don't even go there." Luke's upbeat mood had gone, and with it our moment's intimacy. "Tell your friend Tilly, and her PR machine: the answer is 'No comment'. About anything. Period."

"I'll give her a ring later—" I began, but he interrupted:

"Oh, and this has come for you: hand-delivered, look, no stamp. At least they use the mailbox, didn't come prying down here and shove it under our door." It was always Luke who went up the lane, first thing, to collect our letters.

The envelope was embossed with the dark brown logo of the Norfolk Heritage Society.

"Hey, d'you fancy a trip up to Holt?" I asked. "See the shops, all Christmassy?" Unknown to Luke, I had a special order to collect from Picturecraft, the art suppliers.

"Aye, it'll blow away the cobwebs."

Luke threw on a puffer jacket and got Boo ready in his winter coat.

"See you out there," he said.

Hand-delivered, I thought. Maybe a belated thank you for my contributions to the drama of the Gala Opening? I opened it up. More than a page of dense typing, it was signed with the initial 'K'. I was addressed, ominously, by title, initials and surname.

The start was friendly enough, trusting I was 'back in rude health' following my 'black-out at our presentation'. But I read on...

... with Samphire Hall poised to become a major tourist attraction, the Board, at December's AGM, made a significant decision concerning the unadopted way that connects the annex – your boathouse – to the A149 coastal road.

Signposting this lane and providing a metalled surface will not only benefit present and future residents of 'Wood Feels', but will also provide a convenient and hazard-free route for our paying visitors – and there will be many, thanks to your notable researches and discoveries – who wish to view the unique and historic building, and contemplate its integral relevance to the history of the Samphire Estate.

'Notable researches and discoveries'. I read that phrase again, aloud: true recognition at last, and from a highly-regarded academic. But what kind of academic would want to tarmac over Alice's 'scented alley'?

Our legal team advises that your own conveyancing solicitor, when completing the purchase of 'Wood Feels' on 3 August 2008, did alert you to this Easement, highlighted in red on the Land Registry plan attached. It specifies the Society's territorial options, in perpetuity, over the path in question.

Luke was impatiently sounding the VW's horn now. God, what if he knew that my famous 'researches and discoveries' had neglected to cover our own interests? Wulff's letter hammered that point home:

We understand you may not have expected the dormant right of way to be re-activated so soon during your tenure of the boathouse. If you wish to discuss the matter further, please contact me at your convenience.

Every good wish,

K
Karsten Wulff *BSc, MA, PhD, FRHS*
Director, Norfolk Heritage Society

"Bertie, come on," Luke shouted, somewhere up the red-highlighted track.

"Give me a sec'..." I called back weakly.

The photocopied plans, paper clipped to the letter, of course validated Karsten's position. So it was all about money – never mind the poor bastards trying to live normal lives in the boathouse, when it becomes a Disneyfied sideshow to the Samphire Hall Experience. 'Samphire Hell, more like,' I whispered to myself. 'Luke's going to kill me.'

"Bertie! Get your arse in gear..."

"Coming..." I gulped, cramming the letter into my jacket pocket.

I locked up, and strode up to the van, wearing a smile intended to conceal my shock. Yet another tendril snaking forth from James's accursed cedar, looking for its victim. And this time Luke – angrily fighting through the tourists, to reach his own front door – would not be merely a looker-on.

CHAPTER TWENTY-FOUR
LA FÉE VERTE

It should have been a happy afternoon, mooching around the shops in Holt, but all I could think of was that upsetting letter from the Norfolk Heritage Society. With Christmas looming on top of all my other upsets, I had no choice but withhold Karsten's news from Luke until after the New Year.

Luke was a while in the barber's. I collected my piece of oval glass from Picturecraft, the framing shop. I also slipped in a call to our solicitor, who confirmed that the NHS proposal was well within its territorial rights. The tension, the uncertainty, was unbearable. That night, once Luke had gone to bed, I went down to the jetty hotspot, intending to speak to the Samaritans, though I cancelled the call before anyone answered. Things may yet sort themselves out, I told myself.

The following Saturday, trying to get back to some kind of normality, we went to the Theatre Royal in Norwich where *The Tempest* was opening, starring Stephen Fry. My mind wandered most of the evening. In the campervan, going home, Luke claimed Fry had been 'brilliantly convincing'; when I said I knew a thing or two about cruel aristocrats – citing Lord Randolph Newton-Grey – he went mental. Any topic relating to Samphire Hall was off-limits after the upsets of the Gala Opening. Oddly, though, he had invited Tilly and Jud over for Christmas lunch.

With the holiday fast approaching, seasonal preparations kept us occupied: hoping the first Christmas in our new home would be not only special, but also peaceful. But even as we strung up the cards, and wove swags of greenery through the banisters, my mind was playing out various consequences of the tidings I'd have to reveal come New Year. Luke would surely want to sell up. The Norfolk Heritage Society would be the only prospective buyer – no private individual would choose to live amid a major tourist attraction – and we'd be at the mercy of whatever price Dr Wulff was willing to offer.

I kept in touch with Tilly, clandestine calls when Luke was occupied. She'd tried to mention my anxieties to her boss, but Wulff had berated her for 'meddling outside her remit'. I swore Tilly to secrecy, to preserve a happy Christmas for Luke.

Tilly did tell me that Wulff wanted the NHS to strengthen its connections with Clive Massey, already in post as Norfolk's police supremo. The Masons worked quickly, I realised. I didn't tell her about my dark discovery on his smartphone: that was another problem to be addressed straight after the holidays. The Samaritans beckoned again, yet I soldiered on like a Tommy, bottling my troubles, trying to smile, smile, smile.

Despite the cold Luke wanted to play lumberjacks and search the woods around Samphire Hall for a perfect blue Scots pine to be our Christmas tree. I couldn't tell him he was reviving a tradition from Lord James's time. We hacked away – me full of vengeful venom against the NHS – but with well-worn tools. I wished Skipper had left us a decent saw under the stairs instead of an empty picture-frame. At twilight, skulking like poachers, we strapped our booty atop the VW and soon had it set up at the foot of the stairs. We spent the evening decorating it with our collection of vintage baubles. As it warmed up, its piquant scent eclipsed the everyday aroma of cedar, and the boathouse started feeling pretty seasonal.

Christmas Eve passed into a slate-grey dawn. Before Luke awoke, I finally resolved to wrap the present I'd planned for him in happier times, and fitted Skipper Wood's oval frame with the glass and a trimmed picture of our boathouse – one of the master carpenter's blueprints, countersigned by Lord James himself – that I'd captured on my old phone's camera during that first visit to the Audit House. It made a lovely piece: but how Luke would take this double dose of Skipper Wood I couldn't predict. It went back in my drawer for the moment.

We'd shifted the refectory table from the kitchen to the main lobby, next to the stairs, so we could eat beside the festive tree. When I'd finished laying the table, it looked a picture: Leonardo could not have taken more care over the Last Supper.

"Bertie, something more cheerful?" Luke called from the kitchen. Our guests were due soon, and my Gregorian chants CD was probably a tad sedate.

"Old King Cole, *Christmas Classics*?" I suggested.

"Natty!" he shouted back. He hates company in the kitchen until everything's ready to go.

Boo had rootled out his gift-wrapped goodie bag, under the tree.

"Be patient, boy!" Stroking his head, I noticed a small square box for me, Luke's writing on the label. I was about to fetch Skipper's oval frame to lie beside it – we'd chosen identical paper – when the bell sounded.

"Yours!" Luke commanded; he went on stirring gravy, but craned apprehensively to check who'd arrived at the kitchen door. He couldn't have been surprised when Tilly, Jud and Bertie fox terrier sauntered in.

Jud greeted us with a supercharged smile, showcasing the dental repairs that had finally fixed the damage inflicted by Viktor's gang. The ever-mischievous

Tilly handed me a long-stemmed, single white rose. Luke pretended not to notice, and shooed us out of his kitchen.

"But Tilly, it's been sub-zero for days," I said as I showed them through. "Surely this isn't from Lady Oona's garden?"

"Picked this morning. From James, to you, with love."

"How do you know...?" I began. She kissed me fondly.

"Shush sweetie, it's Christmas. Your fantasies are safe with me." As I took their coats, I told Jud how much better he looked.

"Man, I'm cool." We hugged affectionately and I got a strong whiff of dope. Boo and Victoria Albertina excitedly rubbed noses, Inuit-style; then sniffed arses, doggy-style.

I took the drink orders: mulled wine for Jud and alcohol-free punch for Tilly.

"Sit yourselves at the table," I announced.

While Jud took his place, by the wine jug, Tilly pulled some gifts from a carrier bag. She crouched to arrange them round the tree.

"Nice paper," I said, as an excuse to bend down and ask for whispered news about Karsten's legal machinations. But Tilly interrupted excitedly: the Heritage Channel had invited her to London in January, to audition for the pilot of a new TV show. Then, noting the mistletoe on a branch above us, she pouted her lips for a kiss, which I might have supplied had Luke not come back in. She jumped up, straightening her red ski jumper.

"Fab table, guys!"

"Well, you know us designers: we can't do things by halves," Luke replied, setting out various condiments, in the good china his mum had given us for our civil partnership. Tilly was trying to read the chef's apron I'd bought at the theatre in Norwich.

"*'Tis an ill cook that cannot lick his own fingers'*,"
Luke recited, spreading his arms to reveal the full slogan.

"*Romeo and Juliet,* no?" said Tilly.

"You really know your Shakespeare... *darlink*," I said.
Tilly gave me a glittering, Am-Dram laugh.

"That Shake-shite goes over my head," said Jud.

It was hard to read Tilly's expression as she sat down
beside Jud. Surely she would have preferred a more
cerebral partner? Presumably his accomplishments
below the belt made up for the emptiness above. But he
hardly belonged in the world of London media, where
Tilly's brains and beauty were surely taking her.

Crackers were pulled, corny jokes were read, and silly
hats were binned, except in Jud's case: he sported his
gold jester's crown without inhibition.

"Please raise your glasses to Bertie for finding us such
a mint home," said Luke. He put an arm around my
shoulder. Tilly caught my eye; yet she joined in the toast,
now on the non-alcoholic cava, staying faithful to her
sobriety... while Jud knocked back our good red.

Luke left, to fetch the main course: local turkey, the
Norfolk Black.

"So... what legal news from the NHS?" I whispered,
glancing over my shoulder.

"Luke's still in the dark?"

"God, yes!"

"Well, everything's up in the air. Karsten's suddenly
got a slew of mega sponsorship deals on his desk: big
Norfolk names. Won't discuss any of it."

"What aren't we discussin'?" Jud asked, as he refilled
our glasses. I shushed him as Luke returned, at the helm
of a steaming gravy boat.

"Piggies in blankets coming up. You two like stuffing?"
said Luke, his wink more sleazy than flirtatious.

"Yeah man," Jud sniggered. His sober companion
nodded dutifully. Something about Luke today was

troubling me. Perhaps it was Tilly's presence; or perhaps he actually fancied the clean-cut look Jud had managed to maintain since landing his Bygones Museum job.

Boo and Bertie fox terrier began to prowl, as the table filled with Luke's delicious fare. On the verge of joining us he called out – "Boo, BFT, dindins!" – and they obediently trotted to the kitchen to find their bowls.

There was silence a while, as everybody tucked in. But I didn't like the awkward way Luke was holding his cutlery, as if something was making him tense. I hoped I wasn't doing the same. Unaccountable fluttering in my stomach was quelling my appetite, as if this were some kind of agonising Death Row dinner. Nat King Cole continued to croon his festive favourites.

"Cheers!" Luke sounded a bit forced, to my ears, as he raised his glass again. "Sorry, Tilly, to be turning up the pressure like."

"Don't worry about me, guys: I'll survive my first Christmas without a drink." Her voice hovered somewhere between sobriety and martyrdom.

"Happy Chrimbo, everyone!" said Jud cheerfully, and we all chinked our glasses. But Tilly quickly stood up and assumed a serious air.

"Actually, I've got something slightly momentous to tell you." I felt a pang, a qualm. We all watched her intently.

"The first time I came here," she said, "Bertie and I talked about love. Yes. We talked about Thomas Hardy, happy endings, how no one gets to meet Mr Sex-Bomb Right. Do you remember?"

"I do," I said. I couldn't look at Luke. This was unbelievably embarrassing.

"Well, for one of us," said Tilly, her lip quivering, "it's all come right, fate has been very kind. Will you please raise your glasses, and drink, to 'the Expectant Mother'."

Jud, Luke and I all froze in an instant, then glared at each other, a triangle of alarm, reproach and anger. Tilly's eyes were glistening.

"Don't look at me!" I exclaimed. God knows what Luke was thinking. The dogs stood silent in the doorway.

"Not... Bertie?" said Jud.

"Yes!" said Tilly, her face redder and redder, "My darling Bertie!"

"No!"

"It's true." But then a giggle burst through her solemn mask, and she was hardly able deliver her punch line. "And the father is Boo!"

"For fucksake!" Jud exploded. We'd been well and truly had: the most awkward moment of my life, bar none. But Tilly's laughter slowly spread from face-to-face, and soon we were chinking glasses again.

"You're very, very naughty," I said. But I was intensely relieved.

"Happy families!" shouted Jud. We all joined in the toast. But as the words died away, there came a hefty knock on the outside door, which set my butterflies going again.

"You're expecting someone?" Tilly asked.

"No, not at all," Luke snapped, blushing red, then hastening out through the kitchen. Tilly raised her lush eyebrows. Moments later, we could hear him talking with a woman. Hard to imagine a journalist fishing for stories on Christmas Day, I thought. We listened curiously, as the whiny voice grew more and more insistent. She sounded American.

"Excuse me a sec." I got up to join Luke at the door. A cold draught came right through and trembled the baubles on the tree.

"Hi, Birdie!" said a rather plump lady, with a sugary complexion. "I just knew I'd recognise you immediately!" I guessed she was somewhere in her mid-fifties; she was wearing a green woollen suit, and carrying a large leather Gladstone bag, like a doctor's.

"It's Bertie, actually."

"Bertie, we need a word like, now," Luke whispered, grim-faced.

"We can't leave this poor lady outside in the freezing cold," I told him.

"Too right; I've come a long way to see yer." She stepped over the threshold into the kitchen.

"So you know me from somewhere?" I asked.

"Yessiree, like I wrote you, I'll be your Christmas fairy, bringing wonderful presents." She set down her bag – it fell like a heavy toolkit, upsetting the dogs' bowls – and gave me a punishing hug. "Hi, my English cousin!" And then she unwound the emerald-green scarf that coiled snake-like round her neck. Luke wanted to speak, but she wouldn't stop talking. "What with all the PR, Samphire Hall going viral an' all, I just had to meet yer in the flesh."

"I'm not clear," I began, "about this 'cousin' thing."

"You read my postcards?"

"Luke, did we get any American mail from... I don't know your name?" I said, turning to the stranger, who was shaking out masses of red, crinkly hair. Then I saw his crumpled expression, and I knew something was truly amiss.

"Oh for heaven's sakes, where are my manners? My name is Greene, Dr Leira Greene. Seeing as we're family, just call me Leira."

"Perhaps you misspelt our address," Luke offered. "Odd name for a dwelling, 'Wood Feels', hey?"

"No, no, honeybun, I had the address down right. At least six cards. How backward is it out here? How do you guys live without e-mail?"

She had manoeuvred herself deeper into the kitchen, leaving Luke and me on the threshold, as if we ourselves were the interlopers.

"Anyways, as I was saying, I'm a... well here's my card. 'Greene' was my father's name, kinda ironic, in the circumstances, eh Birdie? I thought I'd better meet yer in the same colour!" She twirled around, one chubby hand smoothing the emerald wool of her suit, the other shaking numerous gaudy bracelets. It sounded as if a reindeer had arrived, and – with her knowing emphasis on the colour green – I began to dread whatever present she was bringing. I looked at our unexpected visitor, and at Luke, in bewilderment.

"I honestly had no idea you were coming," I said, "let alone on Christmas Day."

"Well, it is what it is. Cousin Leira has arrived now, and something smells awful good," she beamed.

"You've had lunch?" I asked, hopefully.

"Cousin, I could eat an entire ranch."

"And would you like to order a drink?" asked Luke pointedly.

"Oh please, don't go to any trouble. I'll just get whatever y'all having."

She steamed on through, and I introduced her to Tilly and Jud.

"Room for a little one next to you lovebirds?" Leira cooed. I pulled up an extra chair and removed the empty dinner plates.

"Excuse me a sec," I said. I strode back into the kitchen, and closed the folding doors behind me.

There on the counter Luke had placed a handful of picture postcards, the top one showing the skyline of Salt Lake City. He looked at me, shamefaced. I spread them out: the Mormon Tabernacle, Zion National Park...

"What the hell?" I swallowed in dismay.

"All right, I'm sorry, I hid the whole series. In case you were having some kind of secret affair." He warmed a plate under the hot tap. "Worried it was another Tilly, like. Now I've seen her, admittedly, there's no competition." He started carving Norfolk Black for Leira.

"What?" I tried to keep my voice down. "You're being ridiculous..."

"Am I? I smelt danger the first time you mentioned that lass. When I met her at the Hall, anyone could see why you were so infatuated."

"I didn't know you were so insecure about 'us'," I said.

"You didn't wonder why I wanted Tilly and Jud over for Christmas dinner? I'll tell you Robert, to check if you and she've still got sparks flying." His eyes were moist, his voice urgent.

"Luke, you're the one I'm with, and the one I love, you have to know that..."

"Well fucking show it then... 'cos you seem so locked up in whatever's bothering you."

He put down the plate of food and moved nearer. I looked into his steely eyes. Checked shirtsleeves, rolled to the elbows. Strong, veiny forearms. He pulled me close.

"Look, I am so sorry for everything. These few months..."

"Norfolk not all it was cracked up to be? Shush... don't say anything..." His bristly jaw rubbed mine and our lips met. I swept one hand over his blond crop and began to feel turned on. Not perfect timing, with a room full of guests next door.

"Keep the show going for now and I'll fall on you later," I murmured into his sexy jug ear.

"Promise?"

"Promise," I said, taking Leira's plate, and cutlery in a napkin, to the folding doors, and preparing a smile. Her American voice shrilled out above the background music, and I wanted rid of her, as you would a bad cold.

"Goodness, a feast!" Leira exclaimed. She held the plate while I laid her extra place, destroying the symmetry of my table.

"So Leira, this cousin business: we're talking Anglo-American relations, I take it?" I asked, pouring some red for her in Tilly's unused glass.

"All will be revealed soon, Cousin Birdie. Pudding then proof, and I've got some mighty fine documents for you," she said between mouthfuls. "My congratulations to the cook..." she added.

"Luke's the master chef," I told her.

"And they told me the Brits only do fish and chips!" she chuckled. "Oh Lukey, can you hear me in that kitchen of yours?"

Luke didn't answer: he was keeping out of her way. I watched our guest, her absinthe eyes the replica of Beulah's secret weapon. She felt like bad luck. I could tell Tilly wasn't keen on her, or Jud for that matter: but they were doing their best to be polite. Even Boo shunned the visitor, and had decamped to his basket cuddling protectively up to his partner.

Luke eventually re-emerged, sitting and eating up hastily. The moment I stacked his empty plate on top of Leira's, he retreated again to his kitchen.

"My, that was finger-lickin' good, just like your friend's apron says!" Leira said. The music was drowned, as she dominated the table with details of her long-haul trip out of Utah, via London, on to Europe. She was on some mission to reconnect lost families, part of some 'outreach' work. 'Wood Feels, Norfolk', as she called our boathouse, had been squeezed into her schedule as a special detour, 'a very personal matter.' It felt ominous.

Tilly stood up.

"I'm just going to get some air," she said, and stepped outside onto the deck for a cigarette. She still cut a lonely figure, leaning over the balustrade, looking out over the bleak marshes, while loved-up Jud continued on his course of getting smashed.

Moments later Luke came out of hiding, bearing the flaming Christmas pudding on its silver tray. Leira applauded.

"Bertie, get the custard in? Trifle for Tilly's on the side." Luke wanted to hurry things along.

Leira was telling Jud about some project of her 'long-gone father' – she kept using the phrase – and how she was keeping Mr Greene's work alive as the ambassador for some company he'd started. Glancing for the first time at her business card, I recognised, below her strange name, the familiar word *Sociopedia*. So it was her online family business that had kick-started my research into Skipper's death, and she was their 'Outreach Director'. I just needed to understand why she'd come such a long way to give me something she could presumably just as well have posted.

"Nippy out there," Tilly remarked, rubbing her arms as she settled to her sherry-free trifle. I realised I was just playing with the food in my own bowl. Meanwhile our larger-than-life visitor had found the sixpence in the pudding, and, on being invited to make a wish, she said she just wanted 'a comfort break before we begin'.

"Begin effing what?" asked Tilly, as we heard Leira locking the door to the downstairs loo.

"Search me," I said, "but the key to her visit is apparently in that doctor's bag." Luke had kicked it out of the kitchen.

"Mrs Samphire," she said bitchily.

"Shush Tils, she'll hear!" I'd never heard Jud tell her off before; but he was pretty hammered.

"I don't give a monkey's, she's a PNG," Tilly retorted. Jud scratched his head. "*Persona non grata*," she said. He looked none the wiser.

"Aye, I'm with you there like," said Luke.

Leira came back, and placed her dark bag by the table. Luke got up to make coffee.

"Cream an' one sugar," Leira called. "Now... the fairy on the family tree is open for business! Where should we start?" She pulled out various labelled folders as she searched her bag. "Ah, here we are, cousin: a little keepsake from Granny Alice!"

This 'Granny Alice' – from an unspecified wonderland – had sent me something weighty and flat, wrapped in blood-red paper.

"You have no idea the difficulty I had getting this through airport security. They thought I was some kinda terrorist!"

"What on earth?" Tilly asked.

"Feels like metal," I replied, starting to unwrap it.

"Now y'all be careful: its teeth are still sharp," Leira warned.

"Looks pretty lethal," Luke remarked as he brought in the coffee tray.

"So... a saw?" I said stupidly, watching the wrapping waft to the floor, right where Luke had spent all those hours scrubbing away Skipper's bloodstain.

'*Calma*, Roberto,' said the little *putto* in my head.

"Not just any ol' saw, silly... it's an heirloom, and it's come right home. Your Olympic jock, Mr Skipper Wood: that's his ol' saw. See, it has his initials on? Craftsmen always did that, back in the day." Luke let out a groan, as the object of my obsession invaded the conversation once again.

"'S.A.W.'," I read out to the others. The neat little capitals, stamped into the wood of the handle, were unmistakable. "What's the 'A' stand for?" I asked her. Not 'Antinoüs', surely.

"Why, I expected you to know that," said Leira. "Skipper Anthony Wood, he used this very saw right here, in your beautiful home." She surveyed the boathouse with a proprietorial eye.

"But if this is...?" I trailed off and stared at the brass back, the dull steel blade. I wanted to feel the teeth – but the thought of touching them appalled me. This was no mere sentimental keepsake; if Leira had really done her research she'd have seen it for what it very likely was: the cause of Skipper Wood's bloody death. I felt infected by it, sickened. Placing it at the foot of the stairs, among the other presents under the tree, I turned to face her. "Where on earth did you get such a morbid thing?"

"My granny passed it down. Mercy me... you didn't get my cards, did you? Sheila, my mom – born Beaufort, South Carolina on November 17, 1913 – she was conceived here. And I mean it, Birdie... right here."

"Someone shagged her granny in Bertie's bed?" giggled Jud, whose inhibitions were vanishing as quickly as my good port wine.

"You're so right," said Leira. "Mom, bless her soul, was what we call 'a lovechild'. The lovechild of Skipper Wood," she declared. "You did know that Skipper had an affair with my Granny Alice?"

"*Your* granny?" I was flabbergasted.

"Lady Alice Newton-Grey, Birdie. You've heard of her, no? *Née* Alice Ogilvy-Fitzgerald?"

I looked at Tilly, but her face was buried in her hands. I didn't dare look at Luke. Ideally I'd have tried to reckon Alice's timing, how pregnant she'd been when she fled to New York. But Jud was lurching angrily to his feet, slopping coffee, knocking over empty bottles.

"Listen – liar – whatever you call yourself. I say you're full of shite. The genie... the genial allergy... the real expert on this family's history an' all was my Nanna Pearl, rest her soul."

"He may be pissed," I explained, "but he's got a point. If Skipper's really your ancestor, Jud's your cousin, not me."

"Oh Jud, honeybun," she said, "I could *not* find you online. My web-team will make up your *Sociopedia* entry this week: I'll send them the data from my hotel. Birdie was so easy – being famous – but I was coming for you next, promise! My, it's quite the family reunion, eh?"

"Shut it!" shouted Jud, who then belched immoderately. "Shut it and get an eyeful of this!" He was unbuckling his belt. Tilly tried to stop him, but he shoved her aside. "Nanna Pearl, she paid for my inkin' so Skipper an' his medals and his carvin' an' all would never get forgotten. An' they never will. If you want the full story for your fuckin' Face-page, here's his walkin'-talkin' descendant for you: Skipper Weed, one 'd'!" In a dramatic gesture, that could have been comic in other circumstances, he hoicked up his denim shirt, and let his combats drop to the ground. "The naked truth," he announced with a brazen, angry grin. "*Tattoopedia!*"

He was not wearing underpants.

"For fucksake Jud," Tilly began. But it got worse. Pulling his shirt over his head, he slowly pirouetted so we saw the whole show, front and back: his parents' plane crash, Skipper and his saw, the Blakeney Seal, the Olympic rings... the entire mystery unveiled.

"No lovechild, see!" he shouted, "No bastards in my whole arc... archive! So stick that in your big-headed American pipe or I'll ram it down your..." Tilly managed to get a hand over his mouth.

"Oh my," Leira gasped. "You Brits, what are y'all like?"

Luke saw me peeping at Jud's impressive body of evidence. I'd partly glimpsed it at his Winnebago, after the illegals beat him up. Now I saw it all: the inked key extended from his tattooed neck-chain all the way down to his dick. An ornate escutcheon – clearly representing the hidden lock in the Boleyn Bureau – framed his pubes. The key, with its trefoil loops, was unmistakably based on the one I'd found in the second step off the landing, which had unlocked the Bureau. I was too angry to speak.

"Christ, that must have hurt like," was all Luke could say.

"For fucksake, Jud," Tilly shouted again, "put it away..." And she started trying to drape a napkin – like a Renaissance fig leaf – over his ample member.

"It's your own fault, Tils," said Jud, briefly kissing the top of her head then belching again. "She hasn't seen the family jewels before, 'cos she won't blow me with the lights on."

"Oh my God!" Tilly shrieked. She stood up and smacked his face, which dropped like melting ice cream. "Sod this!" she bawled, "I need a drink." And she took a swig from an opened bottle, quenching her hot embarrassment.

"Tilly!" I scolded, but I could see this was a losing battle. I turned on Jud instead. "You mean I had to go through all this detective shit," I shouted, "when you knew about the Bureau all along? You bastard, after all I did for you..."

"Oh man, I think the world of you," said Jud, wriggling back into his combats. "Nanna insisted I got inked, the bare facts an' all. But she had no idea her ma done Skipper in. You have to believe me! Nanna rattled on 'bout a treasure hunt an' all, but how could she know what the treasure was, the Wotsit Bureau hidin' her Ma's confession? If she'd known that... how would the shock of it kill her?" At that memory, he suddenly burst into tears.

"'Normal for Norfolk'!" Luke muttered.

"Forget it, Jud," I said, moved by his drunken grief and sorry for my selfish outburst.

"Now, now, boys – cousins, I should say – Christmas an' all..." said Leira, keen to regain control of the gathering. I turned on her.

"And why can't you understand? I am not your fucking cousin!"

"Bertie, calm down," Luke demanded. "Everybody just *fucking* calm down! All right?" He smacked his fist on the table, which rattled violently. The poor dogs, shaken from sleep, ran to cower under the tree. Jud fell quiet, Tilly gulped wine, and Nat King Cole continued to croon, '*Have yourself a merry little Christmas...*'

'Don't even start...' I whispered to the little *putto* in my head.

"You burst in here with your bag of fucking tricks," Luke was telling Leira. "Think you own the place, waving your bloody saw, reckon you know it all like? But if we wanted a historical lecture for Christmas lunch, we've got a *real* expert, home-grown like, right here, do you understand?"

It thrilled me that he'd recognised my 'notable researches and discoveries' at last. But only for a moment: Luke was pointing, not at me, but at Tilly. 'He'll never get it,' I told myself, 'how deeply I'm wound up in this utterly dysfunctional family.'

Tilly – far from responding with choice historical revelations – quit the table and slumped on the sofa, to nurse her humiliation and a fresh bottle of the wine that was her only route to a merry little Christmas now.

"Mercy me," said Leira, "all this rumpus, you're not giving me a chance to explain myself and my mission. My professional mission." She knelt down, rummaged again in her bag, and stood up flourishing an old sepia photograph.

"We do know about Stanley!" I told her. For it was the same portrait – Sergeant Sellars in uniform – that had fallen from Lord James's prosthetic design folder in his Samphire Hall sitting room. This copy, however, had been carefully trimmed into an elliptical vignette.

"Why yes, Birdie, well done. Poor, dear Stanley, the half-bro: missing in action, 1917, on the Somme battlefield, France!"

"Wait a sec', half-brother to who? And 'missing in action', that's not right either," I retorted.

"Cousin Birdie, dearest, I do wonder what you really know about the family history." She handed me the photo. "Turn it over."

I grabbed my glasses off the console table. The inscription on the back was troubling: *'This thing of darkness I acknowledge mine'.* It was Lord James's handwriting, and in an instant I realised I was holding the photograph that the precious oval frame, hidden under the stairs, must have been commissioned for.

"What does he mean, 'mine'?" I said. "This doesn't make sense..."

"Did you never wonder why the family gave Stanley that name, 'Sellars', and kept him as a servant below stairs? I figured it was oh-so British, myself. It's only 'cause James's dad Randolph screwed Ida Henderson, the cute nanny, in the goddam cellars under Samphire Hall."

"I don't see..."

"'*Cellars*', Birdie, do I have to spell it out? Granny Alice knew all about this, 'cause James told her the truth. An' in this heartfelt letter, after she'd left him, he tells about his brother's tragic death." She bent down to grovel once more in her valise.

"She's talking crap, Bertie," Tilly gurgled, from the sofa. "He could be a brother, but he didn't go missing. My exhibition had James's diary, open at the exact page. He found Sellars, all smashed up, in a bunker somewhere. Capelle something?"

"Exactly. Poelcappelle! Dog-tags and all," I added, less confidently.

"Birdie, my dear, clever cousin." Leira was growing ever more patronising. "I have it here in plain English: James's letter to Granny Alice. And all our research suggests Sellars never returned to Civvy Street, as you Brits say. I have the whole *Sociopedia* network, hundreds of researchers, to back me on this."

I pored nervously over the letter she handed me. Certainly it was again James's writing:

'You ask after my dear brother Stanley. It pains me to relate that no trace of him was ever found. Either he is one of the myriad unidentified casualties whose flesh now forms the clay of the Somme, or he ended his days among the anonymous ranks of the shell-shocked in some Parisian sanatorium.'

I took off my reading glasses with horror. So all the Newton-Greys were liars? Luke stepped towards me.

"Leave it, Bertie," he urged, with great concern. "She's messing with your mind, it's party games..."

I brushed him away and tried to think straight. Here was James, casually confirming that Stanley had been his close relation, yet flatly denying, contradicting, the final entry in his diary. Of course he had found Sellars: the dog-tag pinned to the photo proved it. Yet here he was, determinedly erasing those traces. So the illegitimate half-brother had become an embarrassment? Or he'd known too much of the intimate truth behind Bacon's blackmailing? I realised I was talking to myself out loud, but I didn't care. So James abandoned Sellars deliberately, not calling the Jack Wagon back for him, stripping him of his name, leaving him fit for nothing but anonymous burial? A 'thing of darkness' all right. As good as killing Stanley... as bad as killing Bacon. This made James – the man I'd so longed to trust – the worst sort of coward! Sharp pain surged through my chest.

"Luke, you have no idea what this means!" I shouted.

"Goodness," said Leira smugly, "I don't know why y'all are so shocked. Every family has a couple skeletons in the closet, for heaven's sake. Look at your Royals!"

I slouched across to my club chair, holding my chest, trying to breathe deeply and beat the tightness. Luke fetched me an indigestion tablet, which I chewed down like a sweet. He handed me another, sensing I still wasn't right.

"Next thang a family historian ought to know: my granny – Alice Ogilvy-Fitzgerald, 'Lady Newton-Grey' – was dying of cervical cancer in her seventies, but on her bucket list she planned a final grand tour of Old Europe. It was to end here, Samphire Hall England, to be exact. Sadly she never made it. Any of you know where she died? I have the certificate right here: December 25 1965, Deauville, France. Not so far from Cherbourg, where she once boarded the *Titanic* with her mama, for that goddam awful vacation."

At this new challenge, I struggled out of my favourite chair, and hurried to my desk.

"Listen, Miss Genealogy, if you want the low-down – the *accurate* low-down – on the *Titanic* business, I have it all here, for fucksake!" I exclaimed. The top drawer crashed to the floor as I pulled it out, spilling all the yellowing newspapers. I flung a mass of cuttings up in the air, letting them fall to earth like withering leaves, the last vestiges of my trust in Lord James, killed by Leira's revelations.

"What's this?" Luke asked, picking up the oval package that had clattered from the drawer, reading his name on the tag.

"Later. Not now," I told him. I'd heard the glass breaking. Luke put it under the tree, beside his own gift to me, by Skipper's saw. Leira was scooping my fallen *Titanic* cuttings into a wallet-file of her own.

"I'll get these into some kind of order for you, Cousin Birdie," she wheedled.

"Listen, it's 'Bertie', Bertie with no 'd'," I snapped. "And for the last time, will you stop calling me 'cousin'?" In a few, painful strides I snatched the wallet from her fat hands.

"I'd best call Leira a taxi," said Luke, obviously foreseeing fireworks. "Tell me where you're staying?"

"Well I do declare..." Leira was momentarily silenced, as we all were by Luke's decisive intervention. "The Holiday Inn, so-called, in downtown Nor-witch. But you absolutely have to hear me out before I leave..."

"Do I really?" said Luke, shutting the French doors behind him as he went out to phone from the jetty hotspot.

"Poor Ber-tie," came Tilly's slurred voice from the sofa. "So in love with dashing Lord James, and now his hero's... cracked." Jud just grunted, looking dazed, then lit up a joint. Leira surveyed her cousin with disdain.

"Okay, Leira, just say your piece and then leave us all alone," I puffed. "I've had enough, for God's sake." As well as the tightness in my chest, my right arm had started to tingle.

"It's this blue blood thang, so often the heart of our mission as *Sociopedia* outreach workers; and this time it's personal, you know." Her green eyes flashed. I felt sick. "You're in for an amazing ride, Cousin Birdie. Trust me: I'm American!"

"You don't say?" Tilly mumbled.

"Fasten your seatbelts," Leira announced, straightening her garish green suit, grinning like a sprite. She had something clasped in her hands, then she stood over me and let it flutter into my lap, another photograph, a final leaf from a blighted tree.

I gripped the arms of my chair and stared down at the square, creased Polaroid. Its colour was bleached, and the figures posed in it – an old lady, an old man with a bundle on his lap, and a younger woman – were indistinct without my glasses. Boo cantered over, sensing my stress, and sat by my feet. A feverish sweat stuck the back of my shirt to the leather chair.

"As I were saying, Granny Alice died in Deauville in 1965. She expected to die in the Old World – like Pocahontas – and this would be her last-ever vacation. My mom, Sheila Greene, went along as her kinda nursemaid. I stayed home in school, what was I, eleven years old? Anyways, they flew, mother and daughter, into Rome, Italy, on to the art city of Florence and then Milan, capital of fashion." She specified each city like a trophy, emphasising the names as if they would be unfamiliar to her British audience. "Mom loved the Italian styles, she were always so well turned-out, like Granny, 'Lady Alice' to you. Anyways, this day they swung by a fashion boutique on the *Via Monte Napoleone*."

'Pocahontas', that could not be a coincidence; how about *Napoleone*, victim of that toxic wallpaper? Behind me the French doors opened, and Luke interrupted.

"Your cab will be here in half an hour." He sat at the table and poured himself more port.

Leira ignored him. Mascara running slightly, she cocked her head, awaiting my response to her little photo. I peered at it again.

Something about the old man attracted my attention: a sickly fear, as if I were diagnosed with a terminal illness. This face stirred me, this faded matinee idol... he rang a bell in my mind, a carillon even. Yes, of course, the scene *was* familiar. I tried to take a deep breath, but it came shallow. I strained to look closer, while my right hand fumbled the crevice of the armchair, looking for my reading glasses.

Then a second wave of memory: that crevice was where I'd found Jud's dope, the night Boo went missing on the marshes. I'd rolled myself a joint, after so many years of abstinence. The weird imaginings that followed. My mother Miranda dancing on the table in an Italian bar. A crowd of leering men. That light, that Mediterranean light, that's what I was recognising in Leira's snap.

"You've got photos, you cow. How come you've got photos of my dreams?" Leira forced a peal of laughter, but I saw for the first time that her eyes were wet with tears. She was witnessing something that moved her.

"Look at it. Look at the old man," she urged me. There was a hissing noise in my ears.

She was right, of course, the old man in the photo *was* familiar: he was absolutely the silver fox from my hallucination, the one who'd been leering at my mother. That was the point when the unreal Miranda had started telling me the truth about my father. All my certainty that I was the child of the pervert, the Secret Admirer, dated back to that moment. Yet now I couldn't remember her actually spelling it out.

"Cousin Birdie, I see yer getting vexed an' all... listen on... so there they are, my mom and Granny Alice, admiring this tailor's shop on Napoleon Street, and in the window is a distinguished gentleman, surely in his seventies, setting up his special fashion mannequins, or at least giving directions to his window dresser. It's all in the letter Mom sent home." She unfolded a sky-blue page and waved it in front of me. All I could focus on was the airmail logo.

"'The old gentleman's eyes were deep-set black'," she read, "'and very flirtatious with his window dresser, 'cause she were so fine an' young an' pretty an' all, in that classic I-talian sort of way. Sounds like your colouring, eh, Cousin Birdie?"

"Sounds a right perv to me like," Luke muttered into his port.

"Then listen to this, now. 'Mercy me: Granny Alice fainted, there and then, on the *Via Monte Napoleone*'. Imagine!"

Oh, I knew what she was about to say, I knew what this letter would reveal, but I needed to get there first: I jumped up, back to my desk in the bay window, switching on the anglepoise, as the afternoon darkened, searching frantically for my glasses, while Leira read on.

"An' the next thang Granny Alice knew, when she came to, was the mighty fine-looking older gentleman – who was holding water to her lips, staring into her eyes with terrible longing – it were none other than her ex-husband, who had supposedly died young, back in England. It was James Newton-Grey!"

"OMG!" Tilly sat up, out of her Rioja-fuelled stupor. "Now we really know you're lying. JN-G committed suicide right here at Bertie's boathouse, out there by the jetty. Fact! It was in my speech!"

"So, honey, where was his body found?"

"Lost at sea. Body and boat – the *Lady Oona* – vanished in a storm," Tilly retorted. "Front page of the *Sunday Times*; 's in my archives at the Hall..."

"Oh my dear, they've bought that crap about the suicide and the smoking pistol, blah, blah, blah," said Leira.

"I don't buy 'crap', thank you!" Tilly slurred, "I front my own show on the Heritage Channel."

"Well, honey, I put the *Sociopedia* A-team on this, just before I flew over. The collected evidence should be online by now – you'll have to look, see where his lordship's boat came ashore, how he made it to Europe, reinvented himself in Milan, founded his clothes mannequin business. Great Crash or no Great Crash, fashion people wanted their windows dressed. *Sociopedia* has it all."

My heart thumped, my pulse raced. I desperately tried to find my glasses, groping through papers and banging each drawer furiously as I failed. I'd had them half an hour before.

"So what's the proof? What's the proof that it was definitely Lord James?" I spun around, trembling.

"Look at the boutique," said Leira, with a watery smile. "See the name, 'Antonio's'? Lord James's I-talian alias, for this new start in Milan, was the middle name of his very good friend, your man, Skipper Wood – my granddaddy."

"Where are my fucking glasses?" I yelled.

"Bertie, calm down." Luke rushed towards me, putting one hand on my shoulder to still my agitation, and sliding his own glasses onto my face so I could get the picture in focus.

'*Calma*, Roberto!' The voice of the little *putto* seemed to be emanating from the very heart of the photograph.

Harrowingly enough, there was no possible question. The old gentleman in the photograph was James Newton-Grey; his face – his history, his character – had preoccupied me these past three months, and I'd have known him anywhere, even in swinging sixties Milan. But my mind was numbed with teeming questions. There he was, sitting with a bundle on his knee, and I could see now it was a baby, wrapped in a shawl against the sun's glare. James had written so sadly in the diaries about his son, Robbie, who'd been stillborn. But here he was with a healthy child, a round-faced, black-eyed *bambino*, the very image of the little *putto* in my mind.

I looked up at the others. They seemed frozen in time, standing round me in grave concern, like witnesses at a tragic crime scene.

"Look," I cried, careless of the tears that started to stream down my face. "Look, it's definitely James, that's his old wife Alice, lost and found, both of them, lost and found. And this young girl, the servant: her job is to arrange the shop dummies – which Lord James designs of course, like the blueprints in Samphire Hall – and you know who she is, don't you?" Nobody spoke. "That's my mother, my beautiful, runaway mother. It's Miranda!" There was no stopping my sobbing now.

Jud exhaled deeply, the sweet stench of weed all around him. Tilly swayed and sank to her knees. And in an instant I felt – not metaphorically, but as an actual, physical sensation – my mind making a crucial connection, bringing together names and destinies, across the generations, making a mockery of time itself. '*Someone to admire at last, face a secret from your past*', Miranda had promised me. And here he was. Lord James must have seemed like an antique to her: fifty-odd years her senior, old enough to be her grandfather.

"God Bertie, you look as if you've seen a ghost..." said Tilly.

Luke tried to comfort me with a hug, but I flinched away, every nerve-ending in my body charged with phantom power.

"So Leira, out with it, who's the fucking baby, perched on James's knee?" I cried.

"The little angel, with the pretty doe eyes?" she whispered. "You know him, Cousin Birdie. You know him so well. You've known him all your life!"

My hands were shaking so much that I dropped the Polaroid on the floor.

"What's the baby's name, tell me his fucking name!" I yelled.

"Roberto! 'Robert'. It's you, Cousin Birdie..." she said, wiping a tear from her puffy cheek.

"No shit!" Luke shouted. He picked up the photo, and examined it through my glasses, which had been on the dining table all the time. Tilly tottered over to him.

"Bertie, darling, you were such a little sweetie. A beautiful doll."

"Yo, fuck!" blurted Jud, as if his joint had induced Tourette's.

"Stop this, Leira," I shouted. "What kind of father do you want me to have?"

"Aw, Birdie, he was a great man, a war hero, and you heard the beautiful way he wrote about his brother..."

"But that's not all he wrote. Stay there and I'll get you his diary..."

"Where are you going like?" Luke shouted.

"Steady on, sweetie," called Tilly, "the diaries are back at the Hall."

'*Calma*, Roberto, *calma ti*!' I told myself. But there was no restraining my distress, and I started up the stairway out of sheer visceral fear. I'd fled upstairs in terror before, long ago, when the Secret Admirer had found me under the stairs, the day he murdered my dog. This new evidence established that the sicko had never been my father: but the truth, the real truth, was so much worse now. And how come Leira held all the cards? I rummaged frantically in the inside pocket of my tux: these stolen diary pages – James's last sight of Stanley – would show her she didn't know it all.

I found myself standing at the top of the stairs, sobbing. Down below everyone was calling to me – come down and chill out – telling me they loved me and they didn't care who my father really was, or what his crimes were...

I waved the loose pages of James's diary at Leira.

"Think you know it all, but you bloody don't!" She waved her arms, bracelets jangling like chains. Boo and his bitch paced restlessly at the foot of the stairs, yelping.

"Face up, Birdie!" she called up to me. "The Milan photo's dated 1965, the year you were born! It's genuine, from my mom's own camera. Lord James is – he was – your father: pops, papa, whatever you want to call him. Accept it, your gift from the Christmas fairy: you're an honest, blue-blooded, kosher aristo, Birdie. Rejoice!"

'*Calma, calma*, Roberto. *Calma*!'

Luke picked Boo up and held him, by the newel post. Our eyes locked in panic. My pain had got through to drunken Tilly too: her face was the image of my horror. This revised proof of paternity just made me the child of a second psycho-killer.

"You know nothing," I cried to Leira. "What you call a present, to me, it's a curse. The man was a monster – not a war hero! Read his confession, in his own handwriting!" And I tossed the diary pages over the banister. They hung in the air like white feathers, suspended outside time.

I was staggering myself now. I saw Leira stooping, but instead of retrieving James's diary pages, she picked Skipper's saw from under the tree and held it up to me.

"Embrace the truth, Birdie!" she called. "Embrace your heritage..."

I started down the stairs to confront her, but it wasn't easy in wearing Luke's glasses, and as I put my foot on the fateful second step – triggering that death click – a violent jolt pierced my chest, sending my whole body into spasm. I was tearing at my soaking shirt, attempting to breathe, gasping. My eyes surveyed Luke and Boo and Tilly – I loved them all, I thought, in my desperation – everyone holding out their arms to receive me – as I was falling – dazed victim of Sheila Greene's poisonous photo – headlong down boathouse stairs – Birdie in flight – on to Skipper's deadly saw – my heritage, my destiny. My notable researches and discoveries – they were ending – at last.

CHAPTER TWENTY-FIVE
RELEASE

When a child is born, released from the mother's body, how helpless he lies! How long until he can hear and make sense of what he hears? Until he can see and make use of what he finds? How helpless he lays, until he grows to movement, and courage to explore this new cage, the world.

In my new station, my new state – released from my own body, as I come to realise – the first sound is the passing of time. How long, I cannot say. Is it the ticking of a clock, so faint, so distant? Then the creaking of timbers. Then the cry of an owl.

How can I name these sensations, having no one to guide me? I knew them already, yet the knowledge was far away. Everything, so far away. How long until it grows closer?

In the beginning there was the darkness, and I comprehended it not; but with the coming of light – how long, I cannot say – I start to make sense of what I hear. Clock, no, but a fine wristwatch, a chronometer, tiny and shiny on a pillow far below me. A present, I know it. Who sent it? How can I ever reach it?

I find I am lodged high in a cupola, what I once called a lantern window. The day, all too dazzling: yet by night I see a treetop, bare branches, and a moon, sometimes full, sometimes new. Someone has lived up here before me; I'm not the first. Yet of my predecessor there is no sign, no sound. He has been released, moved on: I sense his relief.

If I could whistle? I must learn to whistle, now that I have no distractions, quest or mission. I could not whistle in life, but in death I shall learn. How else shall I make myself heard? But what tune shall I whistle? And who is to hear me?

These days there are songbirds, leaves on the tree. I am making more sense of my sight – not eyesight, having no eyes – more like knowing than looking. I know the fine watch has been left for me. I sense its hands moving, though the time it tells has no meaning to me. I slept, once, on that same pillow. How long ago, I cannot say.

My bedroom. It's empty now. And through the floor – the cedar boards, the joists, the downstairs ceiling – I can survey the rooms below. Cupboards bare, stove without ash. Furniture gone, nothing here I know, nothing remembered. Empty cabinets, though, boards for display. It is destined to be a museum. The visitors, they will hear me whistle.

A picture there is, on the mantelshelf. An oval cedar frame, almost a part of the building. A photograph inside it, a formal group, standing dark in snow. A graveside, my graveside? I cannot see their faces, yet I know... I remember... their voices. Don't cry Tilly, Stanley, Clive, Alice, Yurik, Ida... James. Don't cry Caleb, Miranda, Leira, Karsten, Beulah, Tel, Randolph. There's Jud, there's Constance, Little Pearl, Charlie Snyder, so many others. Anna Bolina, there in the centre, with her Secret Admirer. Thank you for coming. I forgive you all. And, you must know, I am still not far away.

Don't cry, Luke! His name comes home to me, rings a bell in my heart. My bedroom, our bedroom. Did we not have a little dog once?

There's hammering, there's sawing. Down the stairs I send my sight, someone at the door. Breaking in? Skipper Wood? The name rings a bell in my soul, a bell of fear.

Scratching, yapping. The door breaks in. Luke with a saw. His face I cannot see, but his spirit is morose, vengeful. I call to him – using what for a voice? He does not call back. Our little dog, up the stairway he comes, luminous searching eyes, he's jumping by the pillow, the watch. He's straining, on his hind legs; he's keening, whimpering, tail still wagging as he calls me to come down from the cupola.

Hello Boo, my sweet friend.

If I could whistle for him? But what tune? *Oh you beautiful dog?*

Luke is busy. He collects the oval frame. He comes up the creaking stairway for the watch, gathers the pillow. He chastises the whippet. 'Nobody's here,' he insists. He stands a while, sighing, maybe crying – how long, I cannot say – his face deep in the pillow. Perhaps he kisses it. Next time I look, all are gone.

I cannot see, I cannot know, beyond this boathouse plot. My new cage, my world. Luke has changed the sign on the door, hammered up a new one. 'Wood's End'. True. Strange name for a dwelling.

Strange name for a strange house. It could have been good. Still my place, though, still my home. Ariel howled twelve years in the cloven pine. Skipper, longer far – how long, I cannot say. And me? I have no thought of time.

Come back soon, sweet Boo. When I can whistle for you, you'll come. You know where to find me. I can wait; I am not busy like before, all those investigations, projects. I shall not fret – *fortitudine prospero* is my family motto – and I'll keep my soul steady as I have always tried to do, in the still, small voice that speaks in times of trial:

Calma, Roberto, *calma*. There's nobody here but you.